THE DEADMAN'S TRIBE  BOOK 4

strong ENOUGH

NICOLE CRAIG

DEDICATION

For Doris...

And for those of you who suffer from chronic pain...
You are not alone. I see you. More importantly? I ***feel*** you.

I was told, "It's simple, Nicole. If it hurts, you just need to realize that it's time to stop doing whatever it is that makes you hurt."

No. I do not accept that.

If I did, I would have had to quit the job I loved. Quit traveling. Quit bowling. Quit acting. Quit cleaning my house. (Wouldn't have minded that so much.) Quit walking. Quit standing. Quit sleeping. Quit everything and resign myself to being a shadow of who I am because it hurts to do fucking **EVERYTHING**.

So no, it's NOT that simple.

It's difficult for anyone who has not been in your situation to truly understand how difficult it is to get up each day. Until they've lived it, they will never understand, so don't expect them to. It's impossible to understand how depressing it is to not be able to do the little things—picking up a paperclip off the floor, reaching for a glass on a shelf, exiting a car, or heaven forbid, taking those first few steps out of bed each morning—until it happens to them.

They can't understand until they live it, which we hope they never do, because pain sucks.

You don't stop because it hurts to keep doing something. *You keep doing something because it hurts too much to stop.*

1

MAY 26, 1998

Esme

"Hey, Dad. I have a couple more revisions." She stood nervously in the open doorway of the home office, tablet clutched in her hand. Her long red hair was in a perfectly orchestrated French braid, and a light dusting of mascara, blush, and lip gloss had been applied.

She watched him remove his glasses as he glanced up at her. Pointing his remote control at the stereo system to lower the volume of the music in the background, he looked at her, an indulgent smile on his face. "Cherry—your speech is fine. You—are fine. I'm sure any minor changes you made between now and an hour ago—are fine. Come here."

She came forward and around the desk to where her father had swiveled his chair to greet her.

He grabbed the hand not holding the tablet, his face reflecting confusion. "Your speech was perfect. What could you possibly have needed to change?"

A frown formed on her face, and she ignored his question, instead posing her own. "What's with the classical music?"

He shifted in his seat. "I'm... broadening my horizons." He paused. "Did you ever study someone by the name of Antonio Salieri in school?"

She thought about it for a minute. "No, the name doesn't ring a bell. Is that who this is?"

With a grunt, her father used the remote to turn the music completely off. "Never mind that. We have a bigger issue here to discuss. What has got you in such a twist over this speech?"

She replied with a shrug, "This is important, Dad."

He raised an eyebrow. "To whom?"

"Being the valedictorian is a responsibility. People there will expect a good speech."

"I noticed you didn't say it was important to you."

"Well, of course it is. I want to make you proud."

"You do make me proud, Cherry. Every day. And it has nothing to do with being valedictorian, or the speech you give, or where you go to college, or anything like that. Although those things are fantastic bonuses, I'm proud of you because you've turned into an amazing young woman who is compassionate, generous, dedicated, and loving. Because of those traits, you are going to do well at anything you put your mind to, and that includes writing and delivering an amazing valedictorian speech."

She blushed lightly, a soft smile on her face. "Thanks, Dad."

He stood and reached to pull her into a tight hug. She felt the press of his lips to the top of her head. "You're the light of my life, Cherry. My only regret is that your mother isn't here to celebrate this milestone with you."

"Me too."

They stood together, holding each other tight for a few moments longer, soaking in the father-daughter time.

She felt him squeeze her microscopically tighter. "Cherry?"

Tilting her head, she had to bow her body back slightly to look at him. His face had no expression, but his mouth looked pinched, his eyes sharp as they roved her face.

"What's wrong?"

He smiled, but it didn't reach his eyes. "I know we're supposed to go see your Uncle Zion when we leave Paris, but... I was wondering if maybe you wouldn't like to skip that and go to Switzerland instead? This is your graduation trip, and we should go where you want to go, not where your father keeps dragging you to."

No trip with her father had ever been a place he'd had to drag her to, but he was correct in that she'd always wanted to go to Switzerland. Chocolate? Skiing? Snow? Umm, yeah! "I'd love it, Dad! But won't Uncle Zion be upset? It's awfully late notice."

It would be a lie if she said she wasn't relieved at the change. She liked her father's best friend, and she loved visiting his banana plantation at the foot of the Pitons. It was just that... the last year or two, she had caught him watching her with a funny expression in his eyes. It was nothing she could put her finger on, but it was weird.

His expression changed slightly. If she had to name it, it looked like relief. "You let me deal with Uncle Zion. When we come back from the ceremony, you'll have to repack your bags a bit, but I'm guessing you won't mind." The smile on his face was bright and genuine. He hugged her tightly again before sitting behind his desk with purpose. "All right. When do we need to leave?"

"Ten fifteen."

"Got it. I'll be ready."

Rolling her eyes, Esme turned and walked toward the door. "Right, Dad. Believe it when I see it."

"Esme!"

She turned with a frown on her face. He never called her Esme.

"I love you, Esme. Always remember that."

Smiling, she replied, "I love you, too, Dad. See you in an hour."

Esme jogged down the stairs, her graduation gown on, her cap under one arm, and her hands fiddling with getting her earring through her earlobe properly. "Dad, it's ten fifteen! We need to leave in fifteen minutes!" It was really ten o'clock, but since her father was always late, she was in the habit of setting the clocks fifteen minutes ahead so when they finally got out of the house— never on the fifteen-minute early time—they did actually leave when they were really supposed to. Most of the time, anyway.

There was no response.

She stood at the foot of the stairs, emitting a huff of frustration. "Dad! Did you hear me?"

Still no response.

"St. Mary Ignatius, you'd think the man could be aware and on time today, at least. Just the most important day of my teenage life. No big deal." With another puff of air through her lips, she turned and walked toward his home office doors, calling out as she went. "Dad, your daughter cannot be late to her own graduation, where she is the valedictorian and giving an important speech!"

She stopped dead in her tracks. The dual doors to the office were closed. They were always open. For them to be closed, even when he took a business call, was not normal. Even when he had a meeting. Never. Never.

Hesitantly, she took the last few steps and stood in front of the door. She knocked softly. "Dad?"

No answer.

She knocked again, this time a little harder. "Dad?!"

Her hand raised to knock again, but something stopped her from touching the door. All the hair on her body felt electrified as she looked left and right down the hallway. A roaring in her ears accompanied her gaze returning to the door, and she swore her heartbeat pumped her blood so hard that the horrific thump-thump of its pulse was echoing through her ears and out into the house.

The noises increased with each beat to a deafening crescendo as she watched herself reach for the handle. Like in that climactic moment of a horror film, everything went into cliché slow motion as she pushed down and in on the handle to open the door.

The office was in shambles. Papers scattered across the carpet like autumn leaves. Books pulled from all the shelves, spines torn, pages ripped. The mounted television and the artwork on the walls pulled down. The curtains over the French windows to the backyard and the rods that held them, ripped from their hardware and destroyed. Someone had been looking for something.

She approached the desk cautiously. In her eighteen-year-old head, she knew she shouldn't enter that room. She knew she should call the police. Her body, however, was acting of its own accord, her feet moving forward at a slow, regimented pace. Once at the desk's edge, she saw a few drops of what looked like red raindrops on its surface.

"Dad?" she whispered, genuine fear in her voice.

There was only silence.

ON AUTOPILOT, SHE'D BACKED OUT OF THE ROOM AND CALLED the police. Then she'd called her Uncle Zion, who was in town to help celebrate her graduation. Since her mother died when Esme was six and both her parents had been the only children of much older parents, there was no extended family. Her father had raised her completely on his own. She was alone, and Zion was the closest thing she had to family.

Hours later, she sat on the sofa in her family home, her arms hugging a throw pillow from the leather sectional. Her graduation ceremony went on without its valedictorian, but Esme didn't give two donkeys and a manger about that. She just wanted her dad. Somebody had kidnapped him, but why?

Zion arrived quickly to be by her side. While the police were doing their thing in her father's office, the two detectives entered the room, and the questioning began.

"When was the last time you saw your father?"

"Just before nine thirty. I came downstairs to his office to ask him to hear my speech one more time."

"What was his mood like?"

"He was his normal self. We had breakfast together around seven o'clock. He was teasing me, saying that as soon as the ceremony was over, he was kicking me out and renting my room since I'm now a true adult.

"About an hour and a half later, I went to his office to read him my speech. I'd made a few changes, and I wanted his opinion. Then I came down again around nine thirty with a couple of other minor changes. Other than seeming to be preoccupied when I walked in, everything was fine."

"Preoccupied?"

"That's maybe the wrong word," she admitted. "'Focused' might be a better word. If you interrupt him, he doesn't mind, but it takes a moment or two to reset his brain."

"He didn't mention any troubles at work, concerns with other people, or anything like that?"

"No. Dad talked about his business with me often. I even worked for him during the summers, so there wasn't much I wasn't privy to. He didn't really work with anything overly secret."

"He said nothing else?"

"Nothing out of the ordinary. He told me he was proud of me and that he loved me. Those were things he told me often, if not every day."

Her brain reminded her that as she was leaving his office the second time, he'd called her by her first name instead of his nickname for her. That had been very odd because she hadn't remembered him calling her Esme in years... or ever, really. But that wasn't the kind of thing the police were asking about.

"There's luggage packed and ready to go on a trip in both your room and your father's. Were you headed somewhere?"

"We were going to Paris and Rome for two weeks, and then we were supposed to join Uncle Zion in St. Lucia. Dad asked if I would prefer to go to Switzerland instead, since I'd always wanted to go there. So we agreed to do that." She bit her lip and flashed a look at her uncle. "Sorry. I hope you're not mad."

Her uncle flashed her a smile and shook his head. "Of course not, my dear. It was your graduation present. It should have been all about you and not business."

The lead detective flashed a look at the well-dressed man beside her. "Uncle Zion?" the detective asked.

The man in question directed his attention to the detectives as he stood. "Zion Norton. I was Grayson Bosworth's partner and, dare I assume it, his best friend. I own Nimbus Corporation," he explained. "My company makes the planes that Esme's father's communication systems go in. That's how we met. We discovered we had many of the same goals, so eventually, our working relationship turned into a formal partnership."

"He's not really my uncle," Cherry added. "My parents didn't have any siblings, but we see him so often that he's like an uncle. We visit him at least twice a year in St. Lucia, and he visits here a few times as well."

The police continued to ask their questions, most of which Esme felt helpless to answer. None of this made any sense to her. While her father was a successful business owner and wealthy in his own right, on top of it, he'd never mentioned business deals that had gone badly or disgruntled employees. She was sure those things had happened, but he'd clearly not been concerned enough to mention them to her.

And yes, when you had money, kidnappings were always a possibility, but again, he'd said nothing to her. People might argue that he wouldn't in order to protect her, but she knew her father. In reality, he'd been very open with her about the dangers of being his daughter. So much so that he'd made sure she'd taken self-defense courses, and he'd had a military friend from the Navy teach her how to escape certain situations. So, no, there were no threats to him she knew of because he would have told her, wanting her to be aware for her safety.

Hours later, she was startled at Zion's soft calling of her name. The police were gone, and it was just the two of them in the room. "Yes?" she replied, her eyes flying to his.

"Is there anyone I can call for you? A friend?"

Shaking her head, she replied, "It's graduation day. Everyone has parties and things. I don't want to bother them with this. I'll be okay."

With a gentle rub to her spine, he encouraged, "Why don't you go upstairs and take a nap? It's been a very trying day, and I'm sure the police will have more questions tomorrow."

"Likely the same questions," she muttered grumpily. "I don't know why they keep asking me the same thing over and over. My answers will not be any different, no matter how they phrase them or who asks me. No, I didn't hear anything. No, I didn't see anything. No, there haven't been any strange phone calls, letters, emails, or anything out of the ordinary. No, Dad wasn't acting strange lately. Yes, Dad was absolutely fine this morning."

"I sincerely doubt that they think you're lying, my dear. Often, though, people don't realize they've seen or heard things, and it isn't until later that something jogs their memory. Unfortunately, sometimes that's the seventh, twelfth, one hundredth time they're asked the same question."

"Doesn't make it any less annoying."

"No, it doesn't." He smiled kindly. "Esme? Would you like to come and stay with me for a while? I know it's probably too soon, but here you'll be alone. It's an enormous house to rattle around in by yourself. At least in St. Lucia at *Les Vergers de la Mer,* you'll be surrounded by people, and if your father is found, I can get you home quickly."

She felt herself stiffen at his words. "When."

"Excuse me?"

"When. You said 'if' he's found. *When* he's found."

A hand over his heart, his expression regretful, he bowed his head. "I apologize, my dear. I didn't think before I spoke. Of course, 'when he's found.'"

She stood from the couch and felt her heart rate race with irritation despite his backtracking. "Thank you for the offer, Uncle Zion. I appreciate you looking out for me, but I'd much rather stay here and be here *when* he comes home."

"I understand." He gave a short nudge toward the door with his head. "Go on. Try to get some rest. This will all be over soon."

But it wasn't over soon. Days passed. Weeks. Eventually, the entire summer. There were no clues other than the destroyed office and a few drops of blood, which were her father's. Every time she thought about it, she questioned where the blood had come from. A hit to the head? A punch to the face? She worried he was in pain and still hurting.

No ransom requests came. There'd been no withdrawals from his bank accounts. Investigators found his phone on his office floor, but after reassembling and examining it, they found no unusual calls or numbers. The detectives had his computer files and drives investigated. Nothing appeared tampered with or removed. He was just simply gone, and he never reappeared.

Throughout the weeks, Zion kept in touch, and he continued to offer his support. He'd hired his own private investigators to look into her father's disappearance. He'd called in favors from people he knew who might have access to resources law enforcement didn't. He'd continued to invite her to his home as a place to rest and wait. She'd thanked him for his efforts, but she continued to refuse his offer to go to St. Lucia. Even if her father wasn't here, she felt closer to him being at home.

Eventually, the police moved on to other cases. Even the FBI had given up. She didn't blame them. Esme was a practical girl. With nothing to work from for so long, they couldn't keep working on his case when there were other cases to be solved. They assured her they would keep trying, but she knew. It was done. While that hurt her heart, she didn't give up hope that somehow he was useful to whoever had taken him and that he'd come back to her somehow.

The week before college arrived. Throughout August, the wheels in her brain had been turning. She had to make a choice. Early in the year, she had accepted offers from twelve universities, including MIT and Stanford, but she chose Georgetown, her local university, to study business and politics, like her father. The thought of heading to classes like a normal high school graduate seemed wrong, and yet she knew it would be what her father wanted.

As she wrestled with her decision, the attorney informed her she was much wealthier than even she had imagined. In the short term, she had a monthly payment from the interest in a trust she inherited when her mother passed. When she turned twenty-one, she'd gain full access to the trust, making her a multimillionaire. Her father also had a vast family fortune at his fingertips since he was an only child. His money was in trust for Esme as well. However, she'd have to wait longer for that money since he'd have to be declared dead in order for it to come to her.

She'd much rather have him back than get access to the money.

The week before classes began, she was sitting behind her father's desk, a habit she had picked up when she needed to think clearly, and she made plans. With no leads on her father's disappearance, the choice became obvious to Esme. Learn everything she could, as fast as she could, in every area possible that might help her find her father—politics, business, languages, communications, computers, law—and then find people whom she could use to put her search into motion.

When classes started, instead of taking part in dorm life as planned, she stayed at home and headed to class. Despite a heavy course load, she excelled in her classes and vowed never to rest until she found her father or brought his kidnappers to justice.

Five years later, with her final exams and papers turned in and her master's degree validated, she walked out of her apartment on graduation day as if headed to the ceremony. However, when it started, Esme Bosworth's seat at the ceremony was empty. When her name was called, she was not there to accept her diploma.

Once a year, she made a call to her Uncle Zion to check in, assuring him she was healthy and safe. To everyone else, Esme simply disappeared. She never told them where she was or what she was doing. She simply followed the plan she'd set in August 1998.

Tribe Corporation and the deadmen were born.

2

SEPTEMBER 9, 2022

Demon

DEMON, HIS SHOULDER-LENGTH BROWN HAIR BLOWING ACROSS his face in the morning wind, pitched his board into the water and began paddling out into the ocean. While he paddled against the surge of the waves, he tasted the surf on his lips—the salty tang of the ocean in the beading water droplets, the sand grains that his feet had kicked up on his jog down to the water—and took in the scent of the sea.

Once he reached his destination, he straddled his board and watched the waves, contemplating nothing other than catching the peak. His hand reached to his lower back, pushing against the verte-brae, and he winced. The drugs were wearing off. His tolerance to them had been building up for some time now, and he knew he was going to face a decision soon. He'd been putting it off and putting it off, worried about how it would affect his work, especially with the team being a man down.

He knew what a certain redhead's opinion would be. It was that thought and not the mini-swell that hit his board that left him cold. Why did she always have to intrude into his private thoughts? As if she were a part of any discussion over choices in his life. Nope. Not her business. His life. His choice. She could "mind her own knitting," as his grandmother used to say when he was a young boy and lived in Ireland.

He focused back on the waves. To allow his mind to wander to other things was disrespectful to the power of the water, which meant danger.

Other surfers had arrived, but he was an expert paddler and the first to reach the farthest out point, giving him priority. It was usually the same surfers each dawn patrol. He knew none of them by name and encouraged no friendships because of his deadman status, but he was always polite and followed the rules. No drop-ins, no snaking.

A glance over his shoulder showed him that his wave was coming in. As the swell approached, he popped up on the board and rode the shoulder from left to right. Toward the end of the ride, the tunnel caught up to him, and he turned his board to move out of the whitewater as much as he could.

When he arrived on the shore, he pulled up and tucked his board under his arm. A short, ripped Latino male with cold silver eyes stood in a wetsuit, waiting for him, and there was a longboard stuck in the sand. Demon knew from experience that the man was often underestimated because of his size, but while Steel was the smallest of the deadmen, he was one man you did not want to cross. His trade as an assassin would easily allow him to turn his surfboard into a weapon of mass destruction in the blink of an eye, and he would show no emotion as he removed his targets from the earth with it. Anything was a weapon in this man's hands.

"D." Steel greeted him with a head nod. "You up to catch another wave?"

Demon looked out into the water, where several other surfers were waiting. There was a meeting scheduled this morning, and a glance at his watch said it might cut it close to head back out, but... feck it. He was late all the time. How mad could anyone get if Steel was on his heels when he finally arrived at the office? The messages he'd received from Waters the last two days had been check-ins, not orders to come in, so Steel probably had something to say. Out in the water, sound traveled, but if they went out farther than the line and kept the volume low, they'd be fine.

Without a word, Demon turned and jogged back out into the water, his pace a beat slower from the tug on his sciatic nerve. He worked hard not to let it show as Steel pulled his board from the sand and followed him. In silence, they paddled together out past the waiting surfers. Demon signaled to the priority surfer that they were going to wait out past the line with no intention of dropping in.

Once in place, they sat astride the boards in the silence, facing frontside to watch the last of the sunrise.

"You haven't been to the office in three days."

"Not required to be until today."

"You're not answering calls or texts. People are worried."

"Nothing to say to anybody." Then he added a derisive snort. It wasn't "people" who were worried. This was his typical MO, and everyone knew that. One person was worried. One person kept trying to insert her nose into his life. Kept trying to fix things that didn't need fixing. "And as far as 'people,' you mean *Cherry* is pissed. My guess is she envisioned me passed out in a narcotic haze, possibly even dead and food for the coyotes. Rather than have Midas turn on my damn tracker, she sent you out here to either dispose of my remains to the sharks or drag my ass back to the office. Well, fine. I'm alive, I'm not high, and I'll come into the office when I'm damn well ready. Or I get a text from Waters that says I have to report early." The last sentence sounded more than petulant.

The next surfer in line took off. There were two more in front of them.

"She worries."

"No, she smothers. I'm a grown-ass man who knows how to take care of himself. I don't need a babysitter, mommy, or anyone else looking over my shoulder."

"Looking over our shoulders is kind of her job."

The next surfer took off, leaving one in front of them.

Rather than blow up in anger, he switched topics. "You want me to take priority, or do you want me to follow?" Demon asked.

"Party wave? I'll take your six in case I wipe out," Steel replied.

He snorted. "You're even less likely to wipe out than I am."

"Yeah, but I don't do this every day like you do."

"Nope. You only come by when you have something to say, or we're dumping pieces of a body as shark chum."

His teammate let a tiny smile tilt the corners of his mouth, but he didn't disagree.

He lifted his face to the sky, then bound his hair into a short ponytail at the top of his head, exposing the fade cut. "Get ready for it," he warned. "Last surfer taking off. With the wind, this next one is going to be bigger. Watch for the break, low tide or not."

"Copy that."

As the swell approached, they popped up and rode in, Demon avoiding the collapsing tunnel and Steel riding through it. He shook his head. His teammate always did like to play with fire, or in this case, water. Shaking the salt water out of his eyes, Steel rode into the beach directly behind him and to the right.

Up on the sand proper, they grabbed their boards and jogged up to Demon's crash pad, a stilted hut on the Pacific Ocean that he rented for cash and no questions asked. Careful not to touch the rails of the stairs, they moved onto the deck and washed off the sand in the outside shower. When finished, he wiped down the shower fixture while Steel wiped down their boards since they'd be unsupervised briefly. You could never be too careful.

Water dripped from their bodies as they crossed the one-room hut, but Demon didn't care. It would dry by the time he returned, and it wasn't as if the place was fancy. Just a futon that doubled as a place to sit and sleep and a small kitchenette. When things became too tight at Tribe, he came here and rode the waves to chill out. He spent more time here than there because things were almost always too tight. He wasn't too proud to admit, to himself at least, that a certain fireball redhead was more than half the problem.

He stripped off his wetsuit, uncaring that Steel was still in the room, and redressed in the board shorts, T-shirt, and flip-flops he'd come here in. "Do I need to change when I get to the office?" he asked. If he did, it meant they were leaving L.A.

"I don't know. My role this morning was more in the line of a welfare check."

Taking a dry cloth, Demon wiped down everything inside that he'd touched. "I take it you're required to take me in, dead or alive?"

"Dramatic much?"

He shrugged. "I'll be ready in five. Touch nothing."

Steel merely raised an eyebrow.

He rolled up the sleeping bag lying atop the futon mattress and tied it tight. Then he double-checked the garbage, bagging up what little was there to incinerate at Tribe. Other than potential fingerprints, none of them would hold DNA. He also grabbed his wetsuit as they readied to leave. When the two men left the hut, he didn't bother to lock up, as there was nothing there except the futon. But he wiped the towel over the handles to obliterate fingerprints, threw it over his shoulder to put in the laundry back at his apartment, then they grabbed their boards and headed to Steel's truck, throwing the boards in the bed.

"Your jeep wiped down?" Steel asked.

Over his sunglasses, now it was Demon's turn to raise an eyebrow.

Once on the road, Steel engaged the soundproofing and frequency scrambler through buttons on the dashboard that looked like they controlled the satellite radio and other amenities. When the red frame appeared over the navigation screen, they were free to talk.

"So what's got Cherry in such a twist that she's looking for me specifically?" Demon asked.

"Don't know. She texted me late last night to come find you and bring you in today. Wasn't there this morning when I came downstairs, so I couldn't dig further. She's been... off... the last few days."

"'Off' how?"

"Closed off. Can't get more than a few words out of her, and she offers nothing unless you ask her a direct question. Even then, I'm guessing some of what she's saying is bullshit."

"You mean lying?" That would definitely be out of character. Like any of the Tribe team, she could hold information tight to the vest if need be, but she would never lie. At least not to the team.

"No. Not lying. Secretive. Like whatever the secret is, she's worried it's going to blow up in her face. Worried. That's what it is. She's worried about what she's hiding."

"Maybe if she just told us what she's all wound up about, then she wouldn't be worried."

Steel flashed him a look. "The person she's most likely to tell anything to has been missing for three days and is now in my truck. Hmmm. I may not be good at math, but two plus two equals four. Still wondering why she's looking for you?"

Demon looked out the passenger window, his fingers absently playing with the leather bracelet he wore. "She doesn't tell me anything anymore."

"Well... I'm guessing she's struggling with trust right now."

They sat at a stoplight. Steel continued, "Look, far be it from me to tell you how to run your life. I've made my own choices that have been less than popular in the past. The point is, you have something in your grasp that could right a lot of the wrongs you're harboring, and you're blowing it. What she's asking of you is such a little thing. Give up the fucking pills already. You don't need them."

"You don't know shit about what I need. And if it doesn't matter to you all, it shouldn't matter to her. Or are you saying it matters to all of you?" The pang in his gut intensified. Were they finally giving up on him? He wouldn't blame them.

"Of course it matters to us, but not in the way you're thinking."

The light turned green, and Steel eased into the intersection. "The oxy? It's how you cope. I've never seen you unable to function. You take them like you've got a prescription because we can set our watches by when you do. It's as natural a part of your system as if you took vitamins. You're never unable to do what you need to do. You probably even have a tolerance built up, and the shit's all in your head."

"I have physical pain," he mumbled. Even to him, it sounded like a weak excuse.

"Okay, but then why do you stop taking them as soon as you're on any type of assignment that requires you to potentially have to do your doctor thing on somebody? Clearly, you're trying to numb something, yet you recognize the drugs could be a detriment in a crisis. You're making rational decisions, so by refusing to give them up, you're also making a rational decision. If it's her *only* condition for the two of you being together, why wouldn't she believe you don't deserve her trust? You're basically throwing in her face that the shit matters more to you than she does."

"Didn't you just say it wasn't your place to tell me how to live my life?"

Muttering in Spanish under his breath, Steel pushed the button on his dash that opened the gate to Tribe's underground parking and pulled into his preferred spot. However, he didn't turn the vehicle off after he put it in park.

"I'm not telling you *what to do*. I'm just telling you *how it is*, pointing out that you have no right to be pissed when you're willfully doing the one thing that's fucking up the possibilities."

Demon opened the truck door, exited, and slammed it behind him. Arriving at the elevator that would take them upstairs, he jammed the button so hard it cracked. Steel followed him into the carriage. Demon knew the man would never press for details, but he felt like he needed to give his teammate some sort of answer. Other than God and Waters, none of them knew much, if anything, about each other's pasts, so they would have no clue what had driven

Demon to his dependency on prescription narcotics to get him through his days.

Making a choice, he hit the emergency stop button on the elevator just before it hit the second floor of Tribe, where the offices were. He stared at the unopened doors.

"There was an accident."

Clearly, Steel knew better than to prod. Instead, he leaned against the elevator wall, not looking at Demon, waiting for whatever was going to come out of his mouth.

"A boy. Caught in a riptide. He was drowning. I promised his parents he'd live, and then I went out to get him. When I got to him, he was already gone, so I had to decide—try to do CPR in the water or swim with him to land and then start compressions. He'd be too long without air if I did the latter and likely have a brain injury, so I started CPR in the water. I chose wrong."

"Losing a child always hurts more than any other death. You made the best decision you could under the circumstances."

Demon heard a note of pain in Steel's voice that he'd never heard before. It was both comforting and frightening to know that even a stone-cold assassin could feel compassion.

"I know. It was a judgment call, something I'd been used to making in all my time as a surgeon. I always understand that I'm taking a chance. But... I'd had a surfing accident the week before. Screwed up my back, and I was on medication to get me through until therapy. I took medical leave because I couldn't stand long enough to operate, so I was on my medication when I went out to the beach that night. I had no business going out into the water in that condition. On top of that, I made a promise I had no right to make because there was no guarantee I could keep it, and it was just one in a long string of promises in my life that I was failing at."

"Do you honestly believe that taking an oxycodone pill was the difference between that boy living and dying?" Steel asked incredulously.

"Well... no," Demon admitted.

Steel opened his mouth, but Demon cut him off as if he knew what Steel was planning to say. "But it *could* have been a factor. Would I know if pain medication was affecting me? I mean, that's part of what it's supposed to do, essentially. Make people not feel the pain."

Shaking his head, Steel made a "tch" noise. "If I'm bleeding out, I'm saying it now. I want your high ass operating on me more than some sober, cookie-cutter mad scientist. You'd know if you were impaired. And even if you didn't... *mierda*, even a stone-cold sober person can make a mistake or a poor decision. No one expects you to be perfect, *hermano*. We're successful most of the time, but we make mistakes. Waters let orders override his spidey senses, and he left Kubrick vulnerable. TB let Flame out of his sight, and we had to rescue her. Nemo let the love of his life get away twice. The difference is, we learn from those mistakes, and they've never happened again."

Demon swallowed hard against the lump in his throat. "I'm untrustworthy. I say I can do things, but I can't always follow through." He shuddered as if he had taken that first step into an ocean in winter. What would Cherry be worried about? What could be so worrisome that it was causing her to close off from the team? To deflect rather than lie? Was she in some kind of danger? He didn't think he could last long against the fear of that. "Some days, I wonder why Waters even hired me."

Steel clapped him twice on the shoulder. "He saw something in you, just like he saw something in all of us. Five fuckups with skills we were putting to use, six if you count him, but in ways that were causing us all to burn up like comets in the atmosphere. We have a purpose now. It wasn't the purpose we envisioned for ourselves, but we have it just the same. This was our second chance. It came at a cost, so now we need to take it. Value it. Keep it alive, unlike our previous selves." He hit the emergency stop button to allow the elevator to continue on its journey. "Grab on to her, D. The love of a woman can heal anything. Fuck. Ninety percent of your work is complete because you've conquered the urges and self-doubts that plagued Waters and TB. You just need to take that last step, and to be honest, that last step is the hardest one to take. It will also be the most rewarding."

The doors opened onto an empty reception area. Steel exited without a backward glance, turning toward their personal offices. Demon glanced at Cherry's abandoned desk, then hit the button to close the doors and travel up to his apartment to change into project gear.

Where the hell was she?

3

———————————

SEPTEMBER 9, 2022

Cherry

"Demon, we need Cherry."

Saints Peter, Paul, and Mary! Not good!

Today should have been so simple, and it turned into nothing but the classic cluster. Step one—pick up Haskell at the airport. Step two —sneak her into Tribe. Step three—hope that she didn't break her promise to Haskell yet still fail to avoid Nemo so that they reunite. Step four—they fall in love, and "Operation Cherry Plays Cupid" is in the bag. But no! Some Judas planted a bomb, and while those two were in the same room together, it was now "Operation Shit Show" with her as supervisor.

Quickly, she clicked out of the audio link she'd turned on in the conference room. No one needed to know she'd been listening in. Her summons wasn't a surprise, necessarily, but it gave her a few seconds to gather her thoughts.

She heard Demon before she saw him. The rustle of his tac pants and the squeak of the rubber soles of his boots as they traveled down the corridor to her desk. Most of the men in the office moved quieter than ninjas. Not Demon. He could, but ninety-nine percent of the time, he didn't care if you knew he was coming your way. Or was it that he just didn't care if *she* heard him approaching? Did he do it on purpose? Some sort of sick "I'm coming for you, so just sit there and think about that" maneuver?

A shadow fell over her and her desk, and the scent of salt and sand hit her nose. "Conference room."

Two words in that deep timbre and the very distant remnants of his Irish lilt were all it took to make a shiver pass through her. Looking up from her seat, she saw Demon in all his glory. Most days, he rambled around the office in beach gear—T-shirt, board shorts, and flip-flops. His shoulder-length brown hair would be in some version of a man bun or wet and tangled around his face, and he'd either have reflective sunglasses on or perched on top of his head.

Not today, and the heat that passed through her had her ducking her head back down and pretending to focus on her computer screen. She couldn't even tell you what was on it. International secrets. Passwords for the entire office. Hell, it could have been an online order for staples, but she was so distracted by him that she couldn't focus on the content enough for it to be an effective hiding place from his command.

Why was she hiding? She was hiding because today was one of the rare days he wasn't in his beach gear, and if he was gorgeous when he was in surfer mode, Lord love a duck, he was devastating when he dressed in project gear. Something had made him decide not to just roll out of the surf like a merman. Instead, he wore a black T-shirt, black tactical pants, and his black boots. Sinners, get on your knees because your king has arrived!

"I have work to do, Demon."

"It wasn't a request."

Looking up at him from beneath her eyelashes, she had to admire his sharp features. Deep-brown hair loose, parted down the middle, sunglasses holding the sides behind his ears. Green eyes boring into hers, a sparkle of fight in them, and a Roman nose flaring just slightly with every inhale like he was trying to maintain his composure. Lips pressed into a thin line, clearly holding back a lot more words than he was currently giving her.

He really was a frighteningly beautiful man.

"You're not my boss," she replied, purposely diverting her gaze to her screen.

A sensory explosion of sun, sand, and salt enveloped her as his whispered reply rolled into her ear from behind. "Your boss sent me."

Well... yes and no. What he didn't know wouldn't hurt him.

"I don't—"

If possible, his voice got quieter. "Now, Cherry. Or I'll pick you up, throw you over my shoulder, and carry you, just like I did earlier today."

Yeah. Volume decrease, threat increase. DEFCON Demon. Only two levels with him. Asshole and major asshole. Why was that so fucking hot?

With a sigh of suffering, Cherry shut down her computer, transferred the phones over to Nova, Midas' AI creation, and tried to walk with as much dignity as possible toward the conference room. Entering the room, she saw that only Demon's regular seat and the one to his right were unoccupied. Steel was sitting to the inside right with Haskell, one-half of the Cupid pairing in Nemo's regular chair. Nemo, the other half of her experiment, was standing behind Haskell's chair, marking her as his territory. At least one thing seemed to be going right. Midas sat to Haskell's left at the head of the table, typing away at his keyboard, followed around the horn by TB, their interrogator, then Waters, the team leader.

As Demon herded her into the open seat, Waters put the office security protocols in place. In the table's center was a starfish-shaped object that looked like a video game controller. He pressed the red button on it, and the room's coloring changed. Floor-to-ceiling windows, tinted to be impenetrable to sight or sound, made the overhead lights harsher. The inset computer monitors on the conference room table had a red glow around their outer edges. At the head of the table, the telescreen displayed the building security map and several key security cameras, and the telescreen at the foot of the table was connected to Midas' computer screen. Meanwhile, there was a thumping sound as the automatic locks on the door from the conference room to the hallway bolted into place.

Waters opened the conversation. "Haskell, I think you better walk us through this from the beginning. You clearly know things we don't, and I, for one, am tired of being in the dark."

Cherry glanced down the table at Haskell Dawson, a blonde, Shirley Temple, curly-haired thief covered in tattoos and piercings. The look on the pixie's face was clearly asking permission from Cherry to answer his questions about the pressure-plate bomb scare they'd been involved in this morning. Things were about to get dicier than tomatoes at a salsa-making contest.

A quick glance at her immediate boss and Cherry didn't blame Waters for his current level of frustration. He was in the dark—well, really, the entire team was—about a lot of things, especially about the origins of Tribe Corporation's foundation. For the longest time, things had been moving at a snail's pace. Now they were moving faster than she had intended. The day had finally come to open the floodgates about what Tribe was really all about. Secrets were going to be told. They would not reveal all the secrets, but they would definitely reveal some of the most fundamental ones. Didn't mean the guys were going to be happy about what they were about to hear.

Cherry gave Haskell a single head nod, permitting her to give Waters what he wanted. Haskell only knew portions of Tribe's shadowy presence, but it was more than the men in this room knew. She hoped Haskell stuck to the basics. She probably would. The woman was savvy that way, and Cherry would then fill in the additional blanks that needed filling.

Haskell explained her escape from Africa after the owners caught her breaking into a diamond mine, her past encounters with Nemo, her connections to Cherry, and her work as a contractor with Mythos —a trio of operatives who disrupted global sex trafficking schemes. With no exit contact in Africa, Haskell had to contact Cherry for help. After picking her up at LAX, Cherry had taken Haskell to a favorite haunt of hers, where Haskell had inadvertently sat on a chair that triggered a pressure-plate bomb. At first, the bomb attempt seemed to carry all the signatures of Cerberus, a well-known bomber and ecoterrorist. The only problem was that Haskell knew the bomb couldn't be his since he was a contractor for Mythos, like her, and he had no reason to blow up a woman who was his friend.

As soon as Haskell relayed what had happened in the café, Cherry knew that the conversation was taking its inevitable, disastrous turn. Obviously, she had known this day would come, but she couldn't have possibly predicted the explosive—no pun intended—situation forcing her hand today. For the first time, she second-guessed her years of preparation.

By now, Haskell had finished her explanation of how she had selected her seat and was finishing up with her assessment of why their conjectures regarding the bomb were in error. The blonde sighed. "I'll admit, I piss people off all the time when I strike, but not enough to blow me into a million pieces."

TB, the team's interrogator and all-around grouch, grunted. He had his six-foot-seven, two-hundred-forty-pound body sprawled in his chair, and he did not look amused. "Executions and assassinations remove individual threats. Bombs are for making statements. Jewel thieves don't inspire that sort of violence."

"Exactly," Haskell agreed. "So, as well as knowing that Cerberus was not behind this bomb, there's only one group of people I can think of who would go to such extreme lengths to remove a single person in such spectacular fashion. Not only are they willing to do it, but it's typical for them to copy other criminals' signatures in order to divert suspicion."

"And who would that be?" Waters asked.

With a sweeping glance at everyone around the table and

studiously ignoring the angry man next to her, Cherry finally spoke. "She's referring to the Salieri."

All the faces around the table stared at her in shock. That name had come up amongst these men before. Just a few weeks ago, they had battled the lowest edges of that group when one of the Salieri's soldiers, a mid-level drug dealer named Gendry, stalked and kidnapped TB's girlfriend, Flame. Tribe and Mythos rescued both Flame and Medusa, a Mythos member, from captivity. Unfortunately, it wouldn't be the last time they heard of the Salieri, whether it was today or months down the line.

Waters fixed their handler with a stern look. "What have you been hiding, Cherry?"

She blew out a breath before answering. "If they intended the bomb for me, the Salieri fit as our bombers," she said. "Haskell heading to the table first prompted the man in the brown suit to stand. Had I been first, his companion in the black suit would have gotten up and offered me the seat. They executed it perfectly."

She swore she felt the vibrations coming off Demon as he went from pissed off to enraged. "Goddammit, Cherry, why do you think the bomb was for you?"

"My real name is Esme Bosworth, the only child of Grayson Bosworth."

"Shit on a shingle with a side order of fries," Midas, their computer guru, whispered.

Demon rolled his eyes. "You've been hanging out too much with Kubrick and Flame. That was the oddest combination of the two of them swearing/not swearing I've ever heard. Why can't you people curse like normal human beings?"

"You can't even pronounce 'fuck' correctly," TB argued. "Who are you to talk?"

"I pronounce feck just fine," Demon grumbled.

"That 'u' sounds an awful lot like an 'e,' dude," Nemo, the blond, tattooed, and pierced operator, pointed out.

"Feck you," Demon said as he threw up his middle finger at his teammate.

"All right, you three, simmer down," Waters warned. "Neither one of you speaks right with those goof-ass accents. Now focus your pea brains and get back to what's important." He turned his gaze onto their handler. With an audible sigh, he ran a hand over his close-cropped, dark-blond hair. "Now explain, Cherry. Why do you think the bomb was meant for you? And how do the Salieri, whoever the fuck, or feck, they are, fit into all of this?"

"I'll try to be quick," Cherry promised. "My father had many friends in the military, even though he himself had never served. Not for lack of trying. He had a heart murmur that disqualified him from enlisting. But he believed absolutely in the military, even though they couldn't use him personally, so he turned his skills in manufacturing to support the service branches in another way.

"The story of the day he disappeared is public knowledge, but what the public didn't know was where I ended up and how I've made Tribe my life's quest. I've spent the last twenty years building, financing, and running Tribe from my computer."

Stunned silence greeted her confession. She pressed on.

"In order to do this right, I knew I had to play the long game. Success depended on relationships being fostered. I knew that would slow things down further—time that my father didn't have—but what other choice was there? His survival was already unlikely, so I accepted that if I was too late and he was dead, I would ensure everything was in place to catch and punish those responsible for his disappearance.

"It also required that I remain in the shadows. I knew I didn't have the skills to do this by myself, so I used my college years to hone my analytical skills. I learned everything I could about history, culture, finances, politics, and anything else I thought would be useful in running an operation like Tribe. Combine all of that with my family's vast wealth, and I could hire people who could. I purposefully scouted out the best of the best, but there was a hitch.

Those individuals had to be free of family ties. They had to be people who could walk away from everything because we couldn't work out in the open. I started with God and worked my way to recruiting the rest of you."

"So we exist because of a personal need for revenge?" TB concluded.

"Justice!" Cherry sniped. She took a calming breath. "My father deserves that." She looked to TB. "Whatever the reason I created Tribe, you've all done a lot of good over these past five years. Good others couldn't have gotten done."

"We've also done some shady-as-fuck work," TB reminded her.

She pleaded with TB to understand her choices. "None of it was assisting truly bad people. I ensured nothing like that ever touched any of you."

Steel, the quiet Latino member of the team, brought the conversation back to the pressing issue. "What's the connection between today's bomb threat and the Salieri?"

"Years ago, when my father disappeared, I was going through his things, desperate to find clues about who might have taken him. Buried in his personal cloud were folders and folders of articles relating to Mozart and his fellow composer, Antonio Salieri. Everything from research articles to reviews of many play performances around the theatrical world of *Amadeus* by Peter Shaffer. I nearly deleted the files because I couldn't figure out why my father would have something like that saved in his drive. He hated classical music, and live theatre was barely one step above it in his estimation."

"The articles were breadcrumbs," Waters deduced.

Cherry nodded. "In truth, I forgot about the files because getting Tribe up and running became my sole focus. When Gendry gave up the name, it triggered my memory of what I'd found, so I started looking closer at those files again. They were all downloads of genuine articles from a worldwide database, but something about them looked... wrong. Recently, it hit me why." She reached for a keyboard under the conference table and pulled up her files from her computer, switching the content from Midas' screen to hers. "What do you see?"

Silence permeated the room.

Midas' voice broke the silence. "The spacing is all wrong."

"Very good," Cherry complimented him. "I figured you would see it right away."

"Pardon my limited brain power," TB interrupted, "but what does spacing have to do with it?"

"The margins are off," Midas explained. "When you download an article off the internet and save it to your drive, it follows the same default protocols to format the file to its new location. Text centers left, right, up, down, and spaces the lines at 1.15 lines."

Haskell chimed in. "It's like how I configure my body in a small space, or if someone played the game of Tetris. The document uses the allotted space as efficiently as possible. When you copy over text from one source to another, unless you tell it otherwise, the formatting follows along with the text. Most internet articles use Chicago style formatting—the style journalists use—where the document justifies the text so that the margins are even on both sides and words are flush with both the left and right margins. In addition, there are rules for when and where a new page can start."

Midas picked up the explanation again. "If you look at this document Cherry pulled up, the formatting is uneven. Also, if I were to print this document in its entirety, there would be"—he counted—"one, two, three extra pages at the end of the article that would be blank. In a professional setting, that wouldn't happen. That it does here suggests hidden text to me."

Cherry nodded. "I finally came around to that as well." She highlighted the entire article, and within the highlighting in the margins, a shadowy character like a medieval-style "S" inside a diamond appeared at the top left and the bottom right of each new page. The three blank pages that followed the end of the article showed shadowy writing in an unreadable font that was colored white and microscopic on the page.

"What are we looking at, exactly?" questioned TB.

"The authors, or the publishers more likely, used extremely low tech to hide a private message," Midas explained. "Microscopic, white-colored font. Unless you knew what to look for, you'd just assume those last pages were extra and probably ignore them."

TB rose from his seat and walked closer to the screen. "It's brilliant," he whispered. "How did no one see this?"

"Sometimes the best hiding place is in plain sight," Cherry acknowledged. "Like hiding a specific needle in a stack of other needles. Hang on." With a few more keystrokes, Cherry placed a second document side by side with the *Amadeus* article she'd used as the example for the group. The entire room could now view the new version of the document with the white text changed to blue and enlarged to size twelve font.

Haskell looked at Cherry. "Is this what I think it is?"

"Looks like gibberish," Demon complained.

"To most people, yes. In reality, it's Middle English," Cherry informed him.

"Wow." Haskell popped out of her chair and joined TB at the screen, her fingers tracing the lettering. "I haven't seen this since I read *The Canterbury Tales*."

"This is... I don't know what this is," Waters whispered.

Haskell swore under her breath. "My Middle English is rusty, but it's good enough to see that this file is an order of purchase. White women between the ages of sixteen and twenty-five. Clean bills of health, no underlying conditions, no history of genetic disease markers. Preferably women with few family ties and few connections to miss them." Her eyes were glassy as she turned to look at the others in the room. "Bloody hell, they wanted three hundred women."

Cherry nodded. "This is why my father disappeared. He was chasing the Salieri long before Mythos. I bet each of these articles he stored in his cloud is a publicly hidden communication between the Salieri and prospective clients. I'm convinced that they figured out he was closing in on them, or at least closing in more than anyone else had in the past. Now I've been poking around in his files again, as well as digging into new areas, and it looks like I inadvertently announced my presence to the Salieri." She cringed. "I've no one to blame but myself for becoming this easy of a target. I broke one of our biggest rules by eating at that café every Friday."

"Cherry," Demon groaned.

"I know, I know! No repetitions! Don't go to the same places; don't go the same routes. Haskell almost paid the price for my mistake."

Waters cut off her self-recriminations. "There's no use worrying about that now. What's done is done. But Cherry, you understand—"

"That my father's most likely dead? Yes. But I can't stop looking, Waters. This is an enormous piece of information I never knew I had until Flame. It's been years with no leads, and now there are thousands of reviews, articles, and files he downloaded off the internet. There are even some video files. I don't know what those are for—"

"Advertisements," Midas conjectured. "I bet that's what they are. Maybe for the services of the Salieri. Possibly advertisements of specific people they had for sale. Embedded images likely exist within those video files. Each one of these files needs to be gone through and translated, reformatted. Who knows what information is in there?"

Waters stared at the screen. "Something tells me we need this information translated yesterday."

"I'll put Nova on it immediately and go over whatever she finds."

Waters nodded tightly.

Steel walked over to Waters and put his hand on his team leader's shoulder. "*Jefe*, we've just all had a shit ton of information dumped on us and no time to process it. Maybe we should take a break, then come back together when we're in a headspace more prone to taking on the more pressing issue at hand."

Guilt swamped her as she watched Waters process the information. "Agreed. I need to... call Kubrick." At that point, Waters hit the security button on the starfish, putting the room back to its normal protocol. "Reconvene at eighteen hundred. Demon, you're on protection detail for Cherry. Nemo, you're in charge of Haskell. Both of you —do not, under any circumstances, allow these women to leave this building."

Waters practically flung himself out of the room, the rest of the team right behind him. When Cherry rose from her chair, a hand gripped her bicep to steer her away from the table and to the elevator. "You and I need to have a conversation," Demon muttered so that no one else could hear.

4

SEPTEMBER 9, 2022

Demon

Could someone be so angry that they self-imploded? As a former doctor, his brain denied the possibility. Rage increased blood pressure, and if someone's blood pressure got high enough, maybe their heart could rupture, but right now, it felt like his entire body was churning with the anger of a Category 5 hurricane.

Tense did not even describe the silent ride in the elevator after the team meeting with Haskell Dawson and all of Cherry's revelations. Everyone was more than a little stunned right now, to say the least. He had a feeling all of them were spinning with the implications of what Cherry had just told them about her father, the Salieri, and how possibly everything they'd done these past five years was interconnected to those two things. Did she have any clue what she'd potentially and inadvertently unleashed?

When the elevator doors opened on the fifth floor, his hand still clutching her bicep, Demon propelled Cherry off the carriage and toward his apartment door. She tried to be quiet about it, but he was sure people in the elevator heard their first few sentences.

Cherry hissed at him. "I can walk, you know."

"I don't want you trying to escape this long-overdue conversation."

"I have nothing to say to you."

He stopped them in front of his door and swung her around to face him. "That's fine because I have a lot to say to you, and I hate being interrupted."

He keyed in his door code.

"I want to go to my apartment," she fumed.

"It's good to want things."

"You're an asshole!"

"And you're being a bitch right now, so we're even."

He saw and felt her flinch at his verbal slap, and he immediately felt bad about what he'd said, but he squashed it down. Being soft on her right now would not fix things. With one hand, he opened the door, and with the other, he gave her a gentle shove over the threshold. He followed behind her, and once the door was closed, he keyed in his code so that it wouldn't open again without it.

"You know I know everyone's code, right?" she asked. Obviously, she'd gathered her wits about her and got back into combat mode.

"Yes, I am aware. However, the three seconds it would take you to enter the code and wait for it to clear would be enough time for me to catch you and keep you from leaving. Now park your arse. On the sofa, in a chair, in my bed, if you fecking like, but sit."

Her arms folded over her chest, Cherry pivoted on her heel and moved to the terrace window instead. Internally, he sighed. She always did the opposite of what he asked. Well, what he told her to do, if he was going to be truthful. Both of them seemed to jump straight to pissed off whenever they spoke to each other lately. He had no doubts it was about to get worse.

Despite his anger at her, which was really fear, Demon admired her silhouette from where he stood in the center of his apartment entryway. She was fecking fire, and he loved everything about her. Every inch of her five-foot-ten frame in those stiletto heels. Every twitch of her tight ass in those pencil skirts. Every strand of her long, fire-engine-red hair. Every stare, warm or cold, from her sea-gray eyes. Every word, whether it was sarcastic, teasing, or straightforward. Every thought in her machinelike brain. She was the whole fecking package and, right now, gloriously pissed, although he wasn't sure if it was at him or herself. Either way, he wanted her more than he'd ever wanted her before.

With a loud sigh, he removed his sunglasses from the top of his head and tossed them on the breakfast bar. "Damn it, Cherry. What the hell am I going to do with you?"

"Excuse me?" The glare warned him he was in dangerous territory, but it wasn't as if he hadn't already known that.

"What were you thinking? Keeping these kinds of secrets gets people killed. It nearly did today."

"It's my life, Demon!"

"No, it wasn't! Jaysus, for someone who's so organized, you sure don't think straight sometimes. You didn't just put yourself at risk. You put Haskell at risk, all the guys, and Scheherazade when we came to bail you out, not to mention dozens of innocent people in that café. And that's just today's antics! What's the matter with you?"

Instinctively, she managed enough control to defend herself. "I can't be responsible for every decision every sick mother—"

"I didn't say you were or that you should even think you could be. What I'm saying, whether you want to hear it, whether it hurts your feelings, is that you knowingly kept us in the dark to manipulate us to a particular result. That's not cool. I can almost guarantee that had you told us up front, we all would have jumped to help you." Closing his eyes, he hung his head, put a hand to his hip, and with the other, he pinched the bridge of his nose. After taking a steadying breath, he looked back up at her. "Whether it was today, tomorrow, next week, next year, whatever. It doesn't matter. Circumstances forced your hand today. When were you going to let us in on this shite?"

"When I was damn good and ready! You don't tell me what to do, Demon. I tell you! God may be the boss, but I'm the chess master. I set up the board! I make the strategy! And I move the pieces! Me! Tribe is my company. Its purpose is my own!" Her hands slapped down against her sides. "You say you can almost guarantee you all would have agreed to help me without knowing all the details? Then what's the goddamn difference, Demon? If you would have agreed to help me with full knowledge, why does it matter if you knew or not? The result would be the same as it is now."

"The difference is that people's lives are at stake! I get playing things close, Cherry, but you can't work in the shadows like this and hope that we'll come to the solution you want! You're good, but what you're hoping for would take a feckin' miracle. We're human beings. We work as a team, and over the years, we've developed a sort of hive mentality, but we also function independently. Those skills are important too. By not sharing information you had, you stripped us of the ability to inject our personal knowledge and strengths. Don't bury them because they don't fit some plan you made in your head."

Her fists were clenching and unclenching, and he was glad that he wasn't a home decor person because otherwise, anything not nailed down would sail at his head.

"I need your 'hive' to find my father, dead or alive. If he's dead, then I need you to find his killers. If I allow you to work on an independent trajectory, you develop personal agendas, and then what happens if your needs don't match mine anymore?"

"Do you even hear yourself? 'Your needs don't match mine'? TB was right. This isn't about justice. We've become your tools for revenge. Only it's the revenge of a teenage girl who's lost her daddy."

"Asshole!"

"Yes, we established that earlier. But who's the bigger asshole right now? Me or you?"

"What the hell are you talking about?" she screeched.

"You've been putting us at unnecessary risk for six years." He took a step in her direction, then froze again when her eyes narrowed.

He cooled things down with logic so she would understand. "Look. While that came out wrong, the fact remains. Every project has to have a purpose, right? And every project we've been out on, we've been going in with only a partial understanding of what the hell it is we've been doing."

"How dare you accuse me of blindsiding you! Is that really what you think?"

How could he get through to her? How could he make her understand that she'd been playing with people's lives? "We may have had the short-term understanding. Steal the diamonds. Kill the drug lord. Rescue the kid. But we never knew the big picture, Cherry, or that there even was one! You can't play a chess game this large and not sacrifice some pieces along the way."

"I know that!"

"Well, did the pieces themselves know they were part of the game?"

She threw her hands in the air in frustration. "What are you talking about? You're not making any sense."

He moved two steps closer to her. "Did you inform the pieces in your chess match with the Salieri what the dangers were? Did you let them choose to be a part of your game? Did they understand what they might sacrifice? Or did you decide what you were willing to sacrifice, and woe be those who were lost in the cross fire?"

She sputtered in rage, but he knew that when she calmed down, she would see that it was raging at herself. Not him. Not the team. Not even the men who'd kidnapped her father and likely murdered him. A rage of impotence at the whole situation.

The next question he asked was going to be a killing blow, but he couldn't hold it back. It was going to hurt her, but it needed to be said, and he'd rather she directed her rage at him than the team at large. Based on how Waters had reacted in the conference room, it was clear he had made the connection between Cherry's tale and the chain of events she'd set in motion. Events that may not have needed to end as they had.

His voice was sad and soft because the damage he was about to inflict was irreparable. "Did Sarah make the choice to be a pawn in your game?" He watched her body rear back as if from a physical blow and her face blanch.

"How dare you?" Her voice was shaking with anger and sorrow and fear. "Sarah was my best friend. What happened to her was not my fault! The kidnapping of Sarah to retaliate against Waters for stopping the shipment of trafficking victims was unacceptable."

"No, fireball," he soothed while continuing to deliver the blows. "It wasn't acceptable. But it wasn't acceptable to make her an unknowing pawn either. And while it may not be your fault—because obviously, you didn't make the choice to kidnap, rape, and kill her in front of her brother—did you ever stop to think about the harm she could come to based on the choices you made?

"How could we possibly have been fully prepared to fight this kind of evil when we didn't know what we were facing? We did not know who we were dealing with when we intercepted that shipment, did we? Would the outcome have been any different had we known? Maybe not," he admitted. "Maybe they still would have taken Sarah. But maybe Waters would have tempered his response and not gone after her on his own. Maybe, with more information, we could have rescued them both, damaged but alive. Maybe we would have been able to strike harder and damage her captors, even decimate them, rather than just go in, rescue Waters, and get out. It's a lot of maybes, but we might have been able to do some of those things. Now we'll never know."

"You think losing Sarah didn't hurt me? You think I didn't feel that pain just as much as every one of you did?"

"I'm not saying you didn't. But I am saying you had knowledge that you didn't share."

"There was no way I could confirm—"

He held up a hand to her. "Stop, Cherry! Just stop! Don't give me the legalese response. You're not a lawyer here, worrying about trapping a client behind a definitive answer. You're not a doctor being held accountable for a result you promised and then couldn't fulfill." He swallowed the pain that was too close for comfort. "You had information that, circumstantial or not, might have made a difference, and you withheld it. End of story. Now that Waters and the rest of us know, you can't expect us to be comfortable with that. It is going to make it very difficult for us to trust that you're not continuing to hold out on information."

Her mouth opened and closed several times, no sound coming out, as her brain tried to wrap around his words. He knew she was going to have a tough time coming to grips with his truths. Her choices would not make the team, especially him, love her any less. But they certainly changed the dynamic, and it was going to be painful for her to reconcile that while she thought she'd been doing the right thing, it was possible she'd done the wrong thing.

"You've been keeping a lot of secrets bottled up. I'm guessing there are more to come."

"If I'm keeping anything else secret, it's because you don't need to know."

"Not willing to learn from the mistake? You're willing to hide behind this armor, crossing your fingers that someone else doesn't get killed? We got lucky today that Nemo saved Haskell. You're gonna keep rolling those same dice? Feck, you've got bigger balls than I do then because even I know not to take that bet. Eventually, that luck is going to go cold, and it won't just be the person who dies who pays the price. Waters is still grieving, and it was three years ago we lost Sarah. Kubrick is the only thing keeping him from descending completely into the darkness. TB is paranoid as shit someone's gonna come back after Flame because we know her kidnapping has a much bigger role than just Gendry's obsession with her, and don't think he won't hold a grudge against anyone who plays any part in hurting her, including you. Even dipshit Nemo. You think he won't burn the world to the ground for that pixie out there he's been mooning over since before Tribe?"

He framed her face in his hands. "Who will be the victims next time? Haskell dodged a bullet today, but who's saying she won't be a victim again? Or maybe it will be someone Midas or Steel comes to care about? Even if it is you—Jaysus, Cherry. None of us could take that, especially me. I wouldn't just burn the world down. I'd implode the universe over that and take all life as we know it with me."

"Then I guess you'd be no better than me, huh? Are you gonna ask every human being on this planet, every case of sentient life in the universe, if they mind being destroyed because you've got a hard-on for something you can't have?"

He knew she was pushing back at him like a wounded animal. Anything to escape the agonizing pain of his truth. "No, fireball. I wouldn't ask them," he admitted. "But that's the difference between you and me. You feel sorrow. Regret. Remorse. Me?" He shook his head. "There's not one thing in the last six years that I've cared about other than you. So if someone takes you away from me, then no price is too great to make them pay. I would welcome an eternity in hell for my actions. The rest of the world can just go feck themselves."

They stood there for the longest time, saying nothing. He, a pillar of calm determination in his confession. She, a tempest of pain and panic working behind her eyes. "Well, I'm part of that world, too, Demon," she whispered. "You say you feel no sorrow, no regret, and no remorse? Fuck that noise! You're the worst of us all because you lie to us and yourself about how you 'handle' yourself. Your fight with your crippling addiction puts all of us at risk every day. When you give up the drugs? Then argue with me about how I handle things. Until then, you have no right to say 'Boo' to me. About anything."

With a sudden burst of energy, she circled him and headed for the door. He didn't move. His brain was screaming at him to go after her. Promise to trust her, help her. Promise her everything she wanted and more. Instead, his legs remained locked, his feet stayed rooted to the floor, and he listened as she punched his code into the door lock, opened the door, and closed it behind her.

Moments later, he heard the soft beeps as she punched in the code to her apartment down the hall, then the computerized click of the unlocking mechanism, then the snick of the closing door behind her.

"Feck!"

In the apartment's silence, he crossed through the living room and into his bathroom. Jerking the right-hand drawer open, he reached for the unmarked pill container, opened it, and shook out two pills. He threw the container back in the drawer, and as he was about to toss the pills into his mouth, he stopped. He stared at the two white tablets, his teeth grinding as he considered them.

She was correct. He had no right to call her on her behaviors when he had no control over his own. He was a hypocrite.

"Feck," he whispered.

With a toss of his hand, the pills shot into his mouth, and he chased them with a glass of water. Then he cursed himself for being twelve kinds of idiot.

5

____

APRIL 7, 2023

Cherry

"NEVER DO ANYTHING HALFWAY," KUBRICK READ OFF THE SLIP of paper.

"In bed!" There was a chorus of giggles from three of the four women having lunch together. Cherry covered up her lack of laughter by shoving a forkful of garlic chicken into her mouth.

Kubrick, Waters' girlfriend, an athletic, long-haired blonde, was a film director in Hollywood. Today, she'd breezed into Tribe's office building with Chinese takeout for the office at large. The men were probably eating in TB's office because it was always open, since he preferred to do his office work standing at the armory table. The women had confiscated the conference room, and Kubrick showed her inner ten-year-old boy by putting a sign on the closed door that said, "No boys allowed!" She'd even found a crayon to write the message with.

The girls usually attempted to get together for lunch on Fridays.

Since Kubrick was about to depart for China in the middle of the following week and rarely took breaks when on location, they were eagerly trying to get in girl time.

Flame, a romance novelist who looked as if she was from some mishmash of the Victorian era with her boned corset tops and a sixties hippie with her long, flowing boho skirts, sat across the table from her. She was picking through her food, culling out the peas and baby corn from her fried rice. Eight months into her surprise pregnancy, morning sickness had been all day long from almost day one and had never stopped, so any sort of food for lunch was a crapshoot, and her "hell no" foods changed daily. Vegetables always seemed to be at the top of the list.

Projected on the telescreen was Gem, Nemo's other half. Currently, she was sitting at a desk in front of a laptop, her feet up, spooning something out of a bowl with what looked like a leaf. Cherry shuddered. Heaven only knew what she was actually eating.

She and Nemo were somewhere in Africa, working on their diamond mine project from a few months earlier. Until the end of September, Nemo had worked for Tribe. They'd been trying to prove where some conflict diamonds and other precious stones were being mined—stones that were being used to fund the Salieri's purchasing of women through the skin trade. When that project had finished, Nemo left Tribe to go work with Mythos, whom Gem contracted for. There had been several reasons for the move, primarily that the playboy thief was head over heart in love with the woman and had been for almost seven years. Tribe was still adjusting to the aftershocks of his unexpected departure, particularly his fraternal twin, Midas.

With a snort, Kubrick laid the fortune from her cookie onto the conference room table. "Never have to worry about that problem myself."

A chorus of fake disgust at her TMI overshare swept through the room.

"I wouldn't say that. Whatever Waters is going to do without you for twelve weeks is definitely going to be 'halfway' since only one of the two of you will be present," Flame teased.

Breaking her fortune cookie into additional pieces, Kubrick tossed one into the air and caught it in her mouth. Her eyes twinkled. "That's what computers are for."

Another chorus of "Eww" came from the girls.

"Oh, hush," Kubrick chastised. "You can't say 'Eww,' Flame. That's how you and TB met."

"Stop it," Flame ordered. Her pale skin blushed deep enough to match her red hair.

Kubrick shrugged. "It's true."

Gem made porn music sounds in the background. "I've got no complaints either. Nemo's still Nemo," she confided. She raised her eyebrows up and down several times, smirking as she ate her next bite of food.

"What was the latest location?"

"More importantly," Flame inserted, "did you get caught?"

"We never get caught. And I can't tell you where we were specifically, but those napping rooms in hospitals for the doctors are not comfortable at all. Someone needs to speak to their union."

A cheer rose from the two women. "I'll add it to my notebook of places he's been," Kubrick told her. "Might get to use some of those ideas in a movie someday. Maybe he can consult on the scene," she teased.

"Yeah, because your last movie consult didn't end up hot and steamy between the sheets as it was. I know you two took a page out of our book and had sex on your set, so you don't need my guy too," Gem shot back.

"Not on the set specifically. No worries here though. Nemo was always more partial to Flame."

If possible, the redhead blushed further. "Maybe I should put it in a book. Although I don't know if hospitals in the 1700s had napping rooms."

"I'm not even sure they had hospitals," Kubrick said. Her head snapped back to Gem on the screen. "Wait. Why were you in a hospital?"

The woman waved off the question, setting her bowl down. "It wasn't a Mythos member, so it's not important. What about your fortune, Cherry?" All eyes were now on Tribe's handler.

Cherry broke her fortune cookie in half. "Your heart will skip a beat."

"In bed!" the women chorused again, followed by long, drawn-out interjections of "ooh" from Gem and Flame while Kubrick emitted obnoxious kissing noises.

Cherry didn't even break a smile. Normally, she was up for all the antics that her friends induced during their lunches, but today? Today, she wished she'd had an excuse to stay at her desk. Cherry shoved another bite of her lunch into her mouth.

There was a pregnant pause. "I saw the moody doctor this morning," Kubrick admitted. "Definitely sporting his BAMF-mode persona today," Kubrick said. "Mm-mm-mm."

Gem wolf-whistled. "I so love when any of them are in BAMF mode."

Flame scrunched up her face. "What the heck'um is BAMF mode?"

In stereo and without thought, Cherry joined Kubrick and Haskell. "Badass motherfucker."

"Oh. Yeah." Flame shuddered. "Demon even gives me the shivers when he's dressed in BAMF mode." She whispered the acronym since she didn't swear and then giggled.

"Don't let TB hear you say that. He'll tie you to the bed and not let you up for days."

Flame shivered again. "You think? Hmm."

Kubrick shoved a chocolate cupcake in her mouth and winked at her bestie.

There was a snort from Gem. "You seriously shoved a whole snack cake in your mouth. Fortune cookies weren't enough? You've had like twelve of those."

"I'll work them off later." She winked. "Just don't come by Waters' office for an hour after lunch."

A ripple of laughter passed among the women.

"So how are preparations going for China?" Cherry asked. Maybe she could deflect the conversation she knew was coming.

"Nope. I won't allow myself to be distracted. Seriously, he was broody before. He's been downright mopey since your little powder-keg party at the café. Why won't you put that boy out of his misery?"

"Because I don't have a gun on me."

Gem barked out a laugh. "Girl, that bloke loves you so much he's bleeding internally. You don't need to insult the poor sod by shooting him too."

"The man's an asshole. On top of that, he's an addict. I refuse to attach myself to that. You can't trust an addict."

A sharp inhale came from Flame, her eyes wide and instantly watery.

Kubrick hissed. "What the fuck, Cherry?" she whispered.

Immediately, Cherry realized her mistake.

Flame's voice was small when she spoke. "I'm an addict. Do you see me differently?"

Setting down her fork, Cherry apologized to her friend. "I'm sorry. That was cruel and thoughtless of me. But your circumstances were completely different," she qualified. "You didn't make that choice. Gendry forced that shit on you, and you haven't had drugs in years. Demon chose to be an addict, and he's still using."

"Does anyone really choose how they cope?" Gem wondered.

Her gaze swung to the woman on the screen. "Now you're defending him? You used to hold it against him."

Gem shrugged. "Let's just say that Zimbabwe changed a lot of things. Besides, we never really know why someone makes the choices they do, and coping mechanisms are like shoes. They match the external circumstances."

"I vetted all the guys personally. I know exactly what his glitch is."

"And yet you hired him anyway," Flame pointed out.

"She's not wrong," Kubrick agreed.

Gem let her feet fall from the desk, and she leaned toward the computer. "Just because you know the order of events in someone's life doesn't mean you know what the cause-and-effect relationship is. Hell, I know that from Nemo firsthand. And you should know that too. Have you ever known Demon to be blotto enough not to do his job?"

"No," Cherry admitted. "But that's not the point. The point is he uses. Period. He doesn't need to; therefore, the reasons don't matter."

Flame put her fork down. "And now we're back to that." Flame stood up from the table and packed up her leftovers. "Sorry, Kubrick. I seem to have lost my appetite. Have a wonderful trip if I don't talk to you before you leave. Be safe." With that, she left the conference room.

Kubrick was silent as she began cleaning up the table.

"Shit," Cherry murmured, her eyes beginning to water. "I don't know what the hell is wrong with me." Flame's drug use was so far in the past, she didn't even consider it as part of her. Drugs had been used to keep her compliant as a teen by a pedophile drug dealer who pimped her out to anyone he owed money to. That wasn't her fault. But by saying it didn't matter why Demon used, she'd just equated him to Flame, and that wasn't fair.

"Spring fever?" Gem asked before taking another bite of her leaf. "People always seem so much twitchier this time of year." A noise off camera caught her attention, and she nodded to whomever was talking to her. "I have to go, ladies. Duty calls. Cherry... don't beat yourself up. Flame knows you don't really mean it like she's taking it. She's hormonal right now. By tomorrow, she'll have called you to tell you she loves you, and it's forgotten."

She nodded. "Thanks, Gem. Be safe."

With a salute, Gem disconnected the video feed, and the screen went back to its wallpaper.

Cherry couldn't bear to look up at Kubrick. She'd fucked up.

Again. She'd hurt Flame's feelings completely unintentionally, but she'd done it all the same. "Kubrick, I—"

Kubrick slammed a container on the table. "Enough is enough, Cherry. This shit with Demon is infecting everything you touch. He will not change. He is who he is, warts and all. You need to let it go. You want to spend your life miserable without him, fine. That's your choice. But your attitude toward him is causing you to say shit that's hurting Flame, and that I will not stomach. Nor will TB if he hears about it."

"It's stupid. I know it is. My mouth just says things, and my brain can't seem to hop in fast enough to slam the lid on it."

It was more than that, though, and she knew it. In truth, it had little to nothing to do with the drugs, although that concerned her. However, many people functioned just fine in all aspects of their lives despite being addicted to things. His illegal addiction, however, wasn't the reason for her anger.

Even that was a lie. She didn't feel anger toward him. She felt anger at herself, and her pride was refusing to allow her to back down. Tensions in the office were at an all-time high, and it was completely her fault. No one said anything, but Demon had been right. Everyone was second-guessing her now because of all the secrets she'd kept.

Waters was talking to her, but it was all professional, and he never hung out at her desk to chat anymore. TB tried, but his paranoia over Flame and the baby coming to any harm was almost comical, and it was as if he felt just talking to Cherry in the office put them at risk. The man had even double-checked and triple-checked all the security protocols himself at lunch today to ensure no one could get at the women in the conference room. Nemo probably would have been the same with her, but Nemo wasn't here. He was with Gem. Midas kept himself in his office almost twenty-four seven, 365, and what about Steel? Steel had never talked to her much to begin with. Now he just stared at her like a cobra waiting to strike.

Kubrick had tried to ask her what the hell was going on. Unfortunately, she couldn't tell Kubrick what it was really about—Demon's accusations regarding putting the team and their significant others in jeopardy for her personal wants—and the drug use was all she could come up with as a reason why she was keeping him at arm's length. It had become an all-consuming excuse. So much so that she was at a point where she'd tricked her own brain into being unable to get past it, and she was the one who manufactured it as a reason. Her pride wouldn't let her let it go, either, because that meant admitting she was in the wrong.

Everything was so fucked up.

"I don't understand it. His issues have been going on longer than you've known him. You never cared before. Everyone knows—has known—he's a functional addict with an on/off switch. You hired him knowing that. Now, suddenly, you're being a right fuckwitch and judgmental about it. What the ever-loving fuck?"

"Do you need to swear that much?"

"See? That! Right there! Now you're doing it to me! You used to find my filthy mouth charming and unapologetic. Called me a boss bitch babe with a smile. Now? You chastise me like a grandmother."

Cherry pushed all her lunch paraphernalia toward the center of the table, and then she placed her forehead flat on the tabletop, arms outstretched straight in front of her. "I don't know what's wrong."

There was a pause. "Are you pregnant? Because being all hormonal would explain a lot of things."

Lifting only her head, Cherry looked up at Kubrick with a frown. "I am not pregnant."

Kubrick snorted. "So what's the deal? Why are you going so hard at this? You're miserable. He's miserable. You could both be 'miserable' together if you'd just let it go. Is it some sort of test you're putting him through?"

Cherry put her head back down, this time with one cheek to the tabletop, her face turned in Kubrick's direction. "Maybe?"

"So you're never going to let yourself love him unless he never takes an oxy again? Because if that's what this is, that's just bullshit.

That would be like Waters saying he's never going to bend me over his desk again until I give up chocolate. Sister, we know neither one of those things is ever going to happen."

"Is that why he keeps the desk in his office? He doesn't use it for anything. He works at that stupid table now because of you."

An evil smile formed on Kubrick's face. "It's the best reason to keep the desk in his office. However, that's not the point here. The point is, you're asking Demon to do something he's never going to do unless you get to the root of what the addiction is all about. Do you even know?"

In truth, she didn't know the circumstances behind why he chose drugs as his coping mechanism. Since it didn't start after any major sort of trauma in his history, she just assumed it was a habit he'd picked up somewhere along the line, working as a doctor. He used prescription pain meds for patient treatment plans, so they would have been easy to obtain. Now he didn't have the normal channels to get prescription medication, so he was buying it illegally somewhere. In all their conversations, she'd never asked him the most important question. Why?

"Of course you don't." Kubrick sighed, then stood, shaking her head. "I'm not even going to bother with trying to talk sense into you because you're not ready to hear it yet." She stood and crossed to the conference room door. "Look. Don't worry about it, Cherry. As far as Flame's concerned, Gem's right. It's not worth beating yourself up over. Flame knows you don't mean it that way, but being pregnant is stressing her out on multiple levels. I think there are some complications with the pregnancy, so both she and TB are worried about that. Plus, she has a deadline coming up, and according to her, her main characters are currently sitting in the corner because they're not talking to her. She's due in a month and absolutely terrified he'll be on a project somewhere when she goes into labor. More importantly, though, is that she's worried about how this is going to affect TB's work at Tribe, and I can't say I wouldn't be worried too."

"Nothing changes for TB on Tribe's end. They're having a baby, not becoming the king and queen of America. She's a borderline recluse, anyway. They're worrying for no reason."

"If they were worried about physically having a baby, that would be fine. They're looking at his situation through a whole different lens. Being a deadman is fine when you're single. It's slightly worrying if you try to maintain a romantic relationship that's open and not necessarily monogamous. Add commitment to it? More challenging. But a child you can't openly acknowledge?" Kubrick shook her head. "No... there are a bazillion fucked-up issues there that make it a genuine worry. In all honesty, I'm surprised he hasn't up and disappeared already."

Cherry frowned. "You really think he will?"

"I think it has a high level of possibility, yes. My guess would be that you have until Ka-Bar's found. After that? Who knows? Between that project still being open and Nemo leaving, he doesn't want to leave the guys hanging."

"God and I were talking about bringing some new blood in—"

"It's not about the deadmen body count. It's the fact that TB wants to be a parent in reality. Having been an orphan, he doesn't want his child to feel abandoned like he did, even if that abandonment wasn't his parents' choice. He'll miss everything—all his child's firsts, all the school shit, all the rites of passage—because he can't publicly be a part of that life. TB starts showing up to things on the regular, people put a face to the father of the child, then they're going to want a name, and soon it will be impossible to be 'dead' anymore. It's one of the things God worried about, I'm sure, and why he said that since Waters and I became a couple, it made it so things would never be normal again. We changed a core dynamic of the company."

"You know he's not mad about that, right? He loves you," Cherry said.

"He can like me and still be pissed at me. The two are not mutually exclusive. Doesn't matter. Waters and I were the catalyst, and he knew that would happen. The dynamic has changed. Three members of the team have hooked up with someone permanently, and then one of them left the corporation because of it. You and Demon, once you figure your shit out, will eventually make four members. At some point, Steel will find someone, I'm guessing. And then Midas will find his... whatever. I don't know if he's into girls, guys, his AI, his rubber cats, or what. TB and Flame are having a baby. Who knows what any of you will create when your turns come around?"

There was a lingering note of sadness in Kubrick's voice. The woman tried to pretend she was tough, but truthfully, she was probably the most vulnerable of the women. Even more so than Flame. Cherry walked over to her at the door, a hand on her friend's arm. "He's not mad. And he loves you unconditionally, from the moment you called your executive producer a 'jizzmop.'" The two women shared a rueful laugh. "There's no blame. You know how the no-relationships rule came about, but he also told you that even he knew the rule was ridiculous. People are not meant to be alone. We both knew that these days would come, and we've discussed what would happen when they did."

"And what will happen now?"

Cherry smiled. "Don't worry. We're not burying them soon. There's time yet, but eventually, the deadmen will be just that. It was one reason Nemo had to follow Gem and not the other way around. I certainly didn't picture him being the first one out the door, but sometimes, the universe gives us a giggle. I honestly thought Waters would disappear the moment God told him to come home while you were working together, but he refused to force you into a life on the run, which it would have been."

The deadmen couldn't marry, yet TB had collared his romance novelist, Flame, as his submissive. Nemo had left his twin and his teammates to follow Gem around the globe for her company. Two couples were settled, but Kubrick and Waters were not.

Despite being the first to meet and become a couple, they kept their own residences—Kubrick's house and Waters' apartment here at Tribe. Both had their own cars—her Corvette and his company-owned pickup truck. Deadmen couldn't own anything, so everything the guys had was in Tribe's name. Even Scheherazade's puppy came via Nemo and was very much hers and not theirs. He never told her she couldn't do something, and he never questioned if she left town for a meeting, a research trip, or a film shoot. She never complained about his long hours or the rare times he disappeared, sometimes with no word other than a text of "Had to go out of town," their code for him going on a project. If ever a deadman was to have the perfect partner, she was it.

But what if her comfort with everything wasn't how Kubrick was really feeling? Was she feeling as if Waters wasn't making some sort of commitment to her?

"Kubrick? Are you okay?"

The film director smiled, but Cherry could tell it was fake by the slight hitch before it slipped into place. "I'm fine."

"Waters is right. You can't lie for shit. Is everything okay with the two of you?"

Kubrick's eyes were glassy. "Waters and I are great," she chirped. "Told you. Never better, and no worries about half measures."

"Stop redirecting. Something's not right. Did he fuck up? I have access to over fifteen poisonous chemicals in the supply closet alone, some of which will dissolve a small planet, let alone a human being."

Kubrick laughed through a strangled tear. She bit her lip, then lowered her voice to barely above a whisper. "That's not how TB got rid of Stapleton, is it?"

"I can neither confirm nor deny that anyone used chemical cleaners at any point in time to dispose of a body."

"Shit." Kubrick's face seemed to turn a little green.

"Relax," Cherry reassured. "No one will ever find even a single strand of DNA from something that should have been swallowed, not birthed. Seriously though." Her voice returned to normal. "I am well-versed in body disposal, so I can definitely make it happen. I know a guy," she teased. "So what did he do?"

"Nothing," Kubrick admitted. "It's... it's stupid. It's stupid, girly, whiney, and pushy, along with being totally unnecessary." She gathered herself back into her director persona and reached out to hug Cherry. "Thank you for caring." When she pulled back, her expression was serious. "Talk to Demon, Cherry."

"Maybe. Go on." She jerked her head toward the door. "Go collect G.I. Joe, but please sanitize the desk afterward. Be safe next week and beyond."

"Always. Email me. I'll answer when I can."

A squeeze of her arms later, Kubrick was out the door and calling out for Waters.

6

APRIL 10, 2023

Cherry

When she walked into the break room to get her tea, his back was to the door, and he had just thrown back two pills and started washing them down with water. An involuntary gasp flew from her mouth, and when he turned to see her, she spun on her heel and speed-walked back to her desk.

Teeth clenched to keep the tears at bay, she sat in her chair, staring at her computer screen, trying to regroup. It was bad enough that she knew he took them, but seeing it was a slap in the face. The drugs truly meant more to him than she did. He wasn't even trying to stop. With a deep breath, she sat up straight, resolved not to give him another moment of her time nor a single thought. Maybe he'd cared for her in the beginning, but he clearly didn't care for her now if he was so blatantly disregarding her one tiny, completely reasonable request.

She must have been sitting, lost deep in thought, for a while because suddenly, a hand reached around her from behind and set her teacup on her desk. Tension filled her entire body when he placed both his hands on her shoulders, smoothing the silk over them and down her arms. She wished she hadn't taken her jacket off, but the office was overly warm this morning, with the sun streaming in the glass doors and windows despite the tint. Now she felt chilled as his hands kneaded her shoulders, his thumbs sweeping across the top of her shoulder blades.

"Don't." She shrugged his hands free from her.

"Why?"

Lucky Lucifer, this man's voice! Even just one word caused another shiver to pass through her. She desperately wanted to reach for her jacket that hung over the back of her chair to put more barriers between them, but that would let him know how unsettled he made her. He needed no more weapons in that arsenal.

"You're angry."

"Why would you think that?"

"Because when you walked into the break room and saw me, you couldn't get out of there fast enough. I brought your tea to you, since you abandoned it after seeing me, and you were sitting here staring at a blank screen. You were so far in your head, you didn't hear the phones ringing. Plus, you're so tense right now, if I so much as breathe on you, I think you'd shatter into a million pieces."

Desperately, she moved to find something to do. Anything. Even if it was just addressing an envelope—something to distract her from him.

"I'm sorry, *a chuisle*. I didn't mean for you to see that. I got lazy and didn't bother to go somewhere private."

She shrugged, trying in vain to make the situation seem inconsequential. "None of my business."

He grabbed the headrest of her chair, pulled it back from the desk, and turned it to face him. "It most certainly is your business. Everything about me is your business."

"Well, I don't want it to be. Not anymore."

In a fit of pique, she swiveled her chair back toward her desk, reached for a stack of folders on its corner, and stood from her chair, pushing it back hard with her legs so that it connected with his front. Heading for the conference room, she couldn't help but grin at hearing the grunt of pain as the chair wheel rolled over his boot and the exhale of air from where the chairback hit his stomach.

It was too much to hope that he would just drop it and leave her alone to sulk. Demon, unfortunately, was the most tenacious of the entire group, absolutely refusing to give an inch in an argument or to back down on an opinion when he felt he was in the right. However, when he finally began moving in her direction, he didn't rush. He casually strolled behind her, knowing he'd catch up with her. It wasn't as if he didn't know where she was going. They had a meeting later this afternoon, and since there were no clients on the schedule, she'd be setting up the room early.

He entered the room moments after her, and he leaned against the door to shut it. She felt his eyes on her as she circled the conference room table, laying out the project folders. She hoped she projected an unaffected demeanor, but the precise way she was lining up the pencils, pens, and highlighters above each folder probably gave away that she was working to keep her equilibrium.

He was also stubborn. He just stood against the door, waiting her out. In some ways, he was worse than TB, whose interrogation silence technique was legendary.

"What's the occasion?" she finally asked.

"What do you mean?"

"Usually, when you come back from your 'sabbatical,' you're still in your beach gear. Today, you're in normal people's clothes."

"If they make you uncomfortable, I can always take my clothes off," he suggested with heat.

Out of the corner of her eye, she saw him stand up straight, drop his hands to his sides, and walk up behind her. Moments later, his hands gently took her biceps in his grip as he stepped in tight to her backside. She stiffened again. This was how all their private altercations had gone in the past. Like it was some sick little game they played of who could rattle the other one first, getting them to give in to a passionate kiss.

Unfortunately, since the bomb scare with Gem, those altercations had changed and now were more like two rival sharks defending their territory—biting, snapping, and tearing at each other.

"I like you like this," he whispered. "All prickly and full of sass. You're always so cool behind your designer clothes, coiffed hair, and perfectly applied makeup. You can be as stone-cold as the rest of us, letting no one see your emotions that you hide under your sleek surface. But when I get a rise out of you, you're the most genuine person I've ever known. So let it out, fireball. If you're going to judge me, give me all your fire. No more holding back with me."

"I just asked why the sudden change in appearance."

With one finger, he pressed a kiss behind her ear. "Spent last night in my apartment, which you would have known if you'd come home after your date."

"Why would it matter to me? I couldn't care less where you were or what you were doing or with whom."

Clicking his tongue against his teeth, he brought his mouth down next to her ear, his lips barely brushing against the shell. "Liar. You can't care less unless you care in the first place." He kissed her again as he wound his arms around her waist to pull her impossibly closer to him. "So. How was your date?"

"Not that it's any of your business, but I wasn't on a date. I was over at Flame's helping her put away things for the baby." Internally, she rolled her eyes at herself. Why was she bothering to explain herself to him? It wasn't any of his damn business.

"And you stayed the night?"

She shrugged. "It got late. I was drinking wine. I didn't want to drive. Pick your reason."

"Another lie. You hate wine. So you didn't stay out because I was staying in last night?"

"Nope."

Slowly, he turned her to face him. He kept one arm hooked around her waist and then took her chin between his thumb and forefinger, raising it to meet his gaze.

She let loose an involuntary whimper, trapped between him and the table.

"What's the matter, Cherry?" He spoke low in her ear. "Uncomfortable?"

"Yes. Please step back, Demon. You're crowding me."

"Your words say one thing, but your body is arching into mine."

His hands cupped her arms, his lips caressed the shell of her ear, and his hard length made a bruising impression on her hip. She might have whimpered again. She wasn't sure.

Why was she mad at him again? In just a few seconds, he had made her forget. All she could think and feel right now was that their arms fit around each other perfectly, like no one else could be the pieces that fit together in the puzzle that was them. She was the perfect height for him to hold tight, her temple perfectly at height for his lips, and when he pulled her tight to his chest, her head lay comfortably on his shoulder. She felt secure there. Like nothing bad could touch her. He was her perfect match.

With a cry of surrender, her hands threaded through his hair, causing the sunglasses to go flying off the top of his head. She felt herself pulled into a vortex of lips, tongue, and teeth. One hand curled to support her neck and tilt her head so he could slant her mouth to better meet his kiss. When his tongue swept into her mouth, her senses went into overload from the overwhelming scents of the ocean that always surrounded him. It was intoxicating, something ineffably Demon.

Before she could protest, he lifted her to place her on the cool wood of the conference table and pinned her underneath him. His mouth moved to her jawbone, then down her neck. Returning his lips to her ear again, he whispered, "What would you do if I took you on this conference room table right now, Esme?"

The whimper now became a moan.

He answered it with words. "Please, fireball. I'm dying here. Tell me you want me."

Something in his words caused the image from the break room to reappear and remind her of where they were, who they were, and why this was all so, so wrong. She retracted her arms from around him and gently pushed at his shoulders. Turning her head from his kiss, she said the one word needed to end this craziness. "No."

He helped her to sit up but then immediately backed up two steps.

"I may want this. Want us. But nothing's changed, Demon. You know why I won't do this."

"You 'won't' do this. At least you admit it's a choice."

"Argh!" She slid from the table and made for the door. When she got almost all the way there, she turned back to him. "It's always been a choice! Just like it's always been a choice for you to ignore my request!"

"That's because it's not a request. It's a demand!" Hanging his head with a sigh, he ran his fingers through his hair, then stood there, hands on hips. When he finally looked up at her, she could see the confusion in his eyes. "It's like this relationship is a fecking whirlpool. Every time we get close, every time I try to bring you to the outside of the current and free us both, you keep fighting it. It's exhausting as hell, and I don't understand why you keep doing it."

Was she the problem? Was holding onto this condition ridiculous? Inside, she was warring with herself. How could she explain her refusal to him when she couldn't even explain it to herself? If he'd just give her something—some rational explanation—maybe she could bend. "Can you explain to me why you won't give up the pills?"

A sigh escaped his lips, and his eyes dulled with pain. Whether it was physical or mental, she didn't know, but the man was clearly in distress. "I've done things, Cherry. Things I can't ever forgive or forget. They make the voices go away."

"The voices?" She was so confused. Was he talking about authentic voices in his head? "I don't understand."

"I know you don't. I hope you never do."

Now she moved toward him, one hand to his chest, the other to the side of his face. "You listen to me right now, Aidan Parker. I get that I have an issue with your personal choices, but there is nothing you could do that would make me care for you less. And yes, you've done terrible things—albeit necessary for the job—since I met you, and it hasn't meant a thing in terms of how I feel about you. You have nothing to feel guilty over, if that's what all this is about. Just tell me," she pleaded.

He bowed his head, turning his face to kiss the palm against his cheek. "I don't feel guilty. That's the problem."

"You need to speak more clearly. I can't read your mind, and none of this is making sense to me right now."

"I made promises, Cherry. Promises I couldn't keep. Although my inability to keep those promises wasn't my fault, I still disappointed people when I failed. So many people. If I give you what you ask, I'm making another promise. I refuse to make any more of them."

Her eyes searched his. "You're worried you'll break your promise? That you'll give up the drugs and then start again."

"Yes." He took the hand that cradled his cheek in both of his, kissed her fingertips, then led it down to her side and backed away from her. "I can't give them up, even for you. I wish I could. But releasing those voices would destroy what little remains of me. It's just better that you know I'm no good at keeping promises. Never have been. To make this one to you? I'll only hurt you when I fail, and then your voice will add to all the others. I couldn't bear that. Why can't you be with me just the way I am?"

"I want to be with you, but I just can't if this is how you're going to continue. I can't explain it. This is nonnegotiable for me. I'm sorry."

He nodded. "I get it, Cherry. I do. What I don't get is that you've known from day one who I am. My life has been an open book to you even before I knew who you were. That's why this sudden expectation, this requirement to change, confuses me so much. If you cared for me, knowing everything you know, then why is it a problem now?"

She opened her mouth as if she was going to answer. How, she didn't know, because she didn't have a reason to give him. She just knew this was how it had to be. He cut her off before she could say anything.

"I don't know how to make it any clearer. I want you, Esme, and have for the six fecking years I've been here. I will always want you. But you need to understand, sometimes people can't change. You have to want me as I am, or we're just going to keep getting sucked down into the depths of our own misery."

He walked up to her, framed her face in his hands, and brushed a kiss across her forehead. It was slow, tentative, and somehow felt so final.

"Maybe it's best if we just walk away from whatever this"—he waved a hand between them—"is. No more meals. No more hang-outs. No more talk unless it's Tribe related."

She was both incensed and mournful. There was no one to blame but herself. She'd made the decision that his usage was a deal-breaker. She'd said it out loud multiple times. To give in and change her mind, no matter how much she wanted to, would make her weak. She couldn't afford to be weak.

Maybe he was right. Pushing their attraction when neither was going to budge was tearing them both apart. If they caved in, ultimately, they'd end up miserable and hurting each other worse than they were already hurting by being apart now. He was right. They had to let each other go. Completely. It was better that way.

With a deep inhale to build her fortitude, she made her decision. "You're probably right. We're both adults. We can keep it professional."

He gave a single nod, but he didn't move right away. He stood, searching her face, rolling his lower lip into his mouth as if biting back something he wanted to say. Then he nodded again, stepped away from her, crossed to the door, and exited the room.

She waited several minutes to give him space to get wherever he needed to go. Running into him in the hallway right after this would be far too awkward. Ignoring him might hurt like hell, but she could hide behind her desk and her work. After all, she'd been doing it for months already since the big revelation of her secrets back in September. She could keep herself away from him. With time, it would get easier for her to move on and for him to quit holding onto a hope that would never become reality.

Unfortunately, as she headed back to her desk, she knew that for what it was. More fucking lies.

7

APRIL 10, 2023

Demon

A FLURRY OF EXCITED BARKS FLOODED THE HALLWAY OUTSIDE the conference room, and the men around the table were grinning and shaking their heads. Last year, Nemo had rescued a street dog off the streets of Sallum, and she'd had two puppies. Prince Ali Ababwa, the one Kubrick had demanded upon his return, was in the building today.

When Waters walked into the conference room where the four deadmen waited, a slobbering puppy flew into the room on his heels, greeting everyone there with yips and kisses. The Total Terror, as TB called him—mostly because Flame had demanded custody of the other puppy, now named Jasmine—finally ended up in Demon's lap, where he went completely belly up begging for pets. Normally, when Kubrick needed a babysitter, the dog went and stayed with Flame so he could have his sister's company. He wondered, since she was going to be gone for twelve weeks, if Waters had asked her to leave the dog with him. Maybe because he needed something of Kubrick's close while she was gone?

Waters whistled, and the dog's head snapped in his direction. Pointing to the chair, he ordered, "Ali, sit!"

Everyone around the table chuckled as the puppy gave a quick, high bark as if to say, "Yes, sir!" and then jumped from Demon's lap onto the conference table, scattering papers everywhere and knocking over coffee cups with the big feet he'd yet to grow into. There was a lot of good-natured grumbling as Ali, blissfully unaware of the havoc he was creating, hopped down into Waters' chair, turned in circles twice, and sat down looking all cute and innocent, complete with head cocked and ears perked at the shouting of his name. More shenanigans were likely to begin soon and keep up through the entire meeting, as they always did when one of the dogs visited. One of them was a tornado, but if both of them were here, it was a storm of epic proportions, as they both had their mother's goofy personality, and everyone spoiled them rotten.

Glancing once more at the puppy, Demon knew for a fact that the dog's devious mind was already in motion because he was hyper-focused on the folder in Waters' hand that moved naturally when he spoke. He expected at least one report was going to need to be reprinted, and somebody's shoelaces were going to need to be replaced because Ali loved to chew things. Demon had already lost a flip-flop to the little monster the last time he was at Tribe.

Waters redirected everyone's attention from the dog. "All right, people, let's get to it. Midas, Nemo should be on the line in two."

Out of his peripheral vision, Demon noticed the tension that appeared in the cyber specialist. He was still recuperating from the loss of his brother, a man he hadn't been apart from since they were in their late teens. It went without saying that the older twin was still salty about the defection.

Apparently, Midas wasn't the only angry one in the group today. By the way Waters threw his folder down and stabbed the starfish controller in the middle of the table to begin the security lockdown of the room, it was clear he was in a mood. He also looked like he was running on no sleep. Not surprising. Kubrick had left in the wee hours of the morning for China and would be gone for twelve weeks. They'd likely been fecking like rabbits for the last two to three days.

The men, including their big boss, God, had already placed their bets on how long their team leader would last before he "asked" God for time off to go see her. God predicted five days. Steel, the resident Nostradamus with betting, said the man would make it the whole twelve. Steel was rarely wrong, but this time, Demon couldn't help but wonder if the sniper had overestimated the man's willpower.

"Mythos online."

Shaking his head with mild disgust, Demon internalized his snorting response. However, the eye roll was unstoppable. The man couldn't even say his own brother's name.

"*Goeie môre!*" Nemo greeted them as he came up on the screen. Since the teams couldn't share where they were when on projects, he had come up with the idea to say hello and goodbye in the native language of the country they were in as a way of updating them. By his greeting, he was back in South Africa. "How's the weather?"

"Seventy, smoggy. Same as usual," Waters replied. He hit another button on the starfish, which piped in their boss. "God is online. What have you got for us, Nemo?"

"You want to head southeast and get your *Kwéyòl* on. Gem was on a nature hike in the Caribbean and found photographic evidence of the elusive species, Kentus Leechus, known in the familiar as Ka-Bar, at a beachside café in Soufrìere. Pictures should be to you already."

"If this Mythos gig doesn't work out, that girl's got a job with the paparazzi," TB muttered.

Nemo affirmed, "All that gorgeous tininess and spectacular thieving makes her good at being places unseen."

Midas muttered, "As opposed to some people who call all sorts of attention to their presence."

The men exchanged glances. The older twin really needed to get over his mad.

Ali's head popped up from where he was lying. Hearing Midas grumbling, the puppy sensed he needed to calm him, so he jumped onto the table, disrupting everyone's paperwork and coffee. When he reached Midas at the head of the table, he threw himself into the computer programmer's lap. There wasn't really room for him, but Midas wiggled around to make space for him, one hand rubbing the dog's ears while he worked.

Nemo grinned. "Hey, Ali! Looking good, dude. Your mama says hi." There was a gentle woof on Nemo's end of the call, and Scheherazade poked her head up from where she sat at his side. She cocked her head, looking for the source of the snuffling sounds she somehow recognized as her child. Midas reversed his screen so that she could see her wayward pup. The mother and son looked at each other. She gave a huff as if to say, "Behave yourself!" and then she sat back down out of sight. Midas put the screen back to normal.

"Any idea what he's doing there?" Waters asked, redirecting the conversation.

"Officially? Not yet. However, he was meeting with two men with military haircuts and posture, but they were trying to look like they weren't military. These are new players to us, so we're working to identify their names. Feel free to give it a go yourselves, and let us know if you find out who they are."

"Nothing like doing your work for you," Midas mumbled under his breath. He gave an emphatic bang to the Enter key on his laptop.

Nemo's face didn't change, but Demon knew the younger twin must have heard both of his comments. Why Midas was being such a piss whistler—Kubrick's nickname for him since Nemo left—was beyond him. You'd think after fifteen-plus years of looking after the shidiot—Kubrick's nickname for Nemo—he'd be glad for the break from having to bail the man out of one scrape after another. That was Gem's job now.

Midas put the pictures on the screen, and the men studied them.

"How old are these pictures?" God asked.

"Yesterday afternoon. We've had our systems working on a higher-priority issue, which is why we haven't had time to figure out who his lunch guests are. They might be dressed like tourists, but they're overdoing it. Pictures we took will show the one guest coming in with a string backpack, but when they left, Ka-Bar had it."

"The guy on the right is American," Steel said. "Former military. Henry Kroll." He looked at Waters. "Used to work in Nicaragua at Site 66."

The team leader grunted. "That could be awkward if he sees you."

"Considering I technically drowned in a river of shit at Site 66? Damn straight. Dude was bad news then and as crooked as a fishhook. Several individuals met creative ends while under his watch. Not surprising he's hooked into something like this, especially if it means earning more money."

"And I know the guy on the left," TB added.

Muttering to himself, Midas continued to punch in the information on his keyboard. "Why am I even here if everyone can identify everybody?"

TB continued, "Portuguese born, Emiliano Carvahlo." He looked at Waters. "Former *Sistema de Informacoes da Republica Portuguesa*, better known as SIRP. He went rogue in 2009 and disappeared. Did some work for him in my early days as The Collector. Last I knew, he was working out of the Central African Republic. He's a contract killer who accepts any target. Rumor has it he took a job on three children and their teenage nanny."

"*Jesucristo*," Steel whispered. "Just the type of shitweasel the Salieri might hire in case their men can't take care of the women and children of their members."

"My thoughts exactly," Waters acknowledged. "Midas, confer with TB and search out whatever info you can find. We might pick up nothing, but then again, if we can find something, it might lead us to a lower-level Salieri member we could use."

"Already on it. If there's something to find, I'll find it," Midas promised.

Steel focused on Waters. "Need me to track these *pendejos*?"

God spoke up. "Not yet. We go where Ka-Bar is. That's the project. Let Mythos handle the other shit. Besides, as far as we can tell, Ka-Bar is the contact between the Salieri and outsiders. Or one of them. Any sightings of the Kaders?"

Nemo replied, "Last we knew, somewhere in Italy, but lately, there isn't even an echo of them anywhere. My guess is they've been 'handled' by the Salieri for their fuckup in South Africa. In the meantime, we've bumped this sighting up in priority because, if you look closely, Ka-Bar's polo shirt has a logo on it for a company that we've been hearing a lot of rumblings about lately. Nimbus Corporation. Gem went there to gather intel on their CEO. She followed these two dirtbags and caught Ka-Bar in the frame."

"She going to meet us there?" Steel asked.

"Yeah. She's still following our two fake tourists, but they appear to be headed out of the country. Once she's verified that, she'll swing back your way and hand over everything to you and rendezvous with us."

"You left her out there on her own?" Midas' incensed words were the first he'd spoken directly to his brother. "What the actual fuck?"

"Calm your tits, grasshopper," Nemo cautioned him. "Gem can take care of herself. My talents were required elsewhere. Besides, Medusa's with her. Give me some fucking credit. I'm not completely stupid."

"Any other intelligence for us?" Waters redirected. Demon was kind of sad about that. Breaking up what amounted to a sibling verbal fistfight might have lightened his mood after this afternoon's mess with Cherry.

"I sent a preliminary report along with the photos. We're hoping that you can go down, hang out, and check out the Nimbus CEO in the process since you've got a better inroad with him than we do."

"Thanks. Take care, Nemo."

"Will do." He shot a look at Midas, but his twin studiously ignored him in favor of playing with Ali and doing whatever he was doing on his computer. "*Baie geluk.*" Nemo disconnected.

As soon as the screen went to the desktop, TB turned his chair in Midas' direction. "Why are you being such a tool?" TB asked. "He's your fucking brother. You can be mad, but don't shut him out. You're the only one of us who still has family. Appreciate that."

"It's none of your business, TB," the other man mumbled. "Stay out of it. He chose pussy over blood. That's not how it works."

Steel took TB's side. "Don't you dare refer to Gem as 'pussy.' You know that's not even close to true. He worships that woman. Has for years and now finally can be with her. And yeah, that's definitely how it works when you find the one meant for you. They always come first. TB's right. We all gave up any ties we had to do this job. You think that was easy for us? You have the gift of having it built into your job, and you're pissing it away."

All of their heads turned toward Steel, varying degrees of surprise on their faces, but Demon noted Waters as the exception. Their team leader had more knowledge of all of them than they had of each other. None of the team had suspected that Steel still had living family members. From the sound of it, the separation was difficult.

God brought everyone's attention back to what was important. "You can all play *Family Feud* later."

Demon held up a hand. "Hang on. What did Nemo mean by we have a better inroad with this CEO than they do?"

There was a knock at the door. With the click of a button, Midas showed the camera on the outer conference room door. Cherry stood there, stiff as a board. Obviously, she was also unhappy at the moment.

"I asked Cherry to join us. Meet your inroad," God explained. "Midas? Get those preparations in motion that we discussed. And gentlemen... for now, say nothing about the CEO being the target of our investigation. Nothing," he emphasized.

Before the men could ask why, Waters clicked a button on the starfish, disengaging the security system for the room and allowing Cherry inside. Once the door closed, he reengaged the system. Ali yipped with excitement at the new person entering the room, and he hopped out of Midas' lap to greet Cherry.

God didn't waste any time. "Cherry, we identified a rogue Portuguese military intelligence officer and a former American military member, both possibly connected to Salieri, together in a Soufrière café. They met with Ka-Bar. We need a contact in St. Lucia. Your father's friend, Zion Norton. Do you think he's trustworthy?"

Demon watched her hesitate, a series of emotions running across her face.

"Uncle Zion? My father trusted him."

"But you don't," TB said, reading her tone.

"It's not that I don't... trust him, exactly."

"Sure as feck sounds like you don't," Demon growled.

Her eyes flickered his way, and even though things weren't good between them, he saw she wasn't able to lie to him to cover up how she was feeling. "He was very close to my father. They spent time together, professionally and personally. We often vacationed at *Les Vergers de la Mer*, and he often spent time at our home with us when he was in the States. It's just..." She searched for the proper words. "He's not really my uncle. I just called him that because he was like family to me since we saw him so much. Sometimes—" She stopped, took a breath, and looked at him again. Then she looked away as she finished. "When I got into my teens, though, he always seemed a little too focused on me when we'd be together, if you know what I mean. Like, even when it wasn't about me, he'd be, I don't know... overly attentive. Pulling out chairs. Opening doors. Expensive gifts or side trips. Things like that. It's just... it sometimes felt... awkward."

Gritting his teeth, Demon had to hold back a growl. Cherry's instincts about people were exceptional. If she'd picked up on his interest, it had definitely been there.

"Did you ever tell your father about those feelings?" God asked.

"I didn't have to. I was planning to study international business and economics and had planned to study abroad after the first year or two. But on my eighteenth birthday, while visiting Uncle Zion, he pushed on both me and my father that I should go directly to study in Italy. He had connections at *Università Bocconi*, which has a very high ranking for both areas, and he had a home there, so he argued I'd have a support system if I needed it. He had even secretly arranged enrollment."

"I take it your father didn't like that?" God asked.

"At the time, he seemed to be open to it. Later on, when we went for a walk, he sounded me out about it. Asked if it was something I might be interested in. I told him I wanted to go to Georgetown, as planned. He seemed relieved." She frowned. "I thought it was because he would miss me, but now I wonder if he didn't sense that Zion had more than just an altruistic offer on the table. For the rest of the year, I never saw or spoke to Uncle Zion, even if it was a video call, without my father being in the room. Well, until the day Dad disappeared."

He felt his teeth unclench slightly. At least her father had been on to the man.

God asked, "When your father disappeared, how did your uncle react?"

Cherry grimaced. "He pushed again, saying I shouldn't be alone, but I wasn't having it. My excuse was always that I refused to take the chance Dad would turn up, and I didn't want to miss him when that happened. Not sure he believed me. Eventually, he gave up asking when I started classes, but it didn't stop him from offering me reasons to 'get away' from stress and all that when I was on breaks from school. Again, I had the excuses ready. I was taking overloads on my classwork; I didn't want to miss Dad on the off chance that he showed up. Then I had my internship, and I was working eighty-plus hours a week."

Waters spoke up. "What about after graduation?"

"I graduated early, and then I left everything behind. The family attorney sealed up the house upon my request, and Esme Bosworth went off 'to find herself,' never to return. It's still there. The attorney goes there once a month to check on it, and a cleaning service does basics to keep it livable, but I haven't been back to it since."

"What about Norton? You still in touch?"

"Barely. Once a year, I check in. Mostly because if Dad needed help, he'd likely go to Zion for it. He has more connections than probably any world leader, especially considering his work with militaries all over the globe. If Dad needed to be rescued and he could get word to Zion, that would be the best bet for success."

"How so?"

"He's one of the biggest manufacturing moguls in the world. He has deals with most of Western Europe, and while his company specializes in military contracts for transport planes, they also have divisions that specialize in helicopters, radar systems, and fuselages. That's how he and Dad met. The communications systems in all of Zion's company's planes were my dad's. In addition, he owns the only truly sustainable banana plantation in St. Lucia. Everything taken is given back. That endeavor is also widely known and highly profitable. Between *Les Vergers de la Mer* and Nimbus Corporation, he's one of the top three entrepreneurs in the world. Possibly number one. Midas could tell you more."

A loud crunching noise came from over the speaker as God separated his iconic favorite candy from its stick. "I'm sending you to St. Lucia. I'd like you to use your family connection to see if you can't get some more info."

"All right."

"Feck no!"

Cherry and Demon's answers came at the same time.

Demon bristled at the idea of Cherry being an active part of a project. Not that she was incapable. If anything, more than capable. She'd done it in the past, but only for short stints, like dinners where she vetted marks or handled some of the more feminine pursuits where the men would tend to stand out. Either way, she'd always had security with her as backup. There was no way in hell she was doing a trip to St. Lucia on her own, especially with someone who made her feel even the slightest bit uncomfortable.

"Don't get your stethoscope in a twist, D," God ordered. "She won't be going alone."

"What excuse am I using?" Cherry asked. "I've been putting him off for years. Now I'm suddenly going to seek him out?"

The unwrapping of yet another of God's god-awful caramel apple suckers came over the line. "St. Lucia is a huge tourist destination, especially romantic for couples. You've recently gotten married, and you're going on your honeymoon there. Might as well bring him to meet the only family you have left."

Waters had been quietly waging war with Ali over his file folder, complete with puppy slobber and teeth marks, but now he smirked, his bad mood suddenly disappearing. Picking up the whining puppy from the floor, their boss was completely unsuccessful at hiding his glee, realizing what God intended. "Oh, this is gonna be good."

Demon gritted his teeth. "Who are you sending with her?"

"Waters will stay here to run the office since Cherry will be on assignment. TB and Steel will be hiding out as security for her. Midas will offer local tech support. You will pose as her other half." There was a hint of pleasure in his voice at his choices.

A gasp came from Cherry. "I really don't think—"

"You may own this company, Cherry, but you gave me the power to oversee the projects. That means my word is final."

"What if he isn't available? He could be traveling."

"He's not," Midas informed her. "Once we had confirmation from Mythos, God had me set the wheels in motion. I sent 'Uncle Zion' an email on your behalf, and he answered almost immediately. He's more than happy to offer his hospitality at his villa." He sounded so proud of himself. "Apparently, he's hosting a large get-together the day after your arrival, so two more guests are not a problem. I hacked into his guest list, and there are a lot of big names on the list. Everything from top one hundred entrepreneurs to politicians to military. Even royalty."

Her eyes were wild with panic, and she grasped at the flimsiest of excuses. "An occasion like that, combined with posing as a honeymoon couple, I don't have any clothing appropriate for a trip like this. All I own are business suits or lying-around clothes."

Demon barely prevented himself from laughing. Wardrobe? Really? That was what she was going to go with?

"Call Flame," TB offered. "She can help you rush order some things and pack."

"Cherry," God barked. "You are going, and D will pose as your husband. All the men will protect you with their lives, but he is the best choice for up close and personal. End. Of. Story."

The quiet in the room was deafening.

"I'll leave Waters to arrange the details," God interrupted. "Keep in communication at all times." With a click, he was gone.

By now, all the men—except himself—were smiling, with no attempts to hide their glee at this recent development.

"Congratulations"—Midas exaggerated his brainstorming face as he came up with identities for the happy couple—"Mr. and Mrs. McCarthy. I'll get working on your passports."

Waters added, "Better get packing. We meet in five hours to give you your itinerary and plan our attack. I want you out of here tonight."

"Jumpin' Jesus," Cherry whispered.

There was resignation in her eyes, and when she glanced at Demon, he couldn't help but feel his own expression was matching hers. How things ended this afternoon meant this would be torturous for both of them.

8

APRIL 10, 2023

Cherry

"THIS IS RIDICULOUS," CHERRY SAID IN FRUSTRATION. "I CAN'T do this."

"Yes, you can," Flame assured her. "It will be good for both of you. Maybe it will give you a chance to work out this malarkey once and for all." Flame smiled as big as the men had earlier as she helped fold and pack the clothing she'd ordered and had rush delivered. With a sigh of what sounded like jealousy, she admitted, "There is nothing better than a fake marriage, one-bed trope. I love writing those stories the most."

"You and TB should go. You don't have to pretend to be in love."

"Yeah. No. Number one, we don't know your family friend. Number two, TB stands out like an ogre in a bar filled with daisies. Number three, I'm eight months pregnant. The beach ball here"—she placed a hand on her stomach—"is still kicking my booty almost twenty-four seven. Only thing I can hold down with any certainty is ice cream. Not very honeymoon-ish if the bride is constantly puking."

Dread welled from the bottom of Cherry's feet up to her stomach, making it roll, then continued up to the top of her head. She hadn't even given a thought to the sleeping arrangements. Could she possibly convince Zion to give them separate bedrooms? What excuse could she give since they were posing as newlyweds? He snored? She snored? None. Absolutely none.

In addition, they'd have to act like a newlywed couple everywhere they went, especially in a place as romantic as St. Lucia. She sat on the edge of the bed and crashed backward, a hand covering her eyes. "Jesus, take the wheel!"

She felt pressure on the mattress beside her. A soft touch on her thigh made her tilt her head up to see the other woman's back, her head turned in profile.

"Do you love him, Cherry?" Flame asked.

She sighed. "It's complicated."

"No, it's really not. Not if you're honest with yourself. Let me put it this way. It's a yes or no question. Do you love him? What if he became seriously ill after you were together? Would you leave him for it, or would you stand by his side, even if he never recovered?"

"I'd never abandon someone just because they became ill."

"Isn't addiction considered an illness?"

She remained still, the queasy feeling returning as she anticipated where the conversation was going. "Yes," she admitted reluctantly.

"What about if something happened to him on a project? What if he died? How would you feel then?"

"Devastated," Cherry whispered.

"Exactly. I wonder if you wouldn't feel worse than I would if something happened to TB."

"But you adore that man!"

"Oh, I didn't mean I wouldn't be bereft or that I don't love him. I do undeniably love him. But the one consolation I would have is that

I had him for a little while, which is better than never. Right now, the two of you are suffering needlessly. Think of all the time you're wasting holding him at arm's length. And all over something that, in the grand scheme of things, is essentially all wrapped up in when it occurred."

Cherry sat up beside Flame, gripping the woman's hand in hers. "You know I don't feel this way about you, right? Never once have I looked down upon you. I adore you, and I'd miss having you in my life as a friend. Please believe me, I would never hurt you intentionally. But something holds me back from him, and this is what I always seem to latch onto."

"First off... I know you hold me to a separate set of circumstances. Do your comments still hurt my feelings? Yes. I can't deny that. But after a while, I find my Zen and let it go. There's no point holding onto it. And I've never let TB know, so don't stress there.

"As far as Demon goes, assess whether it's worth holding onto this irrational fear you have about loving him, because that's exactly what it is. Fear. The pills are a distraction, and he will give them up, but not until he's ready. Should you have to be the one who bends the knee? No.

"He strikes me as being a lot like Nemo, and I probably know that man-child better than anyone, except maybe Gem. Both need someone to have faith in them. Someone special to them. You're Demon's someone." She got up from the bed. "If I could give you one piece of advice, it's to love him for who he is. Love him for how he treats you. It's what I had to do with TB because heaven knows that man is a trial and tribulation some days. Like that grumpy giant does for me, I know Demon does a great deal for you. And Gem is not wrong. He's dying inside."

"I'm not sure I'm strong enough to do what you're asking."

"And that's how I know this isn't really about the pills. It's about something else altogether. So, whatever that is, the two of you clearly have something far more serious going on." She began unbagging more clothing and packing it into Cherry's suitcases. "Okay, you go pack your toiletries, and I'll finish here. You'll have just enough time to get down to the debriefing, and then I'll have a quick few minutes to say goodbye to TB, and maybe him not being home will help me get this book done before my deadline."

Thoughtful of what Flame said to her, Cherry crossed the room to her bathroom and began packing up her makeup and hair products. Packing her carry-on items into her clear travel pouch, she remembered the day they chose Demon for Tribe.

9

———————

JUNE 1, 2016

Cherry

"Good morning." Cherry greeted God as she placed his breakfast down in front of him.

"Morning." He always ate his breakfast on his penthouse patio. He said it helped him focus for the day. As he closed the folder he'd been looking at, he gestured to the seat across from him. "Have a few minutes?"

"Certainly," she said as she sat down.

He put the folder off to the side of his plate on top of a stack of folders that she'd given him yesterday to review. "I reviewed the files Waters gave me. There are seven here. All are acceptable. However, he flagged Kent 'Ka-Bar' Leech as unlikely to leave the military. Up to us if we want to extend the invite to Tribe. My impulse is not."

"Agreed."

"What about the woman? She would make a second sibling in the crew."

"Waters' sister, Sarah, would be invaluable. I know we want no ties for the team, but both Sarah Miller's and Sawyer Newton's skills are better than any others we've found who have no family."

"Sawyer is reckless. Selfish. A clown. He'll hold his brother back."

"Maybe at first, but Kash is far too good at what he does to let it interfere. Despite his personality, I'm confident that Sawyer will be an asset. There are one or two better options, athletically, but his instincts and improvisational skills match his twin's cerebral gymnastics. Besides, I don't think Kash will open the offer without him as part of the deal."

"And we need Kash." He sighed and contemplated the stack of folders. "We're short a medic."

"Not anymore."

She handed him a file with all the details on the proposed hire. She wasn't sure how God would react. It wouldn't take long for him to read the report since it was in Waters' succinct style—choppy and essentials only.

Aidan Ciarán Parker. Born 1979. Age: thirty-seven. Irish. Resident of Galway. Emigrated to the United States age ten (1989). Entered Harvard Medical School (1998). Earned a bachelor's degree in biology. Completed his degree in three years: took overloads and summer courses (2001). Graduated number three in his class. Entered medical school (2001). Graduated number two in his class (2007). Completed his surgical residency and trauma fellowship, Massachusetts General Hospital (2007-2008). Licensed trauma surgeon at Johns Hopkins (2008-2014).

A lawsuit for malpractice was filed against his surgical team (2014). Three women died post-surgery. Investigation documented overload of work hours (thirty-six straight hours on shift; twenty-two hours surgery without a break) as all three accidents occurred within that time period. (See autopsy: reported excessive doses of prescribed medications in their systems.)

Lawsuit dropped, and a settlement agreed upon by the three

families when Parker assumed full responsibility for his team, publicly and financially. The team was allowed to return to full duties. Parker lost his license to practice.

That same year, four months earlier, on a trip around the Cliffs of Moher, Parker's family encountered mechanical difficulties on their private yacht during a sudden storm. Parker could not attend the trip because of obligations surrounding the lawsuit. Parker's younger sister and her boyfriend's bodies remain lost at sea. Parents found trapped and drowned below deck.

What happened to the man's family was a hard hit after the lawsuits.

She remembered reading about his lauded time at Harvard, the flawless reviews of his time at Massachusetts General, and his quick rise to lead on the trauma team at Johns Hopkins. None of it sounded like a man that had been negligent.

What had sounded like him was his acceptance of the blame for what was likely someone else's fault during those thirty-six hours. As the lead surgeon, he would have seen it as his responsibility, whether he made the actual mistakes or his team members did.

There were pages and pages of his recommendations of staff for promotions and jobs, and even letters refuting complaints regarding staff, including some not on his team.

He made more rounds than any other doctor, and he was always willing to go above and beyond for patients. Patients raved about him in reviews, and when the scandal hit that he was being accused of malpractice, a flood of previous and current patients rushed to send letters defending him, all citing how he prescribed narcotics in moderation. Even patients who had asked for medications, and he had refused them.

He was an excellent surgeon. Something was rotten in the state of Dublin, to paraphrase Hamlet, but they had not dug further. Yet. Perhaps she could set the new computer guy, Kash Newton, Sawyer's twin brother, onto it when he accepted Tribe's offer.

It was the add-on page from Waters that would likely give God pause.

On multiple occasions, I witnessed Aidan Parker taking medication. One night while he was out surfing, I entered his beach shack and searched the premises. No prescriptions or over-the-counter medications found, except for what appeared to be a supply of white, circular tablets. Research identified them as oxycodone. Based on the number found, and the number of times I observed him taking the medication, it is my belief he is a functional addict. A comprehensive database search shows no prescription for this medication. He has no medical records showing them as being prescribed at any time. At no time have I observed him unable to function, whether surfing, driving, or out in public.

Despite the revocation of his license and the presumed functional addiction to narcotics, it is my belief that Aidan Parker would be an exceptional addition to the Tribe team as a medic. My recommendation is to offer Aidan Parker the package, but tell him that we are aware of his substance use and will monitor him. If he proves unable to function on the team, we will issue him the final edict and completely erase him as a violation of his contract.

God grunted when he closed the folder and added it to the pile. "What does your gut tell you?"

"That it's inconsequential."

"I agree with Waters' and your assessments. He's an acceptable risk. My hunch is that the report"—he pointed to the folder—"has a lot of missing information that can only be collected from Parker himself. Information he's unlikely to give to us, even if pressed."

God paused and looked toward the wall, but from experience, Cherry knew his true focus was elsewhere. "I get the sense that total erasure will mean little to him. He might even welcome it. Other methods of persuasion may be necessary, but don't be surprised if those fail too."

"Understood." She changed the subject. "Do we have a location on Waters?"

"Nicaragua. Went for Ildefanso Colonel first. He sensed the man was about to make his move out of Black Site 66 and didn't want to miss him. Retrieving the others will be much easier."

"I'll begin processing their erasures in the meantime. One way or the other, they'll disappear by the same methods."

10

APRIL 10, 2023

Cherry

After Flame left her apartment to say goodbye to TB, Cherry wrestled with her conscience about what the woman had asked her to do.

She wanted to. More than anything.

The moment Demon's eyes met hers after he accepted Tribe's proposal, she had felt the pull. She would have been willing to bet that if anyone had been watching, it would have looked like a volcanic eruption compared to what Waters and Kubrick had experienced when they saw each other for the first time, and that first meeting had been scorching.

Traditional flirtation was not Demon's style, but they had their own version with each other, and it wasn't sly innuendos, winking eyes, and smirks. He threw out witty barbs, and she made snappy comebacks. He watched her with heat, and she gazed back with storm clouds. He developed a tic in his cheek when he was working hard not to smile or laugh at her, and she had a nasty eye roll when he managed to one-up her in a conversation or situation. If people weren't watching closely, it looked like they didn't like each other very much or that, at best, they tolerated each other with heavy frustration on both sides.

Not one to lie to herself, as a rule, she acknowledged there was definitely frustration on her side. Her personal shopping account could attest to that. In the past six years, she'd worn out way more vibrators than she should have needed to work through said frustration. And as the office manager of Tribe, she handled all the dead-men's personal accounts. She wasn't sure what Demon's equivalent for that situation was, but if she had to hazard a guess? It had to do with how often he purchased new surfboards. He broke a lot of them. She hadn't even known it was possible to break a surfboard.

Since her father had disappeared, it had been nothing but work. Her focus was absolute. Then one dark-haired Irishman entered the building, and suddenly, she had something else vying for her attention. Her cold, barren workday had heat in it. The thrill of their verbal sparring had been what made most days of running Tribe from behind the scenes exciting.

So when he had pressed a few times for something more, despite the warmth it gave her that he was interested, the thought of pushing past the current dynamic caused her to break out into a cold sweat. What if it didn't work out? Working with him would be unbearable. It wasn't as if either of them could quit and go somewhere else. She'd rather have what they currently had than risk losing it forever.

Reality hit her hard. Demon had a dangerous job. The team members could, and sometimes had, been captured by others who had murder on their minds. Steel had been a SEAL until something from his past caused him to break ranks illegally. Eventually, his actions caused him to be held in several black sites. While on assignment as a SEAL, someone attacked Waters, resulting in the loss of a kidney. Several years later, enemies kidnapped his sister and subsequently captured and tortured him in a rescue attempt. Last year, a near-explosion in a diamond mine nearly killed their former team-mate, Nemo. All the men had suffered bullet wounds, knife wounds, broken bones, and brutal beatings over the course of their work for Tribe. It came with the gig.

Angels above! What if Demon disappeared or died on a project? Something out of her control had taken the only other people Cherry ever truly loved from her—her mother, her father, Sarah. She didn't think she could bear it if it happened again. Was Flame right? Was it better to have him for as long as she could, even with so many unknowns? More importantly, would it be better to have him for even the shortest of times than to never have him at all?

She was an idiot. Instead of having a conversation with him about it like an adult, she thoughtlessly gave him an ultimatum—a Herculean labor. Quit his pain medication, and they could be together. She'd protected herself from pain because she knew he would never give the medication up, so she was safe from having to follow through. Unfortunately, she fell in love with him instantly, and one moment of diarrhea of the mouth doomed her to be alone. At least this way, she'd still be able to see him every day.

Back in September, she thought she'd earned a chance to give in with grace and not look weak. The day she and Gem had nearly been blown up at that café, and he'd gone all Neanderthal on her, initially, she'd thought it would reset their relationship. Then all of her secrets came out, and it had driven them apart. From then on, it felt like her heart hurt a little more every time they saw each other. Although heated stares and a tic in his jaw persisted, their relationship had changed. The witty barbs had morphed into grunts, growls, and conversations with himself in Gaelic, which he knew she couldn't understand. It felt like she'd lost him anyway. These last seven months of bitter sniping at each other had been soul-crushing. She hated it. She wanted the fun version of sniping with Demon back. She wanted to feel her insides get jittery and excited at the thought of seeing him each day.

To compound the problem, she'd been stewing over Demon's

words on the day of the bombing regarding her reckless disregard for their lives. Some would call him cruel, or at the least callous, in his verbal attack. Yes, he'd been far more direct than any of the others would have been. But she knew his purpose had been to impress upon her that she couldn't go it alone anymore, and she'd forgiven him quickly. The awkwardness between them was more about her embarrassment at being in the wrong.

It hadn't been her intention to put them more at risk. She'd just wanted to make sure they didn't lose focus on what she needed them to do so they could get to the endgame of finding out what happened to her father. However, intentions didn't matter if the result was damaging to them.

He was right. She had been managing them without allowing them a say, whether in the form of consent to work on her goals or in terms of how to work with them. He and the rest of the team had every right to be pissed off at her. Painful didn't even describe her daily working experience. How could she even hope for a relationship with Demon when she couldn't respect his most basic right as her co-worker?

By the time she stood in front of the elevator doors with her luggage, she'd convinced herself to let it go. To not act on her feelings. Yes, she was hurting over it, but better now than later. She was so caught up in her own head, when the doors to the elevator opened, she didn't realize there was another passenger until she'd stepped inside. Since he didn't seem to pay attention to her, instead staring at the floor, she turned and contemplated the door.

When the door closed and started its descent, he spoke. "Maybe you should give yourself a break."

Cherry turned and looked over her shoulder into the steel-gray eyes of the man who earned his nickname for them alone. "Excuse me?"

He reached out to punch the emergency stop button, causing the elevator to halt its progress and the emergency lighting to go on. Moving to lean against the back wall, he crossed his arms over his chest, crossed one ankle over the other, and looked up at the ceiling. He muttered to himself, "Having personal conversations in stopped elevators. Feel like that dude on that show."

"Gibbs? On *NCIS*?"

"The redhead with the sunglasses maneuver?"

"Different show."

"Whoever the guy is who's always slapping people on the back of the head."

"Yeah. That's Gibbs. He's either fighting with someone or imparting words of wisdom when he does it. Which is this?"

He pursed his lips, not contemplating the nonmoving numbers above the door. "I just thought maybe instead of beating yourself up like you have been the last few months, you could let it go and move on."

She turned to face the doors. "I don't know what you mean."

"Yeah, you do. It's time to admit you fucked up, and... what's the saying? 'Build a bridge and get over it'?"

She whirled around on him, knocking over her suitcase with the force of the turn. "If you have something to say, just say it!"

With no show of emotion, he leaned over to pick up her suitcase and right it. Standing next to her, he pierced her with eyes no target wanted on them. "Forgive yourself, Cherry. For months, everyone's been walking on their tiptoes around you. The truths you laid on us the day of the bombing? Yeah, we were pissed off. For all of a hot minute. By the end of the day, we'd forgiven you. We have said nothing because there's nothing to say that can change any of it, so it's better to move forward. Well, Waters might have some things to say, but that's a whole other story. You're the one holding on to that fuckery, so let it go."

She ducked her head. "I don't think I deserve to. I kept secrets. I've put you all at risk. I wasn't thinking."

"*Cariño*, we put ourselves at risk every time we go on a project. We know the risks are higher than normal since we signed on. That was driven home clearly when we were told about the final edict."

"You don't feel like I endangered you? I've been told my hubris might have caused Sarah's death. Waters must hate me."

"Look. It's not as if we weren't engaging in behaviors just as risky before Tribe took us in. For fuck's sake, I was breaking out of black sites, then getting thrown back in. If Waters hadn't rescued me from that Nicaraguan drain, they probably would have shot me on sight when they found me again. Cherry... if anything, Tribe saved all our lives from our own self-destructive ways."

He shrugged. "So you didn't share what the motivation for forming the company was. It's not like any of us, including you, even knew that the Salieri existed, let alone the depth of their depravity. I don't know that there's anyone who could have imagined this in a million years. As far as you knew, your father's disappearance could have been a simple kidnapping for ransom that went wrong somehow. Hell, we still don't know the motivation for his disappearance, even if we're pretty certain it had to do with his private investigations."

He put a hand on her shoulder. "As far as Waters hating you, if you're that worried about it, talk to him. Everyone can feel the tension that's strung even tighter between the two of you. Maybe he's waiting for you to open that door, if it's even an issue for him."

Cherry smiled weakly at him. "Thank you. I owe everyone an apology, so for what it's worth, I'm sorry. I never imagined my choice to keep things secret would have these far-reaching effects."

"No matter how much we consider our actions and plan for contingencies, there are always things that can still be unexpected. We know that every time we go out. Why would real life be any different?" He reached up to curl his hand around her neck, pulling her forehead to his. "We're good, *cariño*. You could dig a hole, push me in it, and bury me alive, and we'd still be good."

"That was creepily specific."

The smile and the shrug reappeared. "Probably not less than I deserve. But Cherry... we all have secrets. Tribe doesn't know everything, even about us."

"I know yours," she whispered. "I've been watching. If I see anything about them you need to know, I'll tell you."

His pupils flared, and his tan skin paled for the briefest of moments. Watching him shut down the one and only time she had ever seen him show fear was terrifying in itself. "*Gracias.*" He kissed her cheek, then added, "I need a favor, *cariño.*"

"What?"

"Talk to D too. The two of you are giving me indigestion. I'd call it heartburn, but I think that's more like what you two have." He hit the emergency stop button again to make the elevator continue its journey. When the doors opened on the third floor, he exited. Over his shoulder, he called out, "Consider that your metaphorical slap on the back of the head."

The doors closed, and the elevator stayed put. She realized she'd never hit the button for floor two when she got on the elevator earlier. Needing a moment to think, she stood in the unmoving car, contemplating Steel's words. The man never talked, but when he did? He tended to unload a lot of shit at once, all of it smart, and it could be overwhelming.

Could she do it? Could she ease her own burdens that easily? Just talk to Waters, and that would be enough to make everything okay again? Seemed too good to be true.

And Demon? Three sentences and now she was rethinking her stance of "let it lie."

11

APRIL 10, 2023

Cherry

"Knock, knock."

Waters' hazel eyes looked up from his computer and the slew of papers spread all over the desk.

Biting the corner of her bottom lip, Cherry tucked her rolling suitcase in between the couch against the wall and the doorframe. "You have a few minutes?"

"For you? Always." He sat back in his chair. "Have a seat if the dog will let you have a corner of the couch."

She glanced over to Ali, who was taking up three-quarters of the couch, obviously exhausted from supervising the meeting earlier. He was belly up, legs in the air, body in three directions, eyes half-open, and little doggy snores and drool hanging from his mouth.

She sat down next to the dog in the small space he'd left open and absently rubbed his belly. He didn't even twitch at the contact. "He looks happy for a dog whose mama is going to be gone for twelve weeks."

"Yeah, he just hasn't realized she's gone, gone. You're lucky you won't be here for that. Make sure you put the chocolate away at your desk, or he'll tear into it in a fit of rage. Kubrick will do worse than murder me if I kill her dog. What's up?"

When she dared to look up at him, a long swath of silence had passed. "All this time, you've lived with the guilt—false guilt—that it was your fault Sarah died. I wondered if now you blamed me? Because of all the secrets I kept. Things between us have been very stilted since Gem and I nearly got blown up, and you have every right to be mad at me. I left you in the dark, and you're the leader of the team. Even before, when God made you primarily office-bound, I should have told you, and I didn't. I jeopardized the team all these years—"

"Whoa, whoa, whoa!" He held up his hand to forestall her babbling. "Wow, you've been packing a lot of shit since September. Cherry-bomb, I will always feel guilty about Sarah. Can't be helped. I've physically paid in spades for that shit show, and Kubrick has helped me let go of a lot of that. I don't think it ever goes away, but it certainly has become less of a focus.

"As far as the secrets shit... That's... a bit more complicated. You know my file better than anyone. I have authority issues with people I distrust. Doesn't matter how high up they are. If the shit they do is whack, then yeah, I have a problem. You don't end up with a missing kidney for disobeying an order because you're a sheep."

"I've been playing solo for so long, I guess I forgot that sometimes people need to know things to make good decisions. It wasn't fair for me to hold information back."

He tilted his head, and his mouth made a sideways movement, pulling his lips in an expression that wasn't confirmation, but not dismissal either. "Your company. You don't owe me any explanations. You think God tells us the reasons behind the shit he does? Fuck, the man up and disappeared for almost two months on us with not so much as a 'Hey, see you later.' I'm assuming you know where he was, but it's not my place to question him." He frowned. "Technically, who is my boss? Him? You?"

"I just own the company. He hands out the directives."

"That you push him toward."

Now it was her turn to copy Waters' earlier expression.

He threaded his fingers together over his stomach. "You knew my sister well, Cherry. Do you honestly think she wasn't aware of the dangers of this job? That she didn't understand what kinds of things could happen to her? If she hadn't ended up here, she would have joined an alphabet agency, and she knew that any job she took might put her in danger. I don't think she envisioned her precise demise, but when abducted, she undoubtedly understood the situation's ultimate outcome."

"I loved her like she was my sister. I hadn't let myself get close to anyone like that in years."

"And she loved you too." He looked at his computer monitor, but she knew he wasn't really seeing the screen, and she could see his brain turning. When he spoke again, his voice was quiet. "They kept us separated. They gave me vivid descriptions of what they were doing to her, but because I couldn't hear it or see it, I was never sure if they were lying or telling the truth.

"When I didn't give them the reaction they wanted, they moved her to the room next door. Then I could hear it. Still, it was disembodied, you know? Like, I knew it was her, but as long as I couldn't see her, it was someone else they were hurting. Still rough, but it was the only way I could lock my shit down.

"I kept silent so that she didn't know I was there. I didn't want her to have that on her soul. There were so many times when I wanted to yell out to her, rage at them... but I couldn't give either of them that because of what I feared would happen when they knew I was reacting to it. Unfortunately, by shutting down completely, it only pissed them off more."

He continued after a long sigh. "Then, the ultimate. They

brought her into my cell. Chained her up so she was facing me. Made sure we could see each other. It only took us a single look to know we would not give in on either side. We refused to talk to one another. We refused to give them anything they could use. The entire time we were together, we never spoke a single word to one another. Not until the end. When she screamed at me not to listen. Not to look."

She watched him through the long, painful pause as he lived through those moments again.

Finally, he spoke, his eyes earnest with her. "Cherry, I knew the penalty for going after her. I knew what I was risking for both of us, and she knew when I got caught, no one was coming for us. I know my sister. She didn't blame anyone except the men who took her. Not me for intercepting that shipment. Not you for keeping secrets."

"But maybe if we'd known—"

"But we didn't. And there's no guarantee we would have, even if you'd told us about your past. It's not like you knew the Salieri existed and purposefully withheld that information."

"You were so mad that day."

"Yeah. I was. Not gonna lie. My gut reaction might have been to throw some choice words your way. You can thank Kubrick for kicking my ass for that within thirty seconds of spitting out the whole thing to her. Which, by the way, I will deny to my dying day and beyond that I told her anything because I know that breaks all the rules. But she helped point me in the right direction, and while I struggled initially, it wasn't directly with you. It was more a sense of helplessness."

"Do you forgive me?"

"Cherry. Have you heard a word I've said? Stop, please. It's done. I should have addressed this long ago instead of letting you fester over it, but I figured if it was really bothering you, you'd come to me. Please promise me that if this, or anything else, crops up again, you'll come talk to me right away. If we have to go hash it out in the gym, I'll happily let you kick my ass, and Kubrick can film it for Midas to put in a file for everyone."

"That'll make another nice bonus feature on the infamous video file of you two meeting," she teased.

He barked out a laugh of frustration. "That shit's still around?"

"You know that things on the internet are never really gone, right?"

"Fuckin' Midas. I'm going into his office to steal all his little rubber geegaws and cut their heads off."

They paused.

"We good?" he asked.

She nodded. "We're good."

"Good. You gonna be okay on this trip?"

She knew he was talking about more than working with her uncle as a source without letting him know. He meant being near Demon more than anything else.

"Yeah. I'll be good."

"Okay." He considered her for a few moments, and she could tell he was deciding whether to ask her a question. "You know he loves you, right? Always has. I've been watching him since day one, and his devotion is unwavering."

"It's complicated."

"I've heard that one before. So has TB. So has Nemo. Don't fall for it. Nothing's really all that complicated."

"That's what Flame said."

"And if there's anyone who knows anything about love, it's that woman."

Cherry looked up at him through her eyelashes. "So... you said Kubrick pointed you in the right direction, huh?"

"Repeatedly." He smirked.

"I take it that means you tried out chapter twelve in Flame's last book."

He mimed locking his lips with a key and throwing it away.

That brought out a genuine laugh. "That's okay. I already know Nemo and Gem did. Which is how I heard you two did."

"How is it my woman can keep her mouth shut about what Tribe does but not about her sex life? I hope I come out of it complimentary," he grumbled.

"Oh, you do. Even if you didn't, you shouldn't feel bad. You two may have tried it out. Poor TB was the guinea pig to make sure it was physically possible."

Waters chuckled. "I won't tell him we know."

His smile faded a bit, and he looked back at his watch.

"It's only been half a day. You really miss her already, don't you?" Cherry asked.

He rubbed his chest absent-mindedly. "It hurts to breathe when she's gone," he admitted.

She loved that he could be vulnerable over Kubrick. He didn't even try to hide it from the team.

"I can always tell how much you miss her. You've picked up a lot of her habits since you met. It started the first time you had to separate. When God made you come home from the movie set and you left Demon with her. You began to channel her work style. The level of sprawl on the table has always been the first indication of how difficult it is to be apart. I don't think you've ever been behind that desk again. Well. Not to work, anyway," she teased.

Shrugging, he shifted uncomfortably. "Yeah, well... Makes me feel closer to her somehow. Even stole her damn villain pens." He pointed at them laid out on the table. "I put a note in her bag, but she's probably still gonna search that backpack of death for at least an hour before she sees it." There was another pause. "Does she—?" He blew air out through his lips with a forceful exhale. Looking up at her, he asked, "Is she happy?"

"Kubrick? More than, I would say."

"It's just... She's seemed, well... not distant. More... quiet lately. Like something's wrong, but she doesn't want to make a big deal out of it because she thinks she's being stupid. I've been worrying she's struggling with us. Sorry. I shouldn't put you in that position. I should just ask her outright, but she's had a lot on her mind with this new film, and I don't want to get in her way."

She didn't want to betray confidences, not that Kubrick had said anything directly, but now she had a feeling she knew what was wrong the other day at lunch. Cherry carefully chose her words. "Maybe she wants you to get in her way. Just an observation, but I've noticed that the two of you are more separate than the other two couples. You're too respectful of each other's spaces, careers, and things. Maybe... maybe you need to 'intermingle' more." Cherry glanced down at the dog passed out on the couch. "Like, maybe saying it's 'our dog' instead of 'her dog.'"

She stood up from the couch and headed to the door. When she got there, she turned to him. "You know, once we're on our way, Nova can take care of most of my front-end work. We have other people on the traditional staff who can usher prospective clients into the conference room and set them up to conference with God. You could do the rest of your work in China. It's not like we can't video chat if we need to."

He rolled his lips in as he thought about her suggestion. "You don't think that would be invasive?"

"No. In fact, I think you might get a few more rounds of chapter twelve out of it, and maybe some pages from one hundred thirty-seven to one hundred forty-four in that other book."

"Ah, yes. The infamous *Nature of the Beast* pages." He grinned. "Those are some very good pages." He stopped to think for a moment. "Will I blow up Steel's bet? I know they bet on me and how long it would take before I caved and went over there."

"He won't win, that's for sure. The guys will be grateful, no matter who wins, as long as it's not him."

"You're sure about this?"

"I'm super sure."

"Okay. I'll talk to God tomorrow. Thanks, Cherry."

"You're welcome."

12

APRIL 10, 2023

Demon

As Demon headed from his office toward the elevator, he came upon TB and Flame.

"Waters is going to take you home tonight." One arm was around her shoulders, the opposite hand rested on her belly. He had to bend way down to meet her forehead with his, especially since she could no longer wear her signature five-inch heels. "I'll be back before you know it. Be careful with the beach ball." He pressed his lips to her mouth. Then, with his lips against her forehead, he whispered, "Love you, Flame. With every breath until the last."

"Be safe. I love you too. Every breath until the last."

"*Ayo,*" TB whispered.

When the elevator doors opened, TB brushed one more kiss against her lips, then met Demon inside the carriage. Once the doors closed, Demon apologized. "Sorry to intrude. Didn't know she was still here or that you were saying goodbye. I would have waited."

TB waved him off. "Not a big deal. I don't care if everyone knows I love her or that you all hear me say it. She deserves that."

Demon couldn't help but think of another redhead who also deserved that kind of outward devotion. Quickly, he shut the thought down. There were too many issues there, and it was going to be hard enough for her to get through this surprise assignment with him. He wished she wasn't being forced into this. Steel could have posed as her husband, but he also knew that had God assigned the man to her, the conference room would have burst into flames to make sure it was him instead. He was nothing if not a sea of contradictions.

They met everyone in the armory for a final weapons check. Demon and Cherry would not be carrying to solidify the honeymoon illusion. A driver would drop off TB, Midas, and Steel at various points, so they would arrive separately at the airport. Gem would meet them in St. Lucia to get them weapons and other equipment they might need, avoiding any difficulties with travel. Each of the men had a weapon on them they would not be checking in and would miss detection by the scanners.

When Waters cleared the three men to leave, they took the elevator to the garage and headed to their pickup points.

Turning to the "newlyweds," he handed them their passports as Mr. and Mrs. McCarthy. "Hope you both studied D's new background."

Both nodded.

He looked at Cherry. "Midas kept him as close as possible to avoid slipups, not that you would. He even did a deep dossier on him, including social media presence, so it should stand up to scrutiny. He'll keep adding details as you travel. Should be complete by the time you arrive."

Holding out his hand to Demon, he pulled him in for the one-arm man hug with the two requisite slaps to the back. He whispered so that Cherry couldn't hear. "Take care of her. Maybe try to fix this, yeah? You deserve her."

When Waters released him with a last look of "Yes, you do," he followed with a look at Cherry. Their boss hugged her tight. He whispered something to her, then pulled back. Demon saw her eyes go glassy when they pulled apart, and the soft smile on Waters' face, along with the single affirming head nod, caused her to throw her arms around his neck, hugging him tightly.

She held him like that for a long time, and Waters ran his hands gently up and down her spine as he whispered in her ear. When she pulled herself together, he told them both, "Stay together. Be careful. Trust no one. Make sure you keep in touch with me and the guys. *Ayo.*"

13

APRIL 10, 2023

Cherry

Tribe's traditional security men had already packed their bags in the car and were waiting with a limousine to take them to the airport. The silence inside the car was beyond uncomfortable.

"Need to quiz me?" he asked.

"No, I'm good," she replied.

More silence.

"I've never flown with you before. You fly okay? Anything I should know?"

"I fly fine."

Even more silence.

"Do you sleep on flights or read, or what do you do?"

"Depends."

Every second alone with him was crushing her. She felt like she couldn't breathe.

"Want to join the Mile High Club?"

Her head whipped around to him, shock on her face, and she started coughing as she choked on the saliva that went down the wrong pipe.

Rubbing her back as she hacked up a lung, she heard him say, "Glad to see something got a reaction out of you." She watched him shake his head and look out his own window. "Look, I'm sorry you're unhappy about partnering with me, but you should know, I'm not sorry. I would have demanded it was me rather than Midas or Steel."

She studied her hands in her lap. Quietly, she said, "I'm not unhappy. Given this afternoon's discussion, 'uncomfortable' would be a better description."

She could feel his eyes on her. Things couldn't stay like this between them. Kubrick was right. She'd apologized to Steel and Waters. She'd have to address it with the others later, but this she could fix now.

"I'm sorry," she told him. "You were right. About everything."

Silence. He was going to make her say it all, and he should. Now she respected him even more because he was holding her accountable for her actions.

"When Dad disappeared, I... It was like I was two people at the same time. One was the same serious, practical brainiac I'd always been. I didn't cry. I didn't scream. I didn't demand things. I went about the process of 'losing' Dad the same way I went about preparing for an exam. I made lists of what I needed to do. I gathered information. I followed up on every avenue. I followed through with every decision.

"But there was another me. An alternate me. I'd already lost my mom and had no other family. I felt it was so unfair to have him taken from me too. On the inside, I was seething so hard that I felt like I was on fire. So, while on the surface, everyone saw methodical me, praised me for how mature I was and told me how proud my father would be of me, inside, there was this raging monster that no one knew was there. It didn't matter if I destroyed the city if it meant I got my father back."

She noticed the slight quirk at the corner of his mouth over the *Godzilla* comparison.

Looking at him, though, when she knew she'd hurt him, was painful, so she gazed out the window, seemingly at the buildings, people, and traffic going past, but none of it was truly registering. "When I started at Georgetown, I vowed nothing would get in my way. I fought tooth and nail to get every opportunity, never worrying about who I might hurt. My rationale was they didn't want it as badly as I did if they couldn't compete and beat me. I excelled at everything I did because I burned with this need to find my father and the men who stole him from me. It was all I thought about. I'm sure there are whole days I went without eating, without sleeping..."

Her voice was so quiet, she wasn't sure he could hear her. "TB was right. I wanted revenge. There was nothing unselfish or altruistic about my goals. I wanted my dad back, and I did not give a holy grail who got stepped on or who suffered. I was so certain I knew it all."

"You had to fight, Cherry," Demon told her. "You were alone. No one was looking out for you since you were technically an adult. Your attorney was logging billable hours. Your uncle had his own agenda, biding his time until you decided you needed him. Your friends and fellow students were busy living the last days of their childhood. I don't know that anyone could really blame you."

"Doesn't make it right."

"No. And I'm not saying I don't believe you should have handled it differently, but it wasn't my decision to make. I shouldn't have pushed you like I did."

"No. You were right to say it. Nothing you said was wrong. Being called out embarrassed me, which made me angry with myself, and I spent the last seven months acting like a total fuckwitch and pushing away those who could help. The people I love like my family. May have even gotten one of them killed."

"They're not going anywhere, Cherry. They will always help you, and they will always love you." There was another long pause before Demon added, "I heard you talking to Waters in his office. I couldn't hear what was being said, but you were in there for a while. Did you talk about Sarah?"

"He said there was nothing to forgive." Her throat felt tight, and her head hurt as she worked to keep the tears from falling. "He told me he understood. That he didn't blame me, and Sarah wouldn't have either." A tear fell then. She couldn't stop it. "He told me what happened in Egypt. I knew it was bad, but it was..." She shook her head, wiped away the tear, and tried to collect herself. "It was so much more than bad. But he also told me she would have understood why I kept things secret, and even if it meant she became a victim anyway, she wouldn't have done it any other way."

"Then I would believe him. He would know his sister better than anyone else on the team."

Abruptly, she changed the subject. "I saw you, you know. In the paper. When the paper reported on the lawsuit."

"Not exactly a ringing endorsement," he griped.

"On its own, no. But they interviewed a former patient, and something he said struck me as odd. It's what made me pursue you for the deadmen. He talked about how he would never, ever believe you were responsible for those women's deaths because when he had asked you for pain medication, you wouldn't give it to him. Now there are several things in that statement to unpack, but that doesn't sound like a doctor who's negligent."

She watched as Demon shifted in his seat, putting all his attention out the door window. "Doesn't mean I didn't make a mistake."

"One mistake, maybe. Three?"

"It was a long two days. Almost as many hours in surgery as working in total. People get tired. Tired makes you sloppy."

"Not you, Demon. I've seen you go for almost a week without sleep. All of you do it, and you function just fine. And I've never seen you even close to being sloppy in anything you've done. You're almost anal-retentive about neatness. Worse than Waters. What really happened?"

His nose twitched as he worked his jaw like he was biting down hard on his teeth to keep from responding.

She continued to wait.

He took a deep breath. Let it out. "We were all overworked. As you probably remember from your reports, my team had been on shift for twelve hours when the first accident victim came in, and we worked on fourteen others. Dense fog in the early rush-hour traffic. A tanker truck crossed the center line and hit a string of cars basically parked at a standstill.

"The injuries were horrific. Some never made it to the table. We operated for twenty-one hours. Rules say none of us should have been operating on anyone, but there was no one else to do it because everyone had been called in already. They'd even diverted injuries to other hospitals, but the victims just kept coming, so we kept pushing.

"I trusted my team, but I rotated my nurses out so they could take catnaps. It was my anesthesiologist, though, who I didn't pay attention to. She was struggling, so she took a bathroom break and snorted a couple of lines of cocaine in order to wake up. Apparently, it was something she did occasionally but rarely enough that we never knew. The last three patients we operated on, she fecked up their sedation orders. Between that and the normal medications we used for pain and infection, they overdosed within a few hours of each other."

It would have been so easy to prove he was innocent. "Why did you take the blame?"

"She was a single mom. Three kids. Husband was a total douchebag. Beat her, beat the kids. Was the one who got her into drugs. She was trying so hard to raise her kids on her own while the feckin' sperm donor rotted in jail for dealing. Neighbor lady watched the kids when they weren't in school, and the mom never saw them because she was always pulling extra shifts to pay the bills, whatever. Her kids would have gone into the system. I couldn't let her go down like that."

"Oh my god. You sacrificed yourself for a woman who could have turned around and done it again the next week!"

"But she didn't. I made sure of it. I told her I would take the blame, but she had to get clean. She could never, ever use again. My attorney drew up the paperwork. They tested her every three to four days for six months. Got her into an outpatient rehab program so that she could still work and be with her kids. She's stayed clean all these years, back on her feet, met a good guy, and he spoils them all rotten. It was worth it for that."

She wondered if he saw the irony in his condition for saving her job and ruining his life.

He looked out the window. "It was a long time ago. There's no point talking about it anymore, and I'm not going to. Nothing I do or say now is going to change what happened to me, to my surgical team, and it sure as hell will not change what happened to those women who died."

They rode in silence for several miles, but while inside the car may have been quiet, Cherry's mind was a cacophony of emotions and thoughts. All the events from earlier in the day—the pseudo breakup with Demon in the conference room, the assignment God gave them, her conversations with Flame, Steel, and Waters—had caused a war within her. Somewhere in the space of all that, she'd come up with a solution for the two of them that was so stupid and crazy, she couldn't believe she was about to put it out there to him.

She wanted him. She had powerful emotions surrounding him, but she wasn't in love with him. Because you couldn't fall in love with someone whose endgame was so drastically different from your own, right? At forty-four, her chances of finding someone to settle down with—deadman status notwithstanding—were microscopic. She had set the guidelines for a relationship between them, and he wasn't willing to abide by them. Fine. But why deny herself this opportunity to have him, even on a surface level?

There would be pain later because she'd know what she was missing, but it couldn't possibly be soul-destroying long-term. She'd get over him, he'd get over her, and life would go on. It couldn't possibly hurt worse than it already did. Could it?

She took a quiet, steadying breath, then unleashed her bomb. "I don't want us to fake our way through this newlywed thing."

He turned his head to look at her.

Gazing into the center of his reflective lenses, she said, "I'm as good as any of you when I'm working on a project, but this situation is a little more than I'm used to. We're going to have to maintain this cover for Zion almost every minute of the day. It's not enough to just spout details of a created history, say we're in love, and think that's going to be enough. We're going to have to appear like believable lovers, and I've never had to hop in and out of character. My roles have never been long-term immersive. A couple hours, tops, at a party or a dinner."

By no twitch or sound did he reveal he was tracking what she was proposing. Hell, she didn't even know if he'd believe her words or if he'd see right through them as the bullshit they were.

Finally, he asked, "Where are you headed with this, Cherry?"

This was so awkward. Just hours ago, they had decided to stay away from each other, and now they were being forced into each other's intimate circle. Not only that, but she was about to propose they ignore that conversation and jump into bed together. Literally.

"I'm asking you to help me out by not making me schizophrenic for the next week. We know we both have chemistry, even if we know that we're not willing to commit to one another. But if we don't act like a couple in practice, I'm liable to screw things up."

Turning his back to the corner of the car, he tilted his glasses up on top of his head, the arms sweeping back the longer top strands to reveal the fade cut underneath. His face was still blank. She would have given anything to know what he was thinking.

"Are you saying you want to feck around while on the project as part of our cover?"

"Maybe?" she offered. Suddenly, she was pretty sure this was the stupidest thing she'd ever done. To cover up her sudden fear, she continued, "I mean, this is only going to be a week, maybe less. Who knows? Maybe we even discover that what we imagine is between us isn't really even there, but we just think it is because we have done nothing about it." Crap, that was even weaker than the first set of bullshit she handed him.

"At the risk of sounding like an idiot by repeating myself, you're suggesting that we be an actual couple for the duration of the project, not just pretend to be one? So you want me to hold your hand, kiss you, all that shite?"

"Sure. I mean, I think it's pretty foolish to think we wouldn't have to engage in some form of PDA to sell it, right? And it's not like we can request separate bedrooms because, well, that would be totally unbelievable if we're trying to pass as newlyweds."

"So, you want me to continue that idea behind closed doors? Not just literally sleep in the same bed with you to fool the house staff but actually have sex with you?"

"I guess? Well, yes. If we just... throw ourselves into it completely... it makes it easier for us so that we don't have to head-hop between ourselves and the mythical McCarthys."

"When out and about in public, sure. But behind closed doors, we can turn it off. There's no one to sell the relationship to there. And it's not as if we have to immerse ourselves so far in this that we're at legend status. Waters doesn't expect that. The job's not that deep."

"I know, I just... Look at it this way. It takes care of two problems. The first, we keep our cover as solid as it can be, with no danger of making a mistake. For the second, right now, the timing of this assignment is awkward because of the conversation we had in the conference room today. If we ignore that—just temporarily—we get to act on all the chemistry we have and get it out of our systems with no worries of awkwardness when we go home. It's perfect, really. A clear timeline, clear parameters, and since we're both adults, neither of us gets hurt when it's over, when the objective of the project is achieved."

He hid it well, but his jaw clenched. If she hadn't been watching for the tiniest of signs, she might have missed it. He was mulling it over, looking at the suggestion from all angles, and deciding how badly it could go.

"This is crazy. It sounds like one of Flame's plotlines, only ten times crazier," he finally ground out. He flashed her a weird look. "Those never work out, you know. Someone always ends up screwing it up by falling in love and making a helluva mess out of everything."

She waved him off, injecting as much confidence as she could into her voice. "That's fiction. This is reality."

She watched his jaw clench harder. Baby Jesus on a skateboard! What was he so mad about? He was a guy. She was offering him no-strings sex. Sex he'd clearly wanted if his antics on the conference room table were to be believed. Why was he suddenly now being so sensitive about it? She would be the ruined one, not him.

His voice cut into her mental tirade. "You think you can do that? Be with me for a few days, then when we come home, just shut it off? Pretend it never happened and put our earlier agreement back in place to keep things strictly professional?"

Her confidence was taking an enormous hit. How dare he think she couldn't be an adult about this? Women had needs, too, and she needed him, whether or not he wanted her to. With the determination that she was right in her thought process, she made one final push. "Demon, just treat it like any other project. I know you've all gotten involved with someone as a means to an end on a project. You were all adults and walked away with no hard feelings when the projects were done."

"We also never had to be around for the fallout either," he reminded her.

Well, that sucked, having it confirmed that he'd fucked around on the job. There had been reports that crossed her desk where, reading between the lines, she knew they'd seduced women, and on one occasion even a man, into getting information or access to things. Didn't mean she wanted actual confirmation of the fact that Demon had done that.

He continued, "This is different. We'll see each other for hours on end, day after day. What happens when the project ends and we stop 'being together,' one of us gets hurt?"

One of us, meaning her. "Again. Adults here. We know what we're agreeing to, so no one can say they thought something else was going to happen. No guilt for either party."

All of that was true. What she didn't say was that she knew her proposal was ludicrous. When the assignment was done, and he walked away as planned, she was going to get hurt. She'd just have to deal with it and keep it from him when it was over. But she decided she'd rather have the pain of losing him than the agony of never knowing what it was like to be with him at all.

Muttering something under his breath in Gaelic while shaking his head, he leaned his outside elbow on the window's edge, his pointer finger running across his lips. Was he going to go for it?

A pained expression flashed across his face as he rubbed his fingers across the wrinkles he'd created on his forehead. With a last burst of air, he agreed. "I'm going to regret this. Fine. Under one condition," he finally replied. "We start now. There's been an awful lot of back and forth with us for a while, and we can't afford to make any awkward screwups once we get to your uncle's, so we work on playing the happy couple before we even get there." He hesitated. "Let's start with something small."

She followed his gaze as it went to her lap. Slowly, he reached for her hand, making sure there was plenty of time for her to pull away if she wanted. When she stayed still, he grasped it loosely in his, threading their fingers together.

As soon as he touched her hand, her mind whirled. All the normal feelings she got when he touched her rose to the surface, but now they seemed magnified a hundredfold. What she wouldn't give for him to touch her like this with no subterfuge involved. His warm skin connected to hers, and she felt that warmth travel from where he placed the back of her hand on his thigh to throughout her body.

Studying their connection, she loved the contrast of his tanned skin against her pale ivory, and she focused on their smoothness. His hands were free from calluses, probably from all the ocean water and applications of wax on his board. That, and she imagined that his time as a surgeon had taught him to take care of his hands better than most.

She turned her gaze back to their entwined fingers when she felt his thumb brushing gently back and forth across her own. Something happened to her at that moment, and the air felt charged. It was something she'd never felt before, and it was both thrilling and frightening at the same time. Like she was at the top of a cresting wave, hanging over the precipice and about to free-fall into the water below to a watery grave.

"This okay?" he asked.

She looked up at him. No. It was not anywhere close to okay. There was only one thing to do.

She swallowed, smiled, and nodded the lie.

It was one thing to know she was going to get hurt in the end. It was something completely different to understand that pain now, long before it happened. One consensual grasp of her hand, and she wanted this for real.

They sat quietly, holding hands for several minutes. She knew she must be thinking about something, but her emotions were controlling the show. They made her feel as if her brain was a sea of organized chaos, each thought a fish in a school, all sensing danger but unsure how to proceed through the waters—instead darting this way, then that way, trying to make sense of what she was feeling.

It was Demon's voice that finally scattered the chaos and brought her abruptly out of her blind panic. "You sure about this, fireball? We're both going to get burned. Badly."

"I'll be fine."

"When was the last time you were in a relationship?" he asked. Then, as if sensing he'd stepped over a line, he backpedaled. "It's not really my business, so it's okay if you don't want to tell me."

"No, it's fine. Never, really."

She saw a flash of fear cross his face.

She laughed. "Don't worry, Demon. I'm not some sweet, innocent thing. I've 'dated,' if that's the term we want to use, but rarely, and never more than a dinner, maybe two, if he kept my interest. Couple of times a year, maybe? Tribe doesn't leave a lot of options open." She shrugged. "Never met anyone I liked enough to keep around."

"I'm sorry. I was just surprised. Not about the fact that you'd had lovers. Just that you were a one-night kind of woman."

"It's okay. I get it. Most women aren't one-night types. It's funny," she confessed. "I've never really seen what the big deal was. I mean, I get it. It's a biological function. People get aroused, and they have sex. I don't go looking for it, and I've left plenty of dates without going home or to a hotel with someone. But once it's over? I've never looked back at it."

"Then you're not having great sex."

She shrugged. "I've gotten what I need out of it."

"Definitely not great sex. That's just survival sex. Keeps you in control until the pressure builds up again."

"A vibrator can do the same thing."

"That's even worse than an anonymous, unemotional feck. I'm not saying they don't have their uses, and I'm not saying you have to be in love with your partner, but there does need to be a connection. No one can connect to a device, no matter how many features, speeds, or styles of vibration it has. Rubbing one out is just a pressure valve release, but it wouldn't be enough in the long run. There's no connection. No spontaneity. No learning curve to what someone likes or doesn't like. And that's half the fun of sex. Discovering what turns your partner on."

A horn blaring outside the car disrupted the moment of tension, and it seemed to remind Demon of something. He reached into his pants pocket. "Since we're discussing our real fake marriage, you need this." He opened the box he'd withdrawn so that the contents faced her.

She thought she kept from audibly inhaling, but she didn't dare look at Demon to see if he'd noticed. Inside the box were three rings. One was a simple platinum band meant for a man's hand, a series of waves in infinity engraved on the surface. The other two were a matching set of platinum rings for a woman. The engagement ring was a circle-cut sapphire that interlocked in a band that was shaped like two waves overlapping, the channels filled with diamonds.

"Can't be newlyweds without rings," he murmured as she stared.

She searched for something to say to keep the moment light. "The waves are very you."

"Yeah, Midas has a thing for that kind of stuff. Did you know he recommended the collar designer for Flame to TB? The guy is a hopeless romantic."

As if she were outside of herself, Cherry watched as Demon removed the women's rings, interlocked them, and reached for her hand to put it on her. The entire time, she sat stunned. Afraid to move. Afraid to breathe. But it wasn't in panic. It was a moment she wanted to remember. To seal into the corners of her brain to take out later, when things were dark or desperate or lonely after this experiment known as "Demon and Cherry" failed to navigate the channel between Odysseus' monsters, Scylla and Charybdis. By the end, she would be chewed up, spit out, and swept to the depths with no hope of survival.

His next words broke her thoughts. "Midas put a tracker in the wedding band portion. Even if the sapphire gets damaged, it's still in the ring, so never take it off. You have your internal trackers, but after what happened in Africa with Nemo's secondary tracker, he's paranoid and wanted a third one on you that was on an outer level."

Of course. A tracker. To find her if something went wrong. Not a vow between them. That could never be.

14

APRIL 10, 2023

Demon

WHAT IN THE ACTUAL FECK WAS HE DOING? HE WAS OUT OF HIS goddamn mind, is what he was. Had he really agreed to an affair with Cherry that had a time limit on it? One that was totally going to destroy him when she walked away like she apparently did with every other lover she'd had? He needed his head examined.

The flight to St. Lucia was going to be twelve-plus torturous hours over two separate flights. The first leg took off just before midnight, so maybe she'd sleep through most of it. He'd both hated and loved the two hours of checking in, hanging out in the VIP lounge, and boarding the plane. It gave him all kinds of excuses to touch her. A hand on the back to guide her. Holding her hand as they walked. An arm around the waist while checking in to pull her close and kiss her temple so he looked like a doting new husband. Pulling out her chair and making sure her hair didn't catch behind her. Brushing her hand when he handed her a glass of champagne.

She responded to all of it as if it were the most natural thing in the world.

It was going to be both heaven and hell. Was he going to take advantage of their status? Hell to the motherfecking yes. However, he would be the first to admit that he desperately wanted it to be real.

Once they'd boarded the plane, the flight attendant brought them more champagne. One sip from the glass and Cherry gave a small giggle, rubbing her nose. "Bubbles. They tickle."

"Are you tipsy?" he teased.

"I don't drink much, if ever. I don't like not being in control of my body for any reason."

"Well, let me be in control of it." He noticed an odd look on her face, one he couldn't decipher. All he knew was that it made him uncomfortable in public. "Drink your champagne, Mrs. McCarthy. I promise not to let you get out of control." Even he heard the gravel in his voice.

After they were in the air, it wasn't over thirty minutes before Cherry slipped off her shoes and drifted off to sleep in the chair bed next to him. He reached over and covered her feet with the thin airplane blanket she had draped over herself. A throbbing started in his lower back, so he moved to adjust to a more comfortable position in his seat, then he drew out his tablet and entered the group chat.

—God, Midas, Steel, TB, Waters already in chat
—Demon now online
MIDAS:... 11th for Steel, the 12th for Waters, 13th for me, and 15th for God. That correct?
DEMON: wot u fex bet on
TB: Here we go again with having to decipher the Harvard grad's deplorable spelling.
MIDAS: Nothing.
MIDAS: We were predicting when it would snow in Chicago and cause a flight delay.
DEMON: I dont believe u

DEMON: april u twatz
DEMON: no snow
DEMON: & not flyn thru Chi
MIDAS: Don't care. That's my story and I'm sticking to it.
DEMON: Feck u btr not hav ben bettn on me & C
WATERS: Of course we were, idiot. At least we weren't betting on whether you were joining the Mile High Club like some of us had to endure.
DEMON: So wots the bet
WATERS: If we tell you, that distorts the odds, and you'll fuck all of us over just because.
DEMON: xctly
TB: Fuck, please learn to type like a regular human being. I don't want to work this hard.
DEMON: told u b4 hate txtn
DEMON: mayb if u smartr u cud read
TB: Midas, can you send in a special request to the flight attendants and have one smother him with his cheap airline pillow?
MIDAS: Say 'please.'
TB: 😡
DEMON: Not nice 2 do 2 C
TB: Why? She'd get to dump your sorry, mopey ass for someone who's going to treat her right.
DEMON: 🖕
MIDAS: You're always so negative.
MIDAS: You can tell a lot about people by their emoji use.
MIDAS: Demon, what are your most used emojis? Top 5.
DEMON: 4 fex sake
TB: This oughta be good.
MIDAS: C'mon. Humor me.

DEMON:

MIDAS: Guess those make sense.

MIDAS: Ok everybody share. Top 5.

TB: Seriously? I left my very pregnant sub at home for THIS?

WATERS:Make him call you "Sir"? Does that help? Or maybe now it's "Daddy"?

STEEL: This is better than the other game his genetic material used to throw at us.

STEEL:

MIDAS: The screwdriver one scares me.

MIDAS: Correction. That whole row scares me.

STEEL: It should

MIDAS: Who's next?

MIDAS: I'll do mine.

MIDAS:

WATERS: Ok first one is Kubrick. Third one is Flame. What are the others?

MIDAS: Last four are Flame.

TB: What the actual fuck? How often are you talking to my woman?

MIDAS: When she's writing, she sometimes asks me to put her on a timer so she remembers to take breaks.

MIDAS: The shoe used to be when she was buying new heels and needed an opinion.

MIDAS: Now it's for when she wants my opinion on something she's buying for you.

MIDAS: The face is when she -shows- me what she's thinking of buying.

TB: Well, that's awkward. I know what she bought me three weeks ago.

MIDAS: Tell me about it. I need eye bleach. Again.

MIDAS: Btw you can thank me for the color. I picked that out.
TB: Now I need brain bleach.
MIDAS: Waters?
WATERS: 🤍😨👀🔥😳
MIDAS: What's with the last one?
TB: I don't think they have an emoji for it, so he shows her his "nose" is growing.
MIDAS: There's an eggplant for that, you know. 🥒
WATERS: You asked for the first five. Not number 6.
MIDAS: Think I'm glad I didn't ask for 7, 8, 9, and 10.
WATERS: 😈
GOD: All right. Enough fucking around.
GOD: Knew nothing was ever going to be normal again.
GOD: Be safe. Try not to kill or injure your handler.
GOD: 🖕🖕🖕🖕🖕
—God offline
STEEL: Totally believe those are his top 5 emojis.
WATERS: I'm surprised he knew what an emoji was.
DEMON: C u idiots in 🌴 **Better yet hope u die in** ❄️
WATERS: No time to die. We got shit to do. Take care of her or the women will do worse to you than God will.
—Waters offline
MIDAS: Do you guys think he got Kubrick off on that Houston leg of the trip and just didn't tell us?
TB: Nah. Not his style. Besides, I was watching too closely, and Nemo would never have missed that for a million years.
—Midas offline
TB: He needs to get over this shit with his brother.
STEEL: He will. Give him time.
TB: New bet needed. Who gives in first? Demon or Midas?
—TB offline

STEEL: Is there surfing in St. Lucia?
DEMON: No big 🌊 on W coast
DEMON: E coast bttr
STEEL: So… west coast should be good for beginners. Take Cherry. Teach
her. Might help her see you in a different light.
—Steel offline

Demon exited the chat. He contemplated Steel's suggestion. It might work.

A glance to his left showed Cherry staring at him. "Talking to the guys?"

"Yeah."

"Are they betting on how soon we'll sleep together?"

Feck. This was dangerous territory. He didn't know that's what the bet was since he came in at the end of the conversation, but if he had to guess? Yes, that's what he'd thought it was.

"Possibly. Went online in the middle of the conversation."

"Well, since there's only one bed, and I refuse to let you sleep on the floor, and I sure as Mary-went-to-the-inn am not sleeping on the floor, whoever said tonight is going to win. What did Steel say?"

"That fecker," Demon muttered. "Steel said tonight. That's now what they meant though."

"No, but the phrasing of the bet matters, yes? So Steel will win."

"Again," they said in unison. There was the briefest of pauses before they both chuckled.

"You know what the others predicted, though, and what they're assuming the bet is versus what it actually is."

"My knowing doesn't matter. Nothing happens if you don't want it to, whether we're sleeping in the same bed or not, and I don't give a shite who wins the bet."

She snuggled back into her pillow. "You should rest."

"Are you inviting me to sleep with you, Mrs. McCarthy?" he teased.

"I guess I am, Mr. McCarthy." She knocked on the table that formed a triangle between the two chairs. "This divider thing will keep you safe from me."

"Hmm. I wonder? Will it keep you safe from me though? I mean... You feel any anxiety on the flight, I'm sure I could ease that. Should you need it." He winked.

She smiled. "I'll keep that in mind. Should I need it." Snuggling back under the blanket, she closed her eyes.

While he watched her, his mind raced. She deserved a man who would give her everything. Love her within an inch of her life and beyond it. Walk through fire for her. Burn the world down for her. Absolutely put her first above all else.

Contemplating the seatback in front of him, he acknowledged it was time for him to get his shite together. For six years, he'd hidden his fears and insecurities behind a gentle narcotic veil, even if it was only to himself. He was about to lose the best thing in the world if he couldn't straighten himself out. It wasn't worth holding onto anymore. He could withstand the physical pain for her. His failure to straighten himself out would doom him to a life without her. It wasn't worth it.

A quick glance to his left showed that Cherry was fast asleep. As quietly as possible, he extricated himself from the seat—the throbbing in his back had upped to a dull, constant ache—and headed up to the lavatory. Once behind the locked door, he reached into his pocket and pulled out a container of mints he carried. He dumped out the contents—thirty white pills—into the palm of his hand. Closing his eyes, he gripped the pills tightly in his hand and heaved a sigh of resolution. It felt melodramatic, but he also felt like the moment needed something to mark it.

He flipped the toilet seat lid up and held his fist over the bowl. He opened his eyes, squared his shoulders, and willed his fist to open.

It stayed closed.

He concentrated all of his efforts on visualizing his fingers fanning open, watching the tablets fall in twos and threes into the bowl. But no matter how hard he concentrated, he couldn't make it happen.

Only once he'd turned his fist right side up would his fingers flex open. As he stared at the pile in his open hand, he urged the other to rise and brush the contents off its surface.

Nothing happened.

He'd never prayed so hard for turbulence in his life. A sudden jolt in the atmosphere to cause the tablets to bounce out of his hand and into the toilet so he could flush them away.

The plane's flight continued its smooth travel.

Something pushed forward through the mist in his brain. A glimmer of who he used to be. Confident. Easygoing. Quick with a joke. A memory of standing in the emergency room with his trauma team a few months before the tanker accident. They'd had a hellacious day, but they all stood easily around the nurses' station in the dark hours of the early morning. Typical doctors functioning on too much terrible coffee and stale birthday cake from another doctor, but they were laughing and telling bad surgical jokes. They'd been like a family.

Now that particular work family was functioning without him.

Another memory popped into his brain. His solo form emerging from the sea, the lifeless body of a ten-year-old boy in his arms, the water sluicing off both of their bodies as he stumbled to the beach. A woman screaming at him in Japanese, her tiny fists beating at his back as he laid her boy down gently on the sand. A man yelling promises of revenge for killing his son.

A family in grief over the son they had lost.

Finally, another image presented itself. Not one he'd seen in person, but one he'd envisioned in nightmares. The blackness of a stormy night. Waves battering a tiny yacht. His sister's shriek as she was swiped over the side of the ship. Her boyfriend screaming her name as he reached for her, then was swept over as well. His mother praying in her native tongue as his father held her close, the water rising steadily higher and higher with them trapped below deck.

Another family ripped apart.

He had no idea how long he'd stood there, locked inside his head. When an insistent knocking at the door broke through his living nightmare, he quickly dumped the pills back into the tin, save two, and shoved it deep in his pocket.

Blood roaring in his ears and rushing through his system, he called out, "Just a moment." His voice sounded shaken and vulnerable, even to him. He popped the two oxy into his mouth, swallowing them dry. He lowered the toilet seat, hit the flush button, and made quick work of washing his hands. Before he left the bathroom, he scrubbed his face with the cool water and ran his wet fingers through his hair, trying to find some semblance of calm.

Who was he kidding? The real Aidan Parker was dead. Not just his physical person, whose official death recorded him as being swept away in a surfing accident off the coast of Japan, but everything he had once been was gone. There was nothing left of who he had been, and who had taken his place was a stranger to him. A man consumed from the inside out by the demon of self-destruction. The very entity that gave him his name.

Cherry deserved someone real. Someone good. Someone who could stand by her side and be proud of the man he'd become. Not the shell of a doctor who'd promised to heal people and save lives but couldn't live up to his words. She needed a man who could keep his promises.

Giving the tin inside his pocket a quick rattle to reassure himself that its contents were safely inside, he stood with a last look in the mirror. Fingers through his dark locks one more time, he surveyed the face staring back at him and came to terms with the fact that he was who he was. He would never be anyone else. He couldn't change. Not even for the one woman he wanted most in his life.

15

APRIL 11, 2023

Cherry

A DRIVER MET THEM AT THE AIRPORT TO TAKE THEM DIRECTLY to *Les Vergers de la Mer*. Tall, dark-haired, and built like a truck. She also noticed the telltale bulge of a holstered weapon beneath his suit coat.

She flashed a quick look at Demon, but he didn't seem to be surprised at all. He simply shook the man's hand and carried on.

All the way to *Les Vergers*, she sat stiff and silent, afraid to speak or react to anything. When the car finally arrived at the gated entrance to the estate, their driver slowed and rolled his window down. Instead of stopping the car, a guard dressed in a white, short-sleeved button-down shirt and pressed tan pants waved them through the gate. She wished they would have been required to stop so she could get a better look at the gate attendant and his hut because out of the corner of her eye, she got a glimpse of the old-fashioned address plate mounted to the brick stanchion. The nameplate was a mosaic piece, but something looked off.

Her gaze darted to Demon beside her, his reflective sunglasses hiding his eyes from her, although the turn of his head suggested he was looking elsewhere. The men commonly used this tactic on projects, but she couldn't tell if his current behavior was an act or if he was truly focused on something else.

Coming to a stop, their driver exited the vehicle and assisted them from the cool interior to the warm breezes, lazy clouds drifting at a snail's pace overhead in the blue sky. As he directed two young male servants to unload their luggage and whisk it away, she pretended to admire the flowering bushes along the front of the wrap-around veranda when what she was really noticing were the discreet armed guards at the corners of the second-floor balcony. Their attire comprised white T-shirts and tan pants, much like the gate guard.

Zion Norton stood on the front steps, nodding to the driver as the man disappeared inside the building. "I apologize. Matthew is not very gregarious. *Alo, bèl fi!*" he greeted in his native British accent. Arms outstretched, his hands lightly grasped her upper arms as he placed a kiss on each cheek, his lips lingering just a moment too long on each side. "It's been far too long, Esme," he scolded lightly.

He seemed not to have aged at all. Admittedly, he could be considered handsome, especially judging by all the women she'd watched try to snag his attention over the years, but she'd never seen him dating anyone. Closer to her age than her father's, he was tall and thin, almost stereotypically elvish in a Tolkien sort of way, with a narrow face, prominent cheekbones, and pointed chin. Despite the delicate countenance, she knew from trips on his boat or days at the beach that there was a muscular build under his bespoke suit. His slightly curly, dark-brown hair, currently brushed back from his fore-head and artfully arranged with product to keep it from moving, was just this side of needing a haircut.

While his mouth smiled, it didn't quite meet his eyes, which she knew from experience would seem to change color from blue to green to gold, depending on how the light hit them or what emotions he was feeling. Right now, they peered intently from the recessed sockets as if assessing her. Did he sense this was more than the friendly visit they had presented it as?

"Uncle Zion, it's good to see you."

"Please. Just Zion, my dear. At this point in our lives, 'Uncle Zion' makes me sound like I'm eighty and with one foot in the grave." The words were jocular, but again, the tone had a shiny edge to it. He turned his focus to Demon. "You must be Ciarán McCarthy." He reached out a hand in welcome.

Demon offered his hand in response. "Pleasure to meet you, Mr. Norton."

"None of that 'Mr.' nonsense. You've married our Esme, which means you're family. Zion to you as well."

She noticed he turned up the wattage on his smile a little more, but it still felt forced, especially when he said the word "our," as if he were partially responsible for her existence.

Her uncle's gaze was measuring. "For years, I despaired anyone would capture this young woman's attention permanently." He gestured toward the entryway of the villa. "Welcome to my home. Please. Enter."

As they passed through the doorway, there was a decided difference in temperature. Although mild and in the mid-seventies at this time of year, the direct sun left one feeling warmer than it actually was. "I asked Rayon, my butler, to bring us some refreshments out onto the gallery. Despite being uncovered, it remains shaded."

They passed through the building, across the marble flooring, and out to a stone-raised patio area in the back of the home that looked down over *Anse des Pitons* at the colorful houses and city below, out to the boats in the bay and eventually the majestic peaks of the Pitons themselves in the distance to the north and south of where they sat. "I wasn't sure what you would be hungry for, so I had Rayon bring us a variety of items. Please, sit." He gestured to the chairs at the table, which faced out to the bay. "I know you're probably tired from the long flights, but this will give you a chance to relax and let the staff unpack for you."

A white linen tablecloth covered the round iron table, and a three-tiered stand sat in the center. China cups, saucers, and miniature plates sat at the three positions of the table. All the trimmings of a traditional English tea setting. "Do you have any allergies, Ciarán?"

"No," he replied.

"Well, there goes my hope of absconding with all the salmon sandwiches, then. Our Esme hates anything fish, so we'll have to share between us."

"Yes," Demon agreed. "When Esme and I first met, we were working on an enormous project at work, and I noticed she hadn't taken lunch the previous two days. I thought I was going to impress her by ordering in sushi. I thought she'd never speak to me again."

Something warm bubbled up inside her. He remembered their first real lunch together? She laughed to cover her surprise. "You tried to hide how disappointed you were when I said I wouldn't eat it." She looked to Zion. "I felt so bad about it after he'd been so thoughtful, so I pawned the food off on a couple of our co-workers, and then I took him to a tapas restaurant around the corner."

It was one of her favorite memories with him, sitting on the outdoor patio, sharing *tortilla Española*, *jamón Ibérico*, and chicken croquettes. After that, when he noticed that some days were so chaotic she went without eating, he had the same meal delivered, and they would go sit on one of their balconies and eat it. It had become his way of reminding her not to skip meals.

Zion smiled. "What a lovely memory to carry with you. Well, I have no tapas here, but... there's an assortment of sandwiches—cucumber with cream cheese, ham with mustard, egg and cress, and my favorite, salmon and dill. We have scones with clotted cream and raspberry jam. And assorted pastries to finish the delights—Victoria sponge, lemon tarts, and shortbread. There's black tea for you, Esme, since I know you prefer that unless something has changed?"

Zion flicked a quick glance behind Esme, who sat with her back to the gallery's entryway. She sensed Rayon approach the table, and when she turned toward him, she saw a single plate with an opaque cover on it.

"Rayon will be happy to make coffee for you, if you prefer," he told Demon.

"Tea is fine. I can't escape it since Esme and I are together, so I've gained a taste for it now."

"How charming," Zion noted.

"Thank you, Zion. We appreciate this, even though it's not quite teatime yet," she returned with a smile. "Even in first class, airline food leaves little to be desired, and flying always leaves me ravenous."

With one hand, Rayon cleared the miniature plate in front of her, and he replaced it with the covered dish. Cherry couldn't help the ecstatic gasp that flew from her mouth as a half dozen mini chocolate eclairs appeared. "You remembered!"

"How could I forget, *bèl fi*? Fresh from my kitchen to your plate."

Without unfolding her napkin, she swooped up one of the miniature pastries and bit it in half. The rich pastry cream oozed out from the flaky dough, combining with the rich chocolate icing.

She was about to pop the second half in her mouth when she heard chuckling. A glance to her left showed her uncle unsuccessfully hiding his amusement behind a single finger laid against his lips. A glance to her right showed Demon, also amused but with a distinct twinkle in his eyes.

"What?" she asked, her eyes bouncing between them.

"You were moaning, *a chuisle*," Demon teased.

"Still the same Esme, even all these years later. My only piece of marriage advice, Ciarán," offered Zion, "is never, and I mean never, get between her and an eclair."

Demon agreed. "She's yet to meet one she hasn't enjoyed with abandon."

She could feel herself heavily blushing, but she refused to apologize. Or stop eating. With great pleasure, she popped the other half of the treat into her mouth. When Demon teased her by reaching for one, she slapped his hand. Hands up in surrender, he withdrew them back to his table setting with a grin. "I tried."

Rayon brought out the tea tray and laid it on the table. He bowed quickly and curtly, then stood along the inner hallway wall, ready to assist when needed.

"Esme, will you be mother, please? After all, you'll know best how Ciarán likes his tea."

She wiped her fingers on her napkin to remove any chocolate or cream, and then she served the tea. She poured a small amount of milk into Demon's cup, then poured in the tea. After filling her own cup and Zion's, she added sugar to hers.

Zion leaned back in his chair and took a sip from his cup. "Thank you, my dear. Well, I've tried to make sure that every comfort is at your fingertips while you're here. I must admit I'm surprised by your visit, *bèl fi*. After all, you've gracefully refused me for years. Then suddenly you message me that you'd like to bring your new husband to visit me. While I'm delighted, I can't help but wonder if there's some ulterior motive for your visit?"

She affected an embarrassed look as best she could, hoping blushing cheeks accompanied it. "Soufrière has always been one of my favorite places to visit, and Ciarán has never been here, so I thought it would be a perfect place for us to visit on our honeymoon. So romantic and all. Plus, you know how much I hate hotels—too many strangers too close together. I never feel quite as... private... as I'd like to be."

"So you choose to visit family on your honeymoon? That's even less private than strangers in a hotel," he teased.

"Yes, well, I have another reason for seeking you out, but it can wait. I'd rather get my bearings and relax a little. Do some sightseeing with Ciarán, visit with you, before I bring up business."

"Business? I'm intrigued. However, I won't press. Speaking of business, I mentioned in my email that I have some associates coming in tomorrow. They'll be leaving by Monday, but there'll be a formal dinner tomorrow night, some dancing, the usual party atmosphere, before we have our official meeting on Sunday morning." His attention turned to Demon once more. "Do you have a tuxedo, or should I call my tailor in the city and have you fitted?"

"I have my own, thank you. Esme made sure I was prepared. We'd love to join you, as long as it's not imposing on your business function."

"Absolutely not. There will be plenty of socializing over the weekend, including a luncheon at the plantation on Sunday afternoon. Definitely something not to be missed."

Cherry glanced at Demon. "The plantation really is fabulous," she assured him.

He took her hand in his and brought it to his lips, brushing a kiss across the back of it. "Then I look forward to it."

"Excellent." Zion finished his tea and stood, buttoning his suit coat. "I must apologize, but I have a few phone calls to finish up before dinner. We will eat here on the gallery at eight. It will be very casual and light. In the meantime, please relax and enjoy yourself. If you need anything at all, Rayon will be happy to assist you. If he's not readily available, you can press the green button on any of the house phones, and it will go directly to him. When you wish to go to your room, I've put you in the west wing in the silver suite. You'll have the best views of the bay from there. Rayon can show you if you've forgotten the way."

"Father's suite," she whispered.

Zion frowned. "Will it be too painful to stay there, *bèl fi?* I can move you—"

She smiled, forcing cheer into it. "It's fine, Zion. I doubt Ciarán would be very comfortable in my suite from when I was in my teens."

"Exactly my thinking." Zion looked at Demon. "It's a lot of pink and flowers. Like someone stabled a unicorn there. I have a tendency to put my least favorite business associates in it to make them uncomfortable."

They all shared a laugh.

"Very good. I'll see you both at dinner." With that, he left, his expensive Italian shoes clicking on the marble floors, losing volume with each step.

She waited until there were no more sounds, pretending to be interested in the pastries. After selecting one, she turned to Rayon. "I think it's just a little too warm for tea. Could I have some lemonade, please?"

"*Sètènman, madanm.*" He turned on his heel and headed toward the kitchen.

"That's going to taste terrible combined with chocolate in that croissant," Demon commented.

"I know, but I needed to get rid of him, and there was nothing else on the table," she whispered.

Standing, she gave a slight tilt of her head to him and crossed to the marble balustrade, looking down and out over the fountain below in the gardens. He met her there, stood behind her, and wrapped his arms around her waist, his mouth dropping to her ear. His warm breath passed over the shell, and she shivered when his lips made contact, repeatedly kissing her neck. "What's going on?"

She arched her neck to give him more room and closed her eyes. Ugh. Why couldn't this be real? If someone watched them, they wouldn't guess her pleased expression was fake because it wasn't. Demon kissed like he reviewed injuries on a patient. Slow. Methodical. Gentle. It didn't help that she could tell he was cataloging each response, comparing reactions, subtly changing pressures, all to find the places that would bring the most pleasure.

Keeping her voice low, she told him, "Rayon and Matthew are not his normal staff. He's always used locals, but these men are different. These guys look like security personnel. In the past, he always had a housekeeper, not a butler. Claimed that male servants were too egotistical to run a household. Plus, he never had boys on staff. If he had male staff, they were always older and were typically grounds crew, not house staff."

"Maybe with his important guests coming in, he's pressed them into service to handle luggage?"

"Maybe," she agreed, "but I'm sure it did not go unnoticed that Matthew was packing a Beretta."

He turned her in his arms so that she faced him and framed her jaw between his hands, his green eyes gazing into hers. She felt as if he were trying to sink inside her soul. Heart racing, all she could do was watch as he lowered his mouth to hers, kissing her in between words. "I noticed that. Does Uncle Zion really need protection?"

His actions would destroy yet another pair of expensive panties if he continued. How did she ever think she could play at being involved with him, even just for a few days? With the barest grasp on reality, she slid her hands up his arms, then curled them around his neck to hold him close. "I suppose, given his rise to the richest man in the Caribbean, he might have some enemies. But it seems odd that he would send his personal security guard to pick us up at the airport when a flunkie security guard, because you know he's going to have more than one, would be more logical."

"Maybe because of who's going to be here this weekend?"

She heard a soft groan in the back of his throat as she relaxed against him, and instantly, she felt his hard length press against her. At least she wasn't alone in reacting to the chemistry between them.

"Is this too much?" she asked, her hips arching gently against him.

"Never too much," he whispered, pressing a kiss to the top of her head. "Just don't expect me to control my body's reaction to you. I've spent a good portion of the last six years hard around you, and I refuse to apologize for it. You're fucking gorgeous, and I'll take you in my arms any way I can get you."

"It's okay. I don't mind. I've gone through more pairs of panties in that time frame than I want to count."

He groaned again, this time sounding even more in pain. "You really should not have told me that." His fingers threaded through her long red hair, and he tilted her head to meet his lips in a prolonged kiss. When his teeth nipped her bottom lip, she gasped quietly at the sharp sting. He licked at the spot to soothe her, then dipped his tongue shallowly into her mouth, the tip delicately tracing the inside of her lips, sipping at the tea and cream flavors left from her sampling of the pastry.

When he drew back and hugged her, she laid her head on his pectoral muscle, her face turned the opposite way from the house. She felt him tense for just a moment as if to reset himself, then he settled back in. She whispered, "I counted seven men, besides Matthew, between the entry at the gate and the front of the house. All of them look very comfortable here, like they've been a part of the household for a while, not just hired guns."

His hands never remained still, caressing up and down her spine, teasing her with soft touches. "I saw them. We'll have to assume there are more. I also spotted a camera system. Well hidden in the black marbling of the building, but there all the same. Same for the hallways, where they blend into the features."

"So the question is, why does he feel the need for such stringent security? Is it business-related or safety-related?"

"We'll have to tread carefully," he warned. "No conversations inside the house without the signal jamming system in place, and nothing at all in any vehicles or around any staff. I doubt he's looking closely at us, but we can't be too careful. We could really use Waters' spidey senses right now."

She tipped her head up to look him in the eye, schooling her face into a sultry mask, appearing for all the world like she was propositioning him to go to their room. "He knew I had another reason for being here. Not much gets past him."

He disentangled himself from her arms and took her by the hand as they heard Rayon approach. Turning, he accepted the drink from the butler and passed it over to her. "*Mèsi*. We're going to head upstairs and freshen up. Esme has been fighting a headache since we landed. Would it be too much to ask to get a call an hour before dinner so we can be sure to be ready?"

"*Sètènman, sè*. Do you need me to escort you to the suite?"

"No, thank you, Rayon. I remember the way," she told him.

Cherry took Demon's hand and led him back inside toward the staircase to their suite. She felt Rayon's gaze on her the entire time until she was out of sight, but the feeling of being watched didn't go away. Who was still watching? Zion? Or his security? She wasn't sure which made her more uncomfortable.

16

APRIL 11, 2023

Demon

If there was ever a time when he lived up to his nickname in wanting to do evil, it was now. In fact, he should get an award for how well he was faking his lack of understanding about what Zion was attempting.

He watched Cherry smile at her uncle. "Dinner was wonderful, Zion. Thank you."

The creep smiled indulgently. "You are so very welcome, *bèl fi*. Although, truth be told, I tasted very little of it. I was far too distracted by the shining star at my table."

Good grief. Did women actually fall for that shite? As he thought about it, he realized that they probably did. Most women likely fell for the perfectly proportioned face, carefully orchestrated sense of style, and impeccable chivalry. He bet even men would be susceptible to the cocksucker's charm and wished they could emulate it. They probably tried.

Others might fall for the mask Zion wore, but Demon knew his kind by sight. He saw the snake the man really was. Cold. Emotionless. Ugly. Lethal. This man would hide in the shadows, watching for unsuspecting prey. When the time came for him to strike, he'd come out of his hiding place with the affectation of a chameleon, blending in with whoever was around him, becoming whomever and whatever was needed to accomplish his goals. When all of that was done, he'd seduce his prey in close, then tighten himself around them so there was no escape. He'd squeeze everything out of them he could, and then he'd end their misery with a swift, venomous kill.

Something wasn't right about the man. He couldn't tell what, but he knew this guy was more than what he seemed to be.

How had her father not seen it from the start? Cherry had mentioned that the summer before her graduation, he'd asked her indirect yet probing questions. Demon suspected that the visit might have been the eye-opener to Zion's true nature. Enough, at least, to make him suggest a change of plans for the summer after graduation.

He watched Cherry as she smiled at her uncle. She seemed reserved but open to his compliments. He didn't believe for a moment she was attracted to the man, but he had to admit he wasn't sure if she saw what he saw.

When she'd stepped out of their bathroom earlier tonight, he'd frozen. The dress she was wearing was indecent. It wasn't, really. But for six years, he'd only ever seen her in designer jackets, skirts, and stiletto heels. Tonight, she looked totally unlike the woman he knew and every inch the new bride on a romantic honeymoon to St. Lucia.

Her dress was light and filmy, a blend of natural colors and patterned tightly with flowers. It wrapped around her form and tied at her hip, the sleeves and hem fluttering with every move, the material revealing every curve while covering them. She wore flat sandals that tied around her ankles, the polish on her toes matching the deep purple on her fingernails. She had styled her hair differently too. A knot at the back of her head created a waterfall of curls instead of her typical French twists. She was the most beautiful woman he'd ever seen.

He hadn't been sure he was capable of emotions anymore. Some might call him a sociopath. Possibly. He genuinely used to care about other people's emotions. In recent years, though, he'd felt frozen. Even with taking on the job at Tribe, he'd never really felt comfortable amongst the other men. He'd mourned Sarah's capture and death. Kubrick's attack and Flame's kidnapping had concerned him. He'd also worried about Waters and Nemo's return after their capture on missions.

But now? As he sat here on the gallery with her and Zion? He finally understood how Waters, TB, and Nemo had felt when they found their women. How they would do anything to make them happy. How they would deliver unspeakable pain to anyone who meant them harm.

He loved her.

And he knew... knew without a shadow of a doubt... that Zion meant harm for Cherry. It was in every spoken word, every expression, every gesture. Pure malice under a glaze of political charm.

"So tell me how you met this"—Zion glanced over at Demon—"gentleman."

"Work," Cherry supplied. "I work in the human resources end of the same company. Ciarán is in operations. He passed my desk every day, and the first time we saw each other, we knew it was meant to be." She smiled at Demon as she took a sip from her wineglass.

"How very romantic. I'm heartbroken that I wasn't invited to the wedding."

There was a smile on the man's face, but it was false. He wasn't "heartbroken." He was mad. Furious, even. And he wasn't mad about the lack of an invitation. He was mad they were married.

Well. Fake married, but Zion didn't know that.

"We didn't want a traditional wedding," Cherry explained. "We just went to the courthouse."

Reaching to take her hand, Demon added, "And I couldn't wait however long it would take to plan a wedding. I needed to make her mine as soon as possible." There. He staked his claim, clear as day. Cherry was his, and he wasn't lying.

"We were very lucky that our boss has a romantic heart and let us off for a honeymoon immediately. Coordinating our schedules otherwise would have been a nightmare."

"Well, I hope my house full of guests starting tomorrow won't infringe too much on your trip. The party tomorrow will serve as a reception of sorts. And there are plenty of things to do and see while you're here that do not involve family or business. Far be it from me to impede"—Zion redirected his attention to the knife at his hand on the place setting—"young love."

Cherry laughed. "Waiting until you're in your forties to marry for the first time hardly qualifies as 'young.'"

"This is true. I'll be honest and say I'm surprised you are married at all. You were always so independent, even as a child. Perhaps you just needed to accomplish certain things before you tied yourself to anyone."

"Or she was just waiting for the right man," Demon offered. "Sometimes fate works like that."

Looking up at Demon, Zion gave his brittle smile again, his hand still playing with the knife, turning it onto its opposite side over and over. "Yes. I've found that fate has a way of stepping in when you least expect it to. But I've also found," he continued, "that fate can be fickle with the more tender emotions. When one arrives at this stage in life, sometimes we grab onto things in the heat of the moment that fizzle out quickly. I wonder if lifelong devotion isn't a better source of true feeling than suddenly finding someone."

Message received. Zion would wait him out. He didn't think Ciarán McCarthy was right for Esme Bosworth, but he also thought the man would change his mind. Then he, someone who had wanted Esme for a lot longer, would swoop in and clean up the damage to her broken heart.

While he felt the kick of being deemed unworthy, which he was, the strength of his emotions for Cherry could not be called into question. Ultimately, they might not work out. She called this temporary. He'd agreed to her offer of a physical relationship. If it made her feel better to think he also agreed with the timeline, she had another think coming. Things had changed, and he wasn't letting go unless she decided she was done with him. It would always be her decision, never his. However, that didn't mean that Demon would stop loving or protecting her if she ended things.

Inside, he took back his earlier sentiment regarding doing evil. He wanted to rip this man's soul from his body, eat it, and destroy it. Only then would he feel Cherry was safe from Zion Norton. The man might be rich and powerful. He might be a longtime family friend, given uncle status, but the man coveted her. The man didn't want to allow her to be what she was meant to be. He wanted to make her submit. And as sure as the tides would rise and fall, Demon did not trust this man.

He redirected the conversation. "Cherry tells me you work with many world militaries. I would imagine that would sometimes bring you into conflicts of interest when their goals might be to annihilate each other."

Zion's laugh was one of the most genuine things to come out of the man's mouth since their arrival. "I can see how, to an outsider, it might seem that way. Perhaps it would if I made weapons. But since my focus is on planes, primarily for logistics, even if two nations are not in complete accord, I find it easy to rationalize. Most of my industry is with Western Europe and its allies, which also makes it easier. It's rare to find two countries in those areas out of sync. Spain will never attack somewhere like New Zealand, or probably any country for that matter. None of them are likely to do so. Western nations are pacifists at heart. They respond to attacks; they don't start them."

"But those planes transport troops and their weaponry. Their purpose is not simply to exist. They exist as agents of war, or the possibility of war."

Zion waved him off. "I don't get myself involved in the politics of those I do business with. Truthfully, I don't involve myself in politics anywhere. The entire arena bores me simply because it takes so long to accomplish anything when you stop to consider all factors and allow microscopic issues and what-ifs to help you make final decisions. Businesses cannot operate by those same measures. We must rely upon owners to make the best decisions for themselves and their buyers."

"Isn't politics a business? They sell an idea rather than a product, yes, but it's still a commodity."

Zion leaned forward in his seat, his fingers threading together, hands raised, elbows on the table. "The populace elects politicians to decide issues for them. The majority votes someone into power, and they trust that individual to have their best interests at heart. So yes, I agree, it is a business in that regard. But I don't sit around with my board of directors and argue whether our planes might deliver weapons to a particular base or border or what have you. We don't argue about what color to paint something. We certainly don't worry about others' uses of our products. Frankly, we don't really care how people see us. Sometimes, I see companies walk back choices when they feel the heat of public scrutiny. But at the time of original decision-making, those things are inconsequential to us. Our goal is to make money. If I want to worry about the ethics of a business, I save that for the banana plantation."

Cherry reminded him, "It's not all that different from our business, Ciarán. Our CEO determines the direction of our projects. We trust his intentions are worthy."

Yeah, he got the message. They trusted God and her, based on recent revelations, to choose jobs that, even though they tread the line of ethically responsible sometimes, were on the side of those who were victimized or exploited.

He turned to her. "Yes. But we don't assist or supply the military with anything. I just think it's messy to do so when it comes to people's lives and free will. Not to mention, it sets dangerous precedents." He looked again at Zion. "No offense, of course. Just not my mindset. I'm glad I don't have to make those kinds of decisions."

Zion nodded. "Some men are born to lead. To decide. To take risks. Others follow. We can't all be leaders, or humanity wouldn't survive very long. We'd destroy each other."

"Aldous Huxley's Alphas," Demon murmured. "There must be a place for everyone, and not everyone can be at the top. The social hierarchy is such that the masses must be the lowest rungs, and the higher you rise, the fewer individuals there are. Only the truly great can rise to the top."

He knew that Zion believed he was putting Ciarán McCarthy in his place, possibly even belittling him subtly to his wife, and he knew Zion wasn't completely wrong. Cherry deserved a powerhouse at her side. Someone like God, who led with a firm hand and a belief that he was always right. He was not like that. He knew exactly who he was and where he fell in the food chain of society. Intellectually, it did not make him less than. It just put him in a different category.

"Exactly." Zion unfolded himself from his seat. "Now, if you will excuse me, I have an important conference call in a few minutes. International business has no set hours, and I'm at the whim of time zones. Please. Enjoy the evening and your coffee as long as you like. Rayon will have the staff clear it whenever you're ready to leave. It is no inconvenience, as they will probably work into the early morning hours getting ready for the weekend, so do not rush.

"Might I recommend a walk down to the sea before retiring? Very romantic, I'm sure, for a young couple in love, and private. In the morning, sleep in as the house is likely to enter chaos as the guests arrive and trickle in throughout the day. Tomorrow's festivities will begin with cocktails at six thirty, dinner at seven thirty, and the party when dinner winds down."

He moved closer to Cherry at her position on the round table and reached for her hand. "Have a good evening, *bèl fi.*" He kissed the back of it, glancing at Demon as he held his lips there for just a moment longer than appropriate. As he rose to his full height, he said,

"I hope you realize what a jewel you've gained, Mr. McCarthy. Our Esme deserves only the finest in life." Then he walked back into the house.

The bastard couldn't resist getting one more dig in, could he?

He wasn't out of sight for over three seconds when Cherry whispered, "Ick." She shuddered. "That wasn't creepy at all. I don't think he likes my choice of husband."

"That's okay," Demon assured her. "I don't much like your choice of uncle."

They looked at each other and grinned.

He placed his napkin on the table and stood, his hand reaching for the one Zion didn't kiss. "Care for a romantic stroll on the beach, Mrs. McCarthy?"

Cherry put her own napkin on the table and rose to stand at his side. "I would love that, Mr. McCarthy."

Hand in hand, they exited the patio and followed the path to the stairs that took them down to the beach. When they reached the bottom, they sat to take off their shoes to avoid getting sand in them. He had to admit that he felt better with sand under his feet. He always did. The beach and the ocean were things he understood.

When he finished rolling his pant cuffs several times, he watched Cherry pick up her sandals as if to carry them. "Leave them. No one will bother them here. Probably won't even see them in the light."

"Those are expensive shoes," she told him.

"If they get stolen, I'll buy you five more pairs. C'mon." Reaching out his hand, he pulled her to her feet and down toward the surf.

When she hissed at the first step, he pivoted and swept her up in a bridal carry, moving down closer to the water. "One step and you already hit a shell edge? This beach is mostly sand. You need to toughen up," he teased.

"It was sharp! How come you can walk on them without flinching?"

"My feet are used to it. I spend most of my time barefoot, except at the office. Not every beach is pristine sand. Just be glad it's not a pebble beach. Ireland is the worst."

"You can surf in Ireland?"

"You can surf most places. Just depends on what kind of waves you want. Ireland is one of the most challenging. Winds off the Atlantic are brutal. Plus, of course, water temperature."

When they reached the water, he found he was reluctant to set her down. Her arms were around his neck, fingers laced beneath his ear, and her attention was completely on his face. Unfortunately, he didn't think she'd appreciate him revisiting his caveman impersonation and carrying her throughout their walk down the beach. He allowed himself the torture of letting her slide down his body slowly, feeling every inch of her as she gained her footing.

Yeah. Selfish and it probably made him a bastard, but he didn't care.

He put her between him and the waves coming up on the shore. There were lights in the distance in the public areas, even though the beaches themselves were closed. Didn't mean there weren't still people on them. Just because he didn't see any wanderers near them on the private beach didn't mean he was going to take chances of someone coming at them with no warning.

"Why does the sand look funny?" she asked. "It looks... swirly."

"We're on what's known as Sugar Beach. This used to be a black sand beach, courtesy of the Pitons when they were active. Volcanic ash made the sand rich with minerals, and the sand turned black. Unfortunately, when the millionaires decided they wanted swanky resorts here, they filled in the beach with white sand to cater to the moneymen's fantasies of what a beach should be. In some places, if the tide conditions are just right, the white sand washes away, revealing the black. Makes it look odd."

They had walked hand in hand a short way down the beach when suddenly Cherry stopped and put herself up against his chest.

Again, bastard or not, he would not refuse the sudden turn in her mood. "Cold?" he asked, wrapping his arms around her.

"No." She snuggled in deeper. "We're being watched. From the gallery. I saw the cigarette glow."

He allowed his hands to smooth up and down her back, his head tilted down alongside hers. He kissed the side of her head. "Matthew?"

"Rayon, I think. Do you suppose he's part of the security staff too?"

"Maybe he's just catching a smoke break before he takes dinner away."

"I guess. Nothing outward is out of place." She turned her face up to his. "I don't like it."

"I don't either. Promise me you'll be careful? I'd prefer you weren't alone with anyone, but obviously, I can't demand that."

"Why not?"

He laughed. "Because I don't want my balls impaled by one of your fancy designer death heels."

She laughed. "I would never."

"Mmm. Forgive me if I don't believe that. I watched you chuck one at Nemo once for double-dipping in your salsa one time." He tightened his hold around her, his mood changing to serious. "I can't be with you every second of every day. As your 'husband,' I'll try, but it's probably an impossible task. I know you can take care of yourself, but I don't trust them around you. Particularly Zion. He wants you, and he will not take 'no' for an answer."

"He can want me all he wants, but he can't have me. I can promise you that." Her face went soft, and her hand lifted to push a loose lock of his hair behind his ear. "There's only one man I want. If I can't have him, I don't want anyone else."

Feck. This was dangerous, but he didn't care. She was opening a door for him. He wasn't going to just put his foot in the way to stop it from closing. He was going to rip it off the goddamn hinges so it remained open permanently.

He picked up the hand she had laid on his chest and kissed the palm. After putting it back where she'd placed it originally, he held her gaze with his, making sure he was reading her intentions clearly. Slowly, he lowered his mouth to hers, giving her every chance to turn or move away if he was wrong about what she wanted. If he'd thought he'd have to cajole her into responding, he couldn't have been more wrong.

This was no tentative kiss. She parted her lips slightly, offering an open invitation to sweep inside and explore. Apparently, he wasn't moving fast enough for her because as soon as he touched her lips with his own, she was pressing her tongue inside his mouth, licking along his teeth, the roof of his mouth, and the inside of his cheek.

He felt his pulse ramp up, and his heart sped to match it. Beneath his linen pants, he felt his cock fill with blood. He knew the minute she felt his response because the hand on his chest slid up over his shoulder, clutching him tightly at the back of his neck, her fingers clutching the roots of his hair to pull him closer. Her other hand slipped between them to cup his hardness and stroke him. Inside, he couldn't help feeling as if he was the luckiest man on the planet at this moment. This beautiful, strong, brilliant woman wanted him.

He pulled back from her, sweeping her back up into his arms.

"What the— Why did you stop?"

He strode up from the shore toward the stairwell. "Because, while the thought of laying you down in the surf and making love to you is fecking hot as hell, our first time together will not be on the beach. Anyone could see us."

"It's pitch black out here. I think it's highly unlikely anyone would see us."

"We already know we're being watched from the gallery. Did you look for security cameras along the wall?" he asked her.

"Well, no, but—"

"Neither did I. I refuse to risk Zion having cameras down here, watching our every move. Instead, I'm going to get out of the angle of any potential cameras, brace you up against this wall, kiss the hell out of you, and hopefully have to cover your mouth when you scream out my name."

They had reached the wall, the stairs angling up behind them to the main house. He ducked around the corner into a small grotto that shielded them in darkness, and he pinned her against the brick wall with his hips before reaching underneath her thighs and pulling her legs around his waist. "Put your hands around my neck. Do not move them unless I tell you to. Understand? You move them, I'll stop and leave you wanting."

"Wow. Bossy much?"

"You love when I'm bossy. 'BAMF mode,' I think you ladies call it."

Her mouth opened, but no sound came out, and her eyes were wide.

"Yeah. I know about it. Maybe sometimes even do it on purpose just to get you all excited."

"All of us?" she asked.

"Get *you* all excited."

"Gold, frankincense, and myrrh," she whispered.

He shook his head. "You're almost as bad as Flame. Your swears might be slightly more appropriate, as I can certainly make this a religious experience. Just don't call out to any specific deities," he warned. "I might get confused about who you think you're with."

Now that he had her against the wall, his brain was short-circuiting. It would be so easy to slide up her skirts and plunge quickly inside her silky, warm heat. But despite the conversation they'd had on the way to the airport yesterday, he wasn't going to. Not yet. He refused to rush her offering of a relationship for the length of the project. While she may have said it, and she clearly wanted him, she still had walls up that needed to come down before he'd make love to her. However, that didn't mean he couldn't do other things.

His eyes glanced down and noticed that her dress had dipped low and shifted to the left, giving him a glimpse of the side swell of her breast where a small beauty mark rested. He felt his mouth water, and he couldn't stop himself from leaning down to touch it with his tongue. Pulling back, he repositioned the sleeve that he had displaced when he'd manhandled her into his arms. Once back in place on her shoulder, he trailed his finger down the material into the V between her breasts, following the drape of the cloth and sliding the tip between the silk and her skin.

"Aidan." She sighed.

His lips brushed the small piercing in her tragus. Gem, covered in tattoos and piercings, teased the women about their "blank body slates," easily escalating the situation into a dare to get pierced. The tip of his tongue traced around the stud, then followed the curve of her ear to the matching stud in her cartilage. "All of you women got these to match Gem. Did you pierce anything else, Cherry? Any other hidden spots on this gorgeous body?"

Her hands slid up to his shoulders and into the ends of his hair. She shook her head. "I wanted to, but it didn't seem very hygienic."

A groan issued from the back of his throat. "I wouldn't have minded making sure you kept it nice and clean while you healed," he admitted. "Feck. I can just picture it. You're so buttoned-up and professional. So prim and proper on the outside. I can only imagine what it would be like to undress you to find something sparkling besides your juices in between these gorgeous legs of yours."

"Do... would you want me to do that? I mean... would you want the woman you were with to do that?"

He nuzzled underneath her ear, pushing back the waves of red hair so he could get at her skin better. "A woman should never decorate her body for someone else. If she wants to make her body a canvas, that's something she does for herself. You personally? I'll think you're a work of art no matter what." His tongue reached out again, tasting the traces of perfume combined with the salt in the air that clung to her. Gently, he allowed his lips to make a seal, and he pulled on the skin. Not enough to leave a mark, but enough that she'd feel the suction.

"I think I'm good with just the ear for now," she shakily admitted.

He grinned against her skin. "But the thought of doing it arouses you," he murmured.

"Wh-wh-what do you mean?"

"I mean, I am a doctor. I know the signs of when a body is at rest, in pain, or turned on. You can't hide it from me. I'll always know. And right now, I can tell you're thinking about it. Your flesh is not only pinking, which I can tell because it's warmer than it was a few moments ago, but your pulse is skyrocketing. You're squeezing your thighs together around my waist, and you're squirming ever so slightly to find friction to get yourself off."

He brought his gaze to hers, a finger tracing down the side of her face to drag across her bottom lip. "You have dilated pupils." He inhaled with exaggeration. "And I can smell just a hint of your body creaming for me."

He licked across her lips, his tongue sliding along the slight gap between them as she sucked in air at his admission. "I bet if I put my hand in between these glorious legs of yours, your pretty little pussy would be slick and swelling. All because you're imagining me seeing that piercing you wanted."

While spinning his fantasy, he never stopped touching her. Never stopped brushing his fingertip along the curve of her breast but never reached further beneath the material to cup and mold the flesh he ached to caress. He forced himself to hold back, to tease her with ghosts of touches from his mouth and his fingers, to seduce her with his words.

"I bet you've got a lot of dirty fantasies tucked away inside this put-together, never-mussed woman," he whispered. "Do you play with your pretty pussy, Cherry? Or do you save all of that for your lovers?"

"I told you. I don't date often."

"Mmm. So that means that your fingers are in that pulsing cunt often, aren't they? That those men are just for when the urges get to be too much? When your own touch no longer satisfies?"

She arched her neck, inviting him toward it. "Sweet Mary, mother of the baby Jesus, what are you doing to me?" she whimpered.

Ignoring her question, he put his mouth where she wanted it, speaking against her skin, his tongue flicking out to tease her rabbiting pulse. "I bet that you have a very vivid imagination. What else goes through that sexy mind of yours, hmm? Do you picture a lover peeling the clothes from your body and laying you back on silk sheets? Do you see him pushing your quivering thighs apart, sliding to his knees between your legs, and resting the backs of your legs over his shoulders so you can squeeze his head tightly when you come?"

He'd pushed himself too far to come back from it. Tempted himself too much not to take it one step further. His hands sought the tie at the side of her dress, slipping the knot free so that the two panels separated. She wore the skimpiest bra and panty set he'd ever seen, one shade darker than her pale flesh, her breasts swelling out of the cups, the high Brazilian cut of the panties daring her to move wrong and expose herself. His hands roved to explore the material— all lace except for the gusset of the panties—all thin enough to be ripped and destroyed with the greatest of ease.

Unable to keep from moving anymore, he ground his cock against her, aimed unerringly at her clit through the lace, determined to give her all the friction she'd need. "Such a dirty girl, watching him as he catches sight of that glint of gold. I wonder what he'd see. A bar through that hard little clit? A ring through its protective hood? You'd be creaming yourself as you watch him, all obsessed with that shiny slit. Waiting. Just wanting and waiting for him to touch you."

He raised his head to look into her eyes as the hand at her breast slid up and formed itself around her throat. His grip was light. He didn't squeeze, but if she moved, he'd keep her in place.

"What do you sound like when you release, Cherry? Do you stay silent except for your breath gasping in and out of your lungs as he drags his tongue across your soft skin, tasting the very essence of you, cleaning up every streak? Do you cry and moan when he reaches your core, burying his face in your pussy, exploring every nook and cranny of you, pushing inside you, and making you even slicker when your juices combine with his saliva as that tongue drags along your walls, fucking you in and out like his cock would? Do you call out your lover's name as his teeth nip that piercing? Or do you scream out his name, the walls and windows shaking, your hands fisting his hair as you grind his face against you, letting everyone know who's latched onto your clit and sucked you so hard you squirted all over his face?"

He felt her entire body tighten, and he knew she was a screamer at that moment by the large inhale she took. His hand went from around her throat to cover her mouth and muffle the shriek that issued forth.

Holy feck! When he got inside her, she'd destroy him.

Softly crooning nonsense words, he pulled her close, his hands slipping between her and the wall, taking on her weight as she clutched at him, brushing up and down her spine until she settled.

With a shaky breath, she pulled back from him, but only enough to see him when she spoke. "You scare me, but I can't resist you. A flame I can't resist touching, even though you'll burn me."

He cradled the back of her head with his hand and pulled it tight to his shoulder. His words were soft and pained. "I shouldn't have done that. I wish I could say I'm sorry, but I'm not, and I never will be."

"Why? I wanted you to. I wanted that and more."

"Because I don't want to hurt you. I know we agreed to let things go naturally while working on this project, and trust me, I'm way too selfish to turn that opportunity down, and I will enjoy every fecking moment of it. But we're playing with fire by following through on that arrangement. We both want more than what we're allowing ourselves, and we're setting ourselves up for failure. We're going to get hurt. It's inevitable."

He felt her clutch at him tighter and gasp at his words. He grasped her tighter, as well. "I should put an end to this, but I won't. Can't. I want to give you everything, Esme. Everything you want. Everything you deserve. But I don't think I can, and it's not fair to you when I worry I can never be what you want me to be."

"I don't want you to be anything other than what you are. It's just… if I hold so much power over you, then let me be your drug. Let me cure what ails you, not the pills," she begged.

Afraid to see her eyes when he admitted his weakness, he buried his face in her hair. "I doubt anyone can cure me. My shit runs too deep. If this small taste of your fire is all I ever get, then I'll take it like the greedy bastard I am."

Her hands clutched the back of his neck, and he felt wetness against his skin. Tears. For him. He never wanted to make her cry.

"I can't lose you. You're the only one who makes sense to my heart. You've felt pain as deeply as I have. I know it. Please let me in. I'm begging you."

He swallowed tightly. Lost to her, he finally gave in to what he was sure would destroy them both. He closed his eyes, his forehead touching hers. "I tried, Cherry. I tried to toss them on the plane, and I couldn't do it."

He heard her sharp intake of breath at his admission. To her credit, she didn't make a big production of it, not that he'd expected her to.

Instead, she responded simply and clearly, in true Cherry fashion. "Then keep trying. And if you fall, I'll catch you."

Her promise caused the dull ache that had been sitting at the base of his spine to intensify. The gentle pulse of tension had been there since exiting the plane, but it had been manageable. Suddenly, it made itself known like a quick jab to the bone.

And then the voices started. They tumbled over each other, overlapping and repeating, yet he heard every word as distinctly as if spoken individually and privately to him.

"A head surgeon promises to look out for their team. The leader is responsible for everything their team does. If a member is weak, it's the leader's fault. You protect them, Parker, as if they were your children."

"Dr. Parker, I was so tired. You said we couldn't stop. You told me to figure out how to stay awake. I didn't know what else to do!"

"Aidan, how could you disappoint your mother this way?"

"You're not here, Aidan! You don't have to live with this! Every-

one's talking about what you did! The whole family can barely walk down the street because of the shame of it."

"Your promise is your bond, son. When you break a promise, you lose people's faith. Faith is everything."

"My baby! You killed my baby!"

"You promised to save him! You promised! Now my son is dead!"

His brain went into lockdown mode as he felt himself beginning to twitch. Now the physical pain in his back had the partner of the psychosomatic pain blossoming throughout his body and into his chest and head. The voices reminded him of a play he'd once seen—three people stuck in a room with no doors, no windows, no way out—three families forever doomed to tragedy because of him. The voices were his ultimate *No Exit*—his eternal hell—to carry the pain of families that he couldn't save.

Resolved, he knew what he had to do. If he chose her, he was making another promise. A promise to another family, her and his teammates, a family he couldn't afford to lose. He would doom her to being a part of that same hell. He couldn't bear to do that. It was better to have her and then let her go. Then the hell he created would be his own alone. Instead, he'd give her an even greater gift than what she desired.

Freedom.

He'd give Cherry what she wanted—a short-term affair so she could work him out of her system. He'd ensure that Zion was out of her life and that she was safe to be the powerhouse she was. When she wanted to be released, he would oblige. That meant when the project was over, so were they, and he'd make the break as clean as possible so that it would heal quickly. He'd walk away from Tribe, and then Tribe would come after him and enact the final edict of his erasure. He wouldn't even try to run far. Just his place on the beach, which everyone knew where it was. He'd make it easy. They would never confirm that they'd done it, and she could go on with her life, blissfully unaware of the future she'd successfully dodged.

Difficult as it was, he loosened her limbs from around him and let her slide down his front to the ground. "No, Cherry. Don't make me into some broody, tragic hero from one of Flame's romance novels. Clearly, it's not within me." Gently, he pulled the sides of her dress back in place and tied it closed. "You need to think about this some more. Sleep on it tonight. I can give you the physical release you want, but that's all I can give you. If you can live with the parameters you set, if that's what you really want from me, then we can move forward. But if you try to convince me again to come around to your way of thinking, it's done. Assignment or no assignment, I will pull us both out of St. Lucia and back home, and we'll find what we need another way."

He ensured she was covered before grabbing her hand and pulling her to the bottom of the stairs. He picked up their shoes, then swept her up in his arms, hoping they looked like a newlywed couple on their way to a night of making love.

What he wouldn't give for that to be true.

17

APRIL 12, 2023

Cherry

SHE WATCHED HIM DRY-POP TWO PILLS FROM A CONTAINER, which he then pocketed before stepping back through the curtains blowing in the breeze through the open French doors. He wasn't paying any attention to her because he was struggling to get his cuff-link affixed, so he didn't witness her pained reaction to his taking the drugs.

While the fact that he was actively using during a project was disconcerting, especially since his teammates always swore he detoxed in those situations, she couldn't help but also notice that in all the years they'd worked together, she'd never seen him like this. He was gorgeous in surfer mode. He was panty-destroying in BAMF mode. He was to die for in a tuxedo.

"The devil himself couldn't be more beautiful," she whispered.

His head popped up at the sound of her voice, and it looked like he was going to say something, but then he stopped. She felt his eyes travel from her hair to her toes. Her breathing felt completely restricted in the red halter dress. The bodice of the dress fit so tightly she didn't need a bra because the cups covering her breasts perfectly molded to them, keeping them high and tight. A plunging neckline to the undersides allowed them to swell slightly along the sides. The fitted waist dropped to a long skirt, with slits from floor to just below her hips. She'd never felt more exposed in her life than she did right now, and all because of the hunger in his eyes.

"I thought redheads couldn't wear red."

Bristling, she crossed over to the vanity table and sat down to check her hair and makeup. "I can wear whatever color I want. You don't have to like it." Guess she'd mistaken the look. How dare he? He couldn't just lie and tell her she looked beautiful?

He placed his hands on her shoulders, drawing them down her arms until he bent close to her ear. "So quick to anger." He kissed her cheek lightly. "I meant, people always say it's not a suitable color for women with red hair. They obviously have never seen you in the color."

"Sorry." To cover up her embarrassment at misunderstanding his words, she grabbed her lip pencil and fixed what didn't need fixing. If she didn't do something with her hands, she was liable to grab his lapels, smash her mouth against his, and say to hell with the party.

He chuckled. "I see that look in your eye," he teased.

She peered at his reflection in the glass. "It's not too revealing?"

"Okay. We can ignore my comment and pretend that's what I was talking about." He drew the back of his finger across her shoulder and down her arm. "Yes, it's too revealing. Every man in the room is going to be salivating. Particularly your uncle, which pisses me off. Stand up."

Was something wrong? A rip? A wrinkle? She stood up from the bench and walked around it, twisting around to see the back, looking down the front, and even checking her cleavage.

A smirk playing about his lips, he turned her so that her back was to his front. She felt his hands gather her hair and release the clips that were holding it swept up to the sides.

She protested.

"Shh, fireball. Trust me."

He tossed the clips onto the vanity table and then gently fanned the waves of her hair along the back of her shoulders. Satisfied with his work, he ran his hands down her sides and smoothed the dress over her hips, returning them to span her waist. He exhaled a ragged breath and followed it up with, "Jesus Christ, you're absolutely stunning."

Her heart pounded, and it felt like her blood raced through her system. It was difficult to breathe. Finally, she whispered, "Thank you. It's nice to hear."

"You always look beautiful, Cherry."

She took a step away from him and turned. "Ready to go into the melee?"

"Can't wait." The sarcasm dripping from the response was impossible to miss.

Desperate to touch him, she gave his bow tie an unneeded straightening and then patted him on the chest with a smile. "Just be your usual charming self, and it'll be fine."

"Got it. 'Arsehole mode.' Let's get this over with."

He crossed to the door and opened it, allowing her to pass through ahead of him. As they walked down the hall, she felt the warmth of his hand on her back. When they reached the top of the stairs, she stopped for a moment to make sure she had her feet properly under her. Marble floors were sometimes difficult to navigate in four-inch heels, and when she started down the stairs, he slipped his arm around her waist as if to help steady her. He was always doing things like that for her.

They turned left at the bottom of the stairs and entered the great room through the double doors, where people gathered, holding drinks. His hand once again on her back, he guided her to the bartenders who were set up along the far wall.

"Mai tai for the lady, and if you have Hibiki, I'll have that. Neat. Otherwise, whatever your best option is."

"How did you know what to order for me?"

"I pay attention. Wine gives you a headache, hence why you stayed at Flame's the other night instead of coming back to your apartment. And normally, you do tequila shots with Kubrick, but I figured you wouldn't want to be slamming those back at this sort of event, and this is really the only other cocktail you drink."

"And what's Hibiki?" Her mouth slowed down to pronounce the word.

"Japanese whiskey."

The bartender placed his glass in front of him, and Demon slid a large bill across the bar, which the bartender swept up and put in his pocket. Demon moved the glass slightly in her direction. "Try it."

Cherry took a small sip of the whiskey, cocking her head as she considered it. "It's fruity. Did you find it on a surfing trip?"

"Yes. Long time ago."

"Obviously, excellent memories."

He gave a self-deprecating laugh. "Actually, no. Trip was a disaster. Only thing good was the whiskey."

Drinks in hand, they turned away from the bar and stepped out into the party, mingling with a variety of guests. They'd just begun talking to the manager of the plantation when, out of the corner of her eye, she noticed Zion approaching.

Taking the hand that did not hold her drink, he complimented her. "Esme, you are a rose among thorns this evening." He brought the hand to his mouth and laid a kiss on her knuckles.

"That's very kind of you, Zion."

She could feel the tension bristling through Demon. He really did not like Zion, which she had to admit confirmed her own impressions that something was off with the man and his attention to her. While his dislike could easily just be jealousy, she was certain the rest of the deadmen would feel much the same way.

The host gave a head bow, then stood straight. "Are you enjoying the party so far?"

"We literally just arrived and grabbed a drink, but I'm sure it will be lovely." She smiled and hoped it looked natural. It didn't feel like it did.

"Since you've already become acquainted with Calvin Deschamps, the man who keeps my little hobby venture successful, I'd also like to introduce you to one of my military contract liaisons." Gesturing behind him and to the left, Zion introduced a second man in an army dress uniform with several pins and badges. Cherry recognized some of them. "This is General Elliott Howard, one of the higher-ranking officials in the United States Army. General, this is Esme Bosworth, whom I believe you met, although she would have been in her much younger years."

She flashed a quick look at Zion, then turned her attention to the general, offering him a smile and her hand. "Esme McCarthy, now. I must have been very young, General Howard. I apologize for not recognizing you."

He shook her hand, his grip firm, his gaze intense. "It was over thirty years ago, my dear, back when you were still wearing pigtails and at your mother's funeral. My condolences, once again. She was a lovely woman. You look very much like her." His words were polite, but the inflection was cold.

"Yes, it's amazing how many of her features I carry." She turned slightly, gesturing toward Demon. "This is my husband, Ciarán McCarthy."

The two men shook hands, greeting each other with the usual inane pleasantries of new introductions.

"We're in St. Lucia on our honeymoon and decided to spend a few days visiting my uncle, whom I haven't seen in quite a few years," Cherry explained.

"Indeed, far too many," Zion emphasized. "However, she's here now, and I'm thrilled, no matter the reason for the visit." The fake smile was once again spread across his face. "Ciarán, here, was asking me about my ethical take on working with so many of the world's militaries. I assured him that there were no conflicts, given our peaceful products."

Howard grunted, and his mouth formed a disdainful smirk. "A common concern. Many people talk about things they know nothing about because they don't do their homework."

"I don't think it takes an educated person, necessarily, to see the ethical conundrum itself," Demon replied. "I understand the need for a military, and I also understand that it takes equipment to support that military. My concern is just indiscriminately supporting multiple militaries." He smiled his own fake smile. "I can imagine that if you entered conflict with another nation Zion supported with his manufacturing, that might be awkward."

"Yes, well, fortunately, we've not entered that situation."

When the dinner announcement came, Zion approached and escorted her to his table, leaving Demon to follow alone. Not a surprise. Luckily, despite being seated next to her uncle, her "husband" sat on the other side of her. Waitstaff in white coats and gloves served the meal in the gardens at round tables. The meal was friendly enough, but Zion talked about many things from Cherry's past that her husband would not have been party to, subtly isolating him from the conversation. Luckily, her dossier contained some of the information, preventing his complete exclusion, but she welcomed the end of dinner.

Unfortunately, their brief respite ended when Zion almost immediately approached them in the ballroom.

"Since I do not have a wife or hostess at my side, Ciarán, I'm hoping you will willingly surrender our beautiful Esme to me for the opening dance."

A coldness descended as Demon tensed just a little further at the request. Aside from his general dislike of the man, she could tell that he really did not want her away from his side, even if he'd be able to see her. "While I appreciate the gesture, Esme is her own woman. The request is hers to say yes or no to."

The brittle smile appeared again. "Of course. How old-fashioned I am." He was livid at being put in his place by Demon. "Esme, *bèl fi*, would you do me the honor?"

Approached in that fashion, it was difficult to say "no" with grace, but she truly wanted to. Instead, she inclined her head. "It's the least I can do since we crashed your party with our arrival." At least she could make it count for something if she used the somewhat private moments of the dance to bring up her interest in local contacts.

As he signaled to the orchestra to begin, Cherry allowed herself to be led to the dance floor. He fluidly spun her into his arms, holding her in the traditional waltz pose. Although he kept an appropriate distance, his grip on her hand and waist revealed possessiveness.

"I don't think your husband likes me very much," Zion began.

She raised an eyebrow, but not high enough for anyone to notice if they were looking at them from around the room. "I could say the same for you about him."

Coolly, he shrugged. "I don't have to like him. You're the one who married him. However, it would be remiss of me to say that I doubt I would find many men good enough for you."

"Father would have liked him."

"Hmm. I wonder." He expertly spun her around the floor, and soon, the other couples joined in.

They were silent through several moments when Cherry broached the subject she needed to talk to him about. "I wonder if you'd be able to help me with something."

"Ah, the mysterious purpose for coming to see me." He chuckled. "Does it concern the glowering man at the bar?"

"Ciarán?" She smiled. "No. Not directly. A friend of ours though."

"Color me intrigued. What can I help you with?"

He turned her again so that they blended further into the couples. She pictured Demon grinding his teeth as they would be more difficult to spot in the center of the dancers. There was no way for her to subtly lead him to a more viewable position, so she did her best to relax, get what she needed, and return to Demon's side.

"Our friend… her brother went missing just over a year ago. We heard a rumor that he might be here in St. Lucia. I thought maybe you could use your influence to ask some questions for us."

"I would love to help you, my dear, but I'm not sure my reach extends to missing persons. Who is it you think I could access that could find this… man?"

"I don't really know, I guess. I just knew that you had connections to many people here, and maybe you'd have some ideas."

"Well, since it's you, I will certainly see what I can come up with."

The music ended, and the dancers separated to give the orchestra polite applause. The conductor gave a small bow, turned back to the players, and they began a new piece.

As he turned back to her, she saw Zion look over her shoulder, and his face lit with a more genuine smile. "Ah! General Howard. I'm guessing you'd like a dance with the beautiful Esme? A very strategic move on your part, as I sense her husband will want to swoop in and monopolize her soon since they didn't have a traditional wedding reception at home."

The general offered his hand. "I'd be delighted if you would honor me. It's been some time since I've done a turn on the dance floor, but I think this old man can remember how to waltz." He didn't sound delighted. He sounded irritated.

"Certainly, General Howard," she replied. Although, in truth, she'd been hoping for a dance with someone else.

"Then I shall leave you to it. Get me what information you have on your friend, Esme. I'll see what I can do." Zion nodded at her, at the general, and then weaved his way through the dancers.

The general took a waltz position with her. "Now, young lady, let's see if my military ball days come back to me."

After several turns on the dance floor, Esme still held herself stiffly in her partner's arms. General Howard was an adequate dancer, but her time with Zion made her nervous, and her current partner was cold and stiff himself. Long gone, she still felt as if Zion's attention lingered. Her childhood impressions were vague, but now, in her forties, she understood men better and could identify what had caused them.

Want.

It wasn't desire or lust. While it didn't feel like a sexual attraction, he definitely wanted her. But why? For what?

General Howard also seemed "off," almost as if he was doing reconnaissance for a mission. Internally, she shook herself. He was in the military. A general. He probably gave most people the impression that they were being unofficially interrogated. After all, he probably didn't rise as high as he had in the armed forces without strategizing most everything in his life. She was likely just another person in his path to analyze.

"How are you enjoying St. Lucia?" he began.

"We haven't really explored yet," she replied. "We arrived yesterday, and air travel always makes me so tired, even when I sleep on the plane. Other than dinner with my uncle last night and a short walk on the beach afterward, I have to admit we slept the day away to recover."

He smiled, but it didn't reach his eyes. "Ah, the honeymoon. Young lovers in the Caribbean, I'm sure you'll find plenty to amuse yourselves."

She didn't have to fake a blush at his insinuation. "Yes, well, we're here for a week. It's been a long time since I was last here. We were supposed to come after my high school graduation, but..."

"Yes, quite." His mood became somber. "Your father was a good man. I regret what happened to him."

Cherry stumbled on the dance step. "I'm sorry?"

"His disappearance. Someone clearly abducted him from your home and from you. It's hard to believe that such an upstanding man, someone who gave so much of himself to his community and his business, someone who seemed to have no enemies, should suddenly vanish so mysteriously. After losing your mother, I'm sure it was difficult for you to lose him as well."

"Oh. Yes. Yes, it was." She relaxed slightly. "I never gave up hope he would return. But when college ended, life had to go on. I needed to find my way and continue to live. It's what he would have wanted. Not to give up and mourn."

His mouth turned up at the corners. It wasn't a smile, but it wasn't a grimace either. More like he was trying to keep from saying something.

"And what about you?" she asked. "Is my uncle's business meeting your sole purpose for being here this weekend?"

"While it is the primary reason for my attendance, I'm also here to visit some of our allies. Virtual meetings, while faster, are so much less personal. And in business, being able to see someone's reactions in person is always better than on a computer screen."

"This is true. I also do a lot of my work through digital conferencing, and some individuals I talk to are only a few floors above me. How impatient we've all become that we can't walk to an elevator and go talk to them in person! As if those two or three minutes each way really take away from anything else we might be doing."

They passed the next moments in silence, Cherry surveying the crowd for Demon. Excellent. He'd moved to higher ground at the top of the stairs near the entrance, his eagle eyes on her. She nodded at him slightly and smiled, creating a look of "I'm sorry for the delay" in case her partner was watching her. When she turned her attention back to her partner, her eye caught on a button on his right uniform pocket.

She willed her eyes to keep from flaring and swallowed a gasp. Instantly, her eyes flew over his shoulder, staring at nothing as she regrouped herself. It had to be a trick of the light.

As casually as she could, she drew her eyes back to General Howard's form, glancing down at the button on his pocket. It looked like any other military button. But curved between the eyelets holding it to the material, a letter "S" sat in the center.

A capital letter "S" in what looked like a medieval script, and remarkably like the letter found in the hidden margins of the files on her father's computer.

Could it really be? It was terribly brazen if it was. Would the Salieri be so bold as to actually wear their symbol on their person to identify each other?

Medusa, whom Tribe believed to be the team leader of the Mythos crew they often worked with in the past few months, hadn't mentioned it in any of their reports. Was it possible she didn't know? Maybe she felt it wasn't important enough to share? Or was the lack of information on purpose? With that crew, one never knew.

Suddenly, a hand reached into view, tapping the general on the shoulder. "May I cut in?"

General Howard stepped back with a small nod. "Of course. We mustn't monopolize your beautiful wife's time." He turned to Cherry. "Thank you for the dance, Mrs. McCarthy. I almost felt twenty years younger again."

"You're welcome, General Howard." Her voice sounded breathy in her head as if she still hadn't regained the ability to breathe properly. His comment, innocuous as it was, unsettled her.

As the man turned and left the dance floor, Demon assumed his position, only the arm around her waist pulled her tight, as a lover would, with no space between them. His thumb gently raked back and forth on her back. The hand holding hers curved around it, pulling it close to rest against his chest without letting go, and he brought his head down next to hers.

His voice in her ear was hard and low. "You went white as a sheet," he whispered. "If he hadn't been holding you, I think you would have been on the floor. What happened? Did he say something to upset you?"

"N-n-no. Not exactly. He made a comment. About Dad. That he regretted what happened to him. I was so shocked by the word choice. When I asked him what he meant, he explained it away, but then..." She choked on her words and felt panic rising like a tidal wave inside her. "Aidan, he had a button on his jacket with the Salieri 'S.'"

Demon pulled back just enough to look her in the eye. Again, to hide the severity of their conversation, he put his forehead to hers and put a lover's smile on his face. "Breathe, fireball. Focus only on me. I need you to look at me like you can't wait for me to spirit you out of here and upstairs to our room."

She took a deep breath. Then another. And another. Finally, she got herself under control. "He was friends with my father as well, although I don't remember seeing him at the house. Friends enough that he was at my mother's funeral. What if...?" She almost couldn't bear to finish the question, but she knew she had to voice it. She needed to make it real. "What if he's responsible for my father's disappearance? What if... as part of the Salieri... he regrets being forced to kidnap and kill my father despite their friendship? Or he regrets he had to order it? Or help with it?"

Demon pulled her close again, his head lying against hers as they danced. "Did you sound out Zion about Ka-Bar?"

Her head answered him in what felt like jerks instead of nods. "I have to get him Ka-Bar's information. He said he'd see what he could do."

"Okay. Good girl. Go upstairs, take a warm bath, and crawl into bed. I'm going to stay down here and have another drink. I'll make your excuses."

"Won't it look funny if the newly married couple don't go up to their room together?"

"If anyone asks, I'll tell them you weren't feeling well, and I'm giving you a little time on your own to settle in. Meanwhile, I'll see if I can corner the general into a conversation and confirm what you saw."

She protested.

"Shh, it's not that I don't believe you. I just want visual confirmation because you know God's going to ask for it, and it's not like I can snap a photo. I'll have another drink, mingle, and see if I can find any other buttons like it. The more info we have, the more ammunition we give Midas and the others to work with." He looked down at her. "Can you do this for me? I need you to go gather yourself. You've had a shock. I'll be up as quick as I can, okay?"

She nodded.

"Are you sure? I can come up instead if you need me to."

"No. I'll be fine, and you're right. We need to know if there are others. But—" She gripped his arm extra tight. "Don't be too long. Be careful," she pleaded.

"I'll be all right. An hour at most, okay?" He kissed her forehead, and she closed her eyes, drinking in his touch. "Go on."

She nodded and pulled away from him. She truly had a headache now, so the fingers she applied to her forehead as if to massage it away were more than real. The noises of the ballroom seemed to ratchet up and stir together in a cacophony bent on pounding her brain flat and useless. She couldn't seem to gather her thoughts—her usual composure gone. If anyone looked at her, they would definitely see a woman who wasn't feeling well.

When she reached the stairs, she looked over her shoulder to see Zion engaging Demon in conversation. Both men looked concerned, and then Demon must have excused himself as he headed over to the bar. Her eyes flickered back to her uncle, who stared at her, his frown deepening. She nodded to him, a weak smile on her face as if to reassure him she would be all right, and then she turned and walked out of the ballroom and up to her room.

Once inside, she made to go to the bathroom and run a bath, then stopped in the middle of the bedroom. Slowly, she turned and walked back to the door. Shakily, her hands reached out to the handle and rested there for just a moment, then she quickly flicked the lock in place. Demon would have to knock when he came up, but the locked door made her feel... safer, somehow. From what, she wasn't sure.

18

APRIL 12, 2023

Demon

Thirty minutes later, Demon made his way upstairs. When he tried the door, he found it locked, which he actually found both concerning and reassuring. It bothered him she'd felt so unsafe that she needed to lock him out, yet he was glad she was smart enough to do it.

He knocked softly. Hopefully, she wasn't still in the bath as he didn't fancy trying to scale the wall to get in through the balcony. A few moments later, he heard the door unlock and the handle turn. Cherry stood just behind the door, her long fingers curved around it and one eye peeking out. He slid through, closing it behind him, and flipped the lock.

Before he knew it, Cherry had thrown herself into his arms. She didn't cry. She didn't even utter a sound. Just grasped him close, her head planted in his chest. Her clean scent from the bath drifted into his nose and spread to his lungs, making him dizzy.

It was so difficult to remember why he couldn't love her all night long and make her every promise she asked for. Proposition or not, she wasn't ready for what she'd suggested. Even though he'd agreed to her proposal, he began listing in his head all the reasons it would be wrong and why it would be unfair to her. Yet... each reason he came up with, he took another deep breath, and the space between reasons became longer and longer.

Gathering every ounce of strength within him, he disengaged from her grip. Holding her arms, he ducked down to look into her eyes. "Are you okay?"

She nodded jerkily again. "I'm just glad you're here."

He nodded his head toward the bathroom. Grabbing a small duffle bag from the walk-in closet, he pulled her with him into the room and closed the door.

Once inside the bathroom, he started the shower. They had swept the room for bugs when they arrived and found none, and he'd set up one of Midas' gizmos he'd built that sent an alarm to his watch if any type of surveillance device showed up, but he never trusted the rooms after they'd left them, and he didn't have time to check again before leaving. Anyone could get into their rooms while they were out and about, so it was better to assume the worst and sweep for bugs anytime they returned to the space. Since he didn't have time to sweep the room, the noise of the water should drown out voices if anyone was listening in. Quickly, he ripped his bow tie loose, then slid his jacket over his shoulders. He watched her eyes open wide when he rushed to unbutton his shirt, shuck it off his shoulders, and toss it to the vanity.

Keeping his voice low, he explained, "I need to meet the team. I can't go by the main road or the beach proper, so I'm going to have to swim out. I texted the guys, and they're going to meet me out in the bay."

A look of horror crossed her face. "You're going to have to swim forever. That's not safe!" she hissed.

He kicked off his shoes and pulled off his socks. "I don't have a choice. Besides, it's not that far. Remember who you're talking to here." Rustling in the backpack, he pulled out his night-surfing wetsuit that covered him from head to toe, including the matching hood, to protect him from the frigid temperatures of the water. "Grab the electrical tape out of the bag for me," he ordered.

As she reached into the bag on the counter, she continued her rant. "It's salt water! There could be sharks! You need a board."

He grinned at her. "Fireball, I'm not paddling out there; I'm swimming. Besides, a board will not protect me from sharks."

Electrical tape in hand, she breathed in deeply. "No. You're right. It won't. On a board, you'll look like a nice shark-size appetizer on a fucking plate."

He stopped to consider her worry for a moment. "Raw human equals shark sushi?"

"Don't be a twatwaffle. I'm being serious!"

"I surf in the Pacific Ocean every day. There are sharks there too. I'll be fine."

He unbuttoned and unzipped his tuxedo pants, pulling them and his underwear down. When they pooled around his ankles, he stepped out of them and kicked them to the side.

The gasp he heard, followed by the invective of "Holy hell, horseshoes, and hand grenades!" as he pulled up the wetsuit, made more than his ego swell.

Oops. He was in such a hurry, he'd forgotten who was with him for a second.

Standing up straight, he pulled the suit up over his hips and carefully tucked himself inside the neoprene. "Breathe in through your nose and out through your mouth, fireball, or you're going to pass out." Pushing his arms through the sleeves, he watched her face turn bright red, her eyes still glued to the crotch area of his suit. If he read her lips right, she was murmuring something to herself about being jealous of the sharks getting a taste of him.

Yeah. That didn't help the swelling. Oh well. The freezing ocean water would take care of that issue.

He shrugged himself into the suit, then finished zipping it tight. "I need you to take the electrical tape and help me use it to cover the reflective stripes."

They worked quickly and efficiently to cover the glow-in-the-dark blue stripes down the side, across his front, and across his back. Then he pulled a climbing rope out of the bag.

"I'm going to have to rappel down the balcony, and I need you to pull up the rope when I'm down."

"How the hell did you know you were going to need that equipment?"

"Fireball," he admonished. "The team's been doing this shite for a long time now. We all have basic kits we take when we travel. When I have to swim, there have been enough times I needed alternative means to access the water that this has become standard. When I pack for any trip, climbing gear is always part of it because it's easy to pass off in luggage as a vacation activity."

As she finished the tape across his back, she asked, "Did you see the button on Howard's uniform? Were there more?"

"Yes, I saw it. You're right. It looks just like the emblem on those documents. I only saw one other one while I was down there, but thirty minutes wasn't much time. Howard loves to hear himself talk, and then your uncle introduced me to some Princess Something or other."

She rounded his body to face him, a scowl on her face. "He what?"

He continued like she hadn't asked a question. "I got delayed a few extra moments because he manipulated me into taking her out onto the dance floor, and then it was hell getting away from her. When she found out I was married, she got feckin' worse. Christ, that was a pain in the arse. Woman actually had the nerve to invite me to her room."

"She what?!"

He stepped closer to her and placed his hands on her shoulders. "Aww... jealous?" He grinned. "Don't be. Most of what she said to me went in one ear and out the other, never to be remembered. I don't know where she's even from." He stepped even closer. "On top of that, there's no way she could draw my attention away from my brilliant, sexy new wife."

She seemed to collect herself, if somewhat petulantly. "Don't let me stop you. I mean, it's not like I have any real claim to you. Just be discreet so we don't blow our cover."

Turning on her heel, she made for the bathroom door, but he grabbed her hand and halted her progress. He pulled her back into his arms. "Hey. I'm sorry. I shouldn't have said anything. And you have a claim to me, fireball. You always have."

Her eyes filled with what he thought was hope, and then he watched the emotion extinguish as fast as it had burned to life. "Just be careful tonight, okay? Please. I'll worry until you're back, and it will probably be hours before that happens."

"I'll be careful. I promise." He squeezed her hand. "I need to get this information to the team, and I don't think it can wait." He hugged her, speaking into her hair, "Once I'm down on the ground, pull up the rope and take it inside. Please keep the door to the hall locked, and don't open it to anyone. I mean it. Anyone. We can always pass off you not answering by saying you took a sleeping pill and didn't hear a thing." He pulled back and looked into her eyes again. "After I leave, keep the lights off. Lock the windows and pull the curtains as well. That way, no one on the veranda can see inside that you're awake. Do a cautionary scan for listening devices. I'm sure it's clean, but it pays to be careful. I'll text you when I'm back, and you can drop the rope and let me back in. Okay?"

She nodded.

"Feck!" He pulled her close, hugging her so tightly he thought it might take the jaws of life to pry him from her if someone tried. "I hate the thought of leaving you here by yourself."

"I'll be fine, Demon. I'm a pretty boss bitch babe, per Kubrick, and can hold my own if I have to."

He smiled. "Yeah. I know you can. Doesn't mean I won't still worry." He kissed her forehead. "Show time, Triple B."

He turned off the shower and led her by the hand to the French windows. Before opening them, he hit a button on his watch that would scramble any short-range cameras for about thirty seconds. Then he opened the doors and scanned both ways and up. Seeing no one, he went silently to the balustrade and looked down, as well as scanned the area. The area was clear.

He threw the loop of the climbing rope over the stone finial on the rail and checked the knots in the rope that he would use as handholds going down. Taking precious seconds, he grabbed Cherry's face, kissed her hard, then pitched himself over the wall and down. When he hit the ground, he took off at a run for the beach, hoping that Cherry would quickly haul up the rope and get inside without being seen.

19

APRIL 12-13, 2023

Demon

Every time the countdown on his watch hit twenty-nine seconds, Demon stopped and hit the button on it to jam any nearby camera signals for another thirty seconds. The worst section would be the open beach. He knew, cameras or not, the moonlight would easily reveal him on the stretch of beach between the wall and the water. From the base of the wall, he dared a glance up at the villa. A man stood at the far end of the veranda, but Demon couldn't see which way the person was facing.

Feck!

Sliding along the wall, Demon looked to see if there was any additional coverage he could use to at least get closer to the water or possibly farther down the beach and out of the guard's eyes, but there was nothing.

Loud beeping noises, like a truck backing up, erupted near the kitchen, momentarily distracting the guard. Demon hit the jammer on his watch and sprinted toward the water. As soon as he could, he dove under the low waves coming in and swam beneath the swells until he felt his lungs were about to burst. Even then, he slowly forced himself to breach the surface to suck in air and see if he was clear of the villa. There was no flurry of activity on the beach, so as far as he could tell, he'd entered the water without being seen. Getting back in would be the hard part.

He turned out toward open water. Scanning to the west, he saw two brief flashes of green light. It was impossible to be sure, but he thought it was about a mile out. Distances over water were deceptive. He winced at a cramp that began in his lower back. Forcing himself to ignore the pain, with powerful pulls and kicks, he swam out toward the green lights. When he could make out the silhouette of the boat and the shapes of two men in it, one large, one small, he used the flashlight on his watch to flash twice toward the blob in the water.

Two flashes of green light appeared again, and Demon continued on through the water. About thirty feet out, he did a shallow submerge, swam under the boat, and came up along the opposite side. Two sets of hands reached down, grabbed his arms, and hauled him into the boat. He did his best to keep a groan of pain inside as his teammates manhandled him into the boat, but a soft grunt escaped anyway. He sat for a moment, catching his breath, then removed the hood from his head and shook out his hair. "Where's Midas?" he asked.

TB raised an eyebrow at him. "Computers and water don't really mix. Besides, he was grumbling so hard at himself and so focused on what he was doing, we left him there. Probably doesn't even know we're gone. Gem brought us pictures and video, so now he's canvassing footage from all over the town and comparing shot angles, trying to see if we can follow Ka-Bar's path to or from the café that day. His workspace looks like a murder board on a crime procedural."

"Why is he having so much trouble?"

"Old-world charm and all," Steel replied. "Security cameras aren't nearly as prevalent as they are back in the States. He'll get it, eventually. The bigger question will be how far we can track Ka-Bar. If he gets in a car and leaves town using interior roads, we'll lose him sooner rather than later."

"Well, I've got something a little more pressing he needs to look into," Demon told them.

"We figured, which is why we're out in the middle of the bay in the middle of the night when Steel should be sleeping, I should be talking to Flame on the computer, and you should be cuddled up in bed with your 'wife,'" TB complained.

"Whatever," he muttered. "We need you to look into a man named General Elliott Howard, four-star general in the United States Army, and another guy named Felix Giudici. He's a money guy of some sort. Wasn't able to get the details."

"What's up with them?" Steel asked.

"Cherry spent a dance with the general. While they were out on the floor, she noticed a design on a button on his uniform. Looked like a normal army button, but when you look closer, it's got a Salieri S on it between the eyeholes." He ran his hands through his hair. "She was so freaked out by the army guy, I sent her back to the room. Apparently, he made some comment to her about regretting what happened to her father. Between that and the button, she was on the verge of losing her shite, and she never loses her shite."

TB whistled. "Yeah, doesn't sound like her."

"I looked around some more, and that's when I found the Giudici bloke. He was sporting a button on his shirt. Just like the army guy, it blended in so that you'd barely notice it. Once you know what to look for, I imagine it becomes easier."

"They're using it as a signal to each other. You see any others?"

"No, but I had little time. Cherry's uncle doesn't like me much. When Zion saw her leave, he tried to distract me with some princess whose tits were falling out of her dress, and her ass crack was showing in the back." He snorted. "Like that would be a distraction from Cherry. Was more like a feckin' train wreck."

"*Pendejo*! So she thinks this guy, Howard, had something to do with her dad's disappearance?" Steel asked.

"His wording would suggest the possibility."

Steel looked up from his watch. "Texted Midas the two names. Didn't give him any details, but he'll know we want them looked at. What do you want to do in the meantime?"

"Tomorrow morning is the big meeting. It's out at the plantation grounds. Not sure if I can get out there and get Cyclopes inside to record the meeting, and I don't think Midas would want to risk Nova. He's still working on her nuances. She's pretty sophisticated already for an AI, but she's not done yet."

"Not to mention the potential of you being caught," Steel said. "Awfully risky. You getting caught makes Cherry vulnerable. I could try. I would be more expendable."

TB said, "Neither of you is expendable." Glancing out at sea, TB chewed on his lip. "We have to run it past Waters. Think Midas can hack into something while they're in there? If this meeting is that important, Zion probably doesn't allow electronics in there. Bet he sweeps everyone down beforehand, but he's also probably smart enough to record what happens in that meeting. Maybe Midas can find whatever he uses to record and tap into that."

Steel added, "The system would have to connect to the internet, or at least be a closed-circuit monitoring system that a central computer in their security room controls."

Demon swore under his breath. "Any further idea on whether Zion and Nimbus are directly involved with the Salieri or if they're pawns?"

TB shook his head. "Nothing yet. If Howard is a member of the Salieri, and if he's the US Army's connection to planes through Nimbus, there's nothing to say he couldn't be negotiating planes for the Salieri as well. The question would just be if Zion was aware or not. Sex trafficking requires the ability to transport under the radar. Ground travel is becoming more and more difficult. Airports too. He certainly has an excellent setup if he's part of all of it. He has a multitude of potential players with his global connections.

"Add to that the fact that St. Lucia is one of the more challenging islands to get to, even with being such a popular honeymoon destination and its limited security capabilities, and he's got himself a winning lottery ticket. The interior of the island can easily hide a small private airstrip, especially if you can stomach moving smaller numbers of people at a time. Some of what Gem gave Midas was drone footage of the estate and the plantation. There's a space of land that fits the bill in the back third of the plantation."

A groan came from Demon. "We can't keep from her that we're looking at Zion as a first-tier player, especially given his relationship with her father." He thought for a moment. "You don't think her father would have been involved with the Salieri, do you? Maybe realized too late what he was involved in and tried to disengage himself? Medusa seems pretty sure they eliminated all members who broke their code. Removing people they did business with would be even less of a concern."

"It's possible," TB agreed reluctantly. "I don't get the feeling that Grayson Bosworth would have been that unaware of who he was doing business with though. From all reports, he was a stand-up guy. Ethical beyond ethical. More likely, he was an unwilling pawn, if involved at all. I'd be inclined to believe he stumbled on one of his associates making deals with the Salieri, likely Zion, if they were as tight as she believes, then investigated them before making accusations. It can be a heavy blow when someone you consider a friend turns bad."

"It would explain all the files Cherry found," Steel agreed. "I'm with TB. I'd put my money on the last theory."

TB grumbled, "And we all know how accurate you are with betting. We need to be much more careful about the language we use when making wagers. My kid's college fund is going to be gone at this rate."

Demon chuckled at that. "Feck that. You've got more funds than any of us, hidden away or not. Even after bidding on the hit on Gem."

"Hey, I got paid for that 'job,' and she's still alive, so mission accomplished. I should get a bonus for that from someone."

"I'm sure Nemo's very grateful," he soothed.

"Hasn't stopped the fucking confetti cannons and shit. I always know when they've snuck back into the States. Even when they aren't on our coast, I know he comes specially to set me up. Now he's got Cerberus helping him with timers and shit. The last time those fucknozzles were in town, I opened a drawer in the armory, and he knows I don't close the drawers right away, so five minutes later, when I was in the zone, a swarm of those butterfly things flew out."

Demon shook his head in laughter. "That'll learn ya. Bet you're shutting the drawers right away now, aren't ya?"

"Fuck yeah. What I can't figure out is why he still has his clearance in our building. You'd have thought Midas would have shut that shit down, considering how pissy he's been acting."

"Probably hoping his brother will fuck up with Gem and come home with his tail between his legs. But as far as the pranks, you know you love it," Steel teased. "Means you know he still loves ya. Especially if he makes a special trip."

"Yeah, but the problem is, he also brings Flame presents from wherever they've been. He shouldn't be bringing my woman gifts."

"He does it merely to piss you off," Demon said with a laugh. "And it works, so he keeps doing it. Stop letting him know it bothers you, and he'll stop."

"No, he won't," TB said. "He truly adores her. It's good to know she's got him in case anything should happen to me. He'll take care of her."

"We all will, *amigo*," Steel assured him.

"I know." TB came out of his reflective state. "Okay. So. Meeting tomorrow. We'll check with Waters when we get back to our home base to see how he wants us to proceed, but I agree. I think we need eyes and ears on that meeting somehow. What else?"

"After the meeting tomorrow," Demon told them, "there's a brunch at the actual plantation's main facility. Cherry and I will go along, see if we can scout out any more Salieri members. He's also offered us a tour. Depending on what time we get back from that, I'll text you, and we can set up a meeting to pass on information. Hopefully, you'll have something for us on Howard and Giudici."

"Agreed. You ready to swim back?"

"Yeah. Child's play."

"Be careful, *hermano*," Steel said as he clasped Demon's forearm. "It isn't only the bay that has sharks swimming around. Protect our girl."

"Don't worry. She's always a priority," Demon promised.

"Is she? I wonder," TB said softly.

"Don't start, Thunder Bolt," Demon growled. "I will always protect that woman, no matter what else happens. I'd die for her without a qualm."

"And yet—"

"I said don't." Demon's eyes glared, even in the dark.

TB held his hands up in a gesture of surrender. "Okay. I won't go any further."

"You gonna be able to get back inside?" Steel asked.

Demon just cocked his head to the side as if to say, "Really?" He put his hood back on and tucked it into his wetsuit. "See you soon." Then he was over the side of the boat, not a splash to be heard, and swimming back to the one thing in the world he loved more than life.

20

APRIL 13, 2023

Cherry

Cherry lay frozen in the bed. She was normally unflappable, but the circumstances were far too personal in this situation. General Howard had been friends with her father, per him and Zion. How close? Being at her mother's funeral meant nothing, as there had been many people there. Then again, to a small child, twenty-five people would have been a lot. Given the button on his uniform, was General Howard part of the Salieri then? Was he part of her father's disappearance? If Howard was part of the criminal organization, and he was in business with Zion, did that mean Zion was also part of the Salieri?

The questions kept looping over and over in her head, keeping her from sleeping. It had nothing to do with Demon still being gone. Nope. Not at all. He was a big boy and could take care of himself. That lie became clear when his text notification came in on her watch. He was back!

As quickly as she could, she got out of bed, grabbed the rope coil by the door where she'd left it earlier, opened the French doors, and peered out in all directions. No one seemed to stir. She tiptoed to the ledge, anchored the rope around the finial, and threw the rest over the balustrade. Within seconds, Demon scaled the wall, gathered the rope, and hustled them into the room, closing and locking the doors behind them.

As soon as darkness enveloped them, she clutched him. She heard the quiet clunk of the rope dropping to the floor, and she felt his arms go around her shoulders, one hand cradling the back of her head and bringing it to rest over his heart. He smelled of the ocean, which she always associated him with. A smell that made her feel reassured and safe.

"Missed you, too, fireball." He kissed the top of her head. "Get back in bed. I'll be there in a few minutes."

Not normally one to take orders, in this instance, she felt the need to do what he said. Burying herself in the bedding, she huddled on her side, watching the bathroom door and listening to the shower run. There was no way she would sleep until he crawled into bed on his side. Only then would she truly feel like he was back and safe.

A few minutes later, Demon returned from the bathroom, his skin now warmed from the shower water, and slid into bed behind her. Afraid to turn over or move, she lay frozen again, eyes wide, heart pounding. He was here. He was safe.

There was a slight rustling as he settled himself, and then she felt hands at her waist—one above, one below—pulling her back into his chest. With her head tucked between his chin and the pillow, a gentle kiss to the top of her head, he whispered, "Sleep now. We're good."

Within seconds, her breathing evened out.

Light steps in the hallway, combined with muted voices, woke her. When she tried to reach for her watch on the bedside table to check the time, she was immediately pulled back against a wall of muscle that smelled faintly of sand and sea. Every muscle in her body went so tight that if someone flicked her, she'd shatter.

"Go back to sleep," a deep voice rumbled.

Demon! Sodom and Gomorrah, why did he have to be so strong?

She tugged on the arm banded around her waist, but it wasn't budging. "Let go of me. There are people out there moving around. We can't be late for the tour."

"Fireball, it is way too feckin' early to argue with you. I'm exhausted from playing nice with you, your fecktwat uncle, and all his shiteheel friends. Not only that, I took a two-mile night swim in freezing waters, and my back is killing me, so please, have some mercy on me, and go back to sleep." A set of soft lips came down on her shoulder, and two arms nestled her closer. "I was rather enjoying you all soft and asleep. So much better than you pissed at me."

His back hurt? Did he hurt himself last night? The lips against her skin distracted her, and she sighed in exasperation. "Well, if you would be nice instead of a raging asshole, you wouldn't be tired then, would you?"

"Nice is not my strong suit, but I'll give you raging asshole. I excel at that."

Ugh. It was so difficult to fight with him when he just kept agreeing with her. She lay stiff and still for a few moments before her self-preservation kicked in. "What time is it?"

He rearranged his head on the pillow so that he tucked the crown of hers under his chin. She seemed to spend a lot of her time positioned like this with him. She didn't hate it.

"Don't know, don't care, but definitely too fecking early."

However, it really sucked that she was the perfect fit there. Her body wanted so desperately to give in. Relax and enjoy the cozy warmth of his muscles sheltering her. However, her brain was racing and refusing to let go of her need to be as far away from him and his sex voodoo as possible, which was stupid given her proposition to him. "What. Time. Is it?" she growled.

With a sigh of resignation, he raised one arm from around her waist to glance at his watch. "It's eight thirty. Again. Way too feckin' early to be awake. They've probably barely started their meeting, so it's hours until we need to go out there. Now lie down and stop wiggling."

"I am not wiggling. I'm trying to get out of bed, and you're keeping me here against my will." Since she couldn't break his hold, she tried to slide out from under his arm. All she could do was turn so that she was facing him, which turned out to be a much more compromising position to be in. Twisting and turning her hands to his chest, she tried to push away from him, but it was useless.

She gave a gentle squawk as the hand along the small of her back drifted lower and grabbed an ass cheek, pulling her core to his very hard erection. "Then stop grinding on me. I'm getting ideas about how you really don't want to get out of bed, and you're just saying that because you think you're supposed to," the deep, rumbling voice teased.

"I was not grinding on you," she hissed in embarrassment.

"Sweetheart, you have your legs wrapped around mine. You're nonstop wiggling, there's a wet spot on my thigh, and you're making these sexy little noises. It's no wonder my hands wandered."

Gasping, she took full notice of the situation. Yeah... they had become tangled. And judging by the uncomfortable state of her silky sleep shorts and the dryness of her mouth? She'd definitely been dry-humping him and making noise.

"Oh sweet Jesus, Mary, and Joseph! I'm sorry."

"I'm not. Does this mean you're no longer interested in that mutual chemistry experiment you propositioned me with?" His voice was muted since he'd now switched their positions so that his head was buried between her neck and her shoulder.

Completely mortified, she tried once again to untangle from him.

He refused to let go. Instead, his other hand slid down to curve under her ass and pull her even tighter to him, then rolled them so he was on top of her. "I'm sincerely not complaining. This was the best way ever to wake up."

His hands slid out from underneath her so that he could brace some of his weight on his forearms on either side of her shoulders. Still embarrassed but curious to see his reaction, she dared to look at his face. The water from his post-ocean shower, combined with sleep, tousled his hair. His face was blank, but his eyes were bright green in the morning sun that streamed into the room as they surveyed her face.

He lowered his mouth to hers. For the briefest of moments, she froze. When he was a breath away, she came to her senses and slipped a hand up over his mouth. "No."

He quirked an eyebrow.

"I haven't brushed my teeth," she offered lamely.

A deep chuckle rose from behind her hand. Lips and teeth nibbled on her palm, with one nip getting just enough purchase to sting. When she pulled her hand back in shock, he swooped in, his lips pressed against hers, his tongue plundering inside her mouth, tasting every nook and cranny he could find. He pressed and swiveled his hips against her core, sliding his body between her legs and positioning her so her feet were flat on the bed. Whatever he was doing down below was slowly turning her anger into an ache.

Leaping Lucifer, this man could kiss!

There was no option but to hang on and enjoy the ride. Once she melted into him, her fingers spearing through his tangled hair, he eased back with the intensity. Instead of one long, soul-stealing kiss, it became a series of soft, sensuous licks and touches. She couldn't say that the tension became easier to bear because it didn't. He had her craving more.

When he stopped kissing her altogether, her eyes fluttered open to see an expression on his face she'd never seen before. If she had to put a name to it, she'd say it was longing.

"Jesus Christ, you could not be more beautiful than you are right now. Arousal looks good on you, your hair all spread out on the pillow like flames burning out of control, and your skin a soft pink blush from head to toe. What man wouldn't want to wake up like this every day? Wouldn't want to watch you come out of sleep under the rays of the sun, knowing that you rested well after he loved you long into the night? And then want to kiss every inch of you until they've got their tongue buried in that hot silk between your thighs, waking you up in a way that makes their name your very first word of the day?"

"You know," she whispered. "It's really not fair for you to ramp me up with all your sexy words and stripper moves, then leave me hanging."

His eyebrows rose in disbelief. "Stripper moves?"

"Whatever you're doing with your hips there."

He repeated the hitch and push he'd been using. "You mean that? Those are surfer moves, fireball."

She wrinkled her nose and squinted at him. "All you do is jump up and stand on a board. It's all about balance."

"And part of balance is hip movement. I'm not standing still out there, you know. My hips help me redistribute my weight so I stay upright. They help me steer the board. My moves are pretty slick."

With a snort, she pushed at him, this time rolling him over easily and sliding herself out of the bed. As she rounded the corner, his chuckle caused her to pause at the foot. She looked back at him. He'd pushed himself to a sitting position, a pillow tucked between his lower back and the padded headboard of the bed, one arm thrown up over his head, resting bent atop it. His fingers absently played with the decorative buttons on the padding as he stared at her. The other hand rested loosely in his lap, where the thick, gray comforter bunched around his waist. Damn, if he didn't look like he'd just spent the night giving some woman the time of her life.

"No bullshit, Cherry." He winked. "But... I bet I could rock a male strip show if I had to. Want to find one and see?"

Shaking her head with laughter, she muttered, "Oh, Mary Magdalene..." Yeah. That image was both funny and swoony at the same time. "Far be it from me to bust your *Magic Mike* moves, but I think we can keep that off the honeymoon list."

He shrugged. "Your loss." The teasing smile remained on his face for a moment, but as the moment stretched between them, it slowly faded. "Why do you use religious phrases when you curse?"

"Huh?"

"You always use religious references when you curse. Isn't that actually worse with people than actual swearing?"

She wondered how to answer the question. No one had asked her about it before, and religion was often a touchy subject for people. She knew her methods of cursing bothered some people, but she didn't let it bother her. "It's..."

He said nothing. He simply lowered his arm to his lap and waited.

"It's related to my mom." All of her energy drained out of her, as it usually did when thinking about her mother. Sharing this with him would be more than she'd ever shared with anyone about her mother's passing. "My mother died when I was six. She developed an aggressive form of lung cancer. Dad said smoking was her one bad habit, and she gave it up when she got pregnant with me, but apparently, that didn't matter in the long run."

She sat back down on the bed, twisting her fingers in her lap. "At the end, she'd been in the hospital for two days when suddenly she just... I don't know how to describe it. It was like she became a zombie. There was no recognition that people were in the room. She obviously didn't eat or drink because she was unconscious. The situation forced my father to decide whether to take her off life support.

"I'm sure he struggled with the decision. He wouldn't have wanted to give up, but he also knew she wouldn't have wanted us to see her like that, and I guess her living will said that after three days, she wanted to be released, so... that's what he did. He took me to see her one last time, and I had to say goodbye to this shell of a woman. I still remember how scary it was. How awful. Her eyes were halfway open, but they had rolled up into her eye sockets so that all you could see was the white portion. It was like those creepy *Annie* comic strips.

"She was taking these overexaggerated breaths, probably because the machines were breathing for her, but back then, I just knew what was lying in that bed was no longer my mom. Dad did, too, so he took me home and then went back to the hospital to be with her when they shut the machines off."

A tear fell. Even all these years later, the pain was still there, just as harsh as it had been when she was a child. She recognized that she never talked about it after that; it was probably why the pain was still so raw. But instinctively, she'd known how hard it had been for her father to take, and she didn't want to bring him more pain over it. The only time he'd ever mentioned her was on her graduation day, which, looking back, seemed terribly prophetic.

"I was so angry," she admitted. "My mother was a religious woman, but not obsessively. We went to church on the bigger holidays. For weddings and funerals. My family expected me to take my First Communion and be confirmed, and as a child, I never questioned it. It was just what we did.

"But even at six, I understood the difference between good and evil, and I couldn't understand why God was punishing her when there were so many bad people in the world. Abusers. Murderers. Rapists. Terrorists. My mother was good. She wasn't like those bad people," she whispered.

Wiping away another tear, she sat up straight, steeling herself against what she perceived as weakness. Mourning wasn't productive. "My father and I continued going to church after she died. I went without complaint. Again, I didn't want to make him upset over it. But I lost my faith the day she died, and I guess the cursing habit became my way of getting back at the entity that took my mom from me. I just never stopped, and it's become so ingrained, I don't even think about it."

He brushed back her hair and kissed her shoulder. At some point, he'd slid behind her to comfort her. "Thank you for sharing something so personal with me. That couldn't have been easy. By all rights, you could have told me to feck off for asking and ignored me. Instead, you trusted me with something I'm pretty sure no one else knows." He reached to grasp her chin and turned it toward him. "I'm sorry, *a chuisle*. I know it was long ago, but no child should be left without a parent. Especially a good one."

Without thinking, she reached across her body and laid a hand on his cheek. "Thank you."

Eyes connected, they sat in the quiet, the soft sounds of the staff walking up and down the halls, putting the final touches on the rooms, the occasional instruction or comment being exchanged between them. The moment ended when a door slammed too hard.

Cherry shook herself, finally remembering his mission last night. "What happened last night? Any news or theatrics?"

"Only theatrics were the thirty minutes I spent being circled by hungry sharks a mile offshore."

The hand she'd had on his cheek punched him in the shoulder.

He smirked. "Sorry. Couldn't resist. As for news, I shared with them what you and I saw last night. They're going to have Midas look into Howard and the other guy I saw. Steel was going to talk to Waters about doing a little breaking and entering to get ears in that meeting today. No idea if he approved that. They said it was too risky for me to try. Depending on what happens today on the excursion, we'll try to meet with them tomorrow to see what Midas digs up. In the meantime, we're going to keep our eyes open and see if we find any additional S buttons."

She nodded. "Sounds like a plan." Standing, she turned to face him directly. "Thank you. For listening about my mom."

He rose from the bed as fluidly as if he were rising from the water like Poseidon. He showed absolutely no self-consciousness about standing in front of her in his form-fitting boxers, the skeleton bunny on the waistband. And why should he? He was freaking perfect. He had the lean build of a powerful swimmer. His abdominal muscles were ridiculous, and his waist tapered to those V-shaped hips that women always went so stupid over. She was in danger of losing more than a few IQ points herself.

Brushing her hair back from her forehead and behind her shoulders, the smile he gave her caused her to lose a few more brain cells. On the rare occasions he did smile, it was more of a smirk or even derision. But this smile? She'd never seen one so soft, so gentle. It made his sharp features even more gorgeous. "Stop it."

"Stop what?" he asked.

"Stop being so beautiful."

One eyebrow went up, but the heartfelt smile stayed on his face. "You think I'm beautiful, fireball?" He shook his head. "You should see my view. Now that's beautiful."

With that oxygen-sucking comment, he gently turned her and gave her ass a gentle slap. "Go. Get even more gorgeous for the trip today. I'm going to call Rayon and order us some breakfast on our patio."

She swallowed tightly, nodded, and began the walk to the bathroom. His voice rang out again. "And, fireball?"

She turned in profile and looked over her shoulder.

"You may not realize it, but I'm always listening. And paying attention, even when you're not speaking."

Afraid to respond, even with a nod, she turned and fled into the bathroom.

Holy Moses!

21

APRIL 13, 2023

Demon

He wasn't ready for "even more gorgeous." A white, sleeveless button-down blouse topped a pair of navy-blue shorts. On her feet were a pair of simple navy-blue tennis shoes, like the kind girls wore in the fifties, and her hair was down but pushed off her face with a matching blue hairband. Why was this sexier than the red evening gown from the night before? She looked... edible. It was the only word he could come up with because all he wanted to do was put his mouth on her.

All of her.

She stopped cold when she noticed he was staring at her. "What?" She surveyed what she was wearing, even trying to look over her shoulder to see if something was out of place or dirty. It was the same thing she'd done when he'd stared at her in her dress last night. When she couldn't see whatever was wrong, she went over to the three-pane standing mirror in the room's corner and tried to find what he was staring at. Looking up at his reflection in the mirror, finally, she asked, "What's wrong?"

"Buttons." It was all he could choke out.

"Buttons?"

"Where are they?"

"Huh?" She looked genuinely confused at the cryptic words coming out of his mouth.

"Your shirt. It's missing buttons."

Frowning, she looked down at it, then back in the mirror. "No, they're all buttoned."

He stalked over to the mirror and stood behind her. The sleeveless blouse mimicked a suit jacket or trench coat; its cut plunged between her breasts, buttoning tightly around her midsection to accentuate her slim torso before flaring loosely over her shorts. He reached over her shoulders to the two lapels of the blouse and pulled them together at mid-chest. "You're missing at least two. Right here." His voice was tight and strangled. He'd never heard himself speak like that.

"I'm not missing any buttons." She gently pried his fingers off the lapels of the blouse and then smoothed the wrinkles he'd made by bunching the fabric together.

"You're showing too much skin," he grumbled.

"I was showing way more skin last night," she chastised. "You didn't seem to mind then."

"That's because when I looked at you, my brain short-circuited when all the blood in my body rushed to my dick. This outfit somehow seems sexier."

"You're right. Bare arms, knees, and shins are terribly sexy," she whispered.

"I'm not talking about your arms, knees, and shins, and you fecking know it," he groused. "Go put another shirt on." He thought better of it. "And one with sleeves. And some pants. Other women's arms, knees, and shins are not sexy. But yours are sexier than I care to think about, and I don't want to be burying bodies of men trying to look at you."

Rolling her eyes, Cherry went to the vanity table and began touching up her lipstick. His eyes automatically and unapologetically went to her ass as she bent over. Feck, he was going straight to hell. He'd assumed that was his lot in life, but now he knew it was.

"Stop staring at my ass." His head snapped up to find her watching him in the vanity mirror.

He didn't bother to deny it. No point. She'd caught him doing it. He shrugged. "It's a nice one."

"That doesn't give you the right to stare at it."

"Nope, it doesn't. But I'm a guy, and it's always on our radar, so... oh well."

"You really can be a dick sometimes."

"Nothing you didn't already know." He glanced around the room. "Ready?"

She recapped her lipstick and ran her little finger along the underside of her bottom lip to remove some excess color. "Did you hear anything from Steel?"

"No, but I didn't really expect to. Not yet, anyway. Maybe something soon when the meeting is finished. No news is good news, as the saying goes." He stopped her movement to the door with his hand. "Cherry, be careful today. Last night? What you saw surprised you. It was easy to pass off your shock as travel exhaustion, but it won't be as easy today. Stay as close as you can, okay? If you see another S button, just note who it is. Don't engage them."

"And what if they're leaving tomorrow? We might just lose our best opportunity to question them. I can handle myself. Been doing it for a while now. Besides, I hired you, so I think I know what we're up against."

"I know you are capable and can take care of yourself. This isn't vetting a client or even a future deadman. I just..." He ran a hand through his hair. "This just became even more personal for you, and no matter who we are, when it becomes personal, mistakes get made. We don't mean for it to happen, but we're not thinking as clearly as we normally do when our emotions are engaged, even when we think we can separate."

As soon as the words came out of his mouth, he knew he'd said too much. Watching her head tilt and the consideration in her eyes, he knew that she'd picked up some note of truth in his voice. They stood in silence—she thinking, he working to affect a blank expression.

"We'll be talking about that," she promised.

"Nothing to talk about," he lied.

"Demon, you can blank your face, but you just went so tight I could bounce a quarter off you into a shot glass. Don't forget. I know you." She walked up to him, her well-manicured fingers threading through his hanging at his side. "I promise. I will play the attentive bride today and stay as close to my adoring husband as the situation allows. But we're here to do a job, and that may mean me asking some questions. Have a little faith in me. I've been doing this a lot longer than you."

With his free arm, he pulled her tight to his chest and pressed his lips to her temple. Even he could feel the tinge of desperation in his act. "I have all the faith in the world in you. Just need you to be careful, fireball," he whispered. "If something happened to you, I couldn't —" He cleared his throat. "If something happened to you, there'd be a long line of people waiting to kick my arse before God put through the final edict." He pressed another kiss to her temple. "Although I'd probably take care of it myself if something happened to you when you were in my care."

He felt her inhale on a gasp, and when her eyes turned up to his, he felt her pain and anger like they were a palpable thing. "Never say that! A million things could happen to me you could never prevent. And no one is worth another person's life."

Loosening his hold on her, his smile pained. "Okay, fireball. Whatever you say."

She made a move to the door, but he stopped her with a gentle tug to her wrist. Her gaze met his.

"You look beautiful, *a chuisle*." He reeled her in for a kiss before they traveled downstairs.

Several of the house staff had used vans to take the overnight guests who weren't part of today's meeting over to the business end of the plantation in groups. Rayon had informed them, however, that Matthew was waiting for them in Zion's private car, which would be a far more comfortable ride, whenever they wanted to leave. On the surface, it seemed like Zion was ensuring nothing but the best for his niece and her new husband, but Demon wasn't feeling an awful lot of warm, fuzzy feelings about the choice. To him, it felt more like controlling their movements, particularly when the clunk of the automatic door locks sounded.

They played the newlywed couple in the back seat of the car Matthew drove. They held hands to start, chatting about things they wanted to see and do over the next week. He snuggled her close to his side under the protection of his arm, and they looked out the driver's side passenger window at the landscape. Periodically, he would sneak a kiss to her cheek or hair, murmuring into her ear, and she giggled at whatever he said.

The plantation rose and fell along the hilly, winding roadways up to the foot of Petit Piton. Seven stone buildings formed the property's center, each structure devoted to a different stage of the banana-farming process. The main building was three stories tall and stood at the center of all the other structures. Stepping out of the vehicle, a young woman greeted them, and in her hands, she had a tray of warm towels to wipe down their faces and skin. Already, the humidity of the afternoon was picking up.

As Matthew closed the car door behind him, Demon felt the vibration of five pips from his phone, which was alerting him that Midas needed to speak to him. Pulling the phone from his pocket, he glanced at the screen for show. He sighed and looked at her. "I'm so sorry, *a chuisle*. Apparently, there's a problem back at the office, and I need to call them. You go on inside. I'll be quick."

Cherry nodded. Zion appeared as he gave his explanation to her. The man's eyes scrutinized him, but when Demon caught him, the stare quickly changed to the typical brittle smile. "Don't be too long, young man. Women don't like to be kept waiting," he warned. Zion put Cherry's hand through the crook of his arm. "Come, my dear. I see a cocktail in your immediate future."

Together, the two went inside the main building. Demon spared a glance at Matthew, who stood, one hand clasping the wrist of the other in front of him, no expression on his face. Mirrored sunglasses hid the security man's eyes from view, but he was pretty sure the man was watching him closely.

He pointed at a large tree in the courtyard. "Is it okay if I step over there?" he asked innocently. "I don't want to move anywhere I shouldn't."

"*Wi, se konsa.* Just watch your feet. The ground can be treacherous if you do not look where you are stepping, sir."

Once he was underneath the branches of the tree, he hit the button on his watch that would actually connect him to Midas. While they talked, he would hold the phone up to his ear so that he looked as if he were actually talking on the phone. Should anyone confiscate it, the call history would show a call to the phone number of the fake company he and Cherry supposedly worked for, even though the actual communication was working through his watch.

The phone had barely rung when Midas picked up. "You alone?"

Demon looked over to where Matthew stood in the shade of an eave of the main building as he lit a cigarette, looking like he'd be standing there for a while. Knowing he'd have to be careful despite the distance he'd put between himself and Matthew to make the call, he couched his answer as generically as he could. "I'm calling from the luncheon. What's going on?"

"Just wanted to let you know Steel wasn't able to get inside the meeting room itself, but he managed a Cyclopes eye on the outside window of the meeting room. Quality is shit, but it's the best we could do with limited reconnaissance. I'll try to clean it up some today and see if there's anything new to catch. As far as I can tell, they discussed issues typical to purchasing of planes and other related items."

"But?"

"I haven't had a lot of time to compare the discussion to the financial and physical movements, but Waters said his spidey senses were going off, and he found something weird about the numbers. He's going to let me know when he's done looking into the data I gave him."

"Sounds good. And the other issues?"

"I got the applications for the two men recommended to me."

Howard and Giudici. "Bad references?"

"Questionable is more like it. Elliott Howard, married to Hannah Black in 1978. Daughter, Valerie, born in 1979, hit by a car riding her bicycle in 1986. No other children. Here's the juicy bit. The last time anyone saw Howard's wife was May 26, 1998. That date important to you?"

"Shite," Demon whispered. He turned his back to Matthew. "Cherry's graduation?"

"Ding ding ding! Bonus point question. Guess who was the best man at Grayson Bosworth's wedding in 1979?"

"Howard."

"He wasn't a general then, but yes, it was him. Even more interesting? He never reported his lovely wife missing. He transferred across the country almost immediately after that, and no one really thought to question it, I'm sure, because military people move all the time."

"No one? Wouldn't she have called, at least, to let someone know she wouldn't be around anymore, rather than just leave?"

"Nope. Apparently, she hadn't really become close to anyone, as they'd only been there about nine weeks. Like I said, they moved a lot. If you look at this guy's transfer rate after that, it's like reading a train schedule for the London Underground."

Paper shuffled in the background. "Giudici had a partner some years ago for around a year. Still digging on those details, but other than her name, I haven't found any record of her once they broke it off."

"Feck! Do you suspect a connection between the two terminations?"

There was a snort from down the line. "You don't think they're connected?"

Demon ran his free hand through his hair, then put it on his hip. He stared at the rows of banana trees stretching out to the volcano. "No, I do. It's just this creates a much bigger mess than we suspected."

"Should have more for you tomorrow morning. The guys said I need a wetsuit?"

"Yeah. Taking Esme surfing. Booked her some 'lessons' in the bay."

"Gotcha. Should make for a good cover story so we can all meet publicly. Nova and I are working on additional avenues of information. I'm hoping my searches tonight will shed some light. See you soon. And bruh, be careful, yeah? After this recent development, we've all got a case of the... what does Flame call them? The jinkies?"

Demon laughed despite the situation. "No, 'jinkies' is a swear word for her. I think you mean 'heebie-jeebies.'"

"Right. Well, either way, we've got a 'shit show,' so be on the lookout."

"Take care."

After he hung up, he stood still, tapping the phone's edge against his chin, staring out into space. To anyone watching, he'd look like someone contemplating the scenery, probably thinking about whatever problem his phone call from work was about. And they wouldn't be wrong. But more important to Demon right now was how Cherry would take the news that General Howard seemed to have an even stronger connection to her father's disappearance, especially since his own wife disappeared the same day. That felt... ominous.

Pulling himself together, Demon slipped his phone into his pocket and headed toward the entrance to the welcome center. He hadn't gotten over ten steps when a voice called out to him.

"Remember to watch your step, sir."

Demon turned to find Matthew, who hadn't moved since their arrival, the plantation's name plaque behind him, taking a last drag from his cigarette. Once inhaled, he dropped the cigarette on the ground and meticulously placed his heel on top of the butt, grinding out any last vestiges of burning ash.

"It would be most unfortunate if you misstepped."

Demon considered the man carefully. "I'll keep that in mind."

"Best that you do." With that, Matthew put his hands in his pockets and walked around the side of the main building, going off to wherever employees went while the guests all stood mingling while having light cocktails before heading out to lunch.

Demon considered the spot Matthew had been standing before he continued into the building to find Cherry. Removing his sunglasses, he scanned the room. He felt a light touch on his forearm from the right. Looking down, he saw Cherry's manicured fingers resting in his arm's crook. Like a good husband would after being separated from his wife, he greeted her by dipping down to meet her lips in a chaste kiss. The touch complete, he turned his head to put his mouth close to her ear as if whispering something romantic.

"They got audio access to the room. Midas found some information I need to ask you about. And we still need to look around at the guests, but be careful. Matthew might have just warned me off."

He pulled back, his face the perfect picture of a smitten lover. She bit her lip, casting her eyes down, then looking back up at him through her lashes. "We'll have to find a private place to talk."

Brushing his nose back and forth across the tip of hers, he

nodded. "Yes, that would be a good idea." He slipped free of her hold but quickly repositioned them so that his arm was tight around her waist, pulling her as close to him as possible. In a voice loud enough to be heard if anyone was listening, he declared, "I could use a drink, and you appear to need a refresher. To the bar, *a chuisle*."

After securing drinks, they stepped away from the bar and into the center of the room. Despite being a private business versus a public tourist attraction, the main building served as a welcome center for those permitted to visit the property, complete with flagstone floors, exposed stone walls, and dark wood beams that matched the furniture and stairs. An indoor courtyard on the main floor resulted from the arrangement of rooms on the second and third floors, and workers could be seen moving busily about on the third floor.

Her hands wrapped around the delicate crystal glass that held her spritzer, she explained the setup of the room, sometimes using the glass as a pointer to what she was talking about. "Downstairs is where all the public business happens, as well as a large kitchen which caters any food and drink needed." She gestured up to the balconies seen from the center of the room. "On the second floor, individual offices for the sales representatives, marketers, and upper management, and on the third floor is Calvin Deschamps' office, as well as the large meeting room for events like today."

"What about the general workers?"

A voice came from behind him. "They report directly to their individual managers in the other buildings. Each structure focuses on a different portion of the production process."

Zion.

Demon shifted so they were facing their host. "While the farm is impressive from what I could see on the drive in, I hope we'll get to see some of the process as part of the tour."

"You are interested in the process of growing bananas? Most people would rather enjoy alfresco dining, a short walk among the trees, and then leave, instead of enduring a long, hot, dusty walk among buildings and listening to someone drone on about the history and process of banana farming."

"I'm always interested in learning new things," Demon told him. "Lunch and a walk will be wonderful, but I'm always more impressed by the substance of something than I am by the flashy surface. So many things that look wonderful on the outside are often rotten to the core on the inside. Don't you think?" He was probably pushing his luck with his comments based on the pinch Cherry was giving to his waist, but he didn't care. He hated this man.

"Yes, I think that's often true," Zion agreed. "So many things are not what they appear to be. And people."

So. He knew the man didn't like him, but clearly Zion didn't trust him either. Good. He shouldn't.

Deschamps exited the kitchens, spitting out rapid-fire patois over his shoulder. He was probably in his late fifties, early sixties—his body wiry with muscle and tan from working the fields. While his short hair was gray, he wore it shaved close to his head, which was bald on top. He had an infectious smile, an often-seen feature judging by the lines around his eyes and mouth. Unlike the men who had come from the meeting in their designer "casual" wear, he was wearing a blue button-down shirt that hung open over a plain, dusky-blue T-shirt, a pair of tan cargo pants, and brown work boots. Once he had delivered his last instructions, he placed a straw fedora on his head and called out to the guests as he came toward them. "Luncheon is ready if you will all follow me, please!"

The guests moved slowly but en masse toward the French doors at the back of the main building. Zion pardoned himself. "Excuse me. I need to catch up with my foreman for a moment and see about arranging that extended tour for you. I will see you at lunch."

Demon stood still and took a sip of his drink, his eyes narrowing as he watched Zion leave.

"What was that all about?" Cherry asked.

"Later. Stick close." He stared at her. "I mean it. Do not leave my side. If you need to go to the restroom, tell me, and I'll find a reason to excuse myself as well. Go nowhere with anyone but me."

Her eyes flicked back and forth between his. "Something bad is happening."

"Later."

SEVERAL WAGONS ATTACHED TO TWO HORSES EACH STOOD ON the dirt road off the patio. Zion handed Cherry into the wagon, then gestured for Demon to follow her before getting onto the vehicle himself. Once everyone was aboard, the driver clicked his mouth, gave a snap of the reins, and the horses took off down the road. Fifteen minutes later, the groups found themselves at an alfresco dining site amidst the banana trees. Several long tables with seating for twenty on both sides were set up in a naturally shaded area for meals of this kind. Given the large number of guests and how organized everything was moving, he figured they did this often. The few women present oohed and aahed, engaging Cherry in their discussions of the fine china and crystal laid out and the flower arrangements. Although warm, there was a slight breeze, making dining outdoors more than pleasant.

As soon as the guests were seated down the long table, waitstaff began appearing from a small building. Fresh wine was poured all around, and each diner received a chilled shrimp appetizer, while Cherry received a fruit plate due to her dislike for seafood.

Cherry leaned toward Demon at her right. "These are the same individuals we had dinner with last night."

"Mm-hmm," he agreed, biting off a piece of shrimp.

"There were probably three hundred guests at the ball. This is about one hundred people."

"Legitimizing the event as much as possible. The people we need to focus on are the ones here. These are the moneymen." He glanced at the gregarious foreman who had led them to the table. "We met him briefly last night. What do you know about him?"

"Calvin Deschamps. He's been the manager here for thirty years. Took over for his father when he passed. The farm has been in the family for generations."

"Who's the boy?"

"His grandson, Andres. I think he's eighteen? When Calvin retires or passes, he'll take over the groves."

"Not the father?"

Cherry shook her head. "Got the story from one of the women while you were out on the phone. She was all atwitter to share with me the tragic story of Nico and Ava Deschamps. Ava died shortly after giving birth to Andres. Some sort of infection set in." They shared a look. "Apparently, Nico was so distraught, he began drinking almost immediately. Drove his fancy sports car off a cliff."

"Hmm. Wife dies, then a grief-stricken husband? Sounds like the husband wasn't with the program," Demon muttered. "So the grandfather is raising the boy. Where's the grandmother?"

"There isn't one. She died while in labor. Story is, Nico had to be cut from her body in order to be saved." She put a forkful of salad into her mouth.

"This family seems to have very bad luck with having babies."

"Mm-hmm," was all Cherry would say. "Did you see the sign as we came in yesterday?"

Ah. She'd noticed. Was she making the connection of Zion to the Salieri all on her own? "Yes. I especially liked the aesthetic design of the second S in *LES VERGERS DE LA MER*." He decided to test her response to a piece of further damning evidence. "It was in the plantation sign too."

"Yes. I noticed," she said quietly.

Okay. She was putting the pieces together that the team had already been suspicious of before they'd left L.A.

The waitstaff returned with individually covered dishes as they removed the appetizer plates. Under each dome was green fig and saltfish, with the exception of Cherry, who was served tassot. Zion had made sure that she would have a main course that wasn't fish. Demon had to admit that Zion knew how to take care of people. He spared no expense to make them feel pampered in his home, provided unique experiences they could share about their visit, and, in general, charmed them.

Unfortunately, like Demon had noted earlier, the beauty that was outside didn't always match what was within. The most venomous creatures were often the most beautiful in order to attract their prey.

"Why do you want a tour?" she whispered to him between bites of food.

Demon's brow furrowed. "Not sure. Just do. My shite meter is blaring warning signals nonstop. Has been since we left this morning."

"You mean it wasn't prior?"

"Oh, no. It was. Just not as loudly as this morning."

"Ciarán," Zion called, "whatever has caused that frown?"

Lifting his head and turning toward his host, he thought hard on the fly. "I was just thinking about all the things we have on our wish list to accomplish this week and how little time we have to do it. I'm guessing we'll have to rethink our plans a bit. Might need to consider saving some of it for another trip in the future."

"Did you have any definitive plans?"

Demon grinned, looking down at Cherry and taking her hand in his, raising it to his lips for a kiss. "Tomorrow, I have a surprise for my lovely wife. I've set up some surfing lessons for her. She's never been, and it's a hobby of mine, so since the waves here are calm and good for beginners, we've got a semi-private lesson set up in the bay."

Her pupils dilated as she gazed back at him. Interesting. Could Steel be right that it would let her see him in an all-new light? In all honesty, it had been an easy way to arrange for them to have a meeting with the team if they were all in an isolated group on the beach and the water. Maybe this would have dual benefits.

"How... interesting," Zion replied. "I didn't know you had an interest in surfing. Then again, it's been a long time since I saw you last."

"Lots of things change over time," Cherry agreed.

Demon continued, "We also planned to spend some time on the coastline, so that will be good for tomorrow, as well. There was a café recommended to me by a co-worker that we thought we would try, which has some stunning views of the bay. Walk and see some of the shops. That sort of thing. Tomorrow, we'll talk about the next day." Demon flashed a wicked grin around the table. "It's our honeymoon, after all. We do what we want when we want."

Some of the women tittered and ahhed at his gently naughty comment. Some of the husbands winked and raised a glass. He noticed that the men who did not have wives gave somewhat indulgent smiles. Those were the men they needed to concentrate on. He needed to figure out how to get photos without being suspicious.

"You know," Cherry said, "we didn't have a traditional wedding back home. Last night was essentially our wedding reception. This could be considered our wedding supper, despite being out of order in the normal line of events. We need a photo to commemorate the guests at our wedding, don't you think?"

Feck, this woman was brilliant. He knew he loved her for a reason.

"I think that's an excellent idea, Esme," he answered. He gestured to the boy standing off to the side. "Would you mind?"

Andres came forward. Demon tapped the camera button on the screen and turned the phone horizontally. The picture would stay in the phone's album, but it would also immediately pop up into Midas' email. He'd know exactly what to do with its sudden arrival.

"This side of the table can just turn around over their shoulder, and we should be able to get everyone in if we take it in panoramic style."

Everyone turned their faces to the camera, the picture was taken, and the "wedding supper" was memorialized.

Zion walked over to one of the other tables to speak with a guest, and the rest of their table became immersed in a discussion of the best beaches on the island. Cherry crooked a finger underneath his collar, pulling him close in what would appear to anyone watching as a flirtatious move. When he ducked his ear to her lips, she whispered, "You said Steel got a Cyclopes eye stuck to the outside of the window of the meeting room?"

"Yes." Immediately, he knew where she was going with her question. He nuzzled her neck under her ear, answering her softly. "If they activated the eye feature even though they couldn't see inside the room, they'll have video of anyone arriving. That window is on the entryway side of the building."

She turned her face in toward him, creating a veil of privacy when her hair spilled over her headband to shield their faces. "You know Midas," she assured him. "It might've seemed like overkill at the time, but even if he didn't have a use for the video feed, it was running. Probably still is. He should be able to get footage of everyone coming, going, or both."

"If they were in the meeting, that means they'd be in the know most likely." He caressed the side of her face with a single fingertip, and he pressed a soft kiss to her lips. "Notice anything interesting about the married couples?"

"Other than the women who appear to be in their mid- to late twenties, even if their husbands are pushing fifty?"

Yeah, his woman was no dummy. When he broached their theory about Zion to her, he didn't think she'd be all that surprised that he believed her uncle to actually be a member, although so far, no S button appeared on his clothing. And given his interest in Esme, the timing of Bosworth's disappearance on Esme's graduation day was unlikely to be a coincidence. Maybe her father's digging into Salieri business had already put that kidnapping in motion, but Zion had been working toward getting his daughter closer to him. Knowing what they did about the Salieri's use and disposal of women? Esme had lived far longer than Zion had planned for her to originally.

There was the gentle tinkle of silver against crystal, and all eyes were drawn to Zion once again standing at the head of the table. "Family." He raised his glass to Cherry and Demon. "Business partners and friends." Another raise of the glass to the guests at his table. "And let's not forget our enemies." When everyone looked around at each other confusedly, Zion gave a conspiratorial smile as he leaned forward and fake whispered, "I'll give you a hint. They're not here." A chorus of chuckles broke out amongst the guests.

He continued his speech, his wineglass in the air. "Thank you for joining me this weekend. I am honored by your presence, and together, we have hopefully strengthened current business ties as well as forged new ones that will be lucrative to all as we aim to make this world a better, safer place for all.

"My beautiful niece, Esme, and her new husband, Ciarán, have requested a tour of the banana farm's inner workings, so if there are others who would like to join them on the impromptu tour, Calvin Deschamps, my overseer, will be happy to escort you on the long, hot, dusty walk after your desserts, which the waitstaff are bringing now. The saner amongst you who choose to refrain, the wagons will be around in approximately thirty minutes to return you to the main building, where I promise you more wine." Again, laughter rose up from his attempt at humor. "Please. Enjoy yourselves this afternoon at my expense, and the vans will return passengers back to *Les Vergers de la Mer* at your pleasure." With a further raise of his glass into the air at his guests, Zion inclined his head at the applause and drank a sip of wine.

As his guests' focus returned to their socializing, Zion reached for Cherry's hand. He kissed the back of it. "Once again, *bèl fi*, I hope you will excuse me. While it is social time for my guests, I have some business to attend to with regard to the end results of our meeting this morning. I hope you enjoy your tour today. There is no hurry. Take as long as you'd like to explore when the tour is complete. There are some lovely walking paths that loop around the first grove closest to the center buildings. As long as you stay on those, you cannot get lost or too far away. Matthew will wait for you until you are ready to return to *Les Vergers.*" A flash of his trademark smile, another kiss to the back of her hand, and he was striding off to a golf cart that had pulled up to take him back to the main building.

22

APRIL 13, 2023

Cherry

As the entrée plates disappeared, the staff replaced them with dessert bowls with a banana mousse laced with rum, topped with a meringue, cinnamon, and a shortbread cookie embossed with the plantation's banana tree logo. When they had finished their dessert, a voice came from behind them.

"Mr. and Mrs. McCarthy."

Both turned to see Calvin Deschamps behind them.

He gestured to another golf cart along the path. "If you have finished your dessert, I am happy to give you the tour you requested."

Cherry rose from her seat, and Demon did as well, pulling her chair back to make exiting from the table smoother. With a hand to the small of her back, he walked beside her as the manager led them to their transportation. Behind the wheel sat the teen, Andres, who returned Demon's greeting with a nod of his head, and then blushed furiously when she smiled at him and said hello.

Demon handed her into the golf cart, then slipped in beside her on the other side, sitting behind Calvin, who was in the front passenger seat. "I hope this tour doesn't put you out, Mr. Deschamps."

"*No, no, pa ditou,*" he assured them. "I'm always pleased to share *Bananato del Sole* with those who are genuinely interested in what we do here. I had Andres bring down a cart to take us to the center court, and we will walk from there, *si?* Save you some of the heat and dust."

The smile on the man's weathered face felt genuine. Perhaps he was truly one in a long line of banana farmers? And yet... the lack of living female influences in the family hinted at more.

"Do you go to school, Andres?" Cherry asked.

"No, ma'am, I am what you would call homeschooled. However, I may go to university when I finish my secondary studies next month. I have not decided yet."

A gentle pat on the shoulder from Calvin caused the boy to smile. "Andres has always been a homebody. I think it comes from having lost his mother. He's always been more comfortable here, and many of the workers' children come to work with their parents and attend classes here with him. We actually have a small virtual-based school of our own that is open to them while their parents are under our employ."

"It's odd," she replied. "I hope you don't find this rude, but... I don't see many female staff."

Calvin turned sideways in his seat, one arm folded over the back of it as he replied to her comment. "Yes, it is true. We do not have as many women on staff as we do men. Unfortunately, we still hold on to a lot of the 'old' ways, and it is difficult for our older managers to be as open to women in higher positions. As younger managers step into place, we see more women. Slow to change, but... there are more women who work in the kitchens, on the farm, and in other facets of our business."

She held her tongue regarding this not being just an issue of tradition, outdated customs, or even misplaced chivalry. This was the Salieri. Their misogyny wasn't something that would ease with education and time. It was an abomination. It needed to be rooted out and burned to ash so it could never rise again, and she hoped it had yet to touch the sweet young man driving the cart.

Before she knew it, they were in the central outer courtyard. Although she admitted it was less charming, the golf cart was infinitely faster traversing the distance than the horse-drawn wagons and also provided more of a breeze on the ride. The return trip felt like it took mere moments after the original fifteen-minute ride earlier. Upon arrival, another member of the staff stood ready with warm washcloths to wipe down their hands and faces from being outside.

With a clap of his hands, Calvin began the tour. "When Mr. Norton invested in *Bananato del Sole*, we could enter a new age of sustainable farming never possible before."

"They're willing to advance their success through technology and money, but not through women. Oh, the irony!" Demon growled low enough under his breath so that only Cherry heard him.

She agreed with him but played her part. "I thought your family owned the farmland for generations?" she asked.

Calvin gestured for them to proceed to the smallest building on the property. "Yes, all the way back to before the islands were under French control in the 1600s, and through all the skirmishes between the French and the British for control, up through to today. But owning the land was not enough. Come! You've already seen the offices today, or building 1. We will go through the buildings counter-clockwise so you can see the process from start to finish. Building 2 is where we take individuals to see the history of the farm and the conception models for what we are today."

Cherry followed the man and his grandson, but Demon lagged for a moment, his hand on the hood of the golf cart. "Ciarán? Everything okay?" she called.

He gestured for them to go forward. "Yeah. Think a piece of rock worked into my shoe. Be right there."

They turned and proceeded toward the building. Moments later, Demon had returned to her side. Deschamps ushered them into the small stone hut, where cool air immediately blasted them. Cherry hugged herself, and suddenly a warm body pressed up against her side, with an arm around her shoulders to pull her tightly to it. Demon had noticed her shiver. Did the man ever not notice things about her?

"I am sorry." Deschamps' smile was apologetic. "We keep this room quite cold because of some documents housed here. It will be a brief stop, and then in a few minutes, you will wish for the air-conditioning again." He stepped to the center of the room, where a giant 3D concept map stood on a pedestal table. It sat inside a plexiglass box. "You will notice the centerpiece diorama of Soufrière, the Pitons, and the surrounding area. You can see *Bananato del Sole* at the foot of Petit Piton."

Along the bottom quarter of the mountain were rows of trees flanking a dirt road, which led to several small buildings that formed the original homestead and outbuildings. "Scientists believe the last known eruption of the Pitons was forty thousand years ago. We believe the event provided the plantation with its rich soil, perfect for successful banana farming. In addition, it is responsible for Sulphur Springs. While the Pitons are dormant structures, there is still much geothermal activity here, and it has produced a major tourist attraction of taking the mud baths.

"My family has possessed this property since the earliest recorded history. Like many businesses in the agricultural world, the farm has existed through periods between destitution and success. Banana growing has waned dramatically in St. Lucia over the years. However, when your uncle came and offered his financial backing, *Bananato del Sole* could do much more than just produce and sell bananas. We became a beacon for environmental experimentation and sustainable farming practices."

He gestured in a circle around the walls. "Based on the diorama, you'll notice that they added this building to the existing structures. That is because we needed updated wiring for all the technology in here. These screens and interactive displays walk our prospective clients, investors, and business visitors through our history, current practices, and future goals, which they can listen to as a group, plug in with provided headphones, or link to their phones. We also have cases that are kept at low temperature, low humidity, and low oxygen levels to preserve the family documents associated with the groves."

They followed him out the opposite door and into another more modernized building. Cherry made an observation. "It's amazing how well you've done matching the new buildings to the original structures."

Grinning, Deschamps replied, "Yes, Zion was most insistent about that. He had to secure special permission from the government to quarry for limestone to match. I hesitate to think what that cost." He turned to continue walking forward. "In fact, he secured some funding for this project from your father."

She and Demon exchanged a glance.

"This is building 3. Here we do our research and development. Again, a newer building, so added to the original structures. And again, necessary because of the technological needs." The temperature in this building was cooler, and the lighting was harsher. A central hallway passed through the building with glassed-off rooms. Inside, workers in scrubs, booties, gloves, and masks worked with test tubes and other assorted chemistry lab materials. "Here on the main floor, we work with testing seedlings, the suckers which are eventually planted to create the trees, natural pesticide methods, genetics, and all the things that go into selecting the proper fruit, soil concentrations, water levels, and everything that makes our product from the bananas themselves to the by-products from them.

"We dedicate each room to a particular part of the process to avoid cross contamination, and each room features a double-entry system to maintain cleanliness. Employees enter through a separate entrance into a sort of airlock, which blasts them with filtered air to remove microbes and the like that might contaminate our work. They enter a locker room where they shower and don specific clothing. When they enter the room, they seal the doors in the foyer and receive another blast of filtered air, and only then may they enter the research portion of the room."

They stopped to watch one scientist plant cuttings into individual pots with soil from different bags in each one. "We like to keep the product pure to the type of banana, but for some products, we will join genetic material or change it to the specific needs. This gentleman here is testing different soil concentrations on our bananas."

Deschamps checked the sign on the window. "This room is for green fig bananas, which Mr. McCarthy ate with his saltfish at the luncheon."

"That's fine in clean rooms," Demon remarked, "but what about out in the groves? How do you keep the bananas from cross-contaminating each other out there?"

The manager shook a finger at him with a knowing grin. He glanced at Cherry. "You have a smart one here, Esme."

"I have basic biology knowledge from university," Demon grumbled.

"But not everyone would think of the difference between environments. At their foundation, bananas are very similar across the board, so cross contamination is not a large concern. However, pest control and disease are far worse concerns, so we use some netting and roads between the varieties to limit these things."

"I never realized how much work goes into growing bananas," she genuinely mused. "Never thought about it, to be honest. I just peel, bite, chew, and swallow." All three of them chuckled. "I guess it's much the same with beef or other meats. To me, it all comes from packages in the stores, not cows or chickens or whatever. Sobering thought."

"Yes, social consciousness and all of that," Deschamps agreed. "It is why we try to be as responsible here with our methods as possible."

Demon gave a chin lift to the elevator at the end of the hallway they were in. "What do you do upstairs?"

"Ah. That is where we do our work with the organic pesticides. We try to keep that on a separate floor so that we can flush out that air separately."

"And the lower floors? I see there's a basement as well."

"Refuse, recycling, those sorts of things. Several of the stages of banana farming create waste. We separate the compost from the recyclables and waste as much as possible, then burn the waste. We have conveyors that take the compost to one set of trucks, which are then moved to the barns for distribution. The recyclable material is sorted, then distributed into containers to the proper trucks to move to facilities that turn that material into reusable resources such as cleaning bottles, shoe soles, even recycling containers themselves."

"Very efficient."

"All part of your uncle's mission for sustainability. Only if we cannot use it does it leave our grounds, and only then is it distributed to where it must go. We have very little waste here that is completely unusable. We even work with companies that use recyclable materials for shipping, containing, storing, and so forth."

From that point, they moved on through the remaining buildings —the greenhouse they used to plant the cuttings until they were large enough to be planted as trees in their rows; the irrigation mechanics ran miles underground to water the young trees because bananas require extremely moist conditions even during the rainy season. The garage—an original stone and timber barn—where all the machinery and larger tools were kept for the fields at this end of the facility. The building where all the plant food was stored, bagged, and distributed for the groves, and another building for the natural pesticides. Buildings where the bananas were brought to be washed, processed, and packaged, and finally, the building where the product was packaged on a larger scale and sent to customers. He also shared that there were additional harvesting and storage buildings further out for each individual grove.

She noticed that both inside and outside the buildings, Demon was scrutinizing things heavily behind his glasses. Because they were reflective, neither the supervisor nor the boy could see his eye movements. However, she could since she was next to him at all times, mostly because he kept an arm around her shoulders as if he was afraid letting go of her or letting her walk two feet away would cause her to be in danger. He also never let his face show his reactions to what he observed, something she figured was a doctor's skill, cultivated particularly for when having to deliver unhappy news to patients and loved ones. However, she noticed a tightening around his eyes, and there was a wince as if he was in pain when they stood in one place too long.

Throughout their entire tour, Deschamps did most of the talking. Sometimes, he would defer to his grandson on a question asked, partially, she was sure, to test his knowledge and partially to get him used to speaking about the business to clients and potential customers. Otherwise, the boy stayed silent, following close behind her. Every time she glanced at him, his attention was on her, or when he answered a question, even if Demon asked it, he seemed to spend most of his time directing his answer to her. While it was sweet that he seemed a bit mesmerized by her, it was also a little unnerving. She supposed it was that way for most adults who found themselves the subject of interest, even adoration, of much younger people.

"This is quite the operation," Demon commended, breaking into her thoughts. "No small amount of capital is involved to do things, let alone do them at this level of technology and sustainability. Those methods aren't cheap, and your profit margins must be low still."

"We get by." The foreman winked. "But yes, the start-up was monumental, and the profit growth was slow. It took men of vision— like Zion and your father, Esme—to believe in what we hoped to achieve and help us get started. However, it has been more than a few years now since we have achieved a level of financial stability or, dare

I say, success. We are now the largest and highest-earning sustainable banana farm in the world."

He clapped his hands, a habit he had of doing when changing from one topic to another. "I imagine you've had enough of my prattling on about our work here. Perhaps you'd like to take a stroll? I imagine as newlyweds, you might like some time alone to discuss your plans for the future, your hopes, your dreams. A little romance among the trees."

Cherry looked up into Demon's face, her smile matching his. "I think that sounds wonderful."

"Excellent!" Deschamps gestured to his right. "The path here will lead you on a short loop through our closest field. There are water stations along the way. Please partake. I've been told that Matthew awaits you at the main building at your pleasure. I've heard he is sweet on one of the cooks, so I'm sure he's in no rush." With a chuckle and a wink, he reached out a hand to Demon. "So pleased to make your acquaintance, Mr. and Mrs. McCarthy. Your uncle has mentioned how happy he is to see you after all this time, and of course, we all hope you will visit again sometime soon. Come, Andres! We will leave the two lovebirds to their romantic stroll!"

With that, they both walked back to the main building. Cherry noticed, however, that Andres was slower to turn and follow his grandfather after a last glance and a shy nod at Cherry.

An arm wrapped around her shoulders, guiding her toward the path. "You have quite the admirer there, fireball." He kissed the side of her head. "He has good taste."

"He's far too young for me," she admonished, "but I bet he'll break hearts if he goes to university. He has that look about him. Girls love the quiet ones. They're almost as much of a challenge as the bad boys."

23

APRIL 13, 2023

Demon

They walked in silence until they were around the first curve in the path, out of view of the buildings. "So... what did you see?" she asked him.

"The security is pretty high for a banana plantation. They even had cameras out in the lunch area."

"Looking for tells on business deals? Or just general paranoia?"

"Definitely the former. Probably both." He paused, turning her into his arms and ducking his head into her neck just below her ear. "They also have them here on the path. If we keep our voices pitched lower and obviously quieter, they won't be able to pick up sound. I'll keep us turned so they can't read our lips."

"Got it."

"Not that making love to your neck is a hardship," he admitted. His lips traveled down the cord from under her ear to her throat.

"Just my neck?"

"I don't think you want the rest on camera. I'm saving my best moves for later in private."

After grabbing his earlobe with her teeth and giving it a soft nip, she whispered, "I look forward to it. Besides cameras, what did you see?"

"They hustled us through that tour. Nobody asked us if we had questions. It took effort to insert them in Deschamps' monologues. And everything felt very much for show."

"You think all those people we saw working were acting?"

"No. I don't mean that way. If I were a betting man—"

"Which you are," she reminded him.

"If I were a betting man," he repeated, "I'd say those were honest-to-god workers. But there's something else going on here, Cherry. You remember those boxes Nemo and Steel found in Sallum? And the one they found Flame in back home?"

She buried her face in his chest as his hands wandered to her spine, his fingertips lightly dragging up and down the vertebrae. "You saw some here?"

"Yeah, pretty sure. They were traveling in that elevator. I was watching the numbers. The carriage came from upstairs, and the main door opened briefly on the main floor. I think it was an accident because as soon as the guy in the elevator saw us, he inhaled pretty sharply, and his eyes went wide. He couldn't manually close those doors fast enough. Then it continued downstairs."

He kissed the top of her head, then framed her face. He was within a breath of touching her lips when he spoke, his palms hiding that he was talking. "Think about it. The main floor is a clean facility. Place is soundproofed. The building is new and modernized. Lots of scientific equipment." He turned her sideways, his arm over her shoulder, and pulled her tight to his side, tucking her face into his chest again. "I suspect those elevators go to more than one underground floor. They probably have tunnels connecting the buildings underground. They could easily move anything that way.

"Plus, boxes were being loaded *out* from a truck out back. He passed it off as a truck moving compost. You wouldn't use a box truck for that. You'd use a dump truck. Plus, the boxes had markings showing medical supplies. You wouldn't need any of that for splicing plants and developing natural fertilizers."

She thought about his observations and conclusions for a moment, drawing the lines from A to B and all the way through to Z. "So they're using purchased women for breeding, and they're using the upper floor as a hospital where they're delivering the children. When the children are born, they kill the mothers. Then they remove the bodies through the same coffins to what? A burn facility?"

"Probably right here on the grounds. Less they have to move off the grounds, the better. We need to get on those other floors and look around. Need to think about how to manage that." He kissed the top of her head again. "I need you to stick extra close, fireball. Between Zion's focus on you and the lovesick puppy who just left us, this is making me nervous having you here."

She looked up into his gaze. An eyebrow quirked at his suggestion. "You think they'd want to get their hands on me as a breeder? I get the Zion concern, maybe, but don't you think I'm a little old, not just for that, but for an eighteen-year-old boy?"

He looked at her over the top of his glasses. "Sweetheart, you'll be even sexier when you're sixty."

He watched her pupils expand and felt her pulse increase under his thumb, where it stroked her pulse point. Her lips were slightly parted, and her tongue darted out to lick them.

Tipping his sunglasses up to sit on top of his head, he stopped in the middle of the path, his hand pulling her face close to his mouth. He dipped his head to bring her lips the final distance to his. Mouth closing on hers, he slid his tongue inside. Her hands clutched his biceps, making his fingers thread through her hair at the base of her neck, pulling tight at the roots to tilt her in the direction he wanted so he could seam their mouths tighter together. When she clutched him even harder, her manicured nails dug into his skin, and a whimper came from the back of her throat. He knew he needed to slow them down, or before long, he'd have her up against one of the trees. Given the cameras in the electric wires above, he refused to give anyone a show. And he certainly couldn't jam the cameras, or security would be on to him.

Reluctantly, he pulled back from her. "We should keep moving," he told her, the regret clear in his voice.

She closed her eyes and nodded.

"Sorry," he whispered. "I promise to pick this up later."

"You'd better," she warned. "Or I just might have to go find some hot security guy to take care of me. Maybe even Matthew."

"Oh, hell no!"

He pulled her along the path again, turning into the last curve, the main building just visible through the branches in front of them.

"Do you think..." she began.

When she didn't continue right away, he asked, "Do I think what?"

"If your suspicions are correct, then *Bananato del Sole* is Salieri property. Probably being used to launder money, at the very least. Given all the evidence so far, it would appear that my uncle is at least aware, more likely complicit. While that's disturbing, it doesn't... well, I won't say it doesn't surprise me, yet it does."

He waited out what he knew was coming.

"My father's disappearance tied up his money because there was no proof of death. Until I turned twenty-one, the family attorney paid all the bills, oversaw the investments, and I lived off the interest of the trust my mother left for me. Then, on my twenty-first birthday, I received control of that trust. I had to wait another four years so I could declare Dad legally dead and get hold of the rest of our family's money. I needed it to put forward my plans for Tribe. We went through everything, but I saw nothing about an investment in the plantation.

"Do you think...?" She blew out a breath and shook her head, a determined look on her face. "No. He wouldn't. He wouldn't have invested money with Zion if he knew what they were connected to."

"Remember. Deschamps said he was a start-up investor. He may have only given a lump sum at one time. But no, fireball, I don't think your father would have been a part of something like the Salieri. Not on purpose. The guys and I discussed this last night. I didn't want to bring it up until I saw what was happening here. Didn't want to get you wound up for nothing. But we're all of the same mind that your father was an honest investor in the property with no knowledge. Probably some men here this weekend are as well. The closer illegal activities run to legitimate ones, the easier it is to hide. And their money is just as good."

"But he was investigating the Salieri when he died, based on the files on his computer. Do you think he figured out they were involved with the plantation, and that's why he started looking into things?"

"I do, and so do the guys."

She seemed to relax in his embrace slightly. "Good. Good. I could never imagine him being a part of something like what's happening to these women."

"Maybe that's why there's no record of the investment either. Maybe as soon as he realized what was going on or became suspicious, he pulled his funding. Maybe the Salieri electronically erased the investment to prevent it from being traced back to them. Could be what put your father on their list of loose ends to tie up. Can't have uncommitted people who know what you're doing running around. This isn't the kind of thing you can expect an NDA to keep quiet." He kissed the top of her head, and they passed out of the trees and onto the circular driveway. "Let's head back to the estate. We could go spend some time on the beach. Or we could…" Did he dare push? "We could hide out in our room like the newly married couple you suggested we be on the way to the airport."

Their eyes locked.

The tip of her tongue peeked out between her lips, swiping across the flesh. "All that good food, the heat, the walking. I feel the need for a nap."

Yeah. There'd be no napping.

24

APRIL 13, 2023

Cherry

The ride back to *Les Vergers de la Mer* was silent except for the sound of the vehicle itself passing over the roads. Staring out the rear passenger window, she felt stiff as a board beside him, her hand engulfed in Demon's resting atop his thigh. She worried her palm would be sweaty or clammy. That wasn't very attractive.

Suddenly, a whisper entered her ear, the breath attached to it soft and warm. "Stop overthinking."

Turning her face to his, he was hiding behind the reflective sunglasses again but clearly looking at her. Biting her lip, she paused and then nodded. She was acting like what was coming when they got back to the estate was new to her. It certainly wasn't. But it felt new. Maybe because it was him. Maybe because she was opening herself up to someone for the first time since her father's disappearance, even if it was temporary. Whatever the reason, she felt like she was spending the night with a man for the first time.

She laid her head against his shoulder and closed her eyes.

Well, in theory, she was. Yes, they'd slept side by side the past two nights in the same bed. Yes, she'd woken up both mornings in his arms, her back tight to his front. But they hadn't had sex yet, and she'd never spent the night with a partner before. She'd gone back to their places or a hotel. She'd fucked them. Maybe she'd hung out for a bit or even gone another round with them, but the time had not been intimate other than the sex itself. She was about to have sex with a man she'd wanted for going on six years, then sleep next to him. Stop overthinking? How could she not overthink what she was about to do?

When they arrived back at the villa, she was still lost in her own thoughts. She heard him thank Matthew, and the driver replied, but the words themselves were merely mumbles. As they entered the building, she registered Rayon appearing and Demon talking with him for a few moments. About what she had no idea. Then he was guiding her up the stairs to their suite. Most, if not all, of the guests must have left because the hallways were silent.

He pulled open the door to their room, gently ushering her inside with a hand to the small of her back. Without conscious thought, she whirled into him and pressed her mouth against his. He clearly wasn't on board with her attack because his hands slid through her hair at the scalp and pulled tight, forcing her neck to arch. The action pried her mouth from his, and that tautness of the muscles caused her lips to remain parted and her eyes to open wide. He must have realized he had her strung tight because he let go with one hand and reached up to rip the sunglasses off his face and throw them to the side.

"You realize you provoked the monster, yes?"

"Yes," she hissed when she felt the slight twist at her hair roots. Now she really couldn't move her head. She didn't want to move. She needed him to be the one in control. There was just too much to process. Too much worry. Too much unknown. These were things she was unfamiliar with in her role at Tribe. She knew more than anyone except maybe God. She was the puppeteer, controlling the projects they took on. Controlling their actions by directing them where she wanted them to go. Controlling the office from her computer station. Not tonight. Tonight, he had control.

"Good. So long as it's understood."

Forcefully, yet careful not to cause her to trip, he backed her up to the edge of the bed. She felt the back of her legs hit the padded bench at the foot, and when he suddenly let go of her hair, she collapsed onto it. "I warned you, fireball. I won't be gentle. I may start easy, but by the end, you'll be wrecked. If you don't want me to own all of you, now's the time to speak."

"I don't want gentle," she admitted. "I want you just as you are."

"Then that's what you'll get." His hand raised in front of her face, one finger laid against her lips. "No talking from this point forward unless I ask you a direct question. I'm going to go downstairs. I'll give you twenty minutes alone. Strip the covers and the top sheet off the bed. Do whatever else you need to do in the time I'm gone, but when I return, your ass better be naked and lying on your back in the middle of the bed. Every stitch of clothing needs to be off your body, and I want your hair down and spilling all over my pillow. Your hands will be up alongside your head. Your eyes will be closed. Nod your head if you understand."

Reflexively, she swallowed and nodded. Apparently, BAMF mode was more than just his project gear.

"Good girl." Immediately, he turned on his heel and went out the door, shutting it behind him without looking back.

Stupefied, she sat there for two minutes, trying to process what the hell had just happened. She had to work to shake herself free of the trance he'd put her in and get moving. She was down to eighteen minutes before he'd be back.

There wasn't time for a proper shower, so she stripped off her clothes as she moved with purpose to the bathroom. She made a pile of them on the vanity next to the sink, heedless of the wrinkles they'd have from not being folded and put away neatly. Now was not the time to worry about that kind of trivia. Instead, she focused on sponging herself down with a cool cloth, lotioning her skin, and brushing out her hair.

With three minutes to spare, she checked to make sure the heat of the day hadn't done irreparable damage to her makeup, and seeing it hadn't, she went into the bedroom portion of the suite. Quickly, she closed the curtains on the French doors, then pulled back the coverlet and top sheet, loosely folding them and placing them on the chair in the corner of the room. Finally, she slid onto the bed and arranged herself as he asked.

And waited.

It was probably no more than a minute, but the way her mind and heart were racing, time felt endless. What would he do? She hadn't taken him for a Dominant in the same way that his teammate TB was. That man actually frequented a kink club. He liked to control Flame through sex with various types of restraints. She'd never seen evidence of that in Demon's past. However, he'd definitely gone all extra alpha on her just before leaving the room, and she was not about to deny that her brain had nearly wept for joy that she wasn't going to have to be in charge or assertive. He clearly was going to be both of those things.

He'd told her there was a darkness in him. A monster. She shivered. God, she hoped so. Not the literal kind. But something subversive. Unrepentant. Dangerous. Feral. Like a dark romance with the most unhealthy of trigger warnings that made a woman's hundred-dollar panties totally unsalvageable, and she wouldn't even flinch at throwing them away. Or letting him rip them off her body and use them to stroke himself off over her while he growled an extremely dirty itinerary for them in his bed. Then once he came all over them, he'd gag her with them while he held her down and fucked her so hard the headboard dented the wall. She shivered again.

"Whatever that thought was, fireball, I want to do that."

So lost in her head, she had missed hearing the outer door to the suite open, then quietly shut. A smile formed on her mouth. Was he hoping to catch her not being ready or not following his instructions? His footfalls were slow, but she knew he was doing it on purpose to heighten the experience. He wasn't just dark. He was twisted in the most delightful way.

Her eyes were closed, as he'd ordered, but she could feel the air around her seem to pressurize. She knew he stood at the foot of the bed, staring at her, but she remained unmoving, unseeing, waiting for whatever move he was going to make. It felt like minutes passed before she heard another sound, but when it did come, it was the rustle of clothing as he moved, a gentle thud on the bedside table, and the clink of metal against a ceramic object.

The bed dipped slightly as he sat at her hip. "Remember. Don't move. Don't make a sound," he commanded.

A single fingertip touched the upturned palm closest to him, and it trailed agonizingly slow down the inside of her bent forearm, inward from her elbow to her shoulder, crossed her clavicle, then downward to her breasts. When he reached the middle of the valley between them, he changed direction again, smoothing over the plump flesh and tracing the edge of her areola, causing her flesh to pebble in response. After several circles around the tip, he dragged his finger back to the centerline and over to the other breast, repeating his touch. Back and forth, he teased her until she felt as if he'd mesmerized her with his touch into a state between asleep and awake.

That's when he struck. As his fingertip moved on its normal trajectory to the breast farthest from him, she was so lulled into the pattern that she didn't expect his warm mouth to close over her right nipple. The shock of his teeth biting around it, the tip of his tongue flicking the nub, and the wet suction around the area made her gasp and arch. In response, the fingers of his right hand grasped her entire breast, his thumb and forefinger giving the nipple beneath a swift, sharp pinch. His mouth let go of her other breast, but it didn't move far because she could feel the heat of his breath on her skin. "That's your one warning, fireball. If you move again, I'll be forced to tie you down. We both know you don't want that."

She whimpered.

"Hmm. Or do you?" His fingers resumed their earlier tortuous course, back and forth, circling. "One of the bonuses of being a doctor is that I'm able to read people's physiological responses well. The easiest ways to tell if someone is aroused are simple sight tricks to pay attention to. Your skin flushes the softest pink in your cheeks. It makes the rest of your fair skin look that much fairer. And the dusting of freckles so faint no one can see them? They pop just the tiniest bit. Especially this one." His lips found the freckle in question on the swell of her breast.

"The most obvious for women, besides blushing, is their nipples hardening. With you at the office, it's hard to tell. You always wear those designer suits that keep everything locked down. But on occasion, when you take your jacket off and show off those gorgeous silk blouses, if I walk in the room, you instantly pop." His hands had captured her smaller breasts, just big enough to fill his palms, and he used his forefingers to lightly abrade the points forming on them. "I can always tell on the days when you don't wear a bra and just wear a camisole because the material brushes against them, and they're even more prominent. I bet it makes them ache to be touched." Again, his mouth came down, his tongue swirling around the nub, his warm breath and then the cool air when he released it, making them harder.

"And your blood pressure rises." His finger brushed her jawline and drew down to her pulse point. "If I watch your throat, I can see your pulse thrumming with the flutters in your neck"—the finger continued down to her chest, and when he reached her heart, he laid his palm flat—"or feel your heart beat faster." His hand disappeared, and then both her wrists were encircled by his fingers as he pushed them down into the pillow, his head lowering to kiss the one closest to him. "I can feel the rabbiting here, as well, when I hold you down and know that you're excited."

He got off the bed. By the sounds, she could tell he had moved down to the foot, centering himself in front of her. She heard shoes clunk on the floor and the slide of material as it passed over skin. The pop of a button and the rasp of a zipper, then his pants joined the rest of his clothing. She heard a quiet creak as he put pressure on the bench at the foot of the bed, and then a hand loosely gripped her feet, the thumbs lightly stroking the soles, applying gentle pressure into the arches, his fingers doing the same to the tops.

"Tension is the most dangerous part of arousal," he cautioned her. "The muscles tighten, and you can actually strain them, even cramp if you tense too hard. We need to make sure these muscles are nice and loose so when they do tighten, they're good and stretched out."

Suddenly, his hands were gone. She heard the snick of a bottle opening, the squeak of it being compressed, and the sound of liquid exiting. After hearing him snap the bottle closed, she heard him rubbing his hands together, then felt them press against her feet again. He worked the warmed oil into her skin, massaging the muscles, making sure no inch was left untouched until he got to her core. There, he made sure to press his thumbs into the creases between her thighs and her pelvis, but he never touched her center.

She whimpered.

"Patience, fireball. I'll get there. Everyone knows you save the best for last."

As he traveled up her body, she felt his legs caging her in—his warm skin against her, the light dusting of hair causing friction as he moved, and the heavy weight of his fully engorged cock against her thigh. It would be a miracle if she didn't combust long before he got inside her. Every so often, he would reach for the bottle to get more oil, always making sure to warm it between his hands before rubbing it into her skin. And instead of flipping her over, he made sure to slide his hands between her and the sheet beneath her, which, of course, brought her body up to his and felt way more erotic.

By the time he had moved up her entire front and was massaging around her temples, she was a raging ball of need. Her fingers began to twitch as she fought the need to move. "Easy, *a chuisle mo chroí.*

Trust me to know what you need." He kissed her forehead, the tip of her nose, then her lips with the barest of touches. So tender and so at odds with how he presented himself to everyone, including her.

She felt him swing his leg over her body and rise off the bed. "Keep those eyes closed. Don't move. Don't speak. I'll be right back." He trailed a finger down her body from forehead to toes as he left the bed.

It was amazing how the lack of sight or the ability to touch with her hands heightened all the other senses. For once, Cherry understood what Flame talked about when she'd shared some of her "research" that TB had introduced to her. Since the woman wrote erotic romance, and her partner was a Dominant and had spent time in the kink community, she'd become somewhat of an expert. This type of play had never been part of Cherry's sexual experiences before, and she found she was glad for that. While it wasn't bondage, it was a power exchange, and Cherry recognized that her being in control of everything all the time needed a release valve. Getting to experience this with him—giving up all the control—made it all the more intense and gratifying.

Moments later, she heard water running in the bathroom. Then he was back, picking something up off the bedside table and repositioning himself, but this time he gently inserted himself between her legs. She could tell he was lying down, propped up on his elbows, and he placed something cool and rounded next to her on the bed.

"Remember. No moving. No sound."

Why would he need to remind her again?

Then she understood. The sensation of something cold dripping onto her bare lower lips nearly sent her skyrocketing off the bed and gasping her surprise. Had he not reminded her, she probably would have. The consistency wasn't liquid, but it was definitely not solid. He continued to swirl his fingers through the bowl, then hover them over her mound, allowing the substance to drop onto her, slide through all her folds, and down to the sheets.

"Sensations during sex should be the focus. Not the technical movements. I could be doing this same thing with you watching, and it might be sexy, but this way, you're forced to truly feel what I'm doing to you. Associate the pleasure with the sensation itself. That's always what I want for you. I want you to feel what I do to you and know the emotion behind it."

He shifted, likely placing the bowl on the floor. "I have a terrible sweet tooth and didn't get nearly enough dessert today. Rayon had some delivered to the estate. Lucky me."

Oh shit. The banana mousse. He'd spread it all over her pussy.

She felt him reach for something else, heard the scraping of a bottle top being turned and the seal breaking, and then liquid poured onto the mess he'd made, running down her body, creating rivulets through the pudding. This wasn't cold. It was room temperature, and it burned slightly, but in a good way.

"There was no rum in this version, so I added whiskey." He began to clean off all the mixture from her mound where he'd spread it, and he made no effort to be quiet about it. His mouth would settle on a patch of skin, his tongue would swipe across it, and then he'd gently suck the last traces, a soft slurping sound as he disengaged. Then he'd repeat in another spot until her entire mound was clean of the sticky treat.

"You taste so good, fireball. Cherry, banana, cinnamon, and whiskey. I didn't think Hibiki could taste any better, but I was wrong."

Then he waged total war on her body. His hands slid under her ass, gripping her cheeks, causing her knees to bend and her legs to open a little further. Raising her to meet his mouth, he delved between the folds of skin to taste the concoction he'd created.

She couldn't hold in the whimper as, with each pass, he went a little lower, getting closer and closer to her channel. When he finally arrived, he pulled her hips up just a little higher, and the pointed muscle swirled around her opening. Finally, he pushed inside until his face was tight against her. He sucked hard to gather any traces of his dessert, then pulled out to swipe up to her clit, circle it, and suck lightly. The next swipe went farther down, ducked inside her cunt, swiped back to her clit, and circled again with the final suck. Again and again, he repeated his pattern until he reached his final goal, his tongue rimming the edges of her back passage. On that final pass, when he reached her clit, he blew on the hard nerve bundle. "Hands in my hair, fireball, and hang on. Now you can move. Make noise. Give me those sounds. I want to hear everything you feel."

Her hands threaded through his hair, now loose from the small knot he'd had on the top of his head at lunch. As soon as his mouth suctioned over her clit, the moan barreled up from the depths of her being. It took less than a half dozen flicks of his tongue to send her over the edge. While one hand scored his scalp and twisted in his hair, the other hand grabbed for a pillow. She'd never been a vocal person since most of her encounters had happened in hotels, and she'd never wanted to give the neighboring rooms an audible show. She smothered her scream in it, her body arching further into his mouth.

His mouth disappeared from her body. Immediately, she groaned at the loss.

The sound registered before the stinging slap on her pussy.

"I told you I wanted to hear you, fireball. I warned you I'd want every fucking thing from you. I don't care if they hear you all the way in the bay. We're newlyweds to the people in this house. It wouldn't be out of place, so let go of that need to control shit and give yourself over. Now I have to start over, and if you don't give me what I want, I'll keep it up until you give it to me, and each time will be more intense than the last."

He rose on his knees, grabbed both of her legs, pulled them up so they cleared his body, then deftly flipped her over. Before she could do anything, he had her kneeling in front of him, and he was settling her between his legs. Both pillows went flying off the bed in separate directions, and a single yank brought her in tight to his hips, then one arm banded around her waist. Using it to raise her hips up to his mouth, he growled against her opening, "Turn your head to the side. Don't you dare scream into that mattress. Now fecking let it out."

He lived up to his word. He licked her from back to front. He fucked her with his tongue, making sure to get as deep as he could, massaging her walls. With a single-inch tip of her hips, his mouth suctioned onto her clit again, and his tongue began flicking hard. While it took a few more strokes than half a dozen, he did not give up until she was wailing at the pleasure-pain from the assault of his mouth.

"One more, fireball," he growled.

"I can't," she panted out.

"You will," he commanded, emphasizing the last word.

He dragged her upright, unfolding himself on his back underneath her. Her knees were like jelly, and her body couldn't seem to respond to her brain's orders. After a few moments, he pulled her up to his head, settling her pussy over his mouth. "Sit," he growled.

She lowered herself lightly, and then the sound and sting of a slap to her ass came. "I didn't say hover. I said sit. Or I'll turn you over and spank that pussy until you come."

Was that really supposed to be a threat? Then again, her clit was already tender. She had a feeling he knew how to slap those nerves just right to keep her on edge for a while before letting her come, and then it would probably hurt more than feel good. Giving up the fight, she lowered herself down, nearly smothering him with her thighs on either side of his ears. Another slap, this time to her thigh, and she finally put all her weight on him. Well... he was a surfer. He did all their underwater work. He could probably hold his breath for a long time.

She gave in to him, and as he licked her lips and sucked her clit and fucked her pussy, she let her body take over and began to grind on his mouth, trying to get exactly where and how hard she needed the friction. It wasn't long before she was keening again, this time calling out nonsensical phrases and praying she didn't pass out.

Her prayers went unanswered.

25

APRIL 14, 2023

Demon

Hours later, the sun was beginning its ascent, causing the light to come through the sheers over the French doors. He lay on his back, one arm bent and folded under his head since the pillows were still on the floor somewhere. His other arm was filled with a warm, sleeping woman sated from a massive release of endorphins. Fingers threading through her long red hair, he contemplated the ceiling.

If someone had told him at any point during the last six years that he'd be where he was right now, he'd have punched them in the throat for tormenting him. He didn't deserve this. But the selfish part of him couldn't regret what they'd done, and he'd do it again in a heartbeat. If she still wanted it to be over after the project was complete, he'd have to accept it gracefully and let her go. But if someone came along and hurt her, he'd gut them like he'd gutted a hundred others before he dumped them into the ocean as shark chum.

There was a light snuffling noise to his right as Cherry burrowed deeper into his armpit in her sleep. He let the ghost of a genuine smile form on his face. His little fireball was a perfect match for him sexually. He needed to be in control, and she needed to let it all go to someone because everywhere else, she needed to run the show. No problem. He could keep her satisfied that way.

The smile turned to a frown. Best not to get too used to it. She might only be his to satisfy for a few days.

Afraid to think about that topic too long, he knew of only one way to distract himself from spiraling. Carefully, he slid his arm out from under Cherry and gently turned her onto her back. She snuffled again but didn't wake. The smile returned. She was fecking adorable, and she'd be mortified if anyone knew that she made these little sighs and moans in her sleep. Her eyes were flicking beneath the lids. She was dreaming. About him? The smile turned wicked. Time to find out if he could insert himself into her dreams, and if they weren't about him, they were about to be.

A gentle push and her legs opened enough for him to slip between them. His cock had been erect most of yesterday afternoon, watching her in the dappled sunlight under the banana tree branches. She was stunning. Always had been. He'd almost been able to trick himself into thinking that he was actually married to this beautiful woman and that they were celebrating being tied to one another. When he'd been kissing her for the cameras on the pathway, he didn't think he'd ever been harder. Apparently, that was a lie because now was that moment since it knew it was finally going to find its way home inside her.

Sliding a hand between them, he tested her channel. Even in sleep, she was wet for him. Feck, he'd never get enough of her!

He notched himself at her opening, slipped one hand beneath the cheek lying flat on the mattress, and turned her face up to his. Moving his other hand to frame her face, he leaned in to kiss her as he slid inside her. She was warm and tight. Her walls hugged him as if recognizing that he belonged there. Braced on his forearms, his hands still cradling her cheeks, his thumbs brushing back and forth across her soft skin, he began to slowly rock back and forth.

"Mmm."

Now she was waking up.

He dropped his head into the curve of her neck, placing open-mouthed kisses along the cord to her jaw, the tip of his tongue dipping out briefly to taste the salt of her skin that had dried from her perspiration while he'd eaten her into oblivion. She tasted better than the ocean, the traces of their scents mingling together to tease his nose as he breathed her in and the fluttering of her pulse beneath his tongue. It didn't get much better than this.

"Demon," she whispered, barely awake.

Picking up his head, he saw that her eyes were still closed. He continued to rock slowly in and out of her, knowing she'd wake fully in a few moments. Her brain was likely beginning to allow the sensations to seep into the remnants of her dreams if the upturn of her lips was any indication. He could speed up and wake her faster, but he was enjoying the lazy pace and getting to watch her come out of sleep for him.

"Oh my god, what a way to wake up." She moaned, eyes still closed. "Every morning. This. Want it."

She wanted this every morning? It was the sleepy haze in her brain forcing out her deepest thoughts, and oh, how he wished it could be their ending. He could just imagine it. Make love to her, catch a few waves, then come back to her smelling of the early morning surf, only to tumble her back into the unmade bed and proceed to love her the rest of the day.

"I would give you the world, fireball," he whispered. He knew she wouldn't hear it, but saying it to himself reminded him how true it was.

Her eyes fluttered open, hazy with sleep, but the smile on her lips was beautiful. "Aidan."

He seamed his lips to hers, not breaching them, pouring everything he was feeling into the touch. His hands moved, sliding down under her arms and gripping her shoulders from underneath. The leverage allowed him to get deeper, go harder, without changing the pace. Instinctively, her hips rose and fell to meet his, her hands moving up his arms, over his shoulders, and curling around his neck to wind into his hair. They pulled with just the right bite, making his scalp sting and tingle, and he hissed as he thrust just a bit harder than before.

"You should see yourself in the sun," he told her, low and deep. "Your hair is like fire against the sheets, your gray eyes like the clouds at dusk. I need you so damn much, Esme."

"Love me, Aidan," she pleaded.

"I am, *a chuisle*. I do. You're like breaking the surface of the water. The air I need to breathe," he promised.

Her walls clenched around him, and her legs drew up alongside his hips, squeezing him tight as she came. The added slickness from her orgasm allowed him to delve just a little bit deeper, so far he swore he reached her cervix. A second, softer release swept through her body, and as he followed her over the edge, his lips met the hollow of her throat. *"Taim i' ngra leat,"* he whispered.

He felt her heart rate begin to slow and knew that there was the possibility that even though she didn't know the language, she would understand the meaning anyway and pull away.

This wasn't a fake relationship. It never had been. They'd been sailing to this point since the day they met. She might deny they were committed to one another based on her condition not being met, but the truth was, they only wanted each other. Would never truly be happy without each other, even if they chose to continue to suffer in misery.

Once she realized that—and she was smart, so she would—he hoped she would embrace it, but he would understand if she retreated. She had fears, and in order to control those fears, she had walls. Meeting up with the team wouldn't help because she wouldn't want to let on that they'd slept together other than in the same bed for their undercover work. It didn't matter. They were "them," and no condition or promise would ever change that.

Rolling off her, he lay on his side. One hand drifted down between her legs where the evidence of what they'd done commingled. He drew lazy patterns on the inside of her thigh, then brought his fingers up to his mouth, licking their fluids from his skin. He knew she was watching him, her expression one of both wonder and confusion.

"Flame has written about people doing that, but I didn't think real people actually did," she admitted.

"Most of it I already tasted earlier. If you've forgotten that, I didn't do a very good job of it. Guess I'll have to keep practicing until I get it right."

She rolled her eyes. "I think you know you did more than okay. I've never blacked out from getting eaten out before."

"Hmm. Definitely need a repeat of that, then. But next time? I want it to be in the surf of the ocean." He tilted his head. "Maybe not here though."

He watched her brow crinkle in thought.

"What are you overthinking about now?"

"It wasn't just the extras and me that you were licking."

"What do you mean?"

"You were part of that mixture."

"And?"

"Isn't that like a hard no for guys?"

"I don't know about other guys. Not for me. It's a natural body secretion. Some protein. Calcium. Citrate. Fructose. Glucose. Lactic acid. Magnesium. Potassium. Zinc. Water. Plasma. Mucus. If it's good enough for a woman to swallow, a man can certainly consume it."

"It's a bit... weird that you know that off the top of your head."

He winked. "Doctor knowledge."

"Yeah, but you were a trauma surgeon. Not exactly the right specialty to need to know that."

"Some things stick with you. Besides, you'd be amazed by what I've had to remove in the ER. You know those warnings on things? 'Do not put into any orifice'? Yeah. People don't pay attention to those."

"Oh my god!" she exclaimed, horrified. Her gaze shifted to curiosity. "What was the worst?"

"Male or female?"

Her mouth formed an "O" before she gathered herself to answer. "Let's start with female and ease into the other."

"I don't know about worst, but it was definitely odd. One of those foldable phones. The ones that open like a book, not a flip phone."

Horrified, she asked, "What in the name of all the animals on the ark did she do that for?"

"I was afraid to ask, but I'm nothing if not curious. She said she wanted to see if she could feel the vibrating motion and hear the ring if she was out at a club and didn't want to take a purse or have pockets in her outfit. People are strange. Ironically, she could feel and hear it because it went off during our exam."

Laughing, Cherry gripped her middle. "That's both disgusting and funny."

"Tell me about it. She actually got that pretty far in there. Had to open her up to get it out. I don't think the warranty covered the repairs."

She blinked. "What about male?"

He grimaced. "I don't think you want to know. It freaked me out, and I thought I'd seen everything someone could shove up their vagina or rectum."

"Come on. Tell me." Her eyes got big. "It wasn't you, was it?"

Now it was Demon's turn to laugh. "Umm, no. If you're asking if I've had something up my ass, yes. But not this."

She blinked.

"What? I treated it like research. If I'm going to put my dick up somebody's ass, I want to know what it feels like so I don't hurt them. And don't pretend you didn't know. I know you read every report that comes across your desk."

She blushed. "I wasn't going to bring it up. In case you're wondering, it doesn't bother me though."

He shrugged. "I figured as much, or we wouldn't be here right now. But I'll satisfy your curiosity. Do it well, and it all feels good, fireball."

Her blush deepened. "While that comment is strangely arousing, let's get back to the patient. Obviously, they didn't have another person stuck inside them."

"Nope." He paused. "It was one of those bristle brushes you use to clean a grill with. Apparently, he and his boyfriend had some issues when they were having sex, and he wanted to make sure he got it all cleaned out. Tore himself up pretty badly. There are no bandages for that either. Told him maybe an enema would be a better option next time."

"Who even—? Ugh. I can't."

There was a long pause, and he watched her brow scrunch up again. He felt movement between them. When he looked down, he saw her hand slip between her thighs and between her labia, scoop up a small part of the mixture, then bring it to her lips. Holy hell, horseshoes, and hand grenades! Hot. As. Fuck.

Without a second's thought, he swooped in and pushed his tongue into her mouth, swirling around to catch their flavors again. When he pulled away, her eyes looked distinctly hazy.

"That was hot," she whispered.

"Mm-hmm." He continued kissing her, licking at her lips, dipping in to drag his tongue along her teeth. "We taste good together, fireball."

She wound her arms around his neck, locking them behind his head, and he reciprocated by sliding his arms around her waist, pulling her tight. He felt himself growing hard again as they kissed.

Several minutes later, he confessed, "I hate to say it, but we should go."

He wished they didn't have to. Keeping her like this, all sated and pleasured, was definitely worth more time, but they had a meeting with the team under the guise of a surfing lesson. They needed intel and to tell the team what they'd found.

He wrapped his arms around her again, pulling her close, his nose in her hair as he took a long inhale. "Mmm, you smell good too. All sex and me." With a kiss to her hairline, he rolled away. "I'll call Rayon and have him bring up some breakfast. Go shower."

"Seems sort of counterproductive if I'm just going into the bay," she grumbled.

That raised an eyebrow. "Much as I love the thought of my cum dripping out of you this morning, I'm not sure you want the guys to know about that."

She wrinkled her nose. "Eww. Yeah. I'll shower." She rolled out of bed but stopped after she stood. "We, umm... didn't use anything. I mean, I'm on birth control, but—"

"I know."

"How?"

He raised an eyebrow at her. "I do your blood tests, fireball, and I do your shot."

"Oh. Yeah. Forgot about that," she mumbled. "Who does yours?"

"My shot?" he teased.

"Dick. No, your blood test."

"I do my own."

"How?" she asked. She turned her arms underside up and tried to figure out how that would work. "Ohhhhh..." She looked up at him.

"Not in a very long time, *a chuisle*. Before Tribe," he reassured her. "I was risky in the year between my dismissal and Tribe in a lot of ways. But as far as you and I are concerned, I tested, and I'm all good."

"It's okay. I didn't exactly take any responsibility either."

Sliding out of bed, he stood in front of her, brushing her hair behind her shoulders. "I'll never put you at risk, Cherry. In any way."

"Have you...?" She bit her lip. "Never mind. None of my business. It's not like I can say I haven't either."

"It certainly is your business, but yes, the test was necessary because there have been a few partners. And don't start feeling guilty or some shite. Sex is normal. It feels good, which is why we do it. I don't care if there were a hundred men since we met. You're with me right now, and that's all that matters." He kissed her again and then gave her a light tap to her ass. "Go. Get ready. There's a wetsuit in my bag for you. The water will be cold, so it'll protect you."

"Hope it looks good on me," she said as she smiled, then turned and sashayed to the door.

Demon grinned and headed to the phone. He didn't miss the extra swish to her hips as she walked away. So naughty. Definitely a match for him.

26

APRIL 14, 2023

Cherry

"Part the Red Sea, this is fucking cold," Cherry muttered. She was paddling her board out to where Midas and TB already were, Steel and Demon on either side of her. "Why can't we do this later in the day when it's warmer?"

"Waves are lowest right now, plus we needed to talk sooner rather than later. Besides, the water is always going to feel cold."

They sat straddling their boards in the bay. Steel—playing the part of surf instructor—had led Midas, TB, Cherry, and Demon through the basics on the beach, and now they were in the water, ready to make their first attempt. Demon had admitted to her in private that he couldn't wait to see TB attempting to hop up on the board with his broad frame and weight. He'd even put a body cam on for the occasion, which the behemoth hadn't appeared to notice yet. She could only imagine the razzing the poor man was going to get as soon as Midas posted the videos to the group chat amongst the guys.

Demon was filling them in on lunch and what they'd seen on the tour of the farming operations, but Cherry couldn't concentrate. Normally, she'd have no trouble shoving distractions to the back and focusing on what needed doing, but yesterday had been a bit overwhelming on multiple levels, and her brain was having trouble connecting the dots.

You're with me right now, and that's all that matters.

That's what he'd said before she got into the shower. At the time, she'd just taken it as a declaration. But after a few minutes alone in the shower, her brain started chasing her own tail. It reminded her that this was temporary. Her proposal and he was only adhering to what she wanted, but damn if it didn't bring home the point that she wanted so much more with him.

"Hey," she said suddenly. "Has anyone talked to Waters since we left?"

There were smirks from all the guys, with the exception of a scowl from Steel. Midas informed her, "We talked to him when we were discussing whether or not to bug Zion's meeting. Guess where his happy ass was? On a plane to China. Didn't even make it two days, the fuckstick. What a pussy."

"You wait until it's your turn," Steel warned. "You'll see what it's like when you can't even make it a whole morning at work, let alone a full day."

"Oh yeah?" Midas asked. "What about you, Mr. High Intensity? Think you'll be any better?"

The assassin grunted, looking out to the waves. "Already had my chance. Fucked it up. That only happens once in a lifetime, *hermano.*"

His eyes came back to Cherry, a flash in them that he'd said too much, and then it was gone. He shut down faster than blast doors on a nuclear bunker.

Cherry made an attempt to rescue him before anyone pushed. "That has to be a cause for celebration for you guys. Steel lost his first bet in a year."

Blessedly, they took the bait. Midas informed them, "God was the closest with his five days. He is never going to let up that he took Steel's money."

"The boss man was prompted," Steel grumbled. "If *somebody* hadn't pushed him, he'd have made it the whole twelve weeks, just out of spite." Steel's words sounded irritated, but when he caught Cherry's eye, he winked and gave her a nod. Good. He wasn't mad. In fact, it seemed he approved and was grateful for the save on his blunder. She smiled back.

Midas had been named leader of the project in Waters' absence, so he rallied them back to the topic of their meeting. "All right. Back to work. So tonight, TB will watch the villa, Steel will take the farm, I'll be monitoring the cameras, particularly the orchards, to help Steel out, and D will search the research building."

"Why can't Demon watch the villa?" Cherry asked. "He's already there."

"I'd prefer to be the one there," Demon admitted, "but I'll know more than TB about the medical equipment that might be there."

"D told us what he suspects about the tunnels under the buildings," Steel added. "We want to see how far they go out and in what directions. Could be dead ends with underground levels, but I'm betting no. If these guys are Salieri members, the diamond mines showed us that they have escape routes in their spaces. I'm betting one comes up in the outbuildings somewhere. Probably several. My guess? The machine barns. D said the one you saw was awfully neat and tidy, including a huge open space in the middle."

"Maybe the machine or vehicles were out in the trees?" she guessed.

"Maybe. Not buying it."

"What about me?" Cherry asked. "What do you want me to do?"

"You?" TB asked with a snort. "You're going to be tucked up in bed behind a locked door."

Cherry felt her teeth clench and her body go rigid. "I am not some delicate fucking flower you need to keep in the hothouse or risk the danger of me wilting and dying. I've been doing this as long as all of you. In some cases, longer. How do you think I recruited God and Waters? I can be just as sneaky and invisible as you."

Demon reached out, pulled her board closer, and put a hand on her arm to calm her. "Hey. No one is saying you're not capable. But what if someone comes looking for us? If one of us is missing, you can distract. If both of us are missing? Suspicious as hell."

She deflated slightly. She didn't like it, but she understood the logic. It was doubtful that anyone would come looking for them in their suite, but depending on when they left and how long they were gone, it might be odd if she were seen without him.

"Couldn't I just say we were playing a newlywed game, hunting each other out for some racy sex?"

The team averted their faces, trying not to laugh, but it wasn't working well.

Blushing, she corrected herself. "Whatever. It's all an act, you gits. Fine. I still haven't gotten that information to Zion about Ka-Bar," she reminded them. "I could cover your exit from the property by distracting him with that after dinner. Is that okay, or is it too dangerous to do without my overprotective 'husband'?"

Demon nodded. "That would work. Distraction would help."

"How much time would you need?"

She could see him calculating time in his head. "Thirty, forty-five minutes? I'd need to get upstairs, change, get out. Should be enough time."

"Okay. I'll plan for an hour. Just in case the security staff is extra diligent."

Steel piped in, "Next wave coming in, D take Cherry in. We'll follow, with me bringing in the back end. We'll catch three or four waves each, then we can seem to agree to go to eat together and head to the café Ka-Bar was last seen at. Gem is going to wander in around eleven thirty and try to give us any intel they found. If they can't get to us directly, we've got plan B to meet with whomever it is."

"What's plan B?" she asked.

"Ladies' room," they said in chorus.

"Well, that's not cliché at all."

"But it works," Steel said with a shrug.

Demon looked out over the water. "Get ready, Cherry. I'll hang back. If you have trouble, I'll be right behind you."

"Just don't run me over," she grumbled. She got into position on the board, and as the wave began to push her in, she popped up onto the board without too much difficulty. Unfortunately, when she stood, her balance was precarious, and she only made it about five seconds before feeling herself start to lose her footing.

"Jump, fireball!" Demon reminded her.

Leaning back and to the right, she gave herself as much push as she could into the air to clear the board, her hands and arms immediately going over her head to protect it. She felt the leash around her ankle pull tight, and then she hit the water. The whitewater passed over her, and it felt like forever that she was underneath, but it was really only a few seconds. When her head burst through the water, she heard a chorus of wolf whistles in the background and clapping.

"Way to go, Esme!" one of them shouted.

Suddenly, Demon was on her right in the water and holding onto his board, his grin huge. "Excellent job for your first time!" he praised.

"I fell off," she sputtered. Her eyes, nose, and mouth were full of salty water, her hair in her face where it got ripped free of the knot she'd had it in to keep it back.

"Yeah, but the pop-up was awesome. Midas and TB probably won't even make it into a standing position the first time." He steadied her board so she could clamber back on it and paddle to shore to be out of Midas' way, who was next.

He defied Demon's prediction, managing to at least get his feet under him in a crouch, but as soon as he tried to stand, he fell off. There was worry for a couple of seconds as the board seemed to flip over right on top of him, but apparently, he ended up deep enough that it didn't touch him. "Remember, dude! Hands over your head!" Demon reminded him.

Midas rolled onto the board, gave Demon an obscene finger gesture, and began to paddle into shore.

Cherry turned her eyes out to the waves where TB was getting ready for the next wave.

"What's the bet?" she murmured.

"He'll make it," Midas said confidently.

"I bet lunch for a week with all that weight and height, he lasts three seconds," Cherry said.

Midas laughed. "Oh, ye of little faith. I'll take that bet. I say he makes it in one go."

Demon chuckled. "You're both wrong. He's not even gonna pop up."

Contrary to Demon's opinion, TB did manage to pop up on the board. He also lasted more than three seconds. But the wipeout, Cherry had to admit, was epic. The best part? He screamed like a five-year-old girl as he went ass over tea kettle right into the impact zone.

"Sweet," Midas commented. "That's so going in the chat tonight."

TB came up from under the water, rolled on top of the board, and began to paddle in. "Don't say it," he growled. Pointing a finger at Midas, he threatened, "And if you post that video I know D just took for you, I will set the first older, unhappily married female I see on you, telling her you're a US Navy SEAL, have a twelve-inch cock, and you can go for over forty-eight hours nonstop with a record of twenty-two orgasms in one night."

Midas blushed and laughed. "That's supposed to deter me?"

Steel had ridden in on the wave behind TB, a perfect surf and dismount, running into the shore like a California lifeguard TV star. "What's a deterrent?"

Midas repeated TB's threat, still laughing.

With a look of total seriousness on his face, the former Navy

SEAL shook his head. "*Hermano*, you have no clue. The first third of that, you'll have a stage-five clinger. But the second and third? You'll probably get roofied, kidnapped, and wake up tied to a bench. We'll never see you again. Women love SEALs. It's actually a curse."

After three more waves apiece—Cherry managing to almost get to shore, Midas wiping out twice and then jumping off once, and TB just in general being a total disaster—they headed up to stow their boards, change, and go to a late lunch at the café. At the truck, the men didn't think twice and began to strip down out of their wetsuits. Cherry slapped a hand over her face.

"TMI, guys! I realize I know your files, which include all kinds of measurements, but this is one I don't need to know."

A body came between her and the men, sheltering her view from through the car with a pull of her head to tuck her face into his chest. "I don't want you looking at anyone but me," he whispered.

Three apologies popped up like a round of "Row, Row, Row Your Boat," and doors opened to create barriers.

Midas added, "We forget you're not one of the guys sometimes." He winced when Steel slapped him upside the back of the head. "Oops. That didn't sound right." He started to speak, then stopped. "Yeah, that was going to sound wrong too. I'll shut up now."

Cherry heard their replies, but her senses were too focused on the salty ocean scent of the man who held her in his arms. Didn't matter if he was in the water, just came from it, or had been out for a while, he always smelled exactly the same. Who would have thought that the beach would be a turn-on just based on smell?

Her voice was muffled unintelligibly when she tried to respond. His grip relaxed, and she repeated, "I don't want to look at anyone else."

"Good. Because going around with a blindfold on would be difficult."

She grinned. "Trust me. I know everybody's measurements. Only one of them comes close in that area."

There was a sort of choking noise in his throat. "I didn't need to know that. But you gonna tell me who?"

"Jehovah, no!" She giggled. "It will be much more entertaining for you all to bet on it, and then imagine you measuring."

"You're so bad, little fireball." He smacked her ass lightly. "You guys decent?" he called over his shoulder.

"Relative term," Cherry murmured.

"No shit."

"Yeah, we're good. Wouldn't want to cause her palpitations," TB teased.

"Yeah, anxiety over how poor Flame survives on your tiny dick could cause that," Demon deadpanned.

A wetsuit came flying from the driver's side of the car, through it, and smacked Demon standing in the open passenger side. They smiled at each other.

"We'll walk a few paces and give you a buffer."

As the driver's side doors closed, Steel left the rear passenger door open as an extra shield for Cherry to change behind. Beach modesty was never at a premium among the surfers, so it had its own unwritten rules that everyone followed—no looking, and if you saw someone in between their doors in the lot, you waited a fair distance until the doors closed.

"Do you want me to turn my back?" he murmured.

Her eyes twinkled with mischief. "It's a little late for that chivalry, don't you think?"

"I dunno. Might be a good idea anyway. Seeing all that gorgeousness that is you, I probably won't be able to keep from kissing you. You ready to do that around these guys?"

She bit her lip, thinking over his words. "I don't know that we're really a secret," she whispered.

"No, my feelings for you have been an open window for anyone to look through. We've never talked about it, but it's a definite shift in our dynamic, and someone might blurt something out that makes you uncomfortable."

"I'm pretty sure I'll survive." Turning her back to him, she ordered him, "Unzip me."

She held her breath as she waited to see what he'd do. Moments later, she swore she heard a soft sigh as he swept her hair over her shoulder, then gently, and making a concentrated effort to only touch the suit, he pulled the zipper down to her waist.

She turned around to face him. "Help me peel this off."

"Feck." His voice was so quiet, she wasn't sure she had heard him.

When she looked up, he'd pulled his sunglasses down over his eyes. She reached up, pulled them from his face, and put them atop her head. "Don't hide from me, Demon. If you want everything from me, I want everything from you."

He inhaled, appearing like he was locked in place.

Would he rebuff her? She knew she was asking too much. He could never give her everything. Kubrick and Flame were right. He was who he was.

He came to his decision relatively quickly by reaching for the neckline of the wetsuit, slowly pulling it from her chest and down her arms. When it dropped at her waist to hang loose, he groaned. His hands reached out to palm her breasts, giving them a gentle squeeze, then used the backs of his fingers to brush up from the bottom of the globes, up over her nipples, and then his lips were moving in time to his smoothing fingers over her shoulders to spear into her hair. The crash of him against her mouth caused her to gasp, allowing his tongue inside to seek and destroy.

She stepped the last centimeters into him, her hands gripping his waist and grinding her stomach against his hard cock. There was a van next to them, which she suddenly found herself lifted up, her back against the side. The weight of his body kept her in place so that he could grab under her thighs and put her legs around his waist. "Well, damn," he mumbled against her mouth. "Forgot you still had the fecking suit on down below. It's like rubbing one out against an inner tube."

She couldn't help laughing out loud, her head tipping back.

A sharp whistle came from somewhere close in the parking lot, signaling a car was coming. Demon set her down, and while Cherry shed the rest of her wetsuit, Demon shook out the airy dress she had brought along to change into. When she stood straight, he threw it over her head, put her arms through the sleeves, and smoothed out the skirt while she protested. "I'm missing some foundational pieces," she told him. She tried to reach around him to at least grab the panties in her bag.

He grabbed her hands, moving them to her sides. "Nope. Don't need them."

He quickly shed his wetsuit, hidden by the door, as the car drove by, a group of girls and surfboards egging him on. Cherry was pissed for half a second, then realized he hadn't even twitched at the praise.

He pulled on a pair of baggy cargo shorts, shrugged into an athletic T-shirt, and shoved his feet into flip-flops. As he ran his fingers several times through his hair to get the tangles out, he realized she was looking at him thoughtfully. "What?"

"You didn't hear that?"

"Hear what?" He looked genuinely confused, scanning the area.

"The girls."

"What girls?"

"Holy Moses! The whistles and invitations? The jeep that just drove past?"

He shrugged. "Nope."

"How the hell are you any good in the field? Don't you need to be able to hear everything? Pay attention to shit so you don't die?"

"I am paying attention," he claimed. Hands on his hips, he looked put out that she was suggesting otherwise.

"They were right behind our truck. You didn't even flinch, and they were loud enough that I did, and I saw them coming."

"Not important noise. I filter shite out I don't need or want." He put one arm around her waist and pulled her close again. "Only one woman in my life right now, and she's gonna keep me plenty busy.

No desire for empty shite that's high-maintenance and as inconstant as the waves."

He began kissing her again, but another whistle brought them out of it. "Hey!" Steel peeked his head around the corner of the van. "Lovebirds! We're gonna be late."

"Later," he promised her. Clearly frustrated, Demon let go of her and turned to slam the door closed. He hung their wetsuits on the rail of the truck as she closed the front passenger door, then threaded their fingers together as she followed him around the back of the vehicles with no intent to let go.

Each of the three team members caught a quick glance down at their hands, and TB muttered, "Four down." Other than that, nothing was said, and nothing was acknowledged. Approval had been stamped on them. If only they knew it was temporary, not that they'd believe her if she told them.

APRIL 14, 2023

Demon

They sat in the restaurant at a table next to the rail, looking over the bay. The conversation had been mostly about Flame's last book and Kubrick's current movie shoot.

"Excuse me, ma'am. You lost your napkin."

Demon, his arm loosely around the back of Cherry's chair, looked up to see a waitress standing next to her, placing the crumpled cloth napkin on the table beside her place setting.

"Yes, thank you."

The girl nodded and refilled all of their water glasses. Under her breath, she told them, "Table by the door." Louder, she wished them a good meal and carried on back to the kitchen, filling water glasses on her way.

TB swore to himself. "Gem couldn't reach us. We're being watched."

Cherry picked up the napkin and laid it in her lap. Demon snuck his hand onto her thigh and felt for whatever the girl slipped to Cherry. It was a room key to a local boutique hotel. Apparently, that's where they needed to meet.

"Yes," Demon agreed, glancing into his lap. "Meetup has moved. Five thirteen at the *Casa del Mare*." He slipped the key card into his side pocket.

"Slick. Room number on the card," Midas praised.

He placed his hand back onto her thigh, his hands unobtrusively bunching up the filmy layers of her skirt and sliding his hand along her mid thigh, curving his hand along the inside. He felt her shift slightly to spread her legs a little more. To put her leg closer to him or to give him more access? Feck. Fun as that might be, he'd leave the surreptitious orgasms during a meal to their exhibitionist former teammate. Instead, he gave her a little squeeze and tapped her skin with his forefinger as if to remind her they were being watched and not just by possible bad guys.

"Midas, you find out anything from your searches?"

"Yeah. None of it good. Felix Giudici. Italian banker. Based out of Rome. Interesting fact—he's the leading donor to *Bananato del Sole* toward the upkeep, as well as being heavily invested in the ongoing sustainability measures. There are also some ruins on the property that he funded the excavation for. His investment is so large he could buy the joint. Red flag central. Not currently married, but he has a son, twenty years old, attending Oxford, and following in dad's footsteps, it appears. Upon diving deeper into his history, the mother is the mystery woman I told you about yesterday. He met and married her while working in Switzerland. Married quick, had the baby, a boy of course, then under a month later, she died after hitting her head against a tree in a skiing accident. No records of her being treated at any hospital. No one in Italy, or elsewhere, had ever seen her." The table shared a look. "Son has a reputation for the ladies, but... no one sticks."

Demon felt Cherry shiver next to him. He removed his hand from her bare leg, smoothed her skirt back down, and he curled his arm around the back of her chair, one hand loosely hanging over her shoulder and a finger tracing back and forth over her clavicle, lending her the warmth of his body. "Let me guess. Almost all of the investors are widowers or single and only have sons for children. Motherfeckers."

"Yeah, that's the bulk of them," Midas confirmed. "There are a few married couples, some with girls, but they're few and far between."

"Cover," TB said behind his coffee cup. "Gotta have some honest investors to hide the real nature of their shit."

"What about General Howard?" Cherry asked. Demon heard the trepidation forming in her question.

"Bit murkier there, but nothing evades me. Widower, no formal children. I'm thinking after the death of their daughter, he removed the wife to pave the way for a future Mrs. Howard, but there's no record of another child or woman. However... he fostered a fellow soldier's son for two years after the father was killed in action. At eighteen, the boy up and left. Moved halfway across the country. No contact with Howard since. Sixteen years now."

"You think he tried to recruit the boy, and the kid resisted? Shades of that kid Andres' father driving his car off the cliff."

"Sounds like it to me," TB agreed. "Must have shown signs he wasn't going to be amenable because he wouldn't be alive if he knew the operation. Think we should reach out to him anyway?"

"Already did. Waters and God approved it this morning when you were first dragging your sorry asses out of bed. No word yet, but it's early hours there. No guarantee he'll return the call. God is fielding it, so he'll let us know if he finds anything."

"What about the plantation manager?" Cherry asked.

Midas looked out into the bay. "Probably the most disturbing of the three. The plantation is registered and semi-protected by the government. Something connected to that excavation I mentioned earlier. They're claiming residency that predates the Arawaks, but there are minimal records, only verified by verbal witnesses in the early years and passed down orally until written records came into play. The land is as close to a national landmark as they can get.

"Banana farming in St. Lucia has taken a nosedive in recent years, except for *Bananato del Sole*, which made a huge recovery. Like most Caribbean countries, their primary economy has been driven toward tourism. In the early two thousands, in walks Zion Norton with a small cadre of investors—Bosworth, Giudici, and Howard among them—with a huge cash investment to take the farm from barely scraping by to profitable. Following the tech advancements, suddenly there's cash to push the product, renovations begin, and by 2006, the groves are the most successful in the country."

Steel grunted. "Can you say 'money laundering'?"

Midas continued, "Most interesting thing I found was in a personal diary." He moved to lean on his forearms on the table. His voice lowered. "A local doctor recorded his suspicions that one of Deschamps' ancestors, back three or four generations, might have murdered his wife shortly after the birth of their son. He suspected she was deliberately exposed to infection and died from it."

"It would not have been a pleasant end," Demon added.

"Back then, it was easier to get away with murder. Things like infection, poisoning by bad food, and unwitnessed accidents happened daily."

"How the hell did you get access to someone's personal diary?" TB asked.

Midas looked at him innocently. "I got a library card, faked some credentials showing I was working on my genealogy, looking to get access to personal records in my family. How do you think I got it?"

Rolling his eyes as if to say, "You are such a nerd," TB shook his head.

Demon asked, "What about the kid? The grandson. Andres."

"That's the creepy part." He confirmed the story Cherry had overheard, then added a new detail. "Turns out Andres disappeared from home for about nine months. When he left, he was a gregarious twelve-year-old. When he came back? His whole demeanor, supposedly, changed. He became quiet. Introverted. Almost to the point of being mute."

"Sounds like him," Demon agreed. "He said very little unless directly prompted. Respectful, but soft-spoken." He flashed the table a look. "He appears to have developed a crush on Cherry."

Steel chuckled. "Some competition for you."

"Please. Like an eighteen-year-old boy could replace the ocean god here."

Demon leaned over and kissed her ear, then whispered, "Ocean god, am I? Remind me to lay you on the sand and rise up naked out of the water for you."

"Stop it!" she hissed.

"Then don't put that image in my head." He kissed her ear again and affected nonchalance as he sat next to her.

The three men on the other side of the table weren't fooled.

"Okay then," TB said. "We've got some time to kill before we meet up with Gem, so what's the plan?"

"I'm going to take Cherry around the town. We mentioned visiting the shops yesterday, so we should follow through. Then, if we enter the hotel, it probably won't be looked at weirdly. Newlywed couple looking for privacy for an afternoon tryst."

"We'll have to scatter," Steel said.

"I'll be back at home base, digging into this stuff," Midas said.

"I'll go back to the beach," TB offered. "Play stupid tourist who ignores signage and wanders 'accidentally' onto *Les Vergers'* private beach and see what happens."

Midas warned, "Be careful not to piss anyone off and get on security's radar."

"No worries," the giant placated their project leader. "I've got a plan."

"That's what worries me," Midas grumbled. "Steel?"

"I'm going to take a ride out of the city. If I head, initially, out toward the plantation, I might pick up a tail. Lead 'em on a little chase this afternoon."

Demon put his sunglasses on and glanced out his peripheral at the table where their observers were sitting. "There are only two of them at the table. They could split up. Send a text if you draw one of them into following you."

With that, the group rose from the table, shook hands as if saying goodbye to their new surfing friends, and left the café.

As expected, the two men trying to look like tourists left shortly after them. Demon and Cherry stopped in front of a shop window so that he could watch them. Steel was obviously aware that the men were intending to follow the couple, so he faked a phone call, purposefully looking like he was doing something shady in relation to them, then hustled into the truck, taking off toward the main highway north. There was a short discussion between the two men, and they decided to split up. One got into a car and followed Steel. The other followed Demon and Cherry down the city streets.

"We're one of the lucky ones being followed. Guess that gives me a lot of excuses to kiss and touch you," he warned.

"You don't exactly need an excuse."

He smiled. "That is correct."

28

APRIL 14, 2023

Demon

At five o'clock, Demon and Cherry stumbled into *Casa del Mare*, cuddling like the perfect newlywed couple. After a discreet stop at registration, Demon had secured a room. When they stepped into the old-fashioned elevator, he pressed the button for the fourth floor. Departing the carriage, he scanned the halls for cameras. Nothing. There was a door at the end of the hall marked Stairs and had no obvious alarms, so they went down the hall, through the door, up to the fifth floor, and knocked on room 513. Gem opened the door, and she let them slip into the room. The other three team members were already there, along with a surprise guest.

Ka-Bar.

Demon and Cherry stood there, dumbfounded.

"Sorry," Gem apologized. "I had no way to warn you. We didn't want to take the chance of anything being picked up on digital channels."

Ka-Bar jumped in before they could ask questions. "I don't have a lot of time, so in-depth explanations and whatnot are going to have to wait for another time."

"You being watched?" Demon asked.

"Always. Plus, they've got me chipped. I'm supposed to be here right now but heading to *Bananato del Sole* to head back to Rome."

"The airstrip," Cherry guessed. "That's how you're getting in and out of places without being recorded. They've got a network, don't they?"

"Yes. Worldwide. I've only seen a few. Here. Egypt. Italy. Russia. Several stateside."

"What do you have for us?" Demon asked.

"I already gave Midas the ID packages on my meet and greet that Gem took pictures of. Confirmation of Henry Kroll and Emiliano Carvahlo. The latter hooked up with the Salieri four years ago and pretty much works side by side with Kroll. Both are not guys you want to mess with."

"Are they in town?"

"No. They're off picking up a shipment." Ka-Bar snarled at the last word, leaving no doubt as to what that shipment was. "The two yahoos following you all are my 'security' with the exit of the Kaders after the South Africa incident."

"'Exit' meaning dead?" TB asked.

"Yup. Had to take care of that myself to prove my loyalty. No skin off my nose. Those guys should have been put down as soon as they threatened Zahra."

Demon turned to Steel. "Did you get rid of Mr. Creepy?"

"Lost him on some back roads heading toward Sulphur Springs. Might have a couple of tires leaking air. Oops. You lose your guy?"

"No. Mr. Crawly is down in the lobby trying to figure out how to bribe the front desk clerk for our room number. I promised the guy twice whatever anyone might offer him if he didn't give it up, since he's my wife's recently spurned, abusive fiancé. We should be good."

"Smart cover story."

Demon looked up at Ka-Bar. "I know why you ended up with these arseholes, but why are you still with them? You can't tell me you couldn't have found a way, given your reputation."

"At first, I stayed because they claimed they had Zahra. I had no way of knowing for sure that it wasn't true until Gem confirmed it. When I knew she was safe with you guys, I figured I might as well stay and see if I couldn't dig around, find out everything I could, then start tearing down from the inside. But this group is so fucking big, I don't know that they can ever be routed out entirely.

"As best I can tell, they've got hundreds of thousands of members on every continent and in every country. Everyone from the rank and file, like warehouse workers at the plantation, to bankers like Giudici. On the surface, they all seem like normal, everyday men. No one questions the sudden deaths of wives or the births of only sons because they're so spread out from each other. I'll probably be able to say I'll never be surprised again by what I've seen because of this. I could never have come up with their bullshit in a million years."

"How do you stand by?" Cherry asked. "How can you watch what happens to these women? Their daughters? Hell, even their sons?"

Ka-Bar had the nerve to look properly chastised. "Because I have to. Believe me, it's sickening. I thought I would become immune with time, but so far, it hasn't happened yet. Protecting Zahra and my son though? I'd do anything for them, even if it means falling in line with these assholes. Hopefully, it won't end this way, and Mythos will extract me at some point. But until they do, my job is here."

"So you're expendable if it gets Loki the information he wants?" TB growled.

The SEAL barked out a laugh. "Loki? You think Loki's in charge? He's more like the enforcer of a motorcycle club. Blunt instrument to take out the trash. He's not calling any of the shots."

"Guess that takes a couple of us out of the betting pool," Midas mumbled.

"Make no mistake though. We're all expendable, really." He

tossed a head nod toward Midas. "Your computer geek here has some more intel on your major players. My biggest thing right now is trying to access shipment schedules. I'm not trusted with any of that, so it's slow going. I've supervised drop-offs, but the logistics people are all privately contracted and intermediaries, not the ones in charge. Hell, some of them don't even know what they're moving, although I think most of them have a good idea. Asking questions just gets people killed, so they probably figure the less they know, the better."

"This fuckery needs to end," Steel muttered. "Did Midas share our intel with you?"

"We hadn't gotten that far yet," Midas admitted. His attention back on Ka-Bar, he said, "We're going to be doing some spying tonight. Demon thinks there are tunnels underneath the banana trees."

"That I can't confirm. I was here strictly to pick up cash exchanged at the meeting yesterday. This is the first time I've been on Norton's property, although I've never met the man. What I can tell you is that their Italy, Egypt, and mine locations all had underground systems. Not a big leap in logic to assume other facilities would have them as well. I'd love to help, but I'm headed to the airstrip as soon as I leave here. I might be able to do one or two things to draw security's attention in the fields and at the estate for you. Not miracles. Just more diversionary so that you can get in easier. You're on your own after that." He cast a look at Demon. "Buildings I can't help you with."

"No worries. Got myself a key card. Snatched it from the golf cart on our tour yesterday."

"Hopefully, they didn't notice it go missing," Midas commented.

"Think positive."

"Who are you, and what did you do with D?"

Demon glared at him.

Rolling his eyes, Midas went back to work on his computer. "I'll dig into their system and see if they made any new cards since after you swiped that one."

"Good idea," Ka-Bar said. "And whatever you do, be careful. These assholes are not people who are going to play by any rules other than their own."

"We will. Take care."

Nodding, Ka-Bar left the room, and the Tribe members reviewed their plan for the evening. When that was done, one by one, they ducked out of the room. Midas was last with the parting shot of "Gem said the room is reserved until tomorrow morning." With a wink, he left.

As soon as the door closed, Demon grabbed Cherry's hand and reeled her into his chest. "Come here," he ordered. His hands ran over her arms, drifting down to palm the small of her back with one hand and tilt her head with the other. "It's been too long since I've tasted you."

"You kissed me stupid in the jewelry store. That was less than an hour ago."

"Exactly. Too long."

Fifteen minutes later, she was prostrate across the bed, hair fully mussed, lipstick gone, and her chest heaving from the mouth that just left between her legs. In the early moments, she'd managed to get his shirt off, but then he'd attacked with his tongue, thrashing at her clit, taking long, hard licks of her slit, then taking his spit and her own fluids and returning to her clit.

He rose up tall on his knees between her legs, and Cherry sat up, pulling him to a standing position. She reached for his belt, making short work of pulling the strap, freeing the prong from the leather, sliding it through the buckle, and pulling it free with the slithering sound giving her gooseflesh. His hands joined hers, freeing the button and zipper of the material and shoving his shorts down to rest around his spread thighs.

After smoothing his palm over the head of his cock to spread the precum welling there, he wrapped his free hand around the base, holding himself steady as he stroked up and down his length. He watched Cherry stare at him, and he could almost see her cataloging how he pleasured himself, noting what spots caused him to hitch his breath, which caused him to moan, and which caused his eyes to glitter with need. She watched the pulls and squeezes, watched where he placed his fingers and how they were tight to the vein on the underside, giving him friction.

When she pried his hands free of himself, she placed one hand on his thigh and replaced his other hand with her own around the base, squeezing tight and burying him in her mouth in one full stroke. He was long. Just too long to take all the way, but damn if she didn't act like she wasn't going to find a way.

She almost undid him when she curled her tongue along the underside of his dick, making sure to hollow her cheeks and suck hard as she dragged her lips along his skin to the tip, then loosened her hold before plunging back down.

"Feck, fireball! Your mouth is as wet as your pussy after I've eaten you."

The hand on his thigh reached for his hand closest to her and brought it to the back of her head.

"You sure?" he groaned. "Your mouth feels way too good. I might lose control and hurt you without meaning to if I go too hard."

Pulling off him, she assured him, "You'd never hurt me. You know I can take it. I want it. I want you so far down my throat when you come, I can't possibly pull back." She dove back onto his cock, pushing until he was at the top of her throat, then relaxed and widened her jaw to take him just that slight bit further. In a few strokes, she'd be able to accept more, and he bet she'd keep going until she helped him give her what she'd asked for.

"Feck!" Both hands cradled her head, gently exerting pressure as she slid back and forth across his dick. "Gonna feck that pretty mouth so hard. Hang on, *a chuisle*."

With each stroke, his speed, pressure, and depth increased until he was sliding into the back of her throat, her face tight to his stomach. He was working up a wetness he'd never experienced when getting a blow job before, and he could see it pouring from her mouth, over her chin, and falling to the floor between them.

"Gonna come, Cherry. If you've changed your mind, pull back now."

She popped off him. "Pull back? Are you nuts? If I were standing in front of St. Peter and I was offered the choice of going through the gates or swallowing your cum, the devil can have us both."

What little tension had been lost from her brief stoppage was instantly back as she swallowed him deep, trying to burrow into his body to get every bit of him inside her mouth. Her hands clutched his ass, pulling him closer, and as he expelled her name with his orgasm, he heard her moan as she swallowed every drop.

When he was done emptying into her mouth, his fingers loosened and reflexively massaged where he'd been anchoring them along the back of her head. She pulled back to look up at him, her eyes still leaking tears from every thrust. Every intimate encounter proved one more way she was his match.

His thumbs brushed away the tears. He brought them up to his mouth, cleaning them off his skin, before he gently shoved her back onto the bed, climbed on it to straddle her bent legs, kissed the hell out of her, and took any remaining traces of his release from the cavern.

Fisting the skirt on her dress, he rucked it up around her waist. He followed that by peeling the loose top portion over her shoulders and underneath her breasts, which he'd been aching to touch all afternoon. Thank god he hadn't let her put a bra on underneath her clothes.

"I do not have time to dirty you up the way I want to. Feck! Knew you'd be beautiful under those suits, but you're too beautiful for this world. It's almost blinding," he admitted. His mouth dropped down over a breast as his hand cupped the flesh, then opened over the areola to take in as much of the flesh as it could. Without letting go, he slid his other hand between them, taking hold of his cock and lining it up to her opening, thrusting hard and fast.

Each pounding stroke caused the bed to shift, the old-fashioned springs creaking with the force. There was a momentary rational thought of being thankful she was across the bed; otherwise, the headboard would be denting the wall, letting the entire hotel know what they were doing. But then it didn't matter because he changed the position of her hips to drag across her G-spot and grind his pelvic bones against her clit, causing her to come with a wail so loud the hotel guests would know anyway.

Oh well.

He felt a wave pass through his body, felt his rhythm stutter, and then he froze, buried so far inside her, it was like they were permanently joined. A shouted curse in Gaelic flew from his mouth, and then he pulled back slightly before grinding against her clit and toppled her into a second orgasm.

Eventually, he pulled free of her and rolled to her side, lying on his back, one arm bent over his eyes, not even bothering to worry that they'd never gotten completely undressed. The other arm slid under her shoulders and pulled her tight to his side. They lay like that, silent, listening to the sounds drifting up from the street as people went to and from the shops, restaurants, and beach.

"I don't want to go back to the estate," she whispered, her finger tracing his abs row by row, then up the centerline only to follow them back down again.

He lifted his arm and rolled onto his side to face her. Grabbing her top leg, he pulled it so her thigh rested over his legs trapped in the shorts still around his legs. He smoothed the sweaty hairs on her forehead back. "I don't want you to go back there either, *a chuisle.*"

"No, I mean, I don't want to leave here. This."

His eyes flicked between hers as if trying to read how serious she was. This moment was huge. Was she saying she was willing to overlook her condition? He seemed to come to some sort of conclusion because he tipped her chin with a single finger so he could place his lips against her forehead as he spoke. "We don't have to leave 'here' or 'this.' 'Here' and 'this' are feelings, Cherry. They're not a physical place. They're just... us."

"For such a BAMF, you sure are philosophical about love."

It was minuscule, but he felt himself tighten. Then it was gone. "Only with you." He kissed her again, and she snaked her arms around him, holding him tight. "Do you mean it?" Even he could hear the vulnerability in his question. It would tear his heart to shreds if it were something said merely in the afterglow. "I don't want you to regret changing your mind. It was important to you."

A tear leaked from one eye to trail down toward her ear. "I mean it," she whispered. "That condition has always been there out of fear. The most important people in my life have been taken away from me by things out of my control. But that's the way it is most of the time, right? If something like that can be controlled, the only one who really has a say is the person who leaves.

"Unfortunately, life takes things, often not caring if you or they deserve it, or caused it, or whatever. I was a child when I promised myself not to allow anyone in who put themself into a position where they could be taken from me by something I didn't have a say in. It's just taken me a very long time to grow up and realize that there's very little in life I can control. But I can control this. I can control having you in my life, and I'd be stupid to let that go." She kissed his shoulder. "Understand. I'm not comfortable with it. I can't promise not to wish for this addiction of yours to be otherwise, but I'm willing to work with it. When you're ready to give it up, I'll be behind you all the way. And I won't be disappointed if you fall. No one will. You're family, and family helps each other when they struggle."

Those three words he so desperately wanted to say lodged in his throat. He'd told her the night they'd made love, but it had been in Gaelic, and she hadn't understood. Probably just thought it was another endearment. He wanted to say the words to her in English, but this wasn't the time. Not in this hotel and not while on this project. But it was coming.

He swallowed hard. Hands holding her head in place so that

their gazes locked, he said what, in the long run, probably communicated those three coveted words in a much better way. "I promise, Esme. I promise I'll do everything I can not to let you down."

He watched tears well up in her eyes. She understood how much it took for him to say those two words. Gathering her close, he urged, "Rest for a bit. We've got time before we need to be back. If you fall asleep, I'll wake you."

29

APRIL 14, 2023

Cherry

"Knock, knock."

Cherry stood in the doorway of Zion's office, papers in hand. It wasn't lost on her that almost twenty-six years ago, she'd done the same thing in her father's doorway the day he disappeared. Only this time, she wasn't seeking the critique of someone she respected. Instead, she was serving as a distraction for Demon to get out of the villa, as well as see if Ka-Bar's picture shook anything loose.

Zion looked up from the eight-by-eleven piece of paper he held. He flipped it upside down on his desk and smiled at her. It was the cold smile he reserved for when he was displeased, but he wanted to keep his thoughts from the witness. "Come in, Esme. What brings you to my dark and dingy office?"

She crossed to the front of his desk but didn't sit. Whatever he'd been looking at was a photo. She wondered if she could lure him out of his office somehow and get a look at his desk.

She extended her hand with the papers to him. "In all of the excitement yesterday, I never got this to you. It's the information on my friend's brother."

Without looking at the papers, Zion reached out his hand to her and took the stack. "Thank you. I'll give the commissioner a call in the morning. No promises, remember, but I'll see what I can find out about your friend, Kent."

It was out of her mouth before she could hold it back. "I didn't tell you his name," she whispered. As soon as it came out, she knew it was a mistake. Archangels and seraphims, he knew Ka-Bar! Obviously they knew who he was because of Zahra and their son, but did they know he was collecting intel on them? She should have held it back. She shouldn't have registered his slipup. Now she was in a lot of trouble, and she knew it.

His eyebrows rose, and he smiled ruefully. "No? No, I guess you didn't." His fingers played with the upside-down photograph on his desk. "You have the innate power to make men act foolishly, Esme."

"I don't understand. How do I make men act foolishly?"

Elbows retracted to the arms of his leather desk chair, he made a pyramid with his hands under his chin. "Simply by existing, my dear. Your father? Yourself? Neither of you had any idea what was being planned for you, personally, in the shadows."

"I don't know what you're talking about," she protested.

"You are the modern-day equivalent of Helen of Troy—making men yearn to possess you, even if it drives them to the brink of destruction. To a point where no sacrifice is too great."

She frowned in confusion.

"Don't worry, my dear. It's not your fault. There are just some women in this world who possess the ability to twist men's minds. They don't mean to do it. It just happens."

Her voice shook as she spoke. "I knew that something wasn't right. Something about you made me uncomfortable. Even after all these years, I second-guessed your interest, trying to convince myself that my father's best friend couldn't possibly be so perverted as to lust after his underage daughter."

He chuckled. "Oh, it wasn't me who wanted you. My tastes run a bit more... exotic. However, I was an inroad to you, which I have always regretted. Because of that, I foolishly tried to intercede in the plans that were being made to take you from your father. I assumed that my standing with the Salieri would be enough to protect you from the danger that awaited you."

"Danger? What danger could I possibly have been in?"

"General Howard."

"Zion, you're not making sense."

"When your mother died, General Howard visited to pay his respects. He was captivated by the precocious young daughter who seemed so composed at the funeral of her mother. He saw you as strong. Resilient. He became fascinated with you."

"I was six years old," she protested.

"Oh, it wasn't sexual," Zion replied. "Did you know he'd had a daughter? She was killed while riding her bicycle, and her death was ripping his marriage apart. The accident happened shortly before your mother died, and she would have been about your age. In his grief, I think his mind suddenly turned you into his daughter.

"Over time, his fascination with you grew. Around the time your father and I became partners, it was clear Howard always knew more about you than he should have, and that should have been a warning to us that it was growing into an obsession. But by the time I realized his feelings were growing into something else, you were turning sixteen, and graduation was looming."

Somewhere in the course of Zion's confession, Cherry had collapsed into one of the chairs in front of his desk. Her eyes were glued to his face, and her ears were burning with the information they were hearing, but she couldn't seem to force any words out of her mouth. The whole situation was ludicrous!

"Howard declared to our elder that he wanted you as his bride. He had plans for the removal of his current wife, whom he was essentially married to in name only since the death of their daughter. He furthered his case by informing the Worthy—our seven leaders—that your father had somehow learned about us and was investigating with the intent to reveal us to the world. That simply couldn't happen, so approval was given as long as taking you for a bride included the termination of your father."

Her stomach heaved. Zion was involved and had known the day he disappeared that her dad was never coming back. Worse yet, he was covering for whoever had taken him.

"Were you involved in my father's disappearance?"

He rose from his chair, tugged his suit jacket down, smoothed it, and crossed to the window. His hands were lightly clasped behind him as he stared out the glass. "Directly? No."

He turned his head in profile. "When I learned what was happening, I tried to intercede without jeopardizing my position. Erroneously, I believed that if I could get you to Italy, studying abroad, living in my home, perhaps you'd fall in love with me. Then I could protect you with my name and position."

He turned to look out the window again. "In the long run, it didn't matter. Given my position as your father's partner, I realize now that I wasn't allowed much information. The events of your graduation day were set in motion without my knowledge. My guess is that either Howard fed your father the information as a means to convince the elders to eliminate him as an obstacle and give you over as a bride, or possibly your father discovered something on his own and decided to confide his suspicions to Howard. Either way, approval was given, with the caveat that your father be terminated.

"I made one final effort on the day your father was taken. I hoped that in your vulnerable state, I could get you away from the house and to St. Lucia, where I could hide you temporarily. At least until I secured your agreement to marry me. I should have known you'd be stubbornly loyal, and because you were eighteen, I couldn't use legal guardianship as a means to force you to come with me."

"Then why wasn't I kidnapped along with my father?"

"That's where I was foolish over you for the first time. I thought I could allow you to live your life without interference and still protect you from any danger that brought you into. You see, I thought I had far more power than I actually did—a common character flaw among young men at that age. But what I did have was money. Lots of it. And since that didn't seem to work to seduce you into my protection, I used it with the Salieri, whom I knew it would work with. Basically, I bought your freedom. My error was in believing that if I just left you alone, you'd be safe. From Howard. The Salieri. Yourself."

There was a click behind her. Over her shoulder, she noticed Matthew had entered the room, closed the door behind him, and stood in front of it. His hands were folded one over the other in front of him, but she didn't mistake his posture as relaxed. He would be ready with a weapon before she could even get to the French doors fifteen feet away.

Zion returned to the desk. He reached to flip over the photo he'd been looking at when she arrived in the room. It was Demon and her at the café the day she and Gem had nearly been blown up, where he had her pulled tight to his chest.

She swallowed hard as he reached for a manila envelope that held about an inch's worth of paper. He pulled them out and revealed a series of photos, which he dropped one by one face up on his desk.

She looked up at him. "Spying on me?"

"Part of what I purchased the day I saved you from General Howard was the responsibility of keeping an eye on you. We had to be sure you weren't aware of what your father had found out. So yes, I watched you.

"Early on, my observations led me to believe that while you were still going to put your brilliant mind to work, you were wracked with grief and totally unaware of what your father had been stirring up. I watched you shield yourself from the world at large. At first, I admit, I was concerned and confused. You never took a formal position anywhere, and I wondered why you were letting your education go to waste. Why did you simply disappear? Why weren't you taking advantage of your gifts with any one of the universities that had to be clamoring for someone like you to teach other brilliant minds? Why weren't you being lured into some corporate think tank or government position worthy of your skills?"

He gave a sardonic laugh. "And then I realized. You weren't grieving. You were plotting. You didn't do any of those things because you had your own plans. You were building your own corporation, independently, silently. Why? What could possibly be so important for you to keep it so secret?

"I started watching a little closer, and as Tribe began to take shape, it became clear that you were building an army. A small one, but an army nonetheless. Your selection of Royal Devlin as the voice of Tribe. The recruitment of the team that, had I been paying attention, I would have seen for the threat they were.

"Still, I didn't interfere. Whether I didn't see it or I refused to see it, I convinced myself that your trajectory seemed to be different from mine. That's where I was foolish a second time. I stopped watching as intently. Shame on me. I let my fondness for you blind me to the danger you represented. I should have known there was only one thing that would motivate Esme Bosworth to work in the shadows as she was. Finding her father."

"Your fondness for me?" she spat. "You may not have wanted to fuck me, but you were a predator just the same."

The hand moved so quickly, she didn't have time to protect herself from the slap across her face. In fact, the assault didn't even register with her until it was over with, and she'd shaken the stars from her vision. When she turned back toward Zion, it was to find his face filled with fury—an expression she'd never witnessed on him before, and it was terrifying.

"Yes, my fondness for you. I could have let Howard take you. You would have become his bride, and when he descended so far into madness that he was a detriment to the Salieri, they would have terminated him and you, simply by association. Instead, you've lived twenty-six years of life you weren't meant to have."

Suddenly, he seemed to remember himself, pulling down his jacket from where it gathered awkwardly from slapping her. Straightening his tie. Smoothing back the hair that had broken free of the confines of its sleek styling.

He continued, much calmer now. "You brought this on yourself now. There's nothing I can do to stop it. When Tribe officially stepped into my world, with your team leader intercepting my shipment five years ago? That was my ticket into elder status of the Salieri, and your golden boy fucked it up but good when he set those people free.

"It was one thing to intercept a shipment when you didn't know what you were interfering with. But combine the fact that it was your team and the setback of years' worth of work to get to that point? I couldn't let that go. I watched and waited for two years to get my revenge. And when I got it? I got it good. Being patient was worth the wait, and I was happy to get at least some satisfaction out of taking it out of his hide, literally, when he tried to rescue his sister."

"You killed Sarah?" She heard the wobble in her voice. The inherent plea for him to deny the truth.

"I wanted to see the devastation on her brother's face when we finally broke her to nothing. I didn't take part in the events that day other than to physically make sure he saw every moment of what was done to her. I wanted him to know that no one was safe if they got in my way. Then his men showed up, and it was a close call for me. Luckily, they weren't interested in chasing anyone away, just killing whoever got in the way of rescuing their boss. I managed to escape to fight another day."

Cherry's heart shattered in that moment, the guilt overwhelming her. Demon had been right, after all. Sarah's death was on her hands, and all because she wanted revenge.

"I had hoped to find a way to leave you unscathed from all of this. The death of Sarah Miller and the destruction of Taylor Miller should have been where it ended. But no. Kent Leech got involved with an old flame who just had to share the nefarious plans of her family, causing Leech to set Tribe on the protection of his sister, setting all of this in motion. What were the fucking odds of that happening? So now? Now, I have a problem."

He added more photos to the desk.

Kubrick and Waters running the obstacle course in Roatán.

TB carrying Flame out of the private room at The Library the night they'd met in person.

Gem and Nemo in the mine the day they'd been captured.

Midas and Nemo coming from somewhere in their tactical gear.

Steel in front of a bank in what looked like a small Midwestern town.

Picture after picture of her... going about her life all the way to the day her father disappeared.

All of his words were sinking in with a weight unimaginable. The Salieri had been watching them from the very beginning. She may have kept her secrets from the team, but they'd never been a secret to the people who most needed to be kept in the dark.

"When you called me up out of the blue to tell me you wanted to introduce me to your new husband, I was instantly wary. After all, you've sidestepped me at every opportunity since the year before you turned eighteen. Now, suddenly, you want to establish a family connection again?" The grimace on his face made him seem devil-like. "Not you. But my curiosity was insatiable, so I allowed myself to be reeled into whatever game you were playing at."

"The problem isn't me or my team, Zion. It's you! You've aligned yourself with the Salieri. You traffic women to breed children, then kill them. And until recently, you killed the daughters who were born, but now you've found a 'sustainable' use for them in the diamond mines. Tell me. When they're too big to fit in the worm tunnels, what happens? Do you destroy them, too, or do they become breeding stock?"

"Nothing is wasted that can possibly be used."

She felt bile rise in the back of her throat. "You're a monster."

He nodded, a look of thoughtfulness on his face. "Quite possibly.

But there are bigger monsters than me. General Howard, for instance. When he was thwarted over you twenty-six years ago, it set forth a chain reaction no one could have dreamed possible. Each new failure has made him that much more difficult to contain.

"In these last years, he'd found a replacement for you, finally. Sylvan Jones. He became obsessed when he saw her, so he made arrangements with Gendry to purchase his ward, but the girl escaped just before the deal could be finalized. Somehow, your team ended up involved in that, as well, and so the general's eye moved back to its starting point. Esme Bosworth. Luckily, he hasn't been able to secure permission to take you as his own. Our elder has something else in mind for you."

Matthew was suddenly at her back, his hands gripping her arms from behind.

With a sigh, Zion looked at Cherry with regret. "I am sorry about this, my dear. I would have loved to spare you the outcome you're about to receive, but... perhaps it's better this way." His last words were to Matthew. "Take her."

As Matthew began to drag her to the door, she fought, pulling at his grip, trying to kick at his legs, but it was no use. She hadn't been paying attention to the silent security guard, and he had her in a hold she couldn't break. That mistake could cost her everything. As Matthew reached the door, a tiny poke in her neck let Cherry know that she was about to go unconscious. It took less than thirty seconds for her to pass out.

30

APRIL 15, 2023

Demon

Demon murmured into his watch speaker, "I know Ka-Bar said he'd help with the distraction of security, but does anyone else think this is too easy? I basically walked out the front door and haven't seen a single security guard at the villa or here."

"There's no one stirring in the groves, but then again, it's late," Steel replied.

TB said, "I'm with D. Something's up. There hasn't been a single patrol since I got into my first position, and I've seen nothing from any of my other watchpoints either."

Midas ordered, "Proceed as planned, gentlemen. I'll work my camera magic and worry about security patrols. TB, what's your location?"

"West side of the villa. Cherry's in talking to Zion. She just handed him the fake Ka-Bar papers."

"Got it. Your footage is a little grainy. Must be some interference. All I can see from your distance is blobs."

Demon felt a small amount of tension leave his body. He'd feel more relief if the cams were working better, but Cherry was in TB's sight, so she was as safe as she could be at the moment. That didn't mean she was clear of danger, but knowing the man could physically see her was something.

He tapped his watch. "I'm at the research building. How's my camera?"

"Grainy as well. Maybe they have some sort of signal interference going. I'll take a look as soon as I can. Steel's is the only one I can see clearly right now. Everybody keep a verbal dialogue going on what you're seeing just to cover our bases."

"Copy. Gonna see if I can get inside the building now."

The three other team members gave affirmative replies and then went silent so they didn't distract each other.

He'd known since the luncheon that he'd need to get into the buildings and have a private look around despite the offered tour. Zion would only allow them to see what he wanted them to see. So when they'd been exiting the golf cart and he noticed a key card in the cupholder, he'd swiped it under the pretense of a rock in his shoe. He was betting it was the grandson's access to things on the site. Hopefully, it didn't trigger alarms when being used and merely recorded the swipes because this could be a real short exploration if security swooped in to see what the boy was doing here this time of night.

"I'm swiping my entry card now," he told the team.

There was a soft chime when the card slid through the swiping mechanism, and Demon reached for the door handle. It turned easily in his hand and opened. He slipped inside the door and closed it behind him. "I'm inside. Waiting ten." He ducked into the shadows off to the side of the door.

Midas came over the line. "I've lost your camera entirely. It looks like it's recording, but it's not broadcasting. Hoping that's the case so I can see it later. I'll keep it on in case it goes in and out, or in case we need the footage later."

After ten minutes had passed with no people arriving with flashlights, let alone guns, Demon slunk up the metal staircase. When he arrived at what would, distance-wise, be two floors above the sealed labs they'd viewed on the tour, he met with a metal door and another lock for a key card to swipe through. However, when he tried the card, a red light flashed, refusing him entry.

"Guys, my card doesn't work in the upstairs door. I may have tripped an alarm. I'm going to leave, watch the building for a bit, then come back in and try the elevator."

"Hang on," Midas interjected. "I'm in their mainframe. Let me see if I can tell why it didn't open." There was silence as Demon waited, frozen in place. "Okay. You're all good. Just a bad swipe. Try again."

He inserted the card into the slit again and tried to run it at a more even pace through the mechanism. This time, he got a green light, and the door handle clicked. "I'm in."

Opening the door as little as possible, he checked the hallway. It was empty. Just like downstairs, there were glass windows on either side, the lights dim, but the hallway didn't go down quite as far. It made a jog to the left at a forty-five-degree angle about two-thirds of the way down. The solid walls straight ahead after that went to the elevator he'd seen earlier on the tour.

"I've looped the camera footage. You've got probably seven or eight minutes before someone starts to think it's odd, which matters not at all if someone comes walking down and sends up the alarm, so don't get seen," Midas warned him.

"Wasn't in the plan," Demon murmured, more to himself than Midas.

He'd taken no more than five steps when he saw what he'd come to see. He hated being right sometimes.

"Visual confirmation. Glassed-in cubicles form hospital rooms. About a dozen beds in all. Each one holds a woman, ages ranging late teens to mid-thirties, and all in what looks like the final stages of pregnancy."

"Can they be moved?"

"Negative. All appear to be heavily sedated."

Demon stepped into the room of one of the younger-looking girls. A clipboard hung on the wall. He looked over her monitor readings. Everything seemed okay on the surface, although sedating a pregnant woman, especially this late in the process, was risky. Still... given the endgame for these women, if they lost them in these final days, it wouldn't matter if they could save the children.

He flipped through the young woman's chart. "I'm in one of the rooms. According to the chart, she's eighteen. Serbian. Due date is in two days. Planning for a cesarean birth." Immediately, he began to take pictures with his watch face of the paperwork on the clipboard. With each page he turned, his rage boiled higher and higher over the thought that Cherry, who when she was the same age as this girl, could have become a victim of the Salieri.

Zion was a dead man, and Demon wanted nothing more than to be the one to put the knife to his jugular that put him down, then carve him up into bite-size pieces for the sharks in Soufrière Bay.

Midas was talking in his ear comm, but a groan of pain echoed from down toward the end of the hall. Carefully and quietly, Demon replaced the clipboard. On silent feet, he crossed down the hall, carefully watching out for staff or guards. No one came. He slipped into the room two doors down to find that the woman in the bed was still sedated but clearly in pain. Her blood pressure was dropping. Her skin was nearly gray.

A quick glance under the bed sheet showed him why. She was hemorrhaging. Badly.

His eyes searched the room for supplies. Donning a pair of latex gloves, he quickly scanned the machines working around her. He didn't have long before one went into an alarm state.

"Midas, I've got a situation here. This woman is about to flatline."

"D, you can't help her! You'll be caught!"

"I can't leave her like this," he argued. "I took an oath, practicing physician or not."

"Think that ship sailed, buddy, the first time you slit a throat," TB reminded him.

"It's not the same thing," Demon argued.

The woman stopped mid-groan and simply seemed to sigh out all the oxygen in her lungs. Her monitor alarm went off. There was nothing for it. He took off down the hall the way he'd come. Swiping his card to exit, he slipped through the door just in time to avoid being seen by the nurse charging into the dead woman's room. Given the high-end equipment and environment, all effort would likely be put into saving the child, but the life of the mother was determined long before he walked into that room. It burned him to leave without trying to save her life, but the rational part of his brain told him there was nothing he could do, especially given how much trauma he'd witnessed her experiencing.

Once clear of the door, he put his ass to the stair rail and slid all the way down the two flights of stairs to the main floor. He was just getting ready to crack open the door leading outside to see if his route was clear to exit when he heard the beeps signaling someone was coming in after swiping their key card. Places to hide were nonexistent, so he would have to rely on the shadows and the men being in a rush and not paying attention to miss his presence. Quickly, he did a one-hundred-eighty-degree turn, got under the metal staircase, and scrunched himself as low and as small as he could in the interior corner.

The two men, one in his mid- to late forties and one in his thirties, speed-walked to the elevator at the opposite end of the hall. The younger man, his voice panicked, asked, "Should I call Mr. Deschamps?"

The second man answered, "No. Not yet. We don't even know

what happened to trigger the alarm. No sense in getting everyone excited over what could simply be a low battery or a faulty fuse."

When the elevator had swallowed them up, Demon remained in his hidey-hole for a few minutes longer, just in case more people would come to see what the alarm was for. It was a long twelve minutes, his back screaming in protest at being cramped into such a small space, but it couldn't be helped. When no one else arrived, he risked extracting himself and stretching to relieve his cramped muscles.

"D, do you copy?"

"I copy, Midas."

"Steel just found something. Two panel trucks pulled into the groves and went down the dirt road to the north end of the fields. He chased after them, but they disappeared. The road dumps out by a shed that holds a tractor. Underneath that tractor is a false floor. He can't see under it without moving the vehicle—"

"It's the diamond mines all over again. Escape paths to the surface large enough for vehicles to disappear into. You want me to go downstairs and see if I can find out who it was and what they're getting ready to haul out?"

"Or what they brought in."

"Nova able to give us some help negotiating movement in the passages? I don't want to have the elevator doors open and be facing a brute squad with guns."

"Routing her into the camera feed now."

With purpose, he moved down the hallway to the elevator. When he got there, he waited for Midas' AI program to clear the gauntlet for him. "Good evening, Demon." Her voice, frighteningly sultry and human, came over the airwaves.

"Nova," he replied. He always felt a little stupid talking to a machine. Especially one with a voice that sexy. "How is the path to the basement warehouse via the elevator?"

"Your current path is clear. When the elevator doors open, press the LL3 button."

He followed her instructions. "Which way after that?"

"The blueprints we have accessed show that the LL1 and LL2 subfloors should maintain the same rectangular shape as the aboveground floors. However, there is some indication that the LL3 floor is much taller, wider, and more open, with air vents that travel from the topmost floor, the main floor, and floors LL1 and LL2. Currently, the internal camera system shows that all activity on LL3 is isolated to the southern corner."

"What about floors LL1 and LL2?" he asked. "Shouldn't we look at those?"

"Those floors are too populated at this time. I am tracking fourteen heat signatures between the two floors, and all are in near-constant motion. They also would not be deep enough for the types of vehicle tunnels you are expecting."

"Got it. Elevator is here. I'm heading in."

"I will ensure that the lights and sounds associated with the elevator moving will be turned off for your descent, and I will only open the doors partially so they do not distract anyone who might be looking in that direction."

"Copy that."

When the doors closed behind him, Demon did a quick check of his gun that was holstered in the back of his waistband and the knife at his hip. At LL3, the doors opened just enough for Demon to slide through and to his left. He found himself behind a stack of long crates, approximately seven feet long and four feet wide, that had been placed in stacks of five. A forklift was heading his way with two similar crates, but it turned at the last second, the lift rose, and it deposited the two boxes on top of three others previously stacked there. When the forklift backed away and drove back to where it came from, Demon slunk to the very last row and stack, then hiked himself up on the uneven corners, daring to look at what was inside the top crate.

A coffin, similar to the ones they'd found when rescuing Flame last year, and exactly like the ones Nemo and Steel had found in Egypt.

"Motherfecker!" he whispered.

Midas barked, "What are you seeing?"

"They've got more stacks of crates down here. Each crate contains one of those sophisticated coffins." He did a quick survey of the warehouse. "Estimated fifty of them. Where the hell are they keeping the women?"

"Irrelevant right now," Midas reminded him. "What else do you see, D?"

"I really hate not having a working body cam," he muttered.

He looked out between the crates, but from as far back in the corner as he was, he couldn't see anything. Slowly, he worked his way around several stacks of crates until he was behind the front-most row toward the center of the room.

"The elevator dumped me into basically a large warehouse. It's just one big empty space. Metal all around, no dirt or rock, so they shored up the hole they dug here."

"They're at the foot of a volcano. Wouldn't the ground be harder there?"

"Depends on the depth we're at, the direction of the lava flows, and a lot of other geology stuff I have shite knowledge of," Demon admitted. "But from what I remember in science class, volcanic soil is perfect for growing things because it leaves the soil full of minerals. Certainly a perfect placement for the banana trees, vineyards, and whatever else people want to grow on the island, and why the family farm had periods of such economic success. The soil would be softer toward the top."

"What else are you seeing?" Midas asked.

"On the surface, a lot of boxes of supplies, crates of equipment, whatever you'd need to run a research facility. I'll try to get closer and see if the items are actually what they are labeled."

"Anything else?"

"Vehicles. Two panel trucks. Those are probably what Steel saw coming into the groves. They're unloading them now. Again... crates say they're things like lamps, clothing companies, probably for clean suits, but could be hospital gowns, scrubs, what have you. I'd need to look closer. Wait. Hang on a minute."

Three men came out of the truck, wheeling a much bigger crate than the others. Demon went back a row in the stockpiles and got closer to the trucks.

"They just wheeled out a large crate that says it's medical equipment. I saw an ultrasound machine delivered once to the hospital. It's about the right size for that." He looked around. "Few more vehicles down here. Some golf carts, open jeeps, that sort of thing. There's also large equipment like air purifiers and generators. I see offshoot tunnels that lead to the north, northwest, maybe? Wide enough for vehicles to go through."

"What's northwest of that building?"

Demon swore silently. "The recycling facility. There's a huge incinerator in that building. How much do you want to bet that's where they're disposing of the bodies?"

"As awful as it sounds, I don't think any of us would bet against you." There was the sound of swearing over the comm link. "We've got a redheaded problem, gentlemen. TB, what's your location?"

"I saw. Already on it. He's going through the house. Turn on her tracker in case I lose him."

Demon froze. There was only one "redhead" they would be talking about. Only one "redhead" TB was watching. "What's going on?"

"D, stay where you are. Chances are, they're bringing her to the plantation somewhere. TB will follow. Steel? Get ready to follow her signal."

"GPS is booted up," Steel replied.

"They're going to move quickly. She's unconscious."

Demon couldn't seem to get a full breath of air. He knew running toward Cherry when he didn't know where she was actually headed was a mistake. Not only that, he wanted to race out into the warehouse, tearing apart limb from limb anyone who was part of this fucked-up shit show, but he'd only get himself caught without backup. That wouldn't help her either. He needed to wait for direction from Midas. But it was so hard not to give in to the impulse.

"TB," he croaked.

"Don't have to say it. Let's go get our girl."

31

APRIL 15, 2023

Cherry

WHEN SHE AWOKE, THE ROOM SHE WAS IN WAS DARK. WHERE the hell was she? She turned her head, but her vision was too blurry to see more than torches burning and that the walls surrounding her were covered in pictures. What exactly those pictures were, she couldn't tell.

The air surrounding her was hot and heavy. There was a dampness that pervaded the space, along with the heat and an odd scent in the air. Not moldy or musty, but more brackish. Like wet earth or a marsh, and it was mixed with brimstone. Light, but still unpleasant, so she moved to cover her nose with her hand.

That slight movement drew her attention to her body. It hurt. Not like she'd been beaten, but more dull, like she was hungover. Laying her hands flat next to her body, she struggled to push herself to a sitting position. It was no use. Her body quickly gave out, and she slipped back into unconsciousness.

The next time she woke, she knew some time had passed. An hour, maybe? The torches were still burning, but they were less bright. There was no sound except for the soft crackling of the flames, and the room had a hollowness to it as if she was entirely alone. It was time to force herself to move. Wherever she was, it wasn't a place to stick around. Blood flow to her extremities was vital if she was going to get out of here, and that was only going to come with movement.

Laying her hands flat at her sides, she gingerly pushed herself to a sitting position. Looking down, she saw she was atop a stone slab in the center of an open, square room. Other than where she lay and the torches, there was nothing in the open space.

She sat for a moment to take stock of her body and collect herself. To compound the pain, she struggled to put thoughts together coherently, like there was a fog suppressing her ability to remember clearly how she might have gotten here. As she sat there, staring at the wall in front of her, slowly, bits and pieces came back to her through the brain fog. She'd been in Zion's office, and he'd revealed he knew who she and Demon were. That they had friends along. That they were pursuing the Salieri, which he was a part of, as well as connected to her father's disappearance when she was a child, Waters' sister's murder and his torture, Flame's capture, and the near bombing that could have killed her and Gem. He'd been watching them all along.

The reveal of his knowledge led to Matthew cornering her, drugging her, and then bringing her here. But where was here? How long had she been gone? Midas had TB watching the villa, but did the men know she was missing yet? Somehow, she doubted that Matthew had taken her out the front door to wherever she was now. It was possible they thought she was back in her room, tucked tightly into bed, and awaited Demon's return from the reconnaissance they'd gone on tonight.

Attempting to escape wherever she was when she was so groggy and physically weak was foolish, so she'd wait. Allow her body to regain some strength, investigate her surroundings, and then make a plan. While she knew the men would eventually figure out she was missing and engage her tracker to find her, she didn't know how long she'd been gone or how soon they'd realize. She'd need to try and help herself in the meantime.

The slab she sat upon was perhaps waist-high for the average person, so there was little difficulty in sliding off it to stand on the floor. She rubbed her wrists and shook out her arms, as well as did some gentle twisting at her waist, bending of her knees, and turning of her ankles to make sure she was at full strength.

Walking down the two steps that led up to the slab, she crossed to the torches spread out about every six feet so that she was closer to the walls to see what was painted on them. The walls depicted several frescoes of women from what looked like the time of the Ancient Greeks. They appeared to be everything from fully dressed to naked, yet artfully posed. Some were preparing food, others were dipping cloths into basins with liquid in them, and there was even a young woman being washed and prepared by other young women.

There was also a scene of a naked man, a sheet draped around his portly figure, his face round and bearded. Several more young women, all naked, were depicted as serving him food and drink, one even appearing to gaze upon him flirtatiously as she knelt at his feet. Behind her, several satyrs played their flutes, danced, and leered at the young maiden.

When the pictures turned the corner, it was to a wall with an open, arched doorway in the middle of it. Burned-down candles dripped wax onto the two votives that sat on carved stone shelves on either side at shoulder height. They appeared to be hands, the thumb and first two fingers extended up, the third and fourth folded down. It was difficult to see it in complete detail, but within the votive, there was a male figure carved as sitting in the palm, holding items in his upraised hands. A knife and a snake. At the base of the votive, a woman and child were carved.

She turned to look at the wall to the right of the doorway. The paintings resumed, this time showing a young woman, her smile almost beatific, her belly round with child, and she was being dressed and cossetted by an older woman while young male servants offered her wine, fruits, and gifts of gold.

The paintings were in excellent condition, but although they were artistically beautiful, she felt a menace behind them. She shivered despite the heat. Something here was very, very wrong.

Grabbing one of the torches off the wall, she stood before the arched doorway, looking at the unfamiliar symbols and glyphs carved into the stone. With a deep breath in and a long, measured exhale, she walked through the archway. She emerged from a hallway less than three feet long only to find herself in another room, this one much smaller than the one she'd been in.

She quickly realized what had seemed wrong in the previous room. There appeared to be no obvious access to enter or exit whatever building she was in. How in the name of all the saints had she gotten in here if there was no way to enter or exit?

The contents of this room were both similar and different from where she'd woken. Here, there were alcoves in one wall where ancient-looking objects—urns, small chests, statues—resided. However, the items appeared to be in pristine condition, the ones with metal shining in the torchlight, and the urns and chests capable of opening and closing on their contents freely with no danger of damage being done to them. There was also another raised slab in the room, only this one was in the center of the space and was reached by descending four steps into a sunken circle. Almost as if an audience would stand around to watch what occurred there. She shivered again, grabbing her biceps and chafing them. Whatever they watched, she didn't think it was anything good.

Circling the pit, she walked closer to the walls to examine what was painted on the remaining three walls of this room, and it didn't take long before the shiver she'd experienced a few moments ago turned into a full-body vibration.

The paintings depicted naked figures in a wide variety of sexual positions. There were men lying on beds, their cocks hard and standing straight up in the air, drawn with great exaggeration to depict them as close to two to three times the length of a normal man. In some images, multiple men were attending to a single woman, or she was stretched to her maximum height and width while bound to various surfaces. And in the background, more men lounged in chairs or leaned indolently against walls, watching as women impaled themselves upon the men in a variety of positions, their faces meant to display the height of ecstasy. Cherry looked upon them and felt as if they were wide-eyed with fear and pain rather than pleasure. They were meant to be erotic, but they had the opposite effect on Cherry.

"Terrifying, aren't they?"

The voice came from the arched doorway. Felix Giudici stood in the arch, the torches placing his face in alternating shadow and light. The flames bouncing off his white hair and sharp features combined with the flickering shadows accentuated his height and gauntness, reminding her of classic horror movie star Bela Lugosi—the icon of monsters. The irony was not lost on her. He was a Salieri. He was a monster.

She stared into his eyes, refusing to show the fear that had her insides turning to jelly. This wasn't the first time she'd been in a dangerous situation, but it was certainly the first time she truly believed there might be no hope of escape. She wondered if this was how Sarah and Waters had felt while being tortured four years ago. Her stomach bottomed out. It would be a fitting end, she thought, for her to end as Sarah had. Fitting punishment for her inadvertent crimes.

"Terrifying and yet erotic, all the same." Giudici answered his own question. Entering the room, he stood directly across the sunken circle from her.

"Where am I?"

"You're on ancestral land."

"You don't exactly look like a native of the island."

"My family settled here long before the Arawaks. I would proudly show off the property to you, but"—he shrugged—"I fear that wouldn't be a very smart thing to do. You might try to run away, and while you wouldn't get very far, it would certainly be quite inconvenient and bothersome to have to retrieve you."

"Well, I would hate to be a bother," she snarked.

He smiled placatingly. "And there is the fire that our brother, General Howard, loves so much." He tilted his head to the side, his brow furrowed and his lips pursed as he considered her. Finally, he said, "I don't see the appeal, myself. But... no matter."

"So if I don't get to see the property, you could at least explain where I am now. This doesn't exactly scream of high-end living quarters."

His mood became that of a professor combined with a cheerful showman. He turned in a circle, hands palm-up in front of him. "This property is an exact replica of our family home in Italy, which is one of seven such properties—one on each continent—that serve as a residence for the direct descendants of the founding members of the Salieri. If you were to look at this estate from above, in the middle of the courtyard, there is a building that serves as the family crypt. In order to protect our ancestors after their passing, this building was sealed, making it impenetrable to the elements. My ancestors learned their lessons from the gods' destruction of Pompeii, which destroyed our home in 79 AD."

"Meaning what?"

"Meaning, back in history, nature was revered. When disasters struck, the people respected the messages. They understood that if a hurricane, a tsunami, or a volcano destroyed a civilization, or a part of a civilization, it was a sign the gods were angry. Scientists today will deliver all kinds of claptrap about wind currents, gas pressure, tectonic plates, climate change, but the truth that we know"—he shook his forefinger at her as if she were a child in denial—"is that over time, the people were letting go of tradition, and that made the gods angry. People become complacent, especially when nothing happens for long periods of time, and they grow to disrespect the power of nature and the old ways as their knowledge allows them to climb closer and closer to the level of the gods. Natural disasters were the punishment for people's loss of faith.

"Like the events of Pompeii in 79 AD would eventually create, in the eighteenth century, St. Lucia suffered its own version of volcanic destruction. The Soufrière Volcano erupted, destroying much of what was in the lava flows' paths. Hundreds of people died in an instant, livestock abandoned and lost, agriculture drowned in debris. This plantation and others were destroyed. The elimination of most of the island was our punishment for our hubris.

"But even in death, there is life." He turned his head to her, the smile on his face appearing benign. "The destruction yielded by the mountain may have buried our home, but this building alone remained standing, mirroring events recorded in the family archives in Naples. *We* were the ones chosen to survive the wrath of the heavens. *We* had been spared. Therefore, it was our responsibility to educate others and bring them into the fold."

"You realize," she said, "the reason the building survived is because it had no entry. It has nothing to do with pleasing the gods or following the old ways."

He continued speaking as if she hadn't interrupted him. "In our gratitude, we dedicated this shrine to our god—the god of the harvest, home, and fertility. On the columns outside, all the family names are engraved to commemorate those who have passed before us. It is here that we honor them, their way of life, and it is here that we perform our most important rituals that perpetuate our kind, for this is our initiation room."

She was pretty sure she didn't want the answer to the question, but she asked it anyway. "An initiation into what?"

"The truth of the Salieri, my dear."

"The truth? You mean the truth that you people are sick, sadistic motherfuckers?"

He walked toward the wall to his left, hands in his pockets, and stood before a depiction of three men holding their exaggerated phalluses, their heads thrown back in ecstasy, eyes closed, mouths open.

They surrounded a young woman, naked, on her knees, her hands behind her back, and her head arched, eyes wide in what looked to be pain. A slim brown line around her neck suggested some type of collar, which Cherry guessed was attached to whatever was holding the woman's hands bound behind her back. One hand left Giudici's pocket so that a finger could trace the outline of the woman's form. Cherry knew it was the flickering of the flames reflecting in the fluid of his eyes, but the orbs appeared to glitter with both malice and joy at the woman's position.

After his finger had traced from the top of the woman's head to her feet, likely also hobbled to her hands behind her back, he turned to her, and the mild-mannered professor seemed to return. He gestured all around him. "Look around this room, and you will see the art and artifacts of a time long before Christianity. A time when polytheism was widely practiced, and the superiority of men over women was uncontested. It was a pure time when things were simple, clean, and accepted as is. Not like today when we struggle to understand even the most basic of life's natural laws."

He took several steps back toward the sunken stage. She countered his steps so that she was directly across from him again. There was no way in hell she was letting this man get close enough to reach out and grab her.

"One man looked at the world around him and saw chaos where there should be control, and so, he formulated a plan. He called himself Salieri, and he made it his mission to tame that chaos. But to do that, he needed to start at the beginning. To rip down the world as it was then and rebuild it in the way he knew it could be.

"He began by surveying the many gods that man worshipped, and he selected the seven whom he considered worthy of worship. He followed that by selecting his seven most trusted men—the Worthy—to form their own tribe dedicated to returning the world to its balance point. They did this by taking the laws he handed down to them, and then each of the Worthy went to the continent assigned to them by Salieri to begin reforming society through their progeny and philosophies."

"And he just expected this to happen overnight? Maybe if he'd had the internet, but communication back then wasn't exactly instantaneous. It could take years for communication to circumnavigate the globe."

"He knew it wouldn't happen overnight. But he believed in his ideals, and he knew that the Worthy would carry out his laws and that their sons would carry out their laws, and so on. Since our originations, we have grown to reside on every continent, every country—including every one of the fifty states of America. If there was a measurable population to be found, the Salieri spread to those places. Our people reside in all walks of life. We have come a very long way in a historically short period of time, even without the internet, and we're not done yet."

"In other words, he made himself a god and gave himself demigods as underlings to cater to his sick fantasies of how the world should work."

Giudici smiled, the expression one of indulgence as if to show her how naive she was. His voice even radiated that of a patronizing teacher when he responded. "He created laws that made sense and gave them a way to correct the wrongs in the world."

"I saw the paintings and the symbols in the main room. The Cult of Dionysus. Sabizia. You're nothing more than a cult."

He made a tsking noise. "Such an ugly word, 'cult.' You make it sound like we're a bunch of backward souls who believe in the end of days."

"What would you call it, then?" she spat. "Your congregation might not be waiting for the mothership to come collect the chosen few after drinking the fruity communion drink to test everyone's loyalty, but you've created an archaic religious dogma and twisted its views on fertility, hearth, and home to rationalize and normalize your own perversions. You're a male-dominated society who, under the guise of some fucked-up utopia, have willfully stolen women from their lives, forced them into sexual slavery, all to bear your children before sacrificing them to your 'god.'

"You grow your numbers by searching out the lost, the abandoned, the disenfranchised, the marginalized, and the twisted. You prey on those who feel like no one understands them, and then you give them a taste of the paradise you sell them. Once they've had their free taste, like a drug dealer, you addict them to your product by ferreting out their weaknesses, convincing them that being initiated into your 'organization' justifies killing their wives, daughters, and other immediate female family relations to feed a disgusting mythology that was created expressly with the purpose of subjugating others.

"I'll give you this. At least you don't discriminate. You recruit rich men into your group, taking advantage of them by encouraging them to invest in your endeavors that are being used to fund your real goals. You bring in the middle class, likely promising them that they, too, can work their way into the upper echelons of the organization if they just follow the plan and work hard, while you work the percentages just enough to make them believe it's possible without actually allowing it to occur. And let's not forget that you exploit the poor and uneducated by showing them that anything you can provide them is better than the life they're living. No cost is too high, no request too great. All they have to do—any of them—is give their soul over to you. Sounds pretty close to a textbook definition of a cult to me."

Giudici shook his head. "It's unfortunate that you feel that way, my dear."

"Why? Because I don't want to become a breeder and then be killed afterward? I can't imagine many women are happy with that prospect."

"They are contributing to a greater world. To be honest, most women don't know the ultimate sacrifice they will make. In ancient times, to be selected as one of the chosen wives for the Worthy was seen as a great honor. However, in this day and age, we have found we must... protect them from modern-day ideology regarding their purpose. We are committed to treating our selected brides with great respect and care while they grow our young. All efforts go to providing them with the best health care, the finest clothing, the finest living arrangements. They want for nothing. In fact, as we prepare them for their roles as mothers of our sons, they see their lives as better than anything they could have achieved in their everyday lives. They don't want to leave."

"Psychological conditioning. You create Stockholm syndrome."

"We provide them with lives they could have never had where they were."

A sudden thought occurred to Cherry. "The women at the luncheon. They were all younger."

"Yes. They are brides of our members. Some are marriages of longer standing from members recruited out of their traditional lives into the fold. Our recruitment is rigorous, and we are clear that the men will serve us well before they are told the price they pay for joining the Salieri. And... whether the marriage comes to us already formed, or it is arranged by us, if the women are considered good stock and they provide a son, or they have shown good breeding capabilities and provide a girl who is miscarried, some are permitted to remain brides for another pregnancy or two."

"The method doesn't matter. Their lives are bought and sold. It's still trafficking!"

"It's true. In recent years, we've had to procure our brides in somewhat nontraditional circumstances, but it has not changed our methods. We still treat them extremely well. And when their confinement comes, they know little of what is happening around them. We keep them medically sedated in a way that is not harmful to them or the child, and they pass blissfully unaware."

"And the women who conceive girls?"

"The joys of modern medicine. Being able to tell the sex of a child early certainly helps with that obstacle. But when it does happen, that is easily taken care of through alternative means. Termination of the fetus through natural methods causes the pregnancy to appear as a miscarriage. Women may even survive the loss of a daughter if they are considered hearty and healthy enough to withstand another pregnancy. However, these days, with the genetic research at our fingertips, we are able to take steps that prevent as many daughters from being conceived as there were in the past."

"This is crazy. You're all crazy. I do not agree to this. I will fight you every step of the way. Do you honestly think my husband will just accept my disappearance? He knows I would never leave him willingly. He will come looking for me, and he won't rest until he finds me. And when he finds you, I guarantee you, you and all of your members will pay for what you've done."

"Come, Esme. Your uncle has already shown you that we know he's not your husband, just as we know he is not Ciarán McCarthy. You do not work for an IT company. You work for Tribe Corporation, a group of mercenaries you put together with the specific mission to find your father."

Two pairs of hands grabbed her from behind. She'd been so caught up in the words of Giudici that she hadn't been paying attention to her surroundings. However people entered this building, they'd managed to sneak up on her from behind. While she struggled against their grip, futile though it was, three more figures walked behind her—Zion, Deschamps, and Andres.

Her uncle was the one who spoke. "I am sorry, Esme. Your father was just a bit too smart for his own good. He was a miscalculation on my part. A trial run of mine, if you will, to successfully include investors with clean money who were not part of the Salieri. Unfortunately, I was proven wrong. He was more savvy than your average businessman and looked deeply beyond the prospectus. Apparently, he didn't trust even his closest friend when it came to financial support."

"He always did have a nose for when something wasn't on the up-and-up."

"Yes, most unfortunate. You should know that he died well, with you as his final thought."

"Where is he?"

"Don't worry. He's buried on the grounds. He was my friend, after all, and I honored his death."

"So now what? I'm going to become a bride and bear a son for General Howard? Not willingly."

He chuckled as he gestured to the young man next to him. "General Howard is too old at this stage to take a bride. Andres has indicated that he'd rather forego university and take a bride. He has selected you."

"He's a child! I'm old enough to be his mother! And forty-four is a bit old for pregnancy."

"Yes, we've apprised him of that. But he is most insistent. You are in excellent health, and he is quite taken with you. And, if things go poorly, he understands the risk that you, the child, or both could be lost during the pregnancy. It's a chance he's willing to take." He directed his attention to the two men holding her. "The women will be here to prepare her shortly. Once they have passed the arch, no one goes in or out until the initiation begins."

Zion, an expression of sympathy on his face, finally spoke. "I had left you behind, Esme. I had no plans to come after you. I tried to honor my fondness for you and your father by allowing you to live happily, unaware of our existence. This could have all been avoided if Kent Leech and your friends with Mythos had refrained from involving Leech's sister and kept their noses out of the Kaders' business. Now we've lost another set of investors, and we're still missing Zahra. Extra work for us, I'm afraid, but... no loose ends, as they say."

Unfortunately, it appeared Zahra and her son were still targets. Cherry knew that Zahra was in a safe house, but given all the information the Salieri had on Tribe, for how long would she remain hidden? And were Mythos aware that they, too, had been found? There was no way to get that information to them either.

The sound of soft footsteps on stone reached her ears, getting louder with every step. Moments later, a line of seven women entered the room, each carrying something in their outstretched arms as they crossed down into the circle at what she now realized was an altar. Bowls with liquid in them. Piles of folded materials. Small chests filled with who knew what. All of them were aware, yet their eyes had a glassy sheen to them. They were obviously drugged.

The two men flanking her began to drag her down into the sunken circle. There was no way she was getting free of them, and even if they let her go, they would be between her and the one and only escape route, which had closed behind the last woman in line. She was well and truly fucked, and the irony did not escape her that she truly would be if Demon and the others didn't find her soon. Hopefully, by now, they had activated her tracker; otherwise, she wasn't sure how they would ever locate her.

"Prepare her. You have one hour."

Her eyes went immediately to Andres. His expression was odd. It appeared blank, but something was working behind the eyes. Her stomach revolted, and she worked hard to keep the bile down. He was barely legal. This whole situation was too weird for words. Could she overpower him when the time came? He was strong from working on the plantation, but she likely had more fight training, given her position at Tribe. Would it do any good? Zion had mentioned her two guards being outside the initiation room until the rite was over. If she did manage to overpower him, would she be able to get to the staircase, find and open the door, and flee before they stopped her? Unlikely, but right now, it was the only plan she had.

32

APRIL 16, 2023

Demon

His back hurt from being crouched behind the crates for so long, but he pushed it down into the far corners of his brain. There was no time to deal with that while Cherry was heaven knew where with who knew what happening to her.

Partially to distract himself, he checked his gun for what felt like the hundredth time, sliding the magazine in and out. Putting it back into the holster at his back, he checked his surroundings in the warehouse. His eyes kept drifting to the hallway tunnel on the opposite side of the warehouse, wide enough to get a golf cart or forklift through, but more often, he saw pedestrian traffic enter and exit. Where did it go? Another warehouse? To another facility on the plantation, or even an extended walkway to another part of the plantation? Both would be convenient for delivering supplies, as well as protection in hurricane conditions.

The only other entrance besides the elevator appeared to be the wide tunnel that inclined to the surface and allowed for the traffic of larger trucks. A semi could probably even get in if it were careful enough. Good information to know in case they needed to get out quickly, as the elevator was too easy to stop and ambush when trying to exit it.

Ducking his head, he checked his underarm holster on his left side of his body. Checking his second gun, he reholstered it. Then he checked his knives—belt buckle, right hip, thigh, boot. Another attachment to his belt held a garotte he could quickly unleash. His pockets held an assortment of things he'd discovered he often needed. Zip ties. Army-style pocketknife. A pen, used more often to do an emergency tracheotomy than to write with. Superglue to temporarily seal small wounds. Climbing gloves. An airplane-size bottle of whiskey for sterilizing wounds. Quikclot, gauze, and tape for bullet wounds. Extra bullets because... well, bad guys. He couldn't even count all the things he had stashed on his person.

Once he'd inventoried everything, he started again, promising himself it would be the last time.

A voice broke into his "final" check. "Dude, you need help. That's the fourteenth time you've checked your kit."

Steel.

"Where the feck are you? And if you've been able to count how many times I've checked, why the hell didn't you say you were here sooner? Feckin' wasting time." He knew his frustration wasn't helpful. Knew he was angry at the wrong person. But it was either voice his frustration this way or start randomly killing people. That wouldn't help Cherry either.

"Look up."

Demon tilted his head back. Steel was crouched on an I-beam directly above him, plainly sitting there, but no one had seen him.

Steel saluted him from his perch. "People look forward, back, left, and right. Sometimes they look down, but people rarely look up."

"You better hope these feckers are as dumb as you think they are." He looked back to the walkway across the way. "How the hell did you get up there?"

"Air shaft. Pays to be small."

"You and Gem would be deadly together."

"That is correct."

"Where's TB?" he asked, unable to keep the tension out of his voice as he began his ritual check again.

"Almost to you. Dude... you check the first aid kits less than you're checking your personal kit. Relax."

A hand dropped onto his shoulder, and he whirled around, knife drawn and against TB's neck. "Shite!" He expelled the air in his lungs. "Don't scare me like that!"

"Then pay attention, leprechaun, because I wasn't exactly quiet. You were being crept up on by one of their workers. You're lucky he didn't warn anyone he saw you. I had to remove him from this plane of existence, or everyone would know we were here. Threw him in one of the coffins, but not sure how long before he's discovered."

Demon looked up at Steel, his expression pissed off. "You could have said something, arsehole. You had to have seen him."

"I did. We had time. I didn't want to take out the worker until I had to, then I saw TB was taking care of it."

Demon sheathed his knife. "What's the plan? We do have a plan, don't we?"

"Midas said he had a location but that it didn't make sense, so he was digging more before he led us in blind," Steel replied.

It was two minutes later when Midas came on the line. "Okay, ladies and jellyspoons, I've got a location on our girl, but you're not going to believe this."

An odd, repeated bell tone began to ring throughout the warehouse. "What the hell is that?" TB asked.

"Look," Steel whispered.

Peering around the stack of crates they were hidden behind, Demon and TB watched as the men currently in the warehouse immediately stopped whatever they were doing and headed toward the mystery hallway. Forklifts were abandoned in the middle of the floor. Boxes were set down wherever the workers had been standing rather than walked the short distance to where they could easily be put away before leaving. While the men chatted with one another as they left, they moved quickly and with purpose.

When all the men were gone, the room remained silent and empty for several minutes. Then, the elevator opened, and a group of women exited, their arms full of assorted items. He couldn't pinpoint why specifically, but there was something odd about the manner they carried the objects. As if they didn't want to hold them close, maybe? They held their arms out directly in front of them, the items balanced on their upturned forearms. In addition, their measured steps were in sync with one another, and their heads were straight ahead as they headed directly for the walkway.

"Okay, that was weird, and we've seen some weird shit," TB commented.

"Let me guess," Midas interjected. "Bunch of young women in white togas carrying things? Saw them coming from the hospital floor of the research building. Pretty sure they're headed the same place you will be. The original schematics I was able to pull up for this facility don't show the hallway D described. However, there are security cameras in the hallway as far as one mile down. Unfortunately, all I can see from those cameras is the actual doors they're pointed at, and none of them are labeled with what those doors go to, just numbers. So I had Nova run some projections as to where that hallway might lead. The last door is exactly one mile away. Guess what else is exactly one mile in that direction from your current location?"

"I don't know, Midas," TB snarked, "a villains-R-us stop and shop? What the fuck?"

"Wow. Someone needs to get laid. Directly one mile down that hallway and up about one hundred feet is a mausoleum. But here's the kicker. I sent a drone in, and the thing has no doors or windows on the outside. It's solid stone, yet Cherry's tracker puts her in the farthest third of the structure."

"Midas," Demon interrupted, "if that's true, then there must be a way up inside from underneath. Find it!"

"Who tangled your stethoscope, Doc? Sheesh. I'm working on it."

"There's no way all those workers fit in that tiny space," TB told him. "You have no idea where the other doors go, Midas?"

"I've got Nova working on some projections, but since all I can see is the door itself and not what side of the hallway it's on, or if it's off a hallway or anything like that, all I can do is guess. I'm thinking that they're exits to various locations in the courtyard—the nearest barn, the shipping area, stuff like that. Makes sense. If one building has subfloors, others might too. Especially the newer ones."

"I don't give a feck where the other doors go. I just want the door that gets me to Cherry," Demon growled.

"And we'll get that," TB assured him. "We need to know where the other doors go though. Never box yourself into only one entrance/exit route. You know that, so keep cool. Can't help her if you pop a blood vessel."

"Relax, D, Nova's working on it," Midas assured him.

"Don't tell me to relax. Can't wait until it's your fecking turn to lose your shite."

"So you admit you're losing your shit? Mark the time, gentlemen. We'll settle up that bet later."

It was some time before Nova's voice came over the line. "Door seven, the final door, is closest to the mausoleum. However, you are too far below ground for a single flight of stairs."

Steel looked at the ceiling. "We're at least four floors beneath ground level."

"If the stairs switch back, the distance could work," TB replied.

Nodding, Steel said, "Like a fire escape."

"Nova, scan for metal under the mausoleum," Midas ordered.

Only a few seconds passed before the AI replied, "There is

enough metal to possibly form an encased stairway within the rock strata."

"Bingo. Behind door number seven, gentlemen, is where your prize awaits."

Demon started to stand from his crouch, but TB pulled him back. "Wait."

"What the feck?"

"Just wait. We need more information. We can't go in there blind. That's not good for us, and it definitely isn't good for Cherry."

He chafed at TB's words and actions, but he knew the man was right. If he wanted his woman back in one piece, he needed to get his head on straight.

Another twenty minutes later, down the hallway and into the warehouse came Zion, Calvin Deschamps, Felix Giudici, and, behind them a few feet, Andres. Demon noticed that the young man was watching those in front of him intently. They all got in the elevator and went upstairs. What the hell were they doing coming from a hallway they just sent everyone into?

"Now where are they going?" Steel asked, a frown on his face.

Suddenly, Demon felt his dummy phone vibrate in his pocket. Sliding it out of his cargo pocket, he looked down and saw an unknown caller.

"Holy shit! D, pick up that call," Midas ordered.

Demon hit the answer button on the watch. "Who is this?"

"I only have a minute. You have approximately forty-five minutes before the ritual starts. Once it does, you won't be able to get in, and she won't be able to get out until it's finished."

The voice sounded familiar to him, like he'd heard it before and recently, but not often. "Who is this?" he repeated.

"It doesn't matter. Esme doesn't deserve this. No one does. You need to get her out of there."

"It's Andres," Midas supplied.

The young man continued talking. "Take the pedestrian walkway all the way to the end. You'll see some stairs. At the top, you'll see a service door—number seven—that says Emergency Exit over it. Punch in the code 177170707077. That will get you through the door. You'll be in a narrow stairwell. On the third-floor landing, there's another panel. Type in today's date, day first. 16042023. It will open a door in the ceiling. Be careful. It will be a blind spot for you because you'll have an entire floor of stairs to get up before you can get in the room, and if the guards see or hear you coming, you'll be a sitting duck in the stairway. Are you alone?"

Demon wasn't sure if he trusted the kid or not. This could be a trap. He went with his gut. "No. I have two others with me."

"Good. Have one person open the doorway while the other two wait at the top. You'll still have to be fast once the door opens, but your odds will be better. When you enter the main room, there's an archway on the south wall. There will be two guards there. Shoot first, don't ask questions. Esme will be in the second room with seven women. The women won't be a problem. They're drugged and compliant. Just grab her and get out of there."

"How did you get this number?" Demon asked.

"Hurry!" Andres urged, ignoring his question. "I'll try and stall, but it won't work for long. I know you'll be safe for forty-five minutes as we prepare. After that, no guarantees."

The line went dead.

"Andres? The kid?" TB asked.

"Yeah," Demon said. "He developed a crush on Cherry while we were touring the plantation. Couldn't keep his eyes off her. He must have just been where she was."

"Do you trust him?" TB asked.

"Hell no," Demon replied. "But do we have any other choice? Intel on this place and these people is as bad as breaking into government databases."

"No," Midas corrected him, "I can get in government databases. The Salieri are worse. It's like 3D printers in reverse. I'm stripping microscopic layer after microscopic layer off and getting nowhere fast. You either trust him, or you run blind."

"I don't like those choices," TB muttered.

"Well, this restaurant serves nothing but shit sandwiches right now, so pick your shit and go. Time's running down."

"Wait a minute." Demon looked blankly at TB and Steel. "What did he mean by 'ritual'?"

"I don't know, but it doesn't sound good," Steel replied. "We better get moving while Midas digs so that we're ready to go."

"I still have no visual on you three, so keep me updated with what's going on. The cameras still show they're recording, so maybe when you get out of there, we'll at least have a record of everything."

They took off running down the hallway, not bothering to be covert. Glances down hallways showed no one moving around. It appeared that the strange tone they'd heard while in the warehouse was some sort of signal to immediately evacuate the area. At least, he hoped that was true. Having to fight off security with a time limit was not on his to-do list right now.

When they reached the door Andres had mentioned, TB updated the time frame. "Minus thirty-eight minutes."

Demon entered the code as Nova repeated it back to him. When the door handle turned in his grip, it opened into a stairwell. It was pitch black except for a glowing wall panel to the left as they entered, likely the only way to open the door and go back into the hallway. Quickly and quietly, they put on their night vision goggles and took the stairs single file.

When they reached the landing where they would need to enter the code, Steel halted them. "We've got time. Let me run point and verify Andres' information before you enter that code." He headed up the remaining stairs. Seconds later, he came over the line again. "Stairs continue up until they hit the ceiling. So far, the boy's honest."

"Kid said two guards inside," TB cautioned. "Even if there's no one right at the doorway, we'll be dead before we even get our heads into the room to see what's going on. We need to see what we're walking into."

"How are we going to do that, TB?" Demon barked. "Midas can't get us eyes in there. Said there are no cameras."

"Midas, can Nova get into the door controls and open it a half inch? Enough to get a flexi-cam in there so we can get eyes on the room?"

"As I've said before, 'Does the Pope wear a funny hat?'" There was mumbling over the airwaves about people asking him stupid questions. "Give us a second." Keys clacked in the background. "Okay, it should pop free in three... two... one..."

There was a tiny click, and Demon could see that the groove showing the door seal now had a slight gap.

Steel dug a flexi-cam out of his kit, connected it to his watch, turned it on, and slid the thin lens through the crack in the door. After turning it three hundred sixty degrees, he removed the camera and packed it away again.

"Two guards, southern wall, all as described. I'll take point, and TB will take the tail," Steel offered. "Your only job, D, is to get Cherry and get the hell out of here. Let us take care of the rest. Don't stop for us. Don't wait. Just grab and go. We'll meet you at the beach."

"Affirmative."

33

APRIL 16, 2023

Cherry

A girl with white-blonde hair flowing down her back approached Cherry. She couldn't be more than fifteen or sixteen years old. Her eyes were mostly black pupils with a thin line of sea blue around them, her stare vacant. She held out a small stone cup with no handles. "Drink this." Only two words were spoken, and Cherry knew the girl was under the influence of something.

Cherry threw her hand out, knocking the cup free of the woman's hold. The girl barely responded to it being dislodged from her hands, and she seemed to watch with abject fascination as the liquid spilled out of the cup where it lay on the ground and along the grooves between the stones on the floor.

Fire in her eyes, Cherry declared, "I'm not drinking anything you give me."

It took only a second for Matthew to grab the girl in front of her, put his arm around her at chest height, and open a wicked, sharp stiletto knife. The girl didn't react to the knife at her throat. She merely continued to watch the liquid flow along the cracks. The man sneered at Cherry. "I won't bother to threaten you because you'll just be stubborn and make me kill you rather than do what I ask. But I doubt you'll stand so firm if I threaten harm to her. I advise you to drink this time." Over his shoulder, he yelled, "Bring another cup!"

A second girl languidly poured another cup of liquid from the pitcher and brought it to her. Cherry dug her heels in. She took the cup from the second girl and locked her eyes with Matthew. "I won't drink it." Slowly, she turned the cup upside down, allowing the liquid to fall to the ground and splash off the stone.

It was over in a flash. Matthew pulled his knife quickly from right to left, and the girl he'd been holding in his arms fell to the floor in a heap, bleeding out at his feet. Her eyes never closed. She never said a word other than the initial soft gasp at the pressure of his knife. However, Cherry knew the exact moment the girl died. It was as if the light that had been her presence suddenly went out, and her eyes went dull. Now her blood mingled with the spilled liquid on the floor.

Matthew grabbed the second girl in the same hold as the first. "Bring another cup," he ordered quietly to the third girl.

His eyes never left Cherry's as she struggled to maintain her composure. She let herself scream internally and mourn for the girl at her feet for all of two seconds before she shored up her defenses.

This time, when the third girl approached, she took the cup from her hands, and without looking away from Matthew, she drank the liquid down. When she finished, she dropped the cup to the floor. "Let her go." The words were soft but filled with anger. If she ever got the chance, she was going to kill him herself.

His smile was smug. "I think I'll hold onto her for a little bit. There are a few more things you need to do before the boss returns, and I want to make sure you're ready when he gets here. Since threatening you has no effect, this little one here will be my insurance that you comply." He pulled the girl tighter to his chest, the knife point nicking her delicate throat but not slicing.

"Bastard," Cherry ground out. "Brave man hiding behind a child."

"Don't need to be brave," he taunted her. "Just need to know my enemy's pressure points. These girls? They're yours."

It took only a few minutes for his partner to come and pick up the body of the dead girl while two of the remaining girls cleaned up the blood as best they could. The other three had Cherry stripped, washed, and redressed in a white robe in a matter of minutes. Based on the paintings on the wall, she had a glimmer of an idea of how her initiation was going to go. Hell no! She'd fight what was about to happen with every breath she had in her. Unfortunately, knowing that she'd been drugged, she had to admit she probably was going to lose that fight eventually. That wouldn't stop her from trying though.

By the time her attendants had backed away, she was freezing. She could tell that the room was still warm, heated by the underground springs, but her body temperature felt like it plummeted, likely an effect of whatever drug they'd given her. Absentmindedly, she rubbed her bare arms, trying to feel any sort of warmth.

When the warmth came, it was like fire was racing through her veins, burning her from the inside out. Her skin even appeared to glow red and orange when she looked at it. Whatever they'd given her was going to cause hallucinations.

There was a sudden tickling sensation in her hands. She gazed in horror at her arms, which she held out in front of her, watching bubbles racing back and forth under the skin. When one bubble bumped into another, they popped, leaving behind a silky fluid on her skin. One half of her was intrigued at what her brain was producing, the other half disturbed. She took in a deep breath and worked to calm the panic trying to claw its way to the surface. Sweat. Chemically, the drug was causing her body to overheat and produce sweat. Already, her brain was struggling to separate reality from unreality. She needed to slow her breathing. Focus. If she allowed panic in, she'd lose whatever small grasp she'd have on what was actually going on versus what her brain tried to create as an alternative.

The room began to feel like it was moving under her feet. Looking down her body, she realized that she was moving, only not by her own power. The women who had come into the room to ready her for Andres were guiding her toward the altar at the center of the circle. Her brain told her to resist, but instead, she kept moving in the direction they pushed her. Head swimming, she felt herself being helped onto the slab, then urged to lie down. She felt so ill, and suddenly she felt tired. So tired. Like weights had been attached to her skin that were gently pulling her down. A tiny little spark inside urged her to fight, but every time she tried to remember why she couldn't just go to sleep, she felt herself get dragged further down into a swirling fog that was filling the room.

In the background of the room, she thought she heard a humming sound, like the drone of working bees in a hive. Not an unpleasant noise itself, but given the darkened surroundings lit only by fire, it was unnerving. There were voices, too, but she couldn't make out what they were saying. Looking around the room, she saw the six girls standing in an arc around the top of the sunken space, hands clasped below their waists, eyes focused on the walls. Their mouths weren't moving. She turned her head toward the archway into the other room. There. The voices were coming from there, the same place where the fog was coming in from. If she could just focus a little harder, and if the bees would just be a little quieter, she knew she'd be able to hear what was being said.

Her head felt as if it were attached to the table. She could move it from side to side, but if she tried to lift it, the weight at the back of her skull was so heavy, she couldn't. Rolling her head to the right, she noticed that the flickering lights from the torches had stopped. The room still lightened and darkened as if they were burning in real time, and the fog continued to move into the room as well, but both had taken on the effect of old-fashioned, two-dimensional stage art for a children's play being pushed onto a stage during a performance.

Behind the stilled flames, the figures painted on the walls began to move. She shuddered at the grotesqueness of shifting images, but she felt rooted to the spot and couldn't seem to look away from the walls. The humming noise increased in volume, and the torchlight was impossibly bright at its source. The figures on the wall continued to move around, change partners, and resume their carnal activities. She could feel reality slipping away with every second, but despite feeling cemented to the spot where she lay, she wasn't so far gone yet that she couldn't feel other thoughts intruding.

Did Demon know she was gone? They'd taken her watch off, and there were no windows to see if it was light outside, so she couldn't tell what time it was, let alone how long she'd been gone. Was her tracker working? She had two placed strategically inside her body. On his last mission, fish boy's... What was his name again? He had a broken fin. Arm? Something. His first tracker had been dug out of him, and the second one wouldn't turn on. Had they pulled her trackers out? She had a third one somewhere. Where was it? She hoped it was working.

The droning sound grew in volume, and the male figures on the walls began to fight amongst themselves, their faces drawn back in anger and pain. The female figures were crying and calling for help, cowering along the walls. There were other sounds, as well. Thuds that weren't rhythmically timed. Grunts.

It was too much. Her head began to spin, and she felt like she was going to vomit, so she closed her eyes. This was better. She felt herself smile. Much better. Behind her lids, her brain imprinted a vision of Demon's face. How he'd smiled at her on their walk through the plantation. His dark hair lifted in the breeze, the gentle uptilt at the corners of his mouth. The deep green of his irises as he'd flipped his sunglasses up to the top of his head and stared straight into her soul before he'd kissed her stupid. She felt his hands grabbing hold of her arms and putting them around his neck like he had the night down on the beach against the stone wall, and she felt swept up like a bride going over the threshold, his arms clutching her tightly to him as he carried her up the stairs to their room.

It wasn't fair. She felt tears leak from her eyes. She swore she could smell the ocean when she breathed in, feel the heat that the sun left on his skin under her fingertips, feel the grit of the sand he could never quite lose from any of his body, and taste the salt of the ocean as her tongue swiped out to wet her dry lips.

"Body shots later, fireball. Hang on tight."

She giggled. What an odd thought to have, and in his voice, even.

Her body felt like it crested on a wave, the water carrying her high above the chaos below the water. The scent of sand, salt, and sun curled around her, blocking out all of the noise. She smiled and burrowed deeper into the wave, then let it take her under into the depths of inky blackness.

34

APRIL 16, 2023

Demon

After pulling the camera back to their side of the door, Steel readied the flash-bang; they opened the door, and he threw it at the same time. The noise it made when it went off was deafening due to the stone walls, and the quirky portion of Demon's brain made a note to test everyone's hearing when they got back home. As the smoke spewed from TB's modified device, the three teammates rushed the room. Steel took care of Matthew's partner, TB took care of Matthew, and Demon went in after Cherry.

His heart nearly erupted from his chest when he ducked into the room through the smoke that was rolling into the antechamber. A woman was lying in the far corner, her dress stained a rusty color. Six other women were standing in a semicircle around a sunken space in the floor. After surveying the room quickly, he leaped down to Cherry's supine form, skipping the stairs altogether, and gathered the redhead lying on the stone table.

When he threw her arms around his neck and pulled her to him, he heard a soft moan and a sigh that sounded like his name, right before her mouth latched onto his neck with a soft swipe of her tongue.

He groaned. "Body shots later, fireball. Hang on tight."

He lifted her off the table, then dashed up the steps with her. At one point, he had to turn sideways with her to clear the arch without banging her legs on the walls, then jumped in order to clear Matthew's falling body as TB finally put him down for good. Steel was already at the doorway, making sure no one was coming up the stairs so they could make a clean exit.

As Demon arrived at the floor entry, Midas gave them a warning. "The goon squad is at the door. Andres has entered the code incorrectly twice. You have maybe ten seconds before they're in."

"*Mierda!* We won't make it." Steel turned and looked at them. "Back into the antechamber. Quick!"

The men rushed back inside the second room to take cover. Once there, Demon ducked to the right inside the archway, plastering himself as best as he could to the wall behind the raised stone lip of the doorway. TB and Steel grabbed the bodies of the two guards and dragged them into the antechamber, dumping them in the corner where the dead girl lay. In an effort to try and protect the drugged girls, the two men herded them down behind the altar and tried to push them into crouched positions as low as they could go.

"You've got eight men coming your way. Giudici is leading the way, followed by Deschamps, Zion, Andres, Howard, and three men I don't know, who are bringing up the rear. I don't see any weapons on them."

Agonizing seconds passed. Demon felt a twitch in his arms, but it wasn't his muscles weakening from holding Cherry; it was the woman herself, seeming to struggle out of whatever haze of drugs she'd been given. The timing was shite. She whimpered in pain, then started to retch. "Feck! Cherry's sick."

Steel dashed to the opposite side of the archway, flattening himself against the wall similar to Demon's position.

Because Demon was holding her in a bridal carry, and she was unconscious, she began to choke on her own vomit. "Sorry, *a chuisle*. This is gonna hurt." In as fluid a motion as he could, he dropped her legs, then turned her over the arm he'd let go of her with. With his other arm no longer needed to support her, he reached forward to her mouth, pried it open, and stuck two fingers as far down her throat as possible, trying to clear the fluid. Now the rest of her stomach contents could exit without going down her windpipe, and she could punch him for the bruised esophagus later.

As soon as she was done vomiting, she hung limp over his arm, still not aware enough to move on her own. He gently propped her up in a seated position off to the side, then resumed his position by the door. As Giudici passed through the door, Demon felt himself trying to press into the wall itself. They needed the entire group to be past them before they moved.

Of course, the odds were shite and didn't work in their favor. By the time Howard hit the doorway, everyone knew something was wrong. If the women crouched and whimpering on the floor weren't a clue, the dead bodies in the corner certainly were.

TB threw another of his flash-bangs toward the door, and as soon as it went off, he rose, both guns drawn and shooting. He connected with Giudici's shoulder, sending the man spinning off to the side.

Howard, being a military man, immediately saw the benefit of retreat and backed through the doorway, pushing those who were behind him into the main room.

Zion managed to draw his own weapon and get off several shots before backing out of the room using Andres as a shield, and he fled down the stairs. The three unknown men followed.

Steel had Deschamps in a choke hold and squeezed until the man was unconscious, put him down on the floor, and took off after Zion and the others, jumping down half the first flight of stairs to try and catch up. He managed to hit the last man in the line as he attempted to clear the doorway, shooting him in the back, then had to jump over him at the bottom of the steps.

After making sure that Cherry had remained untouched in the fray, Demon ran over to Giudici to check his wound. As much as he wanted to murder the man himself, they needed him alive if at all possible. He hauled the man to his feet, the coward groaning and calling out about his pain. "Shut up, you bastard. It's just a flesh wound, which is less than you deserve."

"Midas, we're going to need some help here!" TB informed him. "We are boxed in. Three of us. Four dead bodies. Seven drugged women, if you count Cherry, and two hostages—Giudici and Deschamps."

"I love a challenge," Midas replied. "Okay. Nobody panic, but I'm sealing you in. Nova, reroute power to the computer panels for door seven to my control only."

"Completed, Midas," the AI confirmed.

"All right, you guys need to sit tight. The cavalry is on its way. I'm putting a drone up in the area to pull surveillance, and we'll have you out of there as soon as we can. What kind of injuries do you have?"

Demon rattled off the situation. "Four DOA. One of the girls we saw, Matthew, and two adult males. The other six females appear to be conscious and unharmed but under the influence of some sort of hallucinogen. Cherry is unconscious. Vomiting. Also drugged, likely a hallucinogen. One male, unconscious but otherwise unharmed. One male, shoulder flesh wound." The next comment he issued directly to the wounded man. "Alive, unfortunately." He shoved the man into the wall. Looking at Steel, he told him, "Pressure on it and bind it." Then he turned and went back to Cherry.

As he did a quick visual check of her for any injuries he might have missed, he called over his shoulder to TB. "Make sure none of the girls are hit or have any injuries. If you see any bruising, open sores, signs of malnutrition, or anything that looks like physical harm, document it. We need a photo of each woman, a fingerprint scan, and two pieces of hair with shaft and follicle for identification and toxi-cology purposes. Same for the victims."

TB and Steel went about assessing injuries, taking photos, scan-ning fingerprints, and collecting hair samples. For the most part, now that the effects of the flash-bang had dissipated, the girls were calmer. Depending on how long they'd been continuously drugged and with what, they would probably start coming out of the hallucinations and be frightened, but at least they were safe.

As Cherry's eyelids began to flutter open, he gave a long, loud exhale. Thank god she was waking up. The longer she stayed uncon-scious, the more he worried. Vomiting whatever they'd given her was both good and bad. It got it out of her system, but if it were an allergic reaction, it would be concerning since they were locked down for a while.

"Hey there, fireball," he whispered. "Can you open your eyes for me, *a chuisle?*"

Slowly, her eyes opened to half-mast. "Mmm, my ocean sex god. I smelled you, and I thought it was a dream."

Grinning, he grabbed her wrist to take her pulse. "Nope. No ocean, just me."

Her other hand reached up to cup the side of his face. "You always smell like sun and sand and sea. It's how I always knew you were around before I saw you."

"Well, that's not good. Can't sneak up on my enemies if they can smell me coming. Pulse is a little thready yet. How's your head?"

He watched her frown and roll her head from side to side against the wall. "Everything's really loud. Someone needs to tell those drummers to take it down a notch."

"I'll let them know." She was still feeling the effects of the drug. "How did they drug you? Needle? Drink? Food? Do you know?"

She swallowed. "Drink. Why does my throat hurt?"

"You vomited not too long ago and started choking. I had to stick my fingers down your throat to get you to finish expelling it. You'll probably hurt for a little bit. I'd give you water, but we're stuck here right now without any. I don't want to give you anything they brought in here." He rustled through his pockets and found a piece of wrapped candy he kept for this sort of situation. He unwrapped it and held it up to her mouth. "Open." He popped it in between her lips. "Hopefully that helps. Try not to chew it or swallow it whole, okay?"

"Butterscotch. Eww," she complained, wrinkling her nose. "Better than vomit flavor though."

He chuckled. "I bet."

"I didn't throw up on you, did I?"

"Eh." He shrugged. "My shoes will survive. I'd be more worried about the video Steel took for the group chat."

"Liar," she said with a weak smile. Her eyes closed, her head lolling to the side. "So tired," she mumbled.

He smoothed her hair back from her forehead. "Rest, *a chuisle*. It's better you sleep through whatever this is. We're stuck here for a while until Midas figures out how to spring us out of this tomb, anyway."

"Thank you for coming for me."

He could barely understand her, but he figured it out. "Always, fireball. I'll always come for you."

WHILE HE'D BEEN CHECKING IN EVERY THIRTY MINUTES, IT WAS just over five hours later when Midas came back online with news. "Okay, get ready, boys and girls. I need you all to be gathered as far south as you can. Medusa is coming in hot with some fireworks on the north side. ETA seven minutes."

There was a groan from across the room. "While I'll be glad to get out of this stone abomination, I really hate being in any vehicle that woman is flying or driving," TB complained.

"I don't have any airsick bags on me, so D will have to stick his fingers down your throat if you start puking," Steel ribbed him.

"Hardy-har-har. You don't like flying with her either."

"Yeah. But I don't get airsick when I do."

"Hey, dumbasses, don't let Cherry hear you saying that," Demon whisper-yelled.

"It's okay for you to tease her, but not us?" TB groused.

"Yeah. I'm the one she threw up on."

While TB started moving the girls into the southern corner of the building, Steel came over and crouched down at Demon's side. "How's she doing?"

"Okay. No more vomiting, but she's feverish, and I don't like her pulse rate. She's in and out, but sleep is probably better for her right now anyway. Without knowing what they gave her, it's difficult to say if how she's reacting is normal detox or not."

"Hallucinogen?"

"Yeah. She's been saying some pretty bizarre things in her sleep. Given what's painted on the walls, I can only imagine what she's seeing."

"She's strong. She'll be okay." Steel turned his cold gaze on Demon, and he just barely managed to hold his stare. "You got your head straight and shit sorted?"

"Yeah," he admitted.

"Good. You take care of our girl, and I'll go get the douchebags."

By the time Demon had relocated Cherry with everyone else in the south corner and taken cover as best they could, Medusa was on the line.

"Dropping the payload on my mark, two flight attendants will be available to assist you in entering the aircraft. Three... two... one... mark."

Moments later, a crash shook the building, dust rolling in once again from the main room. The sounds of helicopter blades and machine gun fire filtered through the building. As soon as the shaking stopped, TB and Steel grabbed a prisoner apiece, then hustled the girls out into the main area.

Gilgamesh and Loki stood at the rubble to help the women get on the helicopter. "Please have your boarding passes ready, and no carry-ons allowed. This flight is at maximum," Medusa called out. "We're about to take additional enemy fire, so we need to clear the ground in a hurry."

Demon waited with Cherry in his arms until all of the others were aboard, then, with the help of Gilgamesh, picked his way over the rubble. Loki and TB each took an arm to help him into the helicopter so that he didn't have to let go of the unconscious handler, but as soon as Gilgamesh was halfway in the chopper, Medusa was off and banking steeply. Luckily everyone was strapped in... except for Gilgamesh, who was hanging half out, yelling about spanking Medusa's ass when they got back on the ground, but she pretended she couldn't hear him.

Demon paid no attention to anything else around him but the woman in his arms, still out cold.

35

APRIL 16, 2023

Demon

MEDUSA LANDED THE HELICOPTER JUST NORTH OF MOUNT Pelée on Martinique at what looked like an older estate. From the air, it was well hidden by a canopy of trees, except for a small, isolated patch of dirt that looked no bigger than a schoolyard basketball court. The helicopter literally fit in the space by inches. There, they were met by Midas, who helped them secure Giudici and Deschamps in a basement clearly outfitted as a jail.

"Waters," Cherry mumbled.

Demon pressed a kiss to her temple. "Rest, *a chuisle.*"

Vehemently, she shook her head. "Need to tell him. About Sarah."

He frowned at her pale face, eyes still closed, her mouth pinched with discomfort. "Cherry—"

"Please." Her eyes opened. "It's important."

Something in her tone told him that if he refused her, she'd find a way. He looked up at Midas. "Get him on the computer."

He carried Cherry into the dining room of the estate and deposited her into a chair at the table. Instead of sitting next to her, he crouched at her side, one hand caging her in the chair by holding onto the ladder back, the other hand covering hers in her lap. "You need rest, *a chuisle*."

"I can rest after. This won't take long, but he needs to know. It can't wait."

Moments later, Waters appeared on the screen. "Good to see you upright, Cherry-bomb. Midas said you needed to talk to me. You could have slept for a bit first."

"Sarah." Her voice cracked with pain.

There was a pause. "What about her, Cherry?"

"Zion." Her voice cracked again. "It was Zion."

Demon knew the second Waters comprehended what she was trying to tell him. Everything about the man tightened. The silence felt like time had stopped, and it only started again when Cherry spoke.

"The shipment. In 2017. The one you intercepted. It was Zion's. Something about it was his ticket into the elders. I don't know exactly what that means, but it sounded like it was meant to prove himself worthy of an upper-level position. Maybe like Gendry was trying to work his way higher, only Zion was at a much further stage. When I sent you in to intercept that shipment, it ruined his opportunity, and he had to start over. He took Sarah as his revenge." She paused. Demon could feel her body start to shake. "He was there that day. When you were rescued. He said he was the one who made sure you watched as she died."

If he didn't know better, he would have thought the computer screen was frozen based on how still Waters sat. Someone swore behind him. He heard a thud as someone else collapsed onto a chair. Within seconds, she was collapsing in his arms and sobbing uncontrollably.

"I'm so sorry." It was all she could get out, over and over.

Demon rose, swept Cherry up into his arms, and then sat down in the chair with her on his lap. He clutched her tightly, holding her head to his chest, tucking it under his chin.

They sat in silence for several minutes as Cherry worked through her tears and Waters digested the information. When their team leader's voice came over the speakers, it was gravelly and tight, and everyone knew that there would be no arguing with him. This was the Waters they'd known before his capture. A killer. Demon hadn't seen him like this in years, and he wasn't sure if seeing his boss returned to his former self was a relief or if he liked his boss better on the softer end since he'd met Kubrick. But the man before him? His eyes bored through the screen, his entire focus on Cherry.

"You listen to me, Cherry-bomb, and you listen well. You are not to blame. Don't you dare apologize to me. Ever. That man is not your uncle, and even if he were your goddamn father, you still wouldn't be apologizing to me. He made his own choices and lived them.

"I know exactly what you're thinking right now. Stop it. You couldn't have known what he was. Monsters hide who and what they are until they can't hide anymore. Zion can no longer hide who he is, and we will find him, we will catch him, and he will pay for what he's done. To his victims. To Sarah. To me. To our team. To our friends. To you. And to your father. I promise you that."

"But it is my fault, Waters. You don't know..." she whispered. "General Howard. He fixated on me at a young age. Something about his daughter. When they took my dad, it was his plan to remove my dad to get to me. When he couldn't get to me like he had planned, Zion bought my protection. I suppose I should be grateful, but..." She sucked in a deep breath, expelled it. "He was the buyer. For Flame. When he saw her, she reminded him of me, and he made the deal. Then she disappeared before Gendry could profit off her. Gendry finally found her again, but it was the worst of all coincidences. So when we thwarted him again? I think he snapped. He wasn't looking for a bride anymore. But he definitely wanted his revenge."

A loud crash sounded behind him. By the swear words and the muttering, it was TB. Now General Howard was definitely on TB's most-wanted list. The interrogator would stop at nothing, and he would hunt until his dying day to find the man who threatened his woman.

"Waters," TB growled. "If he's that pissed off, he'll try to take her again."

"I got it, TB. I'm headed home as fast as physically possible, and I will guard her with my life. In the meantime, call one of our trad guys to go pick her up and bring her to Tribe. She'll be safe."

The giant of a man picked something up, threw it, and whatever it was shattered.

"TB!" Cherry cried out as he stormed out of the room, swearing and slamming the door behind him. "He'll never forgive me. I've hurt everyone." She buried her face in Demon's neck, clinging to him as she sobbed.

He didn't know how to help her, and it was killing him inside. All he could do was hold her tighter.

"Cherry. Listen to me," their boss said. When she didn't turn her head, he tried again. "Look at me, Cherry," he ordered her through the screen.

"Sweetheart," Demon murmured. "Look at Waters."

It took a moment, but eventually, her head turned—eyes swollen, face blotchy, exhaustion clear. She needed hydrating, some bland food to soak up what was left of the drugs running through her system, and rest. Lots of rest. He needed to get her out of here and into bed.

Waters had leaned forward on his arms and was staring intently into the camera. "I'm gonna make this short and sweet because I can see D puffing up like one of those spiny fish over getting you checked out and resting. You. Are not. To blame. I will make sure Flame is safe. I promise you, nothing is going to happen to her. Get some sleep. It will be okay."

Demon nodded at his boss, then pressed a kiss to the top of her head. "C'mon, sweetheart. You need rest." He stood with her in his arms, and Steel pulled the chair back so that Demon could turn and carry her away from the table.

He heard quiet voices in the room as he walked out. Likely Steel getting directives from Waters. Didn't matter. He just needed her away from it so that maybe she could shut her brain down for a while and start recovering.

Her exhaustion was so complete, she was asleep before he even made it upstairs to an empty bedroom. He undressed her, sponged off the blood and gore he could get to, slipped a T-shirt on her that someone had dropped off outside the door while he was caring for her, and pulled the covers over her. She'd probably be out for hours, but he scribbled a quick note. He didn't really want to leave her, but he needed to go check on the girls they'd brought back with them.

Demon joined the local doctor Mythos had hired to help them process the girls. After they were examined for acute conditions, they were given rooms on the second floor to clean up, change clothes, and rest. In a few days, Medusa would fly the girls to Gem and Nemo, who would arrive to take them to one of the Mythos schools while they waited to reunite with their families or, if they had no families, give them a safe haven.

WHEN DEMON RETURNED TO CHERRY'S ROOM SEVERAL HOURS later, it was to find her lying in bed, awake, and staring out the open French doors looking out over the forested area. He closed the door and leaned on it, giving his aching back a chance to rest, as well as waiting for her to recognize he was there. He knew she had to be feeling... well, he honestly didn't know what she'd be feeling. An awful lot had happened to her in the last forty-eight hours. It would be enough to mess anyone up. Even a woman as strong as Cherry.

He waited a long time before finally making the first move. "You feeling okay, fireball?"

"I'm fine."

"Can I get you anything? Food? Drink?"

"Not hungry."

"Understandable. I took a blood sample, but you were pretty out of it. They weren't using anything too scary. MDMA. Not very creative, but... given what you were supposed to be put through as part of their ritual, not surprising. The effects should wear off completely by tomorrow."

"And the other girls?"

"They were under something different, and for much longer, probably to keep them aware but compliant. Those results are going to take a little longer, and we're going to wait until we get them to a more secure location to run additional tests since things here are a little more primitive."

"Good."

Her voice sounded so defeated, and he didn't know what to do. She clearly wasn't going to ask him for anything. He wanted to hold her and tell her he was there for her. He wanted to kiss her and take away her pain. He wanted to make love to her and reassure her that she wasn't alone like he assumed she was feeling right now. He needed reassurance, himself, that she was here, that she was okay, and that she was safe. That they were where they had been before Zion took her. But his wants and needs weren't important at the moment, and he wasn't getting the sense that even what he was doing right now was welcome.

Instead, he crossed to the bed, sitting between her and the French doors to the gallery. Her eyes shifted, but to the wall and not to him. "Talk to me, *a chuisle*," he whispered. "What can I do?"

He felt the coldness in her permeate the room. "Don't call me that. I'm not your pulse; I'm not your heartbeat or even your fireball. It's Cherry. Call me Cherry. That's what you can do." She paused. "I'd like to be alone, please."

What the feck? The turnabout from her rescue, not to mention the time in the hotel, was worse than a one-eighty. It was worse than how they'd been the past few months at home. She was cutting him out. He knew she'd struggle, but he hadn't expected this.

"I understand you need time—"

"I don't need time, Demon. I need you to leave."

"Cherry." His mouth stuck on the name. It wasn't what he wanted to call her, but he didn't want to upset her further. "I know this has been a lot. Your dad. Zion. Giudici. Howard—"

"You don't know shit, Demon!" She paused, and then more firmly, she told him, "I want you to leave."

So much for upsetting her less. He was torn. Should he fight her? Refuse to leave? Lord knew that's what he wanted to do. If he let her pull away, he might never get her back. He thought they'd finally come to a point of acceptance. They'd come too far in their relationship to let it all fall apart now. Somewhere along the line, he'd realized she was right and that it was time to put his pain aside. Time to let it drift, like flotsam and jetsam. He'd accepted it. Without her knowing it, he'd given her what she'd claimed she'd wanted. He hadn't let go of the medication, but he had let go of the pain. He knew it would be torture but thought maybe he could withstand the pain. She was worth it.

Now that she had it, albeit unknowingly, she was throwing it back in his face.

He didn't think he'd ever been more confused in his life. "What's going on?"

He understood that she needed some space. Her world had fallen apart once when her father was kidnapped. Now, twenty-six years later, it was like it was happening all over again, except that this time, she had to feel even more betrayed. Men who should have protected her out of loyalty to her father had been her father's downfall, and she had to feel truly alone. If he gave her space, it would let her come to terms with what had happened. Maybe then he could work his way back to her. He'd done it once. Surely he could do it again?

"Don't shut me out. Let me help you," he pleaded.

"You can 'help' me by leaving. Leave, Demon. Leave and don't come back. When we go home, everything can go back to how it was. It will be better for both of us."

He was in shock for the first time in his life. This was not his fireball.

"How is this better for both of us?" He shifted so that he was in her eyeline, unable to avoid looking at him. But she didn't meet his eyes. Instead, her focus seemed to be on his shirt.

"You said you were in this, Esme. Not two days ago. Now, suddenly, you want nothing to do with me? Did you not mean it after all?"

"It doesn't matter if I meant it or not. It won't work. I don't have the energy to work through it. This is all just... too much."

The words came out of his mouth without thought. "When did you become a coward, Esme?"

She jackknifed up in the bed, scuttling away from him, the sheet pooling at her waist.

"You and I are part of this issue, but I'm going to put that off to the side right now because you've been through some serious shite in the last few days." He reached out a hand and placed it on the sheet over her leg. "Right now, you're wallowing in grief. It's not right. It's not fair. I would take it all away from you if I could, but it's yours, so I don't have that power. But all your life, you've been a fecking power-house. Nothing drags you down—not losing your mom, not losing your dad, and not all the challenges you've faced putting Tribe together. You've never backed down from a fight in your life. Don't start now."

She tried to move her leg from his touch, but he squeezed gently, keeping her in place.

"You knew that the events surrounding your father might end this way. You talked about it. After twenty-six years, it was the most probable outcome. Now that it's reality, you're going to crawl into a hole and die like a wounded animal? No. Absolutely not."

He stood up at the bedside, ripped back the covers, grabbed her by her wrist, and pulled her from the bed to stand in front of him. "You can be sad, Esme. You've earned that right. You can be pissed. You've earned that too. But don't wallow in your pain, and don't let your rage consume you."

He threaded his fingers through her hair at the base of her neck to pull her tight to his chest and bent his head to murmur against her hair. "You're strong enough to get through this. Strong enough to get through anything. Fight, Esme! Tell me you hate me if you want. Say you're giving up on us when we've barely gotten started. Claim you're taking back every sweet word you said, every glorious moment we had together. But don't you dare let this change who you are. Because if you do, I will haunt your every moment until it's more difficult to be whatever this shell of a woman is right now than it is to be who I know you are at your core."

She remained unmoving in his embrace. It was her lack of response that scared him more than anything. He dropped her wrist and backed away. "I'll leave this room. I'll give you space. But even if I'm thousands of miles from you, I'm not gone. I'll never be gone. Never. You don't get to break me and build me back up just to shatter me all over again. I won't let you do that to me or to you. To us."

His voice cracked on his last words. "*A chuisle mo chroí.*"

36

APRIL 17, 2023

Demon

Demon was pissed. "We have to go back! We need to catch these arseholes before they go to ground!"

"We will, but we can't rush back without a plan, D. There are way more of them than us," Midas reminded him.

"Since when has that mattered? There were even more douchebags in those mines in Zimbabwe and South Africa, yet we went in there."

"Yes, we did. But we had a plan, and right now, we've been on the ground for all of five hours. You all needed food, hydration, and you should be resting, but instead, we're here trying to figure out the best plan of attack. So sit your fucking ass down and regather your shit."

He threw himself into his chair, his brain divided. One half of him wanted to be upstairs in bed with Cherry, watching over her and helping her through the trauma she was sure to be entering. The other half wanted to race back to *Les Vergers de la Mer*, find Zion and

General Howard, and rip them apart with his bare hands. Maybe inject them with a needle infected with sepsis—something exceptionally painful—then sit back and watch them suffer.

"All right, now that Dr. Jekyll has returned from his Mr. Hyde episode, we can maybe put together a plan."

Midas, TB, Steel, and Demon were joined by Medusa, Loki, and Gilgamesh around the table in the dining area of the estate. A large-screen television on the wall was divided into four squares, holding Waters, Gem, Nemo, and then God's usual black screen with his voice wave when he spoke.

"Midas," God called out, "do we have eyes on any of our players?"

"At the moment, no. Last I was able to see, they had returned to the estate proper and appeared to be doing 'Flight of the Bumblebee' packing up. Demon's right. We don't have a ton of time. But packing up their operations isn't something that can be done in a few hours. There are a lot of moving pieces, not to mention that the plantation is a major source of ready cash funding for them. First thing Zion did when he got back to his office was begin diverting all the liquid assets out of their local accounts. I've got Nova searching globally for where he's stashing it. She'll find it eventually, but it's going to take a little time. We shut down what we could, but he was faster due to our primary focus of getting everybody here safely.

"Luckily, Nova was able to freeze the corporation accounts, at least temporarily, but it won't take them too long to override that. He wasn't able to divert those because it requires at least three board members, sort of like US nuclear deployment. We have their president, Giudici, on ice here. As far as we can tell, the rest of the board is clueless as to what is going on right now, but since we don't know who else on that board is also a Salieri member, we have to tread carefully with any information we leak.

"I've got Cyclopes infected into their systems, listening in on their emails, and where they have their phones attached to the internet. I was also able to hack a number of their cell phones. If chatter starts, we'll know. We've got maybe a week if they've got themselves someone as good as me, which I doubt, but it's always possible. If we want to be able to keep them from those funds permanently, we're going to need to go the legal route for that."

Waters grunted. "No doubt he's likely got contingency funds stashed elsewhere that we know nothing about, so those are another factor. We need to freeze him out as much as possible. If he gains access to the corporation accounts, he could go underground forever."

"Exactly. I've given that task to Nova as a secondary goal right now though. Once we get back to the estate and close that down, then I can put her on it as a primary."

Waters' gaze was assessing, his fingers tapping on the desk. "Smart. It's what I would have suggested. Good choice."

Midas pushed onward. "A little bit harder to do, but not impossible, is tracking Howard. I can't imagine he'd be dumb enough to return to his base, but if his ego is as big as we think it is, he might think he's untouchable. Hacking the American military is something I can do, but I'm going to need immunity if I get caught."

A crunching noise made the voice wave jump on the screen. "I'll deal with that. I may have a channel or two to reach out to. Perhaps we can even farm that out so it doesn't touch us directly. What about the boy? Andres?"

"Zion took him with. Hostage, maybe?" Midas said.

"Another asshole who hides behind children," TB grumbled.

"He's not really a kid. He's eighteen," Midas corrected him.

"Eighteen or not," Demon added, "he's cut off from his family now. From what I could tell, he's pretty sheltered. His grandfather seemed to have a short leash on him. He may have done right by helping in his back-assward way with rescuing Cherry, but he's as emotionally mature as a younger teen."

"He's going to have no footprint to follow. Not even a social media account to follow. He truly was a kid of the land."

Puzzled, Demon asked, "How did he get my phone number then?"

"I think he cloned your phone. Probably on the tour. Luckily, we use our watches for actual communication and our tablets, which he didn't have access to, so it was just the number of the dummy phone and all the other bogus information on it."

Waters brought everyone back to focus on their pressing need. "All right. We've gotten all that shit out of the way. Let's get a plan in place to get back to the estate and see what we can scare up."

Midas shrunk the team members on the screen and pulled up an array of hacked security cameras on the estate. "Security is in the process of activating kill switches on all of their computers. I missed a couple, but Nova is holding the others off for now by placing them in an infinite loop. Won't be long before they work through that once they realize what the problem is. We have twenty-four hours if we're lucky, so we need to get in there before they figure that shit out."

Medusa offered, "I can fly you back in. I was going to fly the girls out to Gem and Nemo tomorrow to get them to the nearest school, but they can wait another day. They can probably use the rest anyway. Three more bodies are extra firepower."

"Agreed," God said. "I would go do your checks, Medusa. I'm guessing once these guys get their plan in place, they're going to want to take off right away. They can always fill you in along the way."

"Will do." The enigmatic logistics expert of Mythos fluidly rose out of her seat and left the room, heading for her helicopter outside.

"All right. Our corner pieces of the puzzle are in place," God said. "Tracking the money, tracking Howard, tracking Zion, and the girls are settled until tomorrow. What about our guests?"

"I'll be talking to them shortly," TB grumbled. "I don't expect it will take long to get them to fold."

"Just don't work them too hard," Waters cautioned. "They do need to be alive to speak."

"Please," the interrogator said with a roll of his eyes. "These aren't some badass terrorists. All I'm going to have to do is loom, growl, and ask questions."

"Giudici is mine," Demon growled.

TB gave him a nod.

"And afterward?" Demon asked.

TB looked at Steel, who looked at Demon. "I'm feeling a little cliché," Steel replied. "I was thinking we could take a field trip to Mount Pelée. Make a deposit."

"He should burn in Hell," Demon snarled. "Poetic justice. Works for me."

"More important than all of this," God interrupted, "how's our handler?"

All eyes went to Demon. He shifted in his seat, working hard to rein in his temper at the men who had hurt Cherry and focus on what he was being asked. "Blood test came back MDMA. She should be out from its physical effects by tomorrow."

"Good."

Silence hung in the room like a weighted blanket. He hated those things. Suffocating, hot, not calming. Calming was the silence of the ocean. The rocking of the waves. The cool of the water.

"What about mentally?"

He shrugged. "Hurting."

More silence.

Finally, there was a crunching noise as God pulverized his sucker. "And?"

"And what?"

"Hurting and…"

With a sigh, Demon ran his fingers through his hair. "I don't know. She's shutting me out. There. Happy?" He stood up, his chair scraping violently along the hardwood floor as he stood. "I'm going to check on the girls. Call me when there's a plan and fill me in."

He fled the room, his brain screaming at him to go back up to Cherry, but he held the voice down under the waves of panic that he was losing her.

Late that night, he made a call to his team leader. He knew the man would be awake since he needed very few hours of sleep, and he was probably on a private flight home to take over Flame's protection detail. Plus he would want to be available if Kubrick called him from China. Demon was close to her, given his time guarding her in Roatán last year, and while she hadn't shared anything, he knew she was struggling with facets of their relationship. While he knew it wasn't a relationship-ending issue, he felt bad because he knew it was stressful for her, especially with them being separated for twelve weeks. He hoped he wouldn't be interrupting one of their calls.

Waters picked up the call almost immediately. "Hey, D. What's up?"

"When we go to St. Lucia, I want to stay behind."

The look his boss gave him was inscrutable. Finally, he asked, "Why?"

"I want to look for Cherry's father's remains. It might be a long shot, but she needs this. Without it, she's going to struggle. Intellectually, she knows he's gone, but she needs closure."

His boss considered the request. "And?"

"'And' what?"

"There's more to this request than that."

Elbows to the table, his hands running through his hair, Demon wondered how much to tell Waters. "I have some shite to figure out. Not about her. That's a no-brainer. She's it for me. But I've been avoiding dealing with a lot of things. It's time. Past time. I can't go to her like this, and it's not fair to the team."

Waters shrugged. "There's nothing to prove to the team, you know. They accept you just as you are. They're not giving up on you. Ever. You've kept your promises to them, unspoken as they are."

"How—?"

"I've always known, D. It doesn't take a genius to see what eats at you." Waters smiled. "Take whatever time you need and come back when you're good."

"I'm sorry. I know we're a man down with Nemo being gone—"

The man on the screen waved him off. "We've got Mythos if we really get in a jam. It's better if you come back to us in a headspace you want to be in. Just don't disappear on us, okay? I mean, we can track you if we have to, but I'd rather trust you to return. If you say you will, I know you'll keep that promise."

A weight seemed to lift off his shoulders. Those words from his boss meant a great deal, a sign of faith he hadn't realized he desperately needed to hear. Almost as much as hearing Cherry say something to that effect. The latter would take time.

"I promise. I'll come back."

Waters smiled. "Then I guess I'll see you when I see you. And by the way, I'm glad you're stepping up for Cherry. We would have gone back to look for her dad, but it will go a lot farther coming from you."

He sure hoped so.

37

APRIL 19, 2023

Cherry - The Decision

SHE HEARD THE TWO SOFT KNOCKS ON THE DOOR, BUT SHE didn't stir from where she lay on her side in the bed. If it were Demon, he would have just walked right in. Maybe if she didn't respond, whoever it was would go away.

She heard the turning of the doorknob behind her and the soft click as the latch gave, allowing the mystery knocker to enter. "Cherry? You awake?"

The soft Northern English lilt of Gem's voice came from the doorway. Cherry didn't move. Didn't respond.

The latch clicked again and was followed up by the footfalls of the thief approaching her bed. "You're a cat burglar. You suck at being quiet," Cherry complained.

"Wasn't trying to be quiet. If I hadn't wanted you to hear me, you wouldn't have."

The mattress dipped as Gem sat on the edge of the bed, then lay behind Cherry and snuggled up to her. "They say you haven't left the room since you got here. You can't stay like this, Cherry-bomb."

Yes, she most definitely could. She was rich. She could buy this estate. She could stay in this room forever. She didn't want company. She wanted to mourn her mother all over. She wanted to wallow in the pain of losing her father again. She wanted to stew in anger at the men who took him from her. She wanted to drown in her guilt for her part in Sarah's death, as well as that poor girl whose throat had been slit due to her refusal to be drugged. She was definitely pissed at herself for pushing away the man she'd learned to love after all these years, despite her fears of losing someone again.

And how did that go for her? He'd said he'd never be gone, but he hadn't come back after that, had he? He clearly decided it wasn't worth the fight, after all, so she'd lost him anyway. Stupid. So stupid! Even though she knew she was being foolish and a bitch, it was like she couldn't hold it back. Her misery sucked her down into a swirling whirlpool of anger, depression, and self-pity, where she lay broken at the bottom, looking up miles above her to daylight and safety but just too damn tired and hurting to try to swim out of it.

"Medusa was supposed to bring the girls to us, but I couldn't stay where we were. I needed to see you. Make sure for myself that you were all right, so we had Janus bring us in. We got in just before the guys got back. They said when they got there that everyone was gone."

"So he got away." Cherry's voice was so small, even she could barely hear it.

"They think they missed them by about an hour. Midas has cut off most of their funds. He wasn't able to get all of it locked down, but an anonymous tip went to the board at Nimbus, detailing what Zion was into. He says two board members vanished within a couple of hours of the email. The rest of the board had an emergency meeting in the wee hours of the morning and locked him out of funds there. In the meantime, Midas has got Nova following trails to offshore accounts and is going to work on shutting those down as well."

"They'll be well hidden. He'll be able to hide for a while."

"Probably," Gem admitted. "But he won't have the power he did. And he won't be able to hide forever from Midas or Nova."

Gem's voice was gentle as she burrowed a little closer into Cherry's back and hugged her friend even tighter. "You're scaring us, Cherry."

Cherry turned in her friend's arms and broke down completely. She clutched at Gem, afraid to let go. Afraid that if she did, the tide of her tears would sweep her away and drown her forever.

Out of the silence, she unburdened her shattered heart.

"The day of the bomb in the café, Demon called me out. He pointed out that my good intentions with Tribe really were the actions of an enraged girl who had a right to her pain but saw only an endgame and nothing in between. He was right.

"I was the one who had gathered the information on the shipment of women that Waters and the team rescued years ago. After the team rescued the victims, we thought we were in the clear. Instead, it put Tribe on the Salieri's radar. Little did we know that Waters became a target. The Salieri, particularly my uncle, were biding their time, waiting for the perfect opportunity to take their revenge. Sarah became their leverage. They knew she was Waters' pressure point, so they took her as retribution for interfering.

"That's what drove Waters to go rescue his sister with such disastrous results. She was beaten, assaulted, and murdered in front of him. He's been wracked with guilt his whole life when really the guilt should have resided with me. My choices led to consequences I never imagined. It never even occurred to me to think of that. How many other decisions have I made that negatively affected the lives of my team and others? After all, I almost got you killed."

Through it all, Gem held her, saying nothing. The sun was just beginning to set when Cherry's tears finally stopped.

"Sarah's death is not your fault. No one is to blame for that except the Salieri. And as far as the consequences of decisions, you lived through a terrible tragedy. No one would be thinking rationally.

Time compounds our bad behaviors, making it impossible for us to see clearly what was never clear to begin with. You can only make decisions based on what information is available. Do not beat yourself up over the past. It can't be changed, no matter how much we wish it could be."

"It cost me Demon," she whispered. "I sent him away. I told him I didn't want him anymore."

Gem gave a single beat of laughter. "No, it hasn't cost you anything, Cherry. At least, nothing but a little more time. You've been dancing around each other for so long, both allowing so many little things to get between you that they became big things. You both made excuses so that you didn't have to face your fears. Now you're faced with having to look yourselves straight on and lay all those fears aside. It's not easy. It's messy. It's painful. But it will be worth it, I promise. He's not going anywhere. Even if he leaves, you're his light. He can't stay in darkness forever."

They lay there in the quiet for some time before Gem gave her a kiss on the forehead. "I'm sorry. I have to go. Nemo, Janus, and the girls are waiting for me." Gem extricated herself from Cherry's arms and headed for the door. "Call me if you need me. I may not be able to answer right away, but as soon as I can, I'll be on the line." Before she closed the door, she added one last comment. "Forgive him, Cherry. He loves you so much. Like Nemo, he's just a man. He's going to fuck up occasionally. But right now, and I'm sorry to say this, but it's true. Right now, you're the one fucking up the best thing in the world. Don't let him get away."

The door closed softly behind the woman's sad smile and wave. Cherry lay there a little longer, thinking to herself about what Gem had said. She hadn't been strong enough to face everything tumbling down around her, and she took it out on him. He didn't deserve that. She had to make it right.

The fight to get out of bed was the most difficult she'd ever faced. Shower. Clothes. Find Demon. Beg his forgiveness if she had to. Lord above, she knew she probably deserved to grovel. Then be the strong woman she'd always thought she'd been before, but this time, be strong enough to ask for his help. Things might just be all right in the end.

When she'd gotten out of the shower and found some clothes that had been left behind for her, she headed downstairs. Mythos had apparently left, so Midas, TB, and Steel were sitting in the dining room, debriefing with Waters and God. All heads turned in her direction.

"Welcome back, Cherry," Waters greeted her. "How are you feeling?"

"Wrecked."

"Not unexpected. We're glad you're back with us."

Her eyes scanned the room, looking for the one man who wasn't there. "Where is he?"

The silence that fell was uncomfortable. She watched them look to Waters before their team leader answered, "He left with Nemo and Gem. Said he wanted to oversee the girls and their fuller examinations." He paused, as if he wanted to say something more, but stopped himself. "We're heading to St. Lucia to do some clean up. We'll be gone two days, then we'll swing back and pick you up. I want you to rest a bit longer."

"He's not going to come back. Are you going to go after him?"

The team didn't look at her, choosing instead to stare at the table in front of them. Waters was the only one who returned her gaze. "Not at this time," Waters admitted.

It felt like an odd answer, but she refused to question it. Tears in her eyes, she begged, "Don't. Let him go. As a gift to me."

She watched as each man looked at each other, then at her. One by one, they nodded.

Cherry turned on her heel, went back upstairs, and crawled into bed. Her eyes glued to the Pitons, which she could see through her open window, she murmured into her pillow, "*A chuisle mo chroí.*"

She didn't sleep until she fell into her bed back at Tribe's headquarters three days later.

38

JUNE 1, 2023

Cherry

For the past six weeks, she'd been a shell of herself. She went about her job with the usual efficiency, her focus undisturbed, but she felt hollow. The guys tried to watch over her without hovering, but they had their own work to do. Projects didn't stop just because their medic was missing.

And that's what he was. Missing. No one seemed to know where he was. She was back to worrying about him like she had the months before they'd gone to St. Lucia. Was he safe? Was he strung out somewhere? Was he alive?

In the face of uncertainty over Demon, the group needed a new medic, so Waters ordered her to search for options. Each folder she started never got completed. Her heart wasn't in it, so they sat there, gathering dust. Waters didn't push, but she knew he would have to start doing so soon.

And every day since their return, she'd tortured herself by

entering Demon's apartment. The first night she walked in, there was a hollowness to the sound of her heels against the floor in the foyer. It didn't take much to realize that the space was clearly unoccupied. All his belongings, such as they were, still remained, but it felt like the apartment was merely a storage space now, rather than a place that housed anyone.

The only sign of life was his signature scent: sand, sun, and sea. She could almost taste it in the air. That first night, she'd collapsed in his walk-in closet and sobbed. When no one could find her, they went into panic mode, and Midas turned on her tracker. Waters eventually found her on the floor, curled into a ball, and held her as she'd cried. He'd said nothing. Just held her, one hand cradling her head to his chest, the other running up and down her back in a soothing gesture. He didn't complain about how long it took for her to cry herself out. But when she finally did, he carried her out of the apartment, took her to her own, sat her on the edge of the bed, undid and removed her jacket, slipped off her shoes, and tucked her into bed.

The next morning, she was back at her desk. Calm. Cool. Collected. As if nothing traumatic had ever happened to her. As if he'd never existed. Midas was still tracking Zion, Howard, and Andres. TB and Steel left occasionally to check out leads. Sometimes they found something, sometimes they didn't, but all three men were still working the case along with other projects. They said nothing to her about it, but she was able to read their reports, so she knew what was going on.

Steel had even gone out to his beach house. Nothing remained there either.

Eventually, over the weeks, his scent had disappeared, but she swore she could still smell him. Her visits to his apartment didn't stop. Tonight, she stood in front of his door, her fingers hovering over the keypad. She didn't understand why she kept going. She needed to stop torturing herself. It wasn't as if anything was going to change.

But not tonight. This would be the last time, and then she would move on.

She entered his code and walked through the door.

Tonight, something was different. A solitary light over the breakfast bar was shining straight down on a piece of paper folded in half once and leaned to create a tent so it stood up. In his bold scrawl was her name.

As if the paper were a wild animal that she feared would bite her, she slowly stepped over to the counter. Her hand shook as she reached out for the paper, pinching it closed with two fingers as she picked it up. She had no idea how long she stood there, staring at the note, afraid to flip it open to its secrets. For a few moments of panic, it was exactly like she'd felt that day her father had been taken from her.

Frightened or not, she needed to open the note and read it. Pretending she hadn't seen it, or ripping it up and throwing it away without knowing what its contents were, was the act of a bratty teenager, and she hadn't been one of those even when she was a teenager.

She flipped open the top half with her name on it.

Open the bag.

That's it? Three words? All the angels in heaven, why couldn't he just say it in a note? Better yet, why couldn't he be a man and tell her to her face?

Next to where the note had sat, there was a small black gift bag about five inches wide and seven inches tall. It wouldn't fit much in it, especially stuffed with the gold tissue paper that was sticking out of the top. She picked it up by the handles, brought it toward her, and peeked inside. Unfortunately, the tissue was artfully arranged so that she couldn't see what was in the bag without opening it up.

She set down the note and the bag on the edge of the counter and wiped her hands on her skirt. Peeling the tissue back gently, she saw what looked like red cloth. Her brow furrowing, she reached into the bag and extracted the contents. Laying out the three scraps of fabric on the breakfast bar, she discovered it was a red bikini and a translucent cover-up in the same color. The swimsuit, if you could call it that, had so little fabric that if she put it on, only the bare essentials would be covered.

What the hell was he up to?

Suddenly, a memory popped up. Something she'd said. His reply whispered hotly in her ear. Involuntarily, she sucked in a breath.

Without a second thought, she grabbed the bag and flew out the door toward the elevator. Multiple stabs to the down button seemed to actually slow the elevator rather than make it rise faster. Fuck! How long had he been waiting? He had ultimate patience, but even the most patient could give up if they thought the person they were meeting wasn't going to arrive.

When the elevator opened, she hadn't learned her lesson. She began to frantically push at the buttons again, swearing at the doors that didn't close fast enough and then at the carriage that seemed determined to thwart her attempts to get to the garage.

The doors finally opened, and she raced to her car. She was barely inside before she started the vehicle and backed out of her spot while simultaneously closing her door. Again, the building seemed to want to keep her inside its confines as she waited for the electric gate to rise enough. Only waiting as long as it took for her car to clear the bottom of the metal door, she gunned the engine, racing through the streets of L.A. like she was escaping the police after starring in *The Italian Job*. Never had she been happier for those defensive driving courses she'd taken.

Miraculously, she avoided every stoplight and didn't get pulled over. When she arrived at the beach near Demon's hut, she rushed out of the car, barely remembering to lock it, yanked off her shoes, and took off running for the building.

Inside, the lights were on. "Demon?" she called out. There was no answer. Okay. He clearly had been here recently.

She began to pull off her clothes, leaving them in a pile on the floor. Her hands shook as she pulled the bottoms on and clipped the chains that held the nearly nonexistent fabric together to the eyelets on either side of her hips. They were still shaking as she put the second set of chains around her neck, clipped them together, pulled the material down over her breasts, and clipped the front together. She took just enough time to carefully arrange the triangles of fabric appropriately enough to cover what needed it, then she slipped the cover-up on and headed out the door to the beach.

To her right was a pier. It was deserted at the moment because it didn't have any lights above it as the other ones did. As swiftly as she could, she walked over to the pier and underneath it. She crossed to the edge of the water, looking out to the horizon where the moon could be seen through the two opposing pylons at the end of it.

She hoped she wasn't making a total fool of herself.

Settling herself on the sand, she made sure to lay her lower half in the water so that the waves crashed between her thighs, wetting the gusset of the bikini bottoms and doing absolutely nothing to cool the fire she felt in her core. She leaned back on her elbows and shook out her hair to trail behind her. Watching the water, she waited.

A few moments later, a long shape dove off the top of the pier, barely making a sound as it cut the water. Then a head popped up in the shallows, and a figure slowly rose from the water, inch by glorious inch. Sweet baby Jesus, he truly was an ocean sex god! His broad swimmer's shoulders, his tight pecs, and the washboard abs she could count even from here, which felt both hard and soft to the touch at the same time.

When he reached waist level, he stopped for a moment, slicking his hair back from his face, then continued his stealthy approach. Naked as he rose from the water, despite the cool temperature of the ocean, his cock was fully erect, curving up to his stomach. Reaching her feet, he nudged them, and as she spread her legs apart, he knelt between them.

His hands slid up her stomach and to her breasts, cupping them from underneath. Sliding his thumbs beneath the material to stroke lightly over her nipples, a deft click of the chains, and they separated at the bottom of the material. With nothing to hold it in place, the material slid to her sides to reveal her to his gaze. She noticed, even in the darkness beneath the pier, his green eyes darkening appreciatively at her form.

"You came back. Where did you go?"

"I stayed in St. Lucia. Unfinished business."

She frowned. "The team said you weren't coming back." She groaned, rolling her eyes. "No. They didn't. I did. I assumed you did, but they didn't correct me. They knew where you were all along."

He nodded. "I had unfinished business. I wanted to see if I could find your father, and I told Waters I wasn't coming back until I found him."

She felt her heart speed up. "Did you?"

He nodded. "It took me a week, but Zion apparently had some feelings toward your father after all. His ashes were in a secondary crypt on the property, his and a lot of others. Mythos is there now, recovering the remains so they can test them and return them to any families they belong to. They may not be one hundred percent successful, but they'll try. Your dad's are the first they'll test."

She threw her arms around him, tears pouring from her eyes. She could hear the echoes of "Thank you" pouring from her mouth as she clutched him to her. He held her through the maelstrom of emotions, not saying anything.

When her tears subsided, she lay back against the wet sand, unmindful of it caking in her hair or clinging to her skin. "I'm still mad at you for disappearing for six weeks."

"Understood," he murmured. "But I couldn't, in good conscience, leave him there. You needed the closure."

"He knew where you were all that time and said nothing to me?"

Demon nodded. "I asked him not to." He blew out a breath. "I had some personal shit to sort through. There was as good a place as anywhere."

"I mourned you every day."

"I'm sorry, *a chuisle*. I didn't want to get your hopes up in case it took longer or he really wasn't there. Plus, I figured you'd snap out of your depression sooner rather than later, and I thought it was better to let you work up a good rage at me for leaving. It was better than no emotion at all."

"Don't you ever not tell me where you're going again!" she admonished him. "I was mad. But mostly? I was scared. I was imagining all sorts of awful things happening to you. Worried the guys were actually out hunting you when they told me they were hunting leads on Zion and Howard."

"I'm sorry. No more disappearances. Forgive me?"

"We'll see."

"Feck, Esme. I want to give you everything you could ever want." She watched him hang his head. There was something defeated in his tone. A bleakness she didn't like. It felt oily. Slimy. Sickly. When he tried to pull away from her, she reached for him, her grasp tight as she pulled him back into her arms.

Her hands reached up to clutch his face between the palms. "Aidan—"

"No. I need to tell you some things. You need to know why I resisted. Why I wouldn't commit. Why I couldn't give you what you wanted."

He sighed and covered her body with his, his forearms bearing the weight so that she felt close to him but not suffocated. "When I was sued for malpractice, I went to Japan. I knew if I stayed in the country, my conscience wouldn't allow me to keep quiet, and the only way to protect her was to remove myself from the area, so I left. I'd been surfing for several days when I got hurt. Rogue wave took me out. Severe concussion. I actually ripped my spine. I was prescribed oxy for the pain to get me through until I could do therapy, but it was going to be a long haul."

"Waters' report said you didn't have a record for a prescription."

"That's probably because I was in Japan at the time I was treated. I'm sure the records are somewhere, but sometimes, international information doesn't transition smoothly. It doesn't really matter. They were legal at one time, but my continued use wasn't. And then there was the boy."

"What boy?"

"About a week after my accident, I was on the beach walking. I couldn't do much else, and even that was painful while taking the meds, but I couldn't sit anymore. The boy had swum out too far and didn't have the skills for the conditions. He got caught in a riptide. His parents couldn't get to him, so I promised his father that I'd get him. I'd save him. I took off into the water, but when I got out there, he was already gone. I had a choice to do CPR in the water or take him back to shore and hope he wasn't too far gone so that I could bring him back. I chose CPR in the water. I chose wrong."

"Why didn't I know about this?"

"My name was never exchanged. I was just a stranger on the beach. I don't even think it made the news. People drown all the time. Steel is the only one who knows, and I told him the day of the café bomb."

"Aidan, you're not to blame," she reminded him.

"No, I'm not, but that's not the issue, Esme." He sighed again, his forehead to her chest. She gently weaved her fingers through the wet tendrils of his hair, waiting for him to go on. "The issue is, I made a promise, and I didn't keep it."

She inhaled sharply.

"As a doctor, I promise people and their loved ones that I can fix them. Heal them. I failed those three girls that day in the hospital because I didn't watch out for all of my team. People I was responsible for. I failed that boy and his parents when I promised to save him. I failed my family when I dishonored them with my actions in surgery the day those girls died, and then I abandoned them rather than go through the awkwardness of the family trip, and then they died when I wasn't there."

He stopped, picked up his head, and looked her in the eyes. "I wanted you so badly. I always have. From the moment I saw you, you were alive with this fiery light. I couldn't look away from you. Despite how messed up I was, you still seemed to want me. I tried not to, but we got closer. I had just convinced myself that maybe we could make a go of it, and then—"

"And then I told you the only way we could be together was if you gave up the meds, which you can't because you actually do need them. It was a sign of another failure to keep a promise because you knew you wouldn't be able to do it." She ran a hand down the side of his face. "Aidan, why didn't you just tell me? I would have understood."

"Maybe, maybe not. But you need to know, I tried to give up the shite, Esme, I really did, but I was all up in my head. My spinal cord was torn in the accident. The discs fused, and the pain is bad. Even surgery isn't going to fix it. I'll always be in pain. Always.

"Sometimes it's okay, but it's never really gone. Standing for long periods of time over a patient or the armory table or any sort of extended activity is excruciating. The meds allow me to function at my work, but when I come down off the adrenaline when the job's done, I can't do anything physical without taking them. I've never been off the meds. It's just that I make sure no one sees me take them because I don't want the team to blame the drugs if something goes wrong on a project. Then I get all up in my head about 'What if something does go wrong?', causing me to get pissy worrying about it, so everyone assumes I'm detoxing."

"It's why you disappear when you come back to L.A. from a project. You're fighting through the pain."

"Pretty much. The beach hut gives me a place to lie low. If I'm at Tribe, I'm accessible. People can just come find me, and I can't hide the pain. At the beach hut, the possibility of someone coming to find me in the early stages of recovering is rare. No one wants to haul their ass to the beach, so they text three or four times before sending someone out to collect me."

"Waters has been covering for you all this time, hasn't he? He knows where you are and why afterward."

"Yeah. Fecker knows everything about everyone. Impossible to hide shit from his spidey senses."

She nodded. "I don't like how you did it, but I guess I can understand. I wasn't exactly listening to what you were saying to me after you rescued me." She stopped. "Wait. You said it took a week to find my dad. Why didn't you come back right away?"

"I just... I needed to get clear. I needed to figure out if I could quit, and I knew I couldn't do that here. Everyone would hover, and I didn't want to disappoint people when I failed."

She bit her lip, afraid to ask but needing to know. She chose a more passive approach to see if he'd open up about what he discovered. "I meant what I said in the hotel room," she confessed. "I want this. Us. I don't care."

"Fireball," he breathed out.

He kissed her lips softly.

"I'm not worthy of your attention, let alone your love." He brushed back wisps of hair that the night breeze was blowing over her face. "I'm always going to be in pain. The only hope I have of being permanently pain-free is surgery, and of course, there's no guarantee it will actually work. I'm not ready for that yet. Not until the Salieri are routed out.

"In the meantime, there's a procedure I tried—radiofrequency ablation—where the doctor severs the nerve. It worked for a while, but the nerves grow back, and then the pain returns; however, I'd only be down about a week before I could return to duty. Probably have to have it done about every six months. As it wears off, I'll have to go back on the meds. Do some more therapy. Then when I can't stand the pain anymore, I'll be out six months to a year to have the surgery and recover. That's assuming it works."

"As long as you want to do it for you, I think you should do it. I meant what I said, Aidan. I'll stand by you. I know I said that once before, and then I went back on it. I was hurting. Not a worthy excuse, but it's true. I did come to my senses, but by then, you were gone."

"I knew you would. You needed space. You needed to find your way on your own, and while I thought it was foolish when you had me to lean on, I know you. It had to be on your own terms. So I thought about you every day and hoped you were making progress."

He kissed her. Gently. It wasn't something she was used to from him. She figured maybe the time apart had changed him just a little. The dark part of Aidan Parker was still there. Always would be. But this moment with him required something different, and he clearly recognized that.

When he broke the kiss, he raised up slightly to look down her body. "Feck, I knew you'd be gorgeous in that suit."

"Thank you for the new suit. Am I a fitting sacrifice for an ocean sex god?" she teased him.

Completely serious, he corrected her, "You're the goddess. It's me who's the sacrifice. You've captured me with your fiery halo of hair and your gorgeous curves. You've ensnared me with your thoughts and words." He swallowed hard and leaned down to cage her between his arms. Within a breath of her mouth, he confessed, "You've enslaved me with your power."

"Well, every goddess needs a god," she informed him. "A male who will elicit her undying love. Make her rage with anger, yet love twice as hard. Someone to worship her."

The first touch of his lips met the skin over her heart, then traveled upward to the cord of her neck, giving nips and sucks she was sure would leave the slightest of bruises, marking her as his. She arched her neck to give him better access. All the while, his hands gently tormented her breasts—brushes of the pads of his fingers around her areolas, gentle pinches of her nipples, soft caresses across the swells, and gentle squeezes of the globes. If possible, her pulse beat faster, the blood rushing throughout her body, making her feel like she was glowing from the inside. It was lava, hot and burning, desire bubbling to the surface, want steadily and swiftly flowing to her extremities.

One hand moved to curl around the back of her head, fingers spearing through her hair, yet he cradled her gently as he lowered the top half of her to the sand. His lips moved now to her jawline, no love bites left behind now, just open-mouthed kisses of adoration. As she turned her head, her mouth met his, eagerly tangling her tongue with his, tasting the salt, sea, and sand that was so much a part of him. The kisses were slow and drugging at first, but after a few moments, his mouth became more insistent with hers. He sucked the tip of her tongue until it was in his mouth, then gently trapped it with his teeth for just long enough to let out a growl of claiming. He let go and swept his tongue around the cavern of her cheeks, teeth, and a final long, slow taste of her mouth before leaving its confines.

His voice was husky. "Will this do, goddess? Or shall I kneel at your feet, prostrate myself, and worship at the altar?"

She moaned, her eyes lowering to half-mast. "Yes, please. That."

She felt him push back against the sand and surf, his mouth becoming level with the small red triangle over her mound. His nose brushed up and down the fabric as hands reached up to slip loose the chains on the bottom of her suit, falling with a light tinkling as they hit each other in the wet sand. His teeth grabbed the corner of material at the front, slowly peeling it back to reveal her pussy to him, the surf lightly crashing against the bare skin. Still, it didn't cool her. It made the burning worse.

"Aidan," she whispered, and with that one sigh of his name, it provided him with the invitation he needed. Hands slid beneath her thighs and under her ass, the palms grabbing so hard as he kneeled upright, she knew she'd see bruises when she looked over her shoulder in the bathroom mirror tomorrow. He pulled her lower half off the ground, making sure she had the support of his knees beneath her upper back. Fastening his mouth to her opening, he thrust his tongue inside to gather the taste of her mixing with the sea.

Both of her hands reached for his head, her fingers threading through the silky wet strands, her palms pressing to the back of his skull, pushing him tighter to her, allowing him to delve further into her pussy. She smiled wickedly, knowing that in his mind, he'd be crowing that he was able to get just that little bit further inside. He wouldn't care that when her back arched so sharply, her thighs squeezed against his ears. Or that her hands tried to press him so far that he drowned in her orgasm. Or that she screamed out into the night when she fell over the top and flew, buffeted on the currents as his lips, teeth, and tongue worked her through until she quieted.

But he wasn't done with her yet, nor was he done destroying her. Gently, he lay her flat on the sand.

She raised a hand to his face and smoothed a lock of his hair behind his ear that had fallen. "Love me, Aidan."

With a slight change of his position between her thighs, with a single thrust, he buried himself as deep inside her as he could go. His right hand grabbed her left, turning it so that he could kiss the ring she still wore since they left for St. Lucia. It was a promise. A promise to be the man she knew him to be. A promise to love only her. A promise of forever. "I can't do anything but love you, *a chuisle mo chroí.*"

In turn, she grabbed his left hand, the one that wore the partnering ring, and returned the gesture. She knew beyond the shadow of a doubt that he would keep that promise. Now everything was one hundred percent right.

ALSO BY NICOLE CRAIG

Good Enough: The Deadman's Tribe Book 1 – B0CJFSW6LZ

Team Leader, Waters, hires on to consult on a movie about Navy SEALs. Director Kai Serrano not only needs his expertise, but also needs his protection as the men of Tribe Corporation search for her missing brother.

Bad Enough: The Deadman's Tribe Book 2 – B0CTHZPN6Y

Interrogator and all-around bad boy TB has been talking in secret to romance novelist Sylvan Jones about the BDSM lifestyle as part of her research for a new novel. But when secrets from Sylvan's past come back to haunt her, the bad boy is forced into the good girl's real world, and he'll burn the world down to protect her.

Never Enough: The Deadman's Tribe Book 3 – B0CZ339NWF

Thief and playboy Nemo partners up with fellow thief Haskell to trace a cache of conflict diamonds through Africa. Will the playboy have his heart stolen by Le Chatte Noire, or will he resist being caught for life?

Strong Enough: The Deadman's Tribe Book 4 – B0F1RBGWHF

Twenty-six years ago, Cherry's father was kidnapped and never found. Her entire life has been a search for those who took him. After all this time, she finally has a lead. Posing as newlyweds, she and Demon, Tribe's medic, travel to the Caribbean, where they uncover ancient secrets that are tied to his disappearance. Those same secrets now endanger the attraction they've finally decided to explore.

The Lucky Rabbit: A prequel spin-off to the series Six Paths to Justice – BoD777NVR5

A short story in *The Lucky in Love* charity anthology. Cosmos, member and part owner of a BDSM club called The Library, meets a woman who intrigues him more than any other woman has. After a memorable night together, he gets called away on an emergency, and their newfound relationship hangs in the balance. (This story is a prequel to a spin-off series from *Bad Enough*, and will connect to the *Operation Alpha: Police & Fire* world of Susan Stoker.)

Justice for Francesca: Six Paths to Justice Book 1 (Operation Alpha: Police & Fire) – BoDTV65N4V

Tripoli and Fleur's story (seen in *Bad Enough*)

Ethan "Tripoli" Evans met FBI agent Francesca McCabe while she was undercover. When her case exploded around her, she was forced to leave the investigation without notice, leaving him hurt and confused. It's now two years later, there's a murdered woman in his nightclub, and Francesca has been assigned to investigate. Tripoli is not about to allow his second chance to pass him by.

<u>Up Next</u>

Midas's Story: The Deadman's Tribe Book 5

RELEASES OCTOBER 2025!

At ten years old, Nicole Craig snuck into a secret box of her mother's books filled with mysteries and romances. Since that day, she has a book (or five) available at all times. At the age of thirty, her husband encouraged her to try her hand at writing. It only took another twenty-five years of teaching high school and a pandemic to do it, creating the types of books she found in that magical box.

Nicole lives in Southeastern Wisconsin. She is a devout Milwaukee Brewers fan, mother of three furry feline children, and married to The One. After twenty-five years as a high school English teacher, she decided to retire to spin fantastic tales, travel, and live the ultimate fantasy: reading a book a day until the end of time.

Please consider leaving a review on Amazon or Goodreads. It's one of the best ways to thank a writer (besides buying their books!) for the work they've done.

Check out her Facebook Reader Group or any of her social media links to get the latest updates on The Deadman's Tribe series or other upcoming projects.

Facebook Reader Group: Nicole Craig's Tribe
Website: https://nicolecraigauthor.com/
Instagram: https://www.instagram.com/nicolecraigauthor/
Newsletter: https://dl.bookfunnel.com/aoslx3defo

ACKNOWLEDGMENTS

SJ Higgins—You knew how worried I was. You took that, soothed that, and made me see what I'd written in a whole new way. You were the medicine that made me feel better. Stronger. Thank you.

Steph White, Vanessa Esquibel, and Kat Wyeth—Thank you for getting the Hot Mess Express through another book. Kat: the graphics are BEYOND words.

CJC Photography—I was okay with using stock footage to finish out the series, but I was in despair when we couldn't find anything even close. Then there was you! Thank you for working with me so fast to get the perfect photo when I was literally days away from the deadline for the cover. You were amazing to work with, and I can't wait to do it again.

Eric Guilmette and Jackie Coleman—I've been looking at your photos for a while, and I can't believe you were "still there" for me. It's like you were waiting for me. The chemistry in this cover photo is totally Demon and Cherry, and I will never visualize these characters as anyone but the two of you ever again.

Nicole Craig's Tribe—Thank you for being a part of my reader group. We are small, but we are tribe.

My ARC Tribe—Thank you for taking some of your valuable time to read and review my novel. I know it's not an easy job. I appreciate your honest reviews.

To Anyone Who Reads This Book—Thank you. You're making a life-long dream come true for me.